THE SENSITIVES BOOKS 1 - 3

RICK WOOD

BLOOD SPLATTER PRESS

ABOUT THE AUTHOR

Rick Wood is a British writer born in Cheltenham.

His love for writing came at an early age, as did his battle with mental health. After defeating his demons, he grew up and became a stand-up comedian, then a drama and English teacher, before giving it all up to become a full-time author.

He now lives in Loughborough, where he divides his time between watching horror, reading horror, and writing horror.

ALSO BY RICK WOOD

The Sensitives
The Sensitives
My Exorcism Killed Me
Close to Death
Demon's Daughter
Questions for the Devil
Repent
The Resurgence
Until the End

Blood Splatter Books
Psycho B*tches
Shutter House
This Book is Full of Bodies
Home Invasion

Rick also publishes thrillers under the pseudonym Ed Grace...

Jay Sullivan

Assassin Down

Kill Them Quickly

The Bars That Hold Me

A Deadly Weapon

THE SENSITIVES BOOK ONE

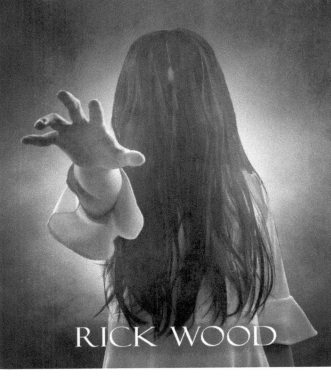

BOOK ONE IN THE SENSITIVES SERIES

THE SENSITIVES

RICK WOOD

1

YOU NEVER EXPECT A SWEET, DARLING LITTLE GIRL TO BE THE source of a man's deepest fear.

Yet all Detective Inspector Jason Lyle could get from his colleague was gibberish. Eccentrically formed, incoherent, insubstantial gibberish.

"She – she – her eyes… her eyes…"

"For Christ's sake, pull yourself together," Jason demanded, rolling his eyes and folding his arms.

"You don't know," retorted the constable. "You weren't there…" He threw his arms around his body, shaking in a frenzied huddle, his bloodshot eyes staring wide-eyed at a vacant corner of the room.

With an exasperated sigh, Jason nodded at the nearest officer and the constable was led away, leaving Jason alone in his office.

Sitting back in his grand, leather office chair, he picked up a mug and sniffed it. It smelt like coffee. He needed coffee.

He took a sip.

He almost retched as he spat it back out. He hated cold coffee. It was all he ever seemed to find around his office –

cold bloody coffee. Where was that constable who said he was bringing Jason a decent, hot cup of coffee?

Probably blubbering with the other pathetic excuse for a police officer, he thought to himself, shaking his head. *Is that what passes the training nowadays?*

Jason cast his wizened, cynical eyes upon a photo frame at the edge of his desk. His wife and his daughter stood, proudly smiling back at him, and he considered his sweet daughter's face. Nine years old, the same age as the girl who had mortified his officer into a blubbering mess. His daughter's face was so innocent, full of such impenetrable virtue. How could a girl, like his daughter, ever be considered as volatile as they were making this witness out to be?

"Fuck it," he coughed, springing out of his chair and dropping the remnants of his stale coffee mug into a full waste paper basket leant haphazardly against his desk.

If this girl was really that bad, he was going to have to see it for himself. If an officer couldn't take a simple statement from a child without turning into a pathetic wreck, then it would be up to him to take the responsibility.

Bloody amateurs.

He threw off his jacket, loosened his collar, and rolled up his sleeves as he trooped toward the interrogation room. People tried to say hello as he passed, but he ignored every one of them. He didn't need pointless, going-nowhere conversations – once he had tunnel vision, he didn't care about the chitchat some boring idiot wanted to start with him.

He reached the interrogation room, turned the handle, and was taken aback to find it locked. He shuffled the handle again, checking he wasn't mistaken.

"Oi!" he shouted, expecting someone to hear and come to his beck and call.

As he had hoped, Gus pointed his head out of a nearby kitchen, pieces of yumyum hanging off his fat cheek.

"What's up, Jason?" Gus inquired, his overweight belly sickening Jason at the sight of what constitutes a police officer nowadays.

"Why the bloody hell is that door locked?" Jason commanded.

"That's where we're keeping that Kaylee Kemple girl, boss," Gus replied dumbly, staring back with thick, inquisitive eyes.

"Yes, I know that," Jason spat through seething teeth. "Why is it locked?"

"Have you met her?"

"No, I have not."

"Then you wouldn't understand."

Jason did all he could to contain his rage. His fists clenched, his fingers flexed, his eyes narrowed. His chest throbbed with his accelerating heartbeat and he found his body unconsciously leaning aggressively toward Gus.

"What the fuck wouldn't I understand?" Jason spoke in a hostile but quiet voice – trying adamantly to remain professional and contain his incessant fury. "It is a little girl. What the hell is wrong with you people?"

"Honestly, Inspector, you haven't met her."

"Well then open the door, I would like to."

Despite the obvious intensity of Jason's anger, the throbbing veins on his perspiring forehead, and the bloodshot fever of his eyes – Gus wobbled.

Gus did not want to endure Jason's wrath; no one did. Jason's anger was legendary. But at the same time, he did not want to have to face what was behind that door.

"Gus," Jason began again, slowly, furiously. "I'm going to ask you one final time. Open. The fucking. Door."

Gus' arms shook, his whole body seizing in fear. Taking the keys off his belt, he presented them to Jason, who took them reluctantly.

"Here," Gus offered. "Take them. But please wait for me to go back in the kitchen."

Gus scuttled away like a pathetic little beetle, slamming the kitchen door behind him.

"Fucking charlatan," Jason muttered, placing the key in the lock.

He had barely reached the first rotation of the key before he froze. A murmur reverberated against the door, vibrating with a croaky breath. A low-pitched rumble that sounded like the deep laughter of an old, demented man echoed from within.

Was that the girl?

Fuck's sake, Jason, don't let it go to your head. It's a nine-year-old.

Ignoring his instinct, he turned the key and opened the door, entering the room and shutting himself in.

He regretted his lack of trepidation instantly. His whole body shuddered. His breath was visible in the air – it was the middle of summer, but this room was like the Antarctic.

Two blond pigtails outlined the head of the girl. She sat completely stationary, facing the opposite wall, humming a quietly chaotic low-pitched tune – a repetitive, incessant tune-less song. Jason didn't know why, but this song sent chills firing up and down his spine.

"Kaylee, my name is Detective Inspector Jack Lyle," he introduced himself. "Mind if I speak to you?"

The humming ended.

Intense, unbearable silence screamed from the back of the girl's head.

"I'm sorry, Kaylee's not here right now," she answered. "Can I take a message?"

2

TEWKESBURY. THE PLACE THAT ALWAYS FLOODED, WAS FULL OF old people, and where everyone knew everyone else.

Except for Oscar.

No one knew Oscar. Except for his mum, his dad, and his cat.

And, very briefly, those people he served on the checkout in Morrison's, though his interaction with these strangers was usually short, often involving a grunt for a greeting and a snarl for goodbye.

Oscar hated working on the checkouts, but he couldn't be arsed to stay in school. He had counted down the weeks until the end of year eleven when he could leave; meaning no more work, no more homework, and no more having to deal with annoying teachers. He could just sit around on his arse all day doing nothing. It was a dream come true.

Then he reached eighteen, and his parents charged him rent.

This was where he ended up. Stuck behind the checkout in Morrison's. With eight hours to go. And a lot of customers that he had to pretend to care about.

"Murgh," grunted a man as he placed his Stella Artois on the belt, handed Oscar a crumpled five-pound note, and plodded back to his miserable life.

However miserable the man's life was, Oscar envied it. The guy had a four-pack of beer and didn't need to sit there serving miserable farts for the next seven hours fifty-eight minutes.

Oscar was aware that he didn't have the kind, welcoming face that would encourage someone to engage in conversation with him. And if someone did try to engage him in conversation, he would find it the most tedious few minutes of his day. He really hated small talk; any acknowledgement of another human beyond a "murgh" was immensely tedious. A fully formed "hello" was the extreme limit of the interaction he was comfortable with.

Yet, some people still tried. Why? Why couldn't they just go through their life leaving him the hell alone?

Oscar was a thin, scrawny young man. Lazy and unmotivated, but too lazy to really care that he was unmotivated. He spent most of his time between being moaned at by his parents for doing nothing with his life, playing FIFA, being moaned at by his parents for not washing up, going to counselling, collecting his anxiety medication, being moaned at by his parents for not caring about the fact he was having to take anxiety medication, then being moaned at that he's not caring about the fact that he's being moaned at.

Maybe that's why I'm so lazy. I've numbed my brain with pills.

His parents would claim it was his Xbox that deadened him – but it was the pills.

Or it could be his Xbox.

Who gives a shit, really?

"Hello, dearie," smiled an old lady as she placed a bunch of bananas, some paracetamol, and a jar of coffee on the belt. Before Oscar could get too irritated by the fact that this old lady had forced two fully formed two-syllable words upon him, he noticed her placing her debit card into the machine and entering her pin number before Oscar had even scanned her items.

"No, you've got to wait," Oscar told her.

"What's that, dear?"

"I need to put your things through first."

"Yes, you put them through, dear."

"Now you need to enter your pin."

"I need to do what?"

"Enter your pin."

"But I already have."

"No, you need to enter it again."

"But then you'd charge me twice!"

Fuuuuuuuuuuuuuuucking heeeeeeeeeeeeeell.

"No. It did not go through because it wasn't ready. I need you to do it now."

"Oh, okay then."

"Yes, I need you to do it now."

"Oh, is it ready now?"

"Yes, it is ready."

"Are you sure? Because I've already done it once."

"Please put your pin in."

I'm going to shoot myself.

"Now you need to press enter."

"Do what, dear?"

"Press enter."

"Oh, where's that?"

"In the bottom right."

"Okay."

"No, that's the clear button, you've just cleared it. Now you need to enter your pin again."

"What's that?"

"You need to enter your pin again."

"But I've already done it twice."

Aaaaaaaaaaarrrrrrrgggggghhhhhhhh!!

"Tell you what; why don't we just use contactless?"

He grabbed the woman's card, held it against the machine, and handed it back to her, beaming a huge fake smile toward her confused face.

Seven hours fifty-six minutes to go.

Oscar sat back in his chair – a plastic chair falling to pieces and digging into his back, which was surely against union regulations – if there was a union for dead-end supermarket workers, that is.

He ran his hands through his greasy, unkempt hair.

Was this what his life had in store for him?

Eighteen years old. He was supposed to be in the prime of his life.

Across the supermarket, some guy with a lip piercing, shorts, and a woolly hat on, put his arms around his girlfriend. His girlfriend was stunning – long, blond hair, curvy waist, succulent arse. Oscar couldn't help but stare – but mostly at the guy. Why on earth had a woman like this chosen a man like that?

I mean, the guy was wearing shorts *and* a woolly hat. Which one is it? Was it hot or cold?

Unsure why it was making him angry, he found his arms shaking and his legs wobbling. This bloke infuriated him. Not just because he dressed like an inept idiot – but because he had managed to bag himself a gorgeous girl.

No girl ever looked Oscar's way.

Ever.

The more and more he glared at this man, the more he felt his anger raging, intensifying, multiplying, as the man packed his cereal, his condoms, and his Coke, picking his plastic bag up in his hand and taking it away and – *BANG!*

The man fell to the floor, a bloody hole sent straight

through his body, falling to his knees, clutching his chest. His girlfriend wept over him, desperately clinging onto him, screaming for dear life.

Oscar glanced over his shoulder to see if anyone else was reacting, and looked back, then–

They were fine.

The guy and his girlfriend were absolutely fine.

Everyone carried on like nothing had happened.

What the hell?

The guy placed his sleazy arm around his girlfriend's shoulders, giving her a disgusting open-mouth kiss that looked like he was a frog trying to eat a tadpole.

But he was alive. Perfectly well.

No one else reacted. No one else had seen anything.

Oscar clambered into his pocket for his anxiety medication. He withdrew it, popping out four pills, shoving them in his mouth and swallowing without the need for water.

"Oi, mate, pay attention!"

Oscar's head shot around. An irritable old man was waiting for his shopping to be scanned.

Willing his heavy breathing to subside and his alert mind to calm down, Oscar picked up a loaf of bread and beeped it through.

It was just his overactive imagination.

This was why he took the pills.

Seven hours fifty-two minutes to go.

3

"We were... reluctant" – began the well-dressed lawyer, pulling a face as if he was chewing something disgusting – "to hire you. I mean, what you do... I don't, particularly, believe in it."

April sighed, chewing her gum with an open mouth just to irritate this toffy, privately educated, stuck-up-his-own-arse, insufferable man. Sure, April liked to dye her hair purple. Sure, she had more tattoos and piercings than this man was comfortable with. And sure, she worked in the paranormal investigating business, something perhaps not given much integrity by the educated elite – it didn't mean this pompous arse got to talk to her so condescendingly.

"But, our client," the lawyer continued, "he, er... he insisted on it. If it were up to me–"

"Looks like it ain't up to you, though, don't it?" April responded, forcing a smarmy, insincere smile to her lips. Yes, it was childish to stoop to his level of condescension – but it felt good to get one over on him.

"We're aren't particularly interested in your opinion, I'm

afraid," Julian pointed out, so stern and diplomatic. "Where is Henry?"

"Just through those doors."

"Lovely," Julian confirmed. "Thank you."

Julian made his way through the double doors first, followed by April – who made sure to give the lawyer a huge, fury-provoking grin.

"What a prick," April observed as she and Julian walked toward the bench where their client sat.

"You need to stay more detached, April," Julian replied. "I know the guy's a prick, but we still need to be professional."

As they approached Henry, April was taken aback by how normal he looked. Despite his hands being in handcuffs and being adorned in prison wear, he looked like the average father. A mixture of brown and grey hair, stubble on his chin, and a sensitive frown on his kind face. Henry looked wounded, as if the events were distressing him immensely – something April had no doubt they were.

"Mr Kemple, it's good to meet you," Julian greeted him, always professional.

"Thank you," Henry replied, raising from his seat in respect. "I would shake your hand, but it's a little difficult."

"Not to worry." Julian smiled as they sat down, April taking a seat beside Julian.

"And please, call me Henry."

April couldn't help but admire how good Julian was with people. He was a gifted exorcist and an accomplished demonologist, there was no doubt about that. And the way he'd taken her off the street when she was younger and taught her to hone her powers, moulding her into the strong, nineteen-year-old woman she had become, was nothing short of heroic. He had a natural air of confidence about him that didn't come off as smug, but as warm and inviting. Perhaps this came from him being almost ten years older than she; and maybe April would learn that patience in time.

"My name is Julian, and this is April. The first question is probably the most obvious one, but I'll ask it anyway," began Julian. "How are you, Henry?"

"Well..." Henry shook his head, looking to his feet. He fought off tears, his face scrunching as he visibly willed himself not to break. "Not good."

"Yes, I can imagine. It's pretty horrific circumstances."

"I just... I can't believe I'm here."

"I imagine it must be devastating."

Henry forced an absent nod as he wiped his eyes on his sleeve.

"Why don't you start from the beginning, Henry?"

"My daughter, Kaylee... She's only ninyears-old. We've always been so close, best friends, even. I took her to parks, zoos, did everything a good dad does. Then one day, she just..."

He trailed off again, forcing tears away.

"Take your time," Julian reassured him.

"She just changed. Became nothing short of sadistic. Started doing all these nasty things."

"When did she start doing these things?"

"Three, four months ago."

"And what kind of things did she do?"

Henry stared back at Julian, his eyes widening, his lips pursed together. His body shook. He visibly willed his lip to stop quivering.

"Horrific things," Henry gasped.

"What kind of horrific things, Henry?"

"She stole the razors from my shaver and cut my wife's arms whilst she was sleeping. I woke up and she was unconscious; I had to rush her to the hospital. Kaylee denied it was her, but I knew. She had this, this far-off look in her eyes, like a distant evil. It was a look I'd never seen before."

"Sounds awful."

"She would spy on me and my wife when we made love. We'd do it after she'd gone to bed, of course, check she was fast asleep, be silent – but the door would be open. We'd hear her breathing. When I'd approach she'd run away, then I'd find her asleep in her room. Then, there was the time…"

"Yes?"

"She sawed our cat's leg off. She got a…"

Henry's eyes gave in and he waved his hand to indicate no more. He turned his face away, covering himself with his arm.

"Sorry," Henry muttered.

"It's quite all right," Julian reassured him. "So why are you here? Why were you arrested?"

"She… She told everyone I molested her. She told everyone I touched her!" His face broke, and his whole body convulsed in tears. "How could I? She's my daughter! I'm a doctor, for Christ's sake! I would never touch her, I wouldn't. I love her! I love her so much."

Julian glanced at April, who had remained an intrigued voyeur for the duration of the interview. His eyes indicated it was time to go.

"What we will do, Henry," Julian began, resting a comforting hand on Henry's shoulder. "We will talk to Kaylee. We will see what we make of her, and let you know what our verdict is."

Henry managed to force a nod, but couldn't get out any words between his furious sobbing.

With a nod to April, Julian stood and led them out. They remained silent until they left the police station.

"So," April declared, breaking the silence. "What did you make of him?"

"Either he's a very good liar, or we have a deranged child on our hands."

Julian stared into the distance, distracted by something, his eyes glazing over.

"What is it?" April prompted.

"I can feel something," Julian replied. "There's someone near. A new Sensitive. Someone who's just starting to discover his gift. I can feel it."

April watched Julian, peering at the troubled look taking him over.

"How do you know?"

"Because it feels the same as when I found you."

April nodded. Julian was normally spot on about these things.

"What do we do?"

Julian took a deep intake of breath, held it, and let it go.

"Find him," Julian confirmed. "Before his powers get the better of him... and someone gets hurt."

4

THERE WAS NO WAY TO SIT IN A COUNSELLING SESSION WITHOUT being uncomfortable, or so Oscar decided. He could lay down on the sofa like he'd seen people do in the movies, but that just felt weird. He could sit forward intently, but that would be too intense. As it was, he decided to shift between sitting back and sitting on the edge of his chair, never quite able to get comfortable.

"Tell me about your week," Doctor Jane Middlemore requested, preparing her pen and her pad and peering over her glasses at Oscar.

Oscar shifted again, placing his hands over his lap, covering a poorly timed erection. How could a counsellor be so attractive? Oscar could barely concentrate. She had long, red hair, prominent bosoms, and wore a fitted suit, with a slit in her skirt that traipsed all the way up to her thigh. Oscar knew he was staring at her thigh, and he needed to stop, as it was becoming painfully obvious.

He couldn't help it. Her skin was impeccably smooth, and her thigh was perfectly rounded.

Damn it. I'm being such a perv. Stop it.

"My week's been okay."

"And how are you feeling?"

Horny.

"Tired, mostly."

"How come?"

Oscar sighed.

Who cares?

I mean, honestly, what difference is confiding in this ridiculously hot woman going to make about anything? Is it going to make him feel better? Change who he is? Make him less of an unmotivated arse?

Honestly, the only thing Oscar cared about was going home and playing FIFA.

"Oh, you know. Playing on my Xbox too much."

Then the most peculiar thing happened.

Out of the corner of his eye, Oscar was sure he could see a masculine figure. Someone standing behind Jane with a relaxed, cocky demeanour.

But as soon as Oscar turned his gaze toward the figure, it went. Like a puff of smoke immediately dispersing.

"What about a girlfriend? Have you thought about going out and meeting someone, perhaps instead of sitting alone playing with your Xbox?"

"I'd love to meet someone, except I don't really think anyone would love to meet me."

The cocky strut of some laddish bloke walked past in the reflection of a window. Jane didn't react.

How could she not see him?

He shot his head around to glance at whoever it was, but it was gone. Nothing. Just a passing hallucination out of the corner of his eyes.

Now I'm seeing things? I'm all kinds of messed up...

"And why is it you think no one would like to meet you?"

"I don't know, it's just—"

And just at that moment, as if appearing from nothing, evolving into a fully formed body, appeared a bloke. Standing at Jane's side. Shaved head, pierced eyebrow, and baggy track-suit hanging off a well-sculpted bare chest.

Oscar's jaw hung wide open. He blinked his eyes tightly a few times, as if the man would go away as soon as he averted his gaze. But the mirage was still there, standing prominently in the flesh.

Jane glanced over her shoulder, then back to Oscar, trying to search for the subject of his gaze, but seeing nothing.

How is she not seeing this?

"Honestly, Jane," the guy grunted. "You're doin' ma fuckin' 'ead in. It's like you're more obsessed with your job. I may as well move my shit out."

Oscar's mind was awash with confusion. He stared dumb-foundedly at this miraculously appeared man,spewing abuse at his counsellor.

"What is going on?" Oscar demanded.

"What do you mean?" Jane replied, completely undeterred by the man beside her.

"What is your boyfriend doing here?"

Oscar closed his eyes and shuddered. When he opened his eyes, the man was gone. Completely disappeared, as if he was never there.

But he had been there.

Oscar was certain of it.

Despite Jane furiously looking over her shoulder to the space Oscar had just shouted at, despite her seeing nothing – he had been there. Oscar had seen him.

"Excuse me?"

"With his skinhead, tracksuit, abs, eyebrow piercing. He was there."

"How on earth do you know what my boyfriend looks like? Have you been spying on me?"

"He wanted to know why you're too busy with your job, and whether he should move out."

Jane's jaw dropped. For a few moments she stared at Oscar in bewildered shock, her eyebrows raised, her body stiffened.

Then her body changed. Her eyebrows narrowed, her fists clenched, and she stood suddenly, jabbing her finger toward the door.

"I think you need to leave!" Jane demanded. "And if you come near me or my boyfriend again, I will call the police!"

Oscar froze.

But he had been there! Oscar had seen him. As clear as he saw Jane at that moment, pointing a vehemently shaking arm toward the door.

"Go!" she shouted once more.

Oscar jumped to his feet, scampering to the door as quickly as he could, then striding down the corridor and out of the building.

Once out, he planted himself against the wall. He was panting, his vision going blurry, his head full of manic dizziness.

What was going on?

How had he just seen that man, heard that man – but Jane hadn't?

5

PARANORMAL INVESTIGATORS DEAL WITH PEOPLE WHO HAVE A range of beliefs – from adamant sceptics denying every possibility of the supernatural, to militant believers who wish to force their precarious knowledge on everyone else. Either way, people were usually furiously intrigued in what April and Julian do; although there were, of course, people who flat-out couldn't be arsed to deal with 'weirdos like them.'

Then there were their clients, who came to them with a range of emotions; from hardened outer shells to distraught, inconsolable messes.

Nancy Kemple was the latter.

This was the kind of situation where April was glad Julian was in charge, not her. She didn't deal with other people getting emotional well. She knew, of course, this was because of her own inability to deal with the emotional gravity of her past; running away from a neglectful home at fourteen, then being found by Julian at fifteen, at which point she was taught to move on from her past and harness her gifts.

Or, when she was taught to be a 'Sensitive' – as Julian called it.

But that treatment from her parents was something she had never quite dealt with, and seeing a hysterical mother weeping in front of her was a situation with which she couldn't empathise. Her cold, callous mother never shed tears over her, nor gave sympathy when April was upset, nor even noticed when April would sneak out for a few hours. Sometimes April wondered if her mother, five years later, had even noticed that she was gone.

"At first, I believed her," Nancy sobbed, taking a tissue from Julian and using it to dab her eyes. "I mean, why else would my daughter accuse her father of raping her? It's just not something she would have heard of. How could she make something like that up?"

"Of course," Julian confirmed, nodding. April enjoyed watching Julian at work, observing his caring demeanour. He was sat on the edge of the chair, looking intently at Nancy. It really showed he cared.

This, compared to April's slouched posture as she sunk into an armchair across their living room, made her feel less professional.

But it wasn't a lack of respect. April was vulnerable to the paranormal; she could sense it, sometimes even control it – and she would need both physical and emotional distance from the subject to be completely synchronised with anything that may be present.

"And then, of course, when Henry was arrested, I hated him," she continued, wiping her eyes, visibly trying to keep her composure. "And Kaylee was taken into care. But now…"

"Now what, Nancy?" Julian prompted her, speaking calmly and serenely.

"Well, then I saw my daughter. And now I know Henry is innocent."

"How do you know this?"

24

Nancy's face scrunched into a distorted mess. She covered her face, doing all she could to keep herself together.

"It's okay, in your own time," Julian reassured her.

Her lips pursed tightly together, her resolve strengthening, and she turned her attention entirely to Julian.

"I have looked into the eyes of my daughter every day for the past nine years," she spoke, a mixture of distress and assertion. "That *thing* – is not my daughter."

April tuned out of the conversation, listening for anything not of this world that may be whispering to her. Concentrating. Feeling the room, the house.

There was something odd about the house. It felt like it didn't belong to this family. Like they were just residents.

She closed her eyes, feeling herself sinking into her seat, the soft touch of the cushions enveloping her into a feeble embrace. The arms smelt damp, like old furniture, with a mixture of cat hair. She could taste coffee, an aroma wafting in from the kitchen.

As she opened her eyes she retained her sound mind, focusing on each one of her senses, fixing her eyes on Nancy.

There was nothing behind her, no definite vision or demon she could see. Yet, she could feel something. Something lingering in the air, something remaining from before.

Nancy's cheek transformed and contorted. Something was making an impression.

A hand-print.

The size of a child's hand, but with something thin and coarse exuding from the end of the fingers. Claws.

Closing her eyes and shaking her head, she brought herself out of her trance and refocussed her energy to the room.

"Thank you for talking to us, Nancy." Julian stood and shook her hand that loosely gripped his. "We will talk to Kaylee and see what we can find."

Julian led April outside. They walked down the porch,

along the garden path and out of the gate before they began talking.

"Anything?" Julian asked.

"Yeah," April replied. "There was a paw print on the side of her face. Like it had been made by a child, but with something coming out of the end of it. Long, sharp nails."

"So you're thinking the child is in danger?"

"That's my instinct."

Julian paused beside his car, taking a big intake of breath. April noticed him do this a lot – it was his way of making sense of things. Taking a deep breath and breathing his anxiety out. Despite believing in what he did, the job was stressful, not to mention exceedingly dangerous – you could lose more than your life; you could lose your mind or even your soul. This big intake of breath was Julian's way of uncluttering his mind.

"We need to collect the other Sensitive," Julian decided. "We need him."

"What, today?" April reacted, surprised.

"I have a feeling he'll be a help with this case. He feels like a glimpser."

"Okay, well, where do we find him?"

Julian peered around the estate, watching a group of lads cycle past, going way too fast on their bikes.

Everyone was so unaware of what the true dangers are in this world.

"We'll follow our instincts," Julian declared, getting into the car. April loyally followed.

6

THE PHARMACY QUEUE WAS ALWAYS THE LONGEST QUEUE IN THE world.

Being third in line, Oscar thought he wouldn't have to wait that long.

No.

Because at the front of the queue was an old man who had forgotten his reading glasses and was partially deaf. The pharmacist fulfilling his prescription was talking like he was speaking to a foreigner without a translator, and getting a response that was as clear as if he was talking to a cat.

Oscar still had his lingering eight-hour-shift smell clinging to him. His unfashionable green work shirt stank of dried bread and burnt bacon. It was bizarre how this smell attached itself to him, despite just working at the checkout. He would have thought he'd smell like... well, whatever checkouts smell like. But no. His aroma was that of the café beside the checkout and its wandering smells.

"You take them one a day," the pharmacist spoke slowly and clearly. "One a day. No, no, you take them one a day. Yes, you can take them today, but only take one."

Bloody hell, this is ridiculous.

All he wanted was to get his anxiety medication – and the more and more irritation this clueless old man was giving him, the more he needed it. It was like the old man was the barrier to the anxiety medication he needed because of the old man.

"Do you want a bag? A bag? I said, a bag. Do you want – do you want a bag?"

Aaarrrgggghhhhh.

Oscar sighed and rolled his eyes.

"Hi," came a friendly voice from beside him.

Oscar's head turned like he'd heard a gunshot.

There stood a beautiful, funky woman. Young, purple hair, a nose stud, tattoos, and a punky dress sense consisting of baggy jeans, Converse trainers and a red, sleeveless top. Her tattoos were very niche – of Tim Burton characters, and logos of various rock bands. She was immensely attractive, made even more so by her sexy, grunger image.

Oscar looked back and forth, then over his shoulder, not sure who exactly this woman was talking to.

"Erm, I'm talking to you. Hi?"

He turned back toward her. She leant casually against a shelf stocking various laxatives.

"Hi?" Oscar offered, shifting uncomfortably at the uninvited greeting from this stranger, wondering why a woman this attractive was talking to him.

"My name's April." She introduced herself with a sneaky smile that made her seem a little bit naughty. She grabbed hold of his wrist and turned his prescription so she could read his name. "And you are… Oscar Ecstavio."

She glanced to Oscar, then back to the prescription, then to Oscar. She let his wrist go, sticking out her bottom lip.

"Wow," she stated. "You so do not look like an Oscar Ecstavio. More like, I don't know – a Barney. Or a Glomp."

"I don't think Glomp's a name..." Oscar muttered, barely audible, his introverted nature taking over his quivering voice.

"Right, well, Oscar. I'm going to need you to come with me."

"Sorry?"

"I'm going to need you to come with me. You don't need all this medication and all that. There's nothing wrong with you."

Oscar's head fluttered with a thousand confused thoughts. Who was this girl? Why was she talking to him? Why did she think she knew so much about him?

"How do you know?"

"Because you're a Sensitive," she announced with a knowing grin. "It means that you can see or do things that other people can't see or do."

"Like superpowers?"

"Don't be a geek, Oscar."

The two people before him in the queue dispersed, meaning Oscar was next. He looked from the expectant pharmacist to April's raised eyebrows.

"Sorry, but I have to..." he trailed off, and shuffled forward to the counter. He could feel April behind him, watching him, not moving. He handed his prescription over and collected a bag of medication, then turned to leave. He glanced at her, giving an uncomfortable smile as he made his way to the door.

She scoffed, chuckling at his pathetic demeanour. And he felt pathetic. As he scuttled/ away, hunched over, walking with small steps so no one would notice him, he could feel her laughing.

He stepped into the car park and hobbled away as quickly as he could without actually running.

"It's not going to go away, you know," he heard her say, trailing a few paces behind him. "Just because you deny it, you're still going to keep seeing these things."

He glanced over his shoulder and saw her casually striding

after him. He was already out of breath, but she was just strolling a yard or two behind, keeping pace with ease.

"Leave me alone," he grunted.

"Tell me, have you been seeing things? Things you thought were there, but appeared to not be?"

The douchebag getting shot in the supermarket.

The skinhead man behind the counsellor.

"I take that silence as a yes," she decided, reaching his side.

"I need medication; I have things wrong with me."

She halted and put a hand against his chest, forcing him to come to a complete stop. He kept his head down, facing the floor, avoiding eye contact.

"I was once like you. Ridiculous, thinking there was something wrong with me. But there isn't. There's not a single thing wrong."

"Leave me alone."

"Oscar, you need to listen to me, because we need your help just as much as you need ours–"

"Please, can you just leave me alone?"

Oscar's anxiety took over. His whole body violently shook, his neck twitching. Blots appeared in his blurry vision, his head a haze of uncomfortable thoughts.

He fumbled through the bag, pulled out a packet of pills, popped a few, and shoved them into his mouth.

Still, he did not stop shaking. His eyes transfixed on the cement before him, focussing on the remains of indented gum against the pavement, the stains of human waste.

Finally seeing that he was too distressed to be in sound mind, April nodded. She withdrew a card and handed it to him, forcing it into his hand.

"Look, tell you what," she began. "If you feel like you want to actually find out who you really are, give us a call. If you want to carry on being a waste of space, then…"

She shrugged.

With a condescending pat on the back, she took off in the opposite direction.

Oscar fumbled the piece of card over. As his vision regained focus, he held it up in front him.

APRIL CRISTINE
Paranormal Investigator
07644 970306

PARANORMAL INVESTIGATOR?

He shoved the card into his back pocket and kept his head down as he shambled all the way home.

7

Oscar truly could not be arsed with the barrage of regretful diatribe his mother routinely put him through as he entered the house.

"You're living off our money!"

"You're an adult now, you know."

"You were such a smart child, what happened?"

Aren't parents supposed to encourage you? Make you feel good about yourself? Spark your dreams? It seemed this woman was intent on pulling down every bit of self-esteem he had left, trying to make it clear he would never achieve anything.

Not that he particularly had dreams. Maybe that was the problem. All that potential, such little motivation or ambition to do anything with it.

"Hi, Mum," Oscar grunted, as he did every other day. He continued the daily home-from-work routine, pulling his feet out of his shoes, dumping his bag on the floor, and tuning his mother out until she was white noise.

His father sat in the same place he was sat every day. Across the hallway and in the living room, watching either a rugby match, repetitive soaps that he only watched to perv over the attractive young women, or – if it was late enough – Babestation.

"Why won't you ever just talk to me!" his mum cried out as Oscar stomped upstairs.

Because why would I want to talk to someone who tells me I'm a failure every day?

Slamming the door of his bedroom and feeling like he was fourteen again, he dove onto the bed and pulled the pillow over his head.

It had been a long day. Just as long as every other day.

Soon, he would enter his nightly routine. Masturbate, watch television, play on the Xbox until 3.00 a.m., then lie awake in bed until he had to get up for work.

But something distracted his mind.

That girl. April.

She had told Oscar there was nothing wrong with him.

She was the first person to ever say that.

But she didn't know him. Maybe if she did get to know him, realise what he was truly like, her perception of him would change. Within a few days she would solemnly declare, "Sorry, Oscar, I was wrong – you are a fuck-up, you do need that medication, you are a dick."

It's true. Anyone who thought he wasn't a self-indulgent nobody just evidently hadn't gotten to know him that well.

She was incredibly pretty though. Had that really kooky, punky thing going on. It was sexy.

Checking his door was locked, he slipped down his trousers, laid on his bed and daydreamed about April.

He thought about kissing her. About running his hands down her purple hair, brushing down her unblemished immaculate tattooed skin. Thought about the curves of her body, the way her kooky fashion sense only made her more sexy.

"Oscar."

Oscar's head turned quicker than a bullet. He abruptly lifted his trousers from around his ankles, holding his belt around his waist, fully alert.

But there was no one there.

Just his bedroom, clothes on the floor, and his poster of Megan Fox on the wall.

Taking another moment to survey the room with a scrutinising inspection of every corner, he concluded it was in his head. There was nothing there.

He laid down.

Relaxed once more.

Pictured April. That smile. It had made him melt. It was perfectly curved, making her look cute yet naughty.

Those lips.

Those luscious lips.

Those piercings.

"Oscar!"

He shot to his feet, his eyes wide open, his vision darting to every crevasse and every shadow.

Now I know I heard that!

The voice had screamed his name with a venomously low pitch.

But the voice had gone. The room was empty.

He refastened his belt and searched his room, constantly looking around, lifting up every stray item of clothing and every open video game case.

His room was a confined mess, with little places anyone could hide. After checking in his wardrobe and under the bed, he concluded he was alone.

But he wasn't.

He couldn't be.

Someone had screamed his name. Far too deep to be his

mother's voice, and with far too much vigour for the little energy his dad could muster.

"Get a grip!" he barked at himself.

He knew he was being pathetic. This was why he took medication. His anxiety manifested itself in many ways. Given, he had never 'heard voices' before – but he had seen things in the corner of his eye that disappeared when he looked at them, felt a brush of wind in a sealed room. How was this any different?

Maybe he'd think about April later.

He sat at his desk and opened his laptop lid.

A scream roared out from the speakers so loud it sent him flying off the chair. A dark face stared back at him in place of his email, with gaping holes encompassing hollow shadows and bloody scars ripping its flesh.

Oscar fumbled back to his feet.

It was gone.

With a vigorous pace he shut down the web page, shut down the laptop, and switched off the plug.

It took him a few minutes until he realised he was still stood in the middle of his room, the four small walls closing in on him, his breathing accelerating with forceful unease.

What the fuck is going on?

That guy in the supermarket.

The counsellor's boyfriend.

The disgusting, scarred face taking over the Internet.

Then April. The person who said she had an explanation. The one who said she could tell him what was happening.

The one who said he was worth more than this.

Fumbling his hand through his pocket, he withdrew the card and looked upon it once more.

A paranormal investigator.

This was crazy.

I need drugs, not 'Ghostbusters.'

Closing his eyes with a perturbed sigh, he bowed his head and contemplated.

Weird shit kept happening.

How else could he explain it?

Because I'm crazy.

Still.

This made sense, in a disturbing kind of way.

Fuck it.

He grabbed his mobile phone and dialled the number.

8

TO SAY APRIL WAS APPREHENSIVE WAS AN UNDERSTATEMENT.

Was this kid really the all-powerful Sensitive Julian had sensed?

Had she gotten the right guy?

Because he seemed like a dipshit loser.

He had scruffy clothes too big for him hanging off his scrawny body, ruffled hair that looked like it had never been touched by gel or shampoo, and a nervous disposition, which meant he was too easily intimidated to even look her in the eye.

Then, not to mention, the ridiculous phone call she had received from him.

"Er, this is Oscar, the guy at the pharmacy. Er, I don't know why I'm calling. Er, this is April, right?"

If he had said er one more time, April was pretty sure she would have thrown the phone across the room.

Now there he was, stumbling out of his parents' house, his hands in his pockets and his head down. There was no one around to intimidate him, yet he still couldn't lift his head up to face the world. It seemed like she and Julian had more to mould than just his Sensitive powers – they had to stop him from being such an infuriating mess.

Seriously, how was she supposed to work with this guy?

Even the way he opened the car door and sat down on the seat reeked of social awkwardness. He slouched, sticking his hands into his pockets, staring at the gear stick. It was as if he wanted to look at her, but couldn't lift his head high enough, so he just focussed on something lower down beside her instead.

April raised her eyebrows and smiled, waiting for him to say the first words.

"I…" he began. "I don't know why I'm here."

"Well that's a start," April said, more patronisingly than she'd intended.

"I – I keep seeing things."

"Yes, you do," April confirmed. "That's because you're what we call a Sensitive."

"What's a Sensitive?"

April exhaled with sheer exasperation. Was she this much work for Julian when he'd found her and trained her?

She was a damaged teenager living on the streets, but still – at least she wasn't so irritating.

"A Sensitive is called a Sensitive because they are Sensitive to the paranormal and the supernatural. You are Sensitive to the world of the unliving."

"You mean, dead people?"

"Not exclusively but yes, sometimes. Sometimes demons."

Oscar snorted with amusement.

April did all she could to contain her irritation at his reaction. It would be the same for any sceptic who heard this news for the first time.

"Have you seen anything strange happen, Oscar? Something you can't explain? Maybe you've seen or heard something no one else has?"

"… Yes."

"This isn't because you have anxiety. You don't need this ridiculous medication you're taking. You need to be taught to hone these skills."

Oscar sighed. April could see the thoughts twisting and turning inside him, so clearly torn between whether to take a leap of faith or to rely on his ingrained rational thinking.

"Is it just you?"

"Me and Julian. He's a sound guy; just don't piss him off and you'll be fine."

"And what powers do you have?" He spoke so softly, it was as if he didn't want to believe he was asking it.

"My Sensitive is that I can sense and feel the paranormal. I can also act as a conduit."

"A what?"

"A conduit. It means I let spooky fuckers borrow my body."

"What about Julian?"

"He can see Sensitive powers in others. And he's a kick-arse exorcist."

Oscar raised his eyebrows. She could see he was over-whelmed, entwined with disbelief.

"Yo, Oscar, can you lift your head up and look at me, yeah?" April decided she needed to take a different tact. If only to stop him pissing her off, this was something he was going to need to see to believe.

Oscar lifted his head slowly, but still didn't meet April's eyes.

"A little bit more," she prompted. "Almost there. Look me in the eyes, not the chest."

She grinned as he blushed. He slowly lifted his head, warily making brief eye contact with her, shifting his glance back and forth.

"I'm going to take you to a case we're working on," she

decided. "Maybe when you meet this little girl, you'll be able to see something others can't. Maybe then you'll believe."

"… Okay," he muttered.

Rolling her eyes at his despondency, she put the car into gear.

*Does this guy get enthusiastic about anything? He's about to see a sodding demon, for Christ's sake!*She sped off, smirking as Oscar gripped his seat and quickly fastened his seatbelt.

9

To say Oscar felt awkward was an understatement. The whole drive, April kept shooting glances at him as if she was studying him or trying to figure him out. It was difficult enough that he found her immensely attractive, but trying not to stare at her staring was proving difficult.

After a drive that felt longer than it was, April pulled up outside an old-fashioned building. The summer evening had turned to night, and there was an uncomfortable humidity lingering in the air. The building itself was grand, with spiralling architecture and red bricks covered in green moss.

"What is this place?" Oscar enquired.

"This is the place where social services dump kids they don't know what to do with," April answered in a glumly matter-of-fact tone.

"Why are we here?"

"Because this is where they are keeping the girl we're going to meet."

April hastily stepped out of the car, stylishly using the roof to lever herself out. Oscar did the same, though without the slick manoeuvre. Instead, he stumbled over the door and just about kept his balance.

A man who looked a few years older than April approached, his eyes in a fixed glare at Oscar. Oscar even glanced over his shoulder to check this guy was looking at him. There was no one else there.

"This is Julian," April introduced. "He's the boss."

He was a good-looking guy, no doubt about it. His hair was swept back to his neck; he had a prim, clean-shaven face and a well-toned physique that made Oscar feel instantly inferior. Still, he didn't want to get on the wrong side of this guy, so he offered a hand.

"Nice to meet you. I'm Oscar."

Julian looked at Oscar's hand like he was being offered shit on a cake, prompting Oscar to immediately withdraw it. Julian didn't smile; in fact, quite the opposite. He looked at everything like it was a mediocre speck of dirt he simply needed to tread over.

"Follow us," Julian demanded, his voice assertive, but with a rugged huskiness. "And don't say a word unless instructed to."

Julian turned and strode to the decadently majestic front door, pushing its heavy weight open with relative ease. Even the way he walked was with a superior pace. A natural leader, someone who automatically willed the weak to follow him – the complete opposite of Oscar.

"He takes some warming to," April commented as she followed Julian, and Oscar fumbled after them.

"We are here to see Kaylee Kemple," Julian informed the lady at the desk. This lady glanced at Julian, then averted her wary gaze to April's niche dress sense, then to Oscar's shy exterior.

"That girl is being kept under strict protection," the woman answered.

"I know she is, her lawyers sent us," Julian interrupted

confidently. "We have an appointment to see her. If there's an issue, perhaps you could take it up with her police liaison officer."

Any gumption the lady thought she had faded, and she nodded warily.

"Okay," she confirmed. "But I do warn you, that girl – she isn't right."

"Can you point us the way please?"

"Okay." The woman nodded feverishly, her eyes wide open, as if she was shocked that people were willingly speaking to this girl. "Down the corridor, fourth door on the right."

Julian gave her a slight nod, then strode forward again, leading the way.

Oscar scuffled to April's side.

"Who is this girl?" he asked.

"This girl claims her dad raped her," April answered monosyllabically. "Her mum and dad are claiming she didn't. They want us to see if there is anything 'off' about her."

"Off?"

"As in, anything untoward." They paused outside the door. "Not of this world. Demonic. Keep your eyes open, Oscar – if you can see things, and this girl is surrounded by these particular forces, then you will likely see things in this room that you can't explain. Be wary – if it's the first time you see them, you might be in for a shock."

Oscar's jaw remained open as he nodded with absent eyes and a terror-filled mind. What was it he was going to see?

I don't want to see things!

He wished he was back at home. In his bed. Something he never thought he'd wish in a million years.

Julian knocked on the door a few times, laid his hand carefully on the door handle, and twisted it. The door creaked open, and Julian stepped toward a dark figure in the corner.

April gestured Oscar in and shut the door behind them. She led him to a chair behind Julian and sat next to him.

The room was marginally lit by the moon seeping through a narrow gap in the curtain. Besides that, there were many shadows and many pitch-black corners Oscar grew increasingly wary of. There was an eclipsed figure across the room, sat on a bed made up of a single mattress and a wired, metallic frame. This figure was encased in black and barely moved. The silhouette was in the shape of a young girl, but the way it breathed, moved ever-so-slightly, sinisterly twisting its head – it did not feel like a young girl.

"Julian will try and talk to it," April whispered to Oscar. "We need to sit back and watch, then report on what we see."

"Hello," Julian greeted the dark figure.

A croaky, deep-pitched chuckle responded.

"How old is she?" Oscar whispered to April.

"Nine," April responded.

"Then how is her voice so deep?"

April didn't answer. Oscar was pleased she didn't. As soon as the question escaped his lips, he knew he didn't want it answered.

"Can I ask who I am talking to?" Julian prompted, standing tall a few steps away from the bed the little girl propped itself upon.

"Kaylee," the girl responded in a high-pitched, girly voice – but a little too girly, as if it was someone imitating how a girl's voice should sound. It made Oscar's entire body shudder.

"No," Julian stated, shaking his head. "No, I want your real name."

"Kaylee," it responded again, with the exact same tone of voice. "My name is Kaylee."

As Oscar's eyes adjusted to the light, he could just about make out some of the girl's face. Except, the facial features didn't seem like that of a girl. Yes, they were a girl's nose, a girl's mouth, and a girl's eyes – but something about them was off. As if her features were being manipulated into a knowing snarl.

Cuts marked her face, open slits that were yet to close hanging open upon her.

"My daddy molested me," the girl sang, in a happy-go-lucky sing-song voice. It was strange, how such a dramatic, awful accusation was blurted out with such a playful happiness.

"Molested?" Julian responded, sticking his bottom lip out. "That's a big word. Where have you heard that word before, Kaylee?"

"My daddy does it all the time," she sang out again with a buoyant grin. "He molests me all the time."

Something else was there. Oscar was starting to make it out. Something in the shadows around the girl. Something with hazy, indefinite lines, towering over her, consuming the air that surrounded her fuzzy hair.

"What is it?" April whispered. "Are you seeing something?"

"Are you seeing it too?" Oscar asked, growing scared.

"I can feel it, I can smell it – but I can't see it," April confirmed. "Can you see it?"

Oscar stared at a slight movement in the shadows. A cloud of grey breath became momentarily visible, and it petrified him. His hands gripped the side of his chair, his entire body stiffening.

"Yes." Oscar nodded profusely. "Yes, I can."

"Is Kaylee in there with you?" Julian continued. "Is she in there, right now?"

"I am Kaylee."

"No, you're not. You look like Kaylee. You sound like Kaylee. You may even sometimes act like Kaylee. But you are not Kaylee, are you?"

Silence.

The creature behind her moved once more.

It grew larger. A looming shadow, creeping up the walls, creeping over the ceiling, growing larger, coming toward Oscar, coming toward him faster and faster.

His paralysed body shook, seizing in terror.

That's when he saw it.

A female figure, long, black hair reaching down to its waist, large breasts that consumed half its chest, thick black lips – except its eyes were less female. They curved inward to large, dilated pupils that grew to the entire vicinity of its eyes. Below its navel, its waist turned into a long tail, like that of a snake. This tail slithered out, consuming the room, at least three times the size of its torso.

Then in its arms. A baby. Squeezing tightly onto it. The tail wrapping itself around the baby's neck, lifting the baby up, holding it in mid-air.

Oscar could feel April's eyes on him as his eyes grew wider and wider, and his fingers dug further into the arm of the chair.

He didn't notice her stares, nor the fact that Julian and the little girl had now turned their attention to his screams. He couldn't even feel the screams exuding from his throat. He couldn't feel the soreness they were creating, couldn't hear the echoing of his wails around the room.

"Oscar, calm down," April insisted, but the words just blurred into the background with the rest of the room.

The creature loomed further and further over Oscar.

Then the baby it asphyxiated with its tail moved. Its head rotated toward him, its eyes just like its owner – black, full. Its face a ravenous growl. Its mouth open.

It was an abyss of black matter, thinly pointed fangs curling out, dripping with excess saliva.

Oscar fell to the ground, stumbled to his feet, and ran for his life.

Oscar burst out the door and fell to his knees. Before he could even register his need to gag, he was throwing up over a well-laid flower bed, retching repeatedly.

The acidic gunk of his vomit lurched up his throat once more, forcing him to blurt out another mouthful.

He clambered to his knees and attempted to balance himself. The whole world was spinning around him. The house, the lawn, the gravel, spinning and spinning, until he felt so dizzy he was sick again.

"Yo, Oscar!"

Oscar lifted his head with a jolt, expecting to see the beast once more. But it wasn't the beast – it was April. Crouching down beside him, putting a hand on his back.

He hadn't heard her approaching, but somehow she was at his side.

In that moment, he wished he could be anywhere else. He felt his cheeks burn red. He bowed his head in humiliation that April had to see him puking over a family's garden.

"Oh, Jesus," she declared, frowning at the destroyed flower

bed. "You could have at least aimed it away from the roses. They probably took friggin' ages to do, too."

Oscar slumped onto his arse, grimacing at the pain of the bumps of the drive-way digging into him. He shook his head, willing himself to overcome his embarrassment and ask the questions he wanted answered.

"What was that?" Oscar gasped between hyperventilating pants.

"Just breathe, dude," April reassured him, patting his back. "Just keep breathing."

The door creaked open and Julian took a few judgemental steps toward Oscar.

"How bad is it?" Julian prompted.

"Oh, about five times worse than my first demon," April decided. "About ten times worse than your average pussy. I mean, seriously, dude, the orchids?"

Oscar pushed April's hand off him, not taking kindly to the ill-timed jokes. He felt enough of a tit already. He went to stand in a spurt of anger but only ended up stumbling onto his back.

"What was that?" he demanded once more.

"All will be explained," Julian announced, pressing a button on his car keys to unlock his car. "We need to get you home first. Get you a glass of water."

"You want to take me *home*? After I've seen *that*?"

"Not your home, doofus," April sighed. "Back to our home."

"I don't even know you people."

"Yes, you don't," Julian agreed. "But as it is, we are the only ones who will believe you saw what you just saw. Everyone else will call you a delusional prick. We, however, need to know what you saw to identify what demon we are dealing with – so, to us, you are a helpful prick. So, what's it going to be?"

Julian turned to Oscar and gave an award-winning smile, his white teeth sparkling.

"Are you going to be a delusional prick or a helpful prick?"

Oscar's breathing slowed down. It was nowhere near calm, but he could at least take in his surroundings without becoming nauseous. He glanced from April to Julian, and back to April.

"Fine," he grunted. "Just – take me anywhere but here."

April offered Oscar a hand and helped him up.

"See, bud?" she grinned at him. "You're not as much of an irritating cowardly dick as I thought."

Oscar frowned, not sure whether to take that as a compliment. She helped him hobble to the back seat of the car, which he climbed into and laid down upon.

For the whole drive, Oscar stared at the roof of the car. All he could see were the ghastly eyes of whatever it was that he saw. If following these people meant he was going to see more of that, he wasn't entirely sure it was for him.

11

EVERYTHING HENRY HAD HEARD ABOUT PRISON WAS TRUE.

Even though he was only in holding, being denied bail – it was still full of people that terrified him with a glance. He was a middle-class family man. A doctor. He had never mixed with drug dealers or criminals before, and it was wearing him down.

The constant looking over his shoulder. The knowing there was nothing he could do if he saw something over his shoulder. The unbearable tension of how he might be woken up the next morning.

But the most unbearable thought was knowing that he was innocent, yet still stuck there.

And that there was nothing he could do about it.

Once again, he was restrained and guided out of his cell, down the vacant corridors, to another interrogation room. Another desk, with another tape recorder, with another interview, with a blank police officer trying not to be judgemental despite having automatically presumed him guilty.

This police officer allowed silence to fill the room before he started. He was methodical in his approach – making sure his pad was out, his pen was ready, and the tape rewound to the beginning.

Finally, giving a vacant look to Henry, the police officer began the tape.

"This is Detective Inspector Jason Lyle, interviewing Doctor Henry Kemple. The time is twenty fifty-eight. It is noted that Doctor Kemple has waived his right to have his attorney present. We'll begin."

Henry let out a deep breath he didn't realise he was holding. He tried to relax his tense muscles, only to find that they tensed again a moment later.

"Doctor Kemple–"

"Call me Henry, please," Henry interrupted. "You're not a patient, Henry will do."

"Henry," Jason corrected himself. "Could you just explain briefly why you have waived your right to an attorney, just out of interest?"

"Because I am innocent," Henry pleaded. He thought he was sounding assertive, but in truth, he came across as desperate. His voice was soft-spoken, like a caring father; nothing like the hardened criminal he was being made to feel. "I'm tired of these ridiculous impromptu interrogations. Why am I here?"

"Because I am taking over this case, Henry," Jason answered, noting something down on his pad. "And I just wanted to find out a bit more about you."

"A bit more about me?" Henry repeated, shaking his head, wiping his tears on his sleeve because he couldn't lift his restrained hands to his eyes. "I'm a doctor, a husband – and a father! I love my family. What do you need to know?"

"Your daughter is saying you molested her, Henry. She is nine years old. Why would she accuse you of such a thing?"

"I don't know."

"Could she have heard the word 'molest' in the playground, perhaps?"

"I don't know."

"I just seems a strange thing to accuse–"

"I don't *know*!"

Jason rested the end of his pen in his mouth, his eyes hovering over Henry as if inspecting a difficult clue. Henry did not know what to make of this officer. He was unlike the rest, though Henry couldn't decide how.

"I understand your attorneys have called in a group of paranormal investigators," Jason offered, again keeping his expression null and his voice flat.

"Have they?"

"What do you think they are hoping to find?"

"How would I know?"

"Have you seen your daughter since your arrest?"

Henry's weary face morphed into a passionate frown. Scowling at Jason through gritted teeth, he felt his nails dig into his hands in frustration.

"How the hell would I see her?" Henry's lip quivered, his eyes welling up, his emotions spilling from his feeble mind to his fatigued face. "When you are accusing me of doing such things as – as you are accusing."

"Because I went to see her the other day, Henry."

"Oh yeah?"

"What kind of girl is your daughter?"

Henry vehemently shook his head.

"What's that got to do with anything?" he protested.

"Please, Henry, just answer the question."

Henry closed his eyes, clearing his mind, doing all he could to contain his inconsolable grief at this ridiculous situation.

"She is a happy girl, a delightful girl. Friendly, outgoing, boisterous. The life and soul of the party. Would never say a nasty thing about anyone."

Jason nodded as if this was confirming something, though Henry couldn't figure out what.

"When I met your daughter—" he began, then paused. Taking a moment of clear thought, he stopped the recording.

"What are you doing?" Henry asked, shocked at this lack of procedure.

"When I met your daughter, Henry," Jason continued, ignoring Henry's brief outrage, "she was anything but happy. She was far from boisterous. And she was definitely not the life and soul of the party."

"What are you saying?" Henry pleaded.

"I'm saying, whatever your investigating friends find... It's not that I believe in that kind of thing, it's just... I..."

"Officer, if there is something you are trying to say?"

Jason looked around the room. He straightened his sleeves, smoothed down his collar, and clasped his hands over his mouth. Then, after finally gathering his thoughts, he turned his gaze to Henry.

"Whatever is in that room, it's not... What I'm trying to say, Henry, is that I believe you. I think you're innocent."

12

JULIAN SLAMMED A NOTEBOOK AND PEN ON THE TABLE BEFORE Oscar and stood, arms folded, gazing at him inquisitively.

"What do you want from me?" Oscar pleaded.

"You saw the demon," Julian replied, a dead stare and a flat voice. "Now we need to know what we are dealing with."

"I didn't see a demon!" Oscar claimed. "I just saw something because I have mental issues. I'm batshit crazy, I'm off my rocker, I'm–"

"Oscar," April interrupted, leaning coolly against the far wall, her voice coated with relaxation. So much confidence, so much control; Oscar envied it.

He realised he was sweating. Panting, even. Looking back and forth at these two people. Julian, standing expectantly with a bored look on his face; it wasn't even impatience, it was an expectant wait for Oscar to get his shit together. April was a little different. She had a tinge of a smirk, as if she found the whole thing amusing.

Neither of them were anywhere near as out of sorts as Oscar was.

Finally, he forced his heavy breathing to subside and willed himself to raise himself to their level.

"The demon," Julian demanded. "What did it look like?"

"Erm, okay…" Oscar began, resolved to comply. "It was a woman."

Oscar looked back at Julian expectantly, who returned his stare with a close of the eyes that accompanied a sigh and a raise of the eyebrows.

"There are many, many female demons, Oscar," Julian pointed out, speaking as if he were addressing a petulant child. "We are going to need you to be a little more specific than that."

"Erm, okay, okay." Oscar's thoughts shot through his mind as he frantically tried to make sense of them. He willed himself to somehow focus on the inexplicable image of what he had seen. "Long hair. She – she wasn't wearing her top. I mean, she had breasts out and everything."

Julian raised an eyebrow to April, who sniggered knowingly.

"She had no legs. It was like her bottom half was turning into a tail, like a snake's tail, like she was half-snake, half-woman."

Julian clicked his fingers and instantly picked out an old, broken, leather-bound, dusty book off a shelf behind him and started sifting through the pages.

"Go on," he prompted.

"Okay, I – I don't know what else to say."

"Was she holding anything?"

Oscar paused for thought, thinking carefully.

"Actually, yes," he answered. "She was holding – I think it was a baby."

Julian nodded, opened the book, and slammed it in front of Oscar. It was open to a page that displayed a woman exactly as the one he had described.

"Oh my God," he choked. "That's her!"

April moseyed over and peered at the page. She got very close to Oscar. He could faintly smell her and it made him nervous.

"We got a name?" April prompted, forcing Oscar to return his focus to the demon.

"Yes," Julian replied, smiling as if demonology was his time to shine. "She has had various names, known as Ardat Lili, or Lilitu – or, most commonly, Lilith."

"Lilith?" Oscar echoed. April shushed him.

"She is a succubus, associated mainly with either pregnant women or young children, hence the child."

Oscar feebly raised his hands, and the other two looked at him as if he were an idiot.

"Sorry, but – what's a succubus?" he innocently asked.

"A female demon that shags blokes, often when they are asleep," April answered matter-of-factly.

Oscar nodded, not sure what to make of that information.

"Around 4000 BC," Julian continued, "she was reported as a water-demon. More recently, however, from a stone carving in 2400 BC, it was claimed that she was having sex with various men to unleash her demon-spawn upon the world."

Oscar looked from April to Julian, to April, and back to Julian again.

Was he in some kind of fantasy world?

They were aware this was reality, right?

He shook his head. His thoughts filled with utter confusion.

What the fuck are these people on...

"She has a Sumerian origin," Julian began to conclude, Oscar nodding as if he knew what that meant. "She's a sexual demon, often preying on the young, killing children, drinking blood, and raping men. Most notably, she is part of a pairing, with a similar male demon."

"There's more of them?" Oscar choked, bemused, only to find his irritating comment ignored.

"Lilith is often referred to as a female, but she has a male counterpart – usually referred to as Lilu."

"So where does that leave us?" April asked, taking a seat next to Oscar, not noticing how distracted Oscar was by her smooth skin, her well-fitted strappy top, and her generous cleavage.

Noticing Julian's frown, Oscar quickly diverted his attention away from her.

"Well, knowing the kind of horrific things this demon does to young children, and to men – I'd say we need to act fast. God knows what this thing will have done already."

13

FINALLY, JASON COULD REST FOR A MOMENT. HE'D BEEN RUSHED off his feet for most of the day, solving this and that, answering question after question.

It was part of his job, and it was not a problem – but it was nice to finally be able to get himself a coffee.

The kitchen of the police station was smaller than most cells, with a noisy kettle, an aged microwave, and a toaster where you have to hold the button down to make it work. Unfortunately, updating and repairing kitchen equipment was not the priority of a detective inspector, nor was it within the police budget.

As he left the kitchen, sipping his coffee and thinking how much he detests the supermarket brand stuff, one of his sergeants came bustling up to him.

"Hey," called the man, getting Jason's attention. "Can you sign this?"

Giving his colleague his coffee to hold, Jason traded it for a few pages attached to a clipboard. As he glanced down it, he suddenly became alert.

"What is this?" Jason demanded.

"What do you mean?"

"This is talking about Henry Kemple's release."

"Didn't you hear? His daughter dropped the charges, he's being released."

What?

What could have prompted such a sudden change in the daughter's story?

And how could this information have gone past him?

"No," Jason spat. "I did *not* hear."

Shoving the clipboard against his inferior, Jason marched through the corridors and to the front desk of the station.

"The Kemples?" he barked at the clueless officer sitting at the desk.

"Sorry?"

"The Kemples, being released. Where are they?"

"Er, I think the mum's through there–" he pointed a loose finger down a corridor. Jason had begun marching down the corridor before the officer could say another word.

Storming forward, he looked through the window of every room. Eventually, he reached the one where he spotted Nancy's distraught face and entered.

"Mrs Kemple," Jason began, quietly shutting the door, and taking a seat opposite her. "I've just heard. What's happened?"

Nancy dabbed at her eyes with a tissue as she shrugged her shoulders.

"Kaylee claimed she was lying," she answered, shaking her head as if disbelieving it.

"Do you trust her?" Jason inquired.

Nancy took a moment to consider this question.

"I believe that Henry is innocent. That he didn't touch her. I know that much."

"So, what is the matter then?"

Nancy closed her eyes and sighed, furiously shaking her head. She went to speak a few times, each time producing nothing but dead air. Eventually, she took a deep breath in, composed herself, and answered the question.

"It's Kaylee," she spoke softly. "She's – she's not herself. She's changed. And I don't completely understand why."

"Maybe she's playing up for some reason. Kids can often be naughty."

"Have you met my daughter, Detective Inspector?"

Jason shuddered at the recollection of those few moments he had spent in Kaylee's presence.

"Yes," he confirmed, directing his eye contact elsewhere. "Yes, I have."

"And tell me – did she seem all right to you?"

Jason returned Nancy's adamant stare, considering how to respond to that question. Kaylee hadn't appeared to be your average conflicted or traumatised little girl. The room she was in had turned cold; she gave an aura of menace, and there was a deeply sinister glint in her eye. For a nine-year-old girl, there was nothing innocent or childish about her.

"I – I don't know how to answer that question," Jason answered honestly.

"Well, let me tell you about Kaylee. Kaylee is the kind of girl who would let another child have the last sweet in the sweet shop so that child doesn't get upset. Kaylee is the kind of girl who draws pictures of flowers and gives them to her teacher. Kaylee is the kind of girl who smiles and she lights up the room. Did she smile while you were there?"

"… Yes."

"And what was that smile like?"

Jason shrugged his shoulders despondently.

"It – I don't know how to put it into words."

"Exactly."

Jason tucked his shirt in and pulled his tie up, having to do something with his hands to avoid nervously fidgeting. He knew exactly what she was saying, but still needed to maintain an air of professionalism. Ridiculing a young child was not appropriate for a police officer of his standing.

"Look, Mrs Kemple, maybe things will clear themselves up in time. But you are getting your husband back, and you are getting your daughter back – this is surely a good thing. Just take your time to be happy about that."

Nancy dabbed her eyes once more and dropped her gaze to the floor.

Jason was so convincing, he almost believed his reassurance himself.

14

Nancy could see herself in the eyes of those who walked past her.

Although she could not directly see her reflection, she knew she was a mess. People's faces were etched with discomfort and avoidance, looking at her as if she was a homeless urchin just picked up off the street.

She wasn't a homeless urchin. Nor had she been picked up off the street.

She was a distressed, concerned mother – who simply did not understand what was happening.

Despite initial concerns, she hadn't doubted her husband. Even after Kaylee persisted in her accusations, she remained firm in the belief that Henry had not touched their daughter, nor had the thought ever even crossed his mind.

But she hadn't completely disbelieved Kaylee either. It was as if it was a lie that Kaylee had convinced herself so adamantly was real that, to her, it was a truth.

In a situation when someone isn't being honest with themselves, how are they meant to be honest with anyone else?

It's just… Kaylee had never heard the word 'molest' before.

She didn't even know about sex, what it was, or where she came from; she knew far too little to even approach a subjecti such as rape.

Nancy decided to put her faith in the group her lawyers had contacted – The Sensitives, she recalled them being referred to. As much as she reminded herself she didn't believe in such things, in a time of crisis one's thoughts jump to extreme conclusions.

A girl walked out and Nancy's body tensed. She filled with terror, desperately on edge to see her daughter's face.

Then the girl walked past, with a different face to her daughter's, into the arms of a different father.

And she relaxed.

Is this really how I'm going to be when I see my daughter again? Worried and on edge?

She bowed her head and closed her eyes. Despaired about what kind of mother she was to doubt her family so much. Never had she thought she'd dread seeing father and daughter reunited.

But there she was.

A pair of weakened eyes appeared from a far door. A man once strong, but full of the emotions of weeks in a jail cell, cautiously stepped into the corridor.

Nancy rose. Not sure why, she just automatically stood.

It felt like the right thing to do.

Her eyes met her husband's.

And they broke.

So many nights sleeping in their home alone. No daughter to cuddle, no husband to cry to. Just the sound of late-night television to help her fall asleep.

After all that, this is what she does.

Stands across the corridor of a sparsely populated police station reception, staring vehemently at the eyes of the man she vowed to love, in sickness and in health.

He froze too, casting a solemn tear from his eye, letting it dance slowly down his cheek.

"Henry–" Nancy began, stepping forward to embrace him – but the gesture was cut short by the sound of their daughter running into the room.

"Daddy!" Kaylee cried, a face full of elation. Despite running out the doorway closest to Nancy, she bypassed her and sprinted straight into her father's arms.

Nancy could only watch as Henry fell to her level and clutched his arms tightly around Kaylee. He fell to pieces, his lip quivering and his eyes filling with tears. His arms gripped her, holding her closely, clinging on for dear life. It was an embrace that never ended, one that was flooded with the emotions of the love between father and daughter.

Nancy remained stationary, watching.

It made sense that Kaylee ran past her, and straight to her father.

Didn't it?

Can't think such destructive thoughts now. Pull yourself together.

Willing herself to be strong, to keep faith in her family, she forced a forged smile to her lips. She went to step forward but was stopped as Kaylee and Henry pulled apart.

They remained close and, in exact unison, turned their heads toward Nancy. A sadistic smile crept across both of their faces. Something shared, unbeknownst to Nancy, was passed across in the silent subconscious between father and daughter.

Or maybe Nancy was just being paranoid.

Yes.

Weeks of stress accumulating into bad thoughts. That's all it was.

Just the emotions she had kept bottled up for so long, finally reaching the surface.

Then Kaylee turned to Henry and, keeping her eyes pinned

on her mother's, whispered something gently into her father's ear.

Henry nodded.

And the moment was over.

Henry took Kaylee by the hand toward Nancy, allowing mother and daughter to finally embrace. It wasn't a tight, desperate hug like she had given her father – but rather a reluctant, compulsory hug you would give an aunt you barely see.

Nancy willed the bad thoughts to the back of her mind.

She told herself it was nothing. Just a silly interpretation of a love between Henry and Kaylee that, really, they should be celebrating.

Her father had his daughter back again.

And the mother had her family.

No more sleepless nights alone.

Or so she thought.

15

IF YOU ASKED OSCAR WHY HE ENTERTAINED THE RIDICULOUS notions of him having some special supernatural abilities, he probably couldn't give you an answer. He had no idea why he remained in the same room as Julian and April, listening to them prattle on about demons and exorcisms and ghosts.

Maybe it was because April was really attractive. Maybe that's what it was.

Maybe it was because he had found somewhere he belonged, which was something he'd never had. At school, he'd had plenty of acquaintances, but never many friends. Various social groups he may have had lunch with, but never anyone he would invite to his house for tea, or down the park for a kickabout.

Maybe it was because it finally gave him a purpose. Something these people genuinely believed he could do, no matter how preposterous a concept as him being a 'Sensitive' with special paranormal powers may be. These people actually wanted him there. He hardly had huge ambitions of climbing up the promotion ladder in the supermarket. This gave his insignificant life some significance.

But, most likely, it was because it felt right. Like some-where deep inside of him, it was true. It was a feeling he couldn't articulate – hell, he could barely acknowledge it – but it offered him an explanation. Something that provided reasons to the various mental ailments he had been diagnosed with and medicated for.

So he watched as Julian and April fervently paced the room, distressed about the news of a phone call Julian had received.

"I can't quite believe this," Julian had announced as he returned to the room.

"What?" inquired April, moving to the edge of her chair in anticipation.

"Kaylee Kemple has changed her testimony. She's saying she lied about her dad, and they are both being released."

Oscar watched April for some direction as to how he should act. April's jaw dropped and she looked around the room for imaginary answers, which told Oscar that he should evidently be shocked also.

Though, if this girl was in fact 'possessed,' as they were hypothesizing, surely she'd be erratic in her decisions. Changing her mind and coming up with precarious accusa-tions that would mess with the family seemed like a perfect way to torment them. And why else would a demon be plaguing this family, other than to torment them?

April and Julian were on their feet. They had a huge white-board against the wall, and a dozen pens scattered around various furniture surfaces, and they wasted little time in filling it. Everything they knew went on it. Starting with the basics: the girl, the parents, their ages, their jobs, their family history. Then they mindmapped off Kaylee's name, noting various observations they had made about her.

Oscar became mesmerized with April's buttocks for a short period of time, watching them bounce and wobble hypnotically with a dainty enticement as she wrote various pieces of information on the board. After a few moments, he broke himself out of his daze and forced himself to focus on what she had written.

In a big red pen, she had written in capitalised letters, *LILITH / ARDAT LILI*, and joined it to Kaylee's name. Around these two main headings, various pieces of information had been noted.

Cold room in her presence.

Repeated "Daddy molested me."

Smile unlike child's normal smile.

After the board was full, Oscar watched statically as Julian and April vocally came to life, bouncing questions back and forth. They ignored Oscar sitting there, staring at them.

"So why would she claim he molested her in the first place?" April proposed.

"To mess with the dad," Julian answered. "But then why would she stop messing with the dad?"

"Where's the mum in all this?"

"Has she made any accusations toward her?"

"I don't know, has she?"

"Not that I know of."

"Hey, guys–" Oscar tried to interject, but his timid offering was cancelled out by the relentless wave of questions.

"What's the link here?"

"The link between what?"

"Lilith, the demon, and the accusations?"

"Is there ever really a link?"

"The demon often molested men itself…"

"Maybe it's planning something?"

"Maybe–" Oscar tried again.

"I think–"

"Hey, guys!" Oscar shouted.

April and Julian froze, slowly rotating their heads toward

him in unison, taken aback by the interjection of his impudent voice.

"Maybe she just needs to be closer to her parents to continue her attack," Oscar offered, then sat back in his chair, curling up, retracting back into his introverted shell.

Julian looked to April. It was the kind of look that said, *He's right, but I really don't want to admit it.*

"Of course," April spoke. "If this is just the first wave of attacks, surely she's going to need to be closer to her parents for the rest?"

They continued barking back and forth various ideas and plans and concoctions.

Oscar just sat back in his chair, smiling, glad to actually be of some use.

16

Everyone has their way to escape the troubles of their life. Some sing, some dance, some even turn to drugs. Nancy sewed. Didn't matter what – clothes, bedsheets, even skirts for her daughter's Barbies, she just did it.

So, once she had left Kaylee downstairs to play with her toys, she retreated to the silence of the study to work on a quilt she had begun before the whole ordeal had started. It was nice to finally return to some resemblance of normality.

Henry was at work. Kaylee was playing. Nancy was sewing.

It was as it should be.

Then it occurred to her.

This silence. Kaylee had been quiet for an awfully long time...

Normally, there would be some background noise of Kaylee's voice, acting out some kind of bickering between her dolls. Or at least the sound of her walking around, knocking into various ornaments.

But nothing.

Absolutely nothing.

She turned her head, peering over her shoulder into the darkness of the hallway. Despite it being the middle of a sunny day, the hallway was always dressed in darkness; a lack of windows was the only thing that had originally put her and Henry off buying this house.

She listened.

Not even a murmur.

"Kaylee?" she called out, then remained still as she waited for an answer.

There was no reply.

Maybe she hadn't heard her.

"Kaylee, are you there?" she shouted once more, this time a little louder.

Impeccable silence drifted up the stairs and flooded into the room with a succinct absence.

She shuddered. Not entirely sure why this was so disturbing.

Kaylee was allowed to be quiet if she wanted to.

It was all just so...

Unusual.

Nancy placed her sewing upon the desk and wandered into the hallway. She looked back and forth, scanning every corner and crevasse of the house; not entirely sure why.

It was her daughter, for God's sake.

She needed to stop thinking there was something wrong when there wasn't.

Pausing at the top of the stairs, she strained to listen. The living room was opposite the bottom step, so any hustle or slight movement would carry, and Nancy could take it as a surety that Kaylee was safe.

But the only thing that carried up the stairs was silence and dust clouds.

The creak of the step as Nancy placed her first foot down

71

was far louder than it normally was, but this may have been because quiet noises always sound louder in silence.

Nancy reached the bottom step and cautiously thumped the worn-out carpet of the hallway. The open door to the living room displayed an empty presence.

Edging forward, Nancy slowly peered around the doorway, scanning the room.

A pile of dolls were left scattered across the floor, a half-empty orange juice on a cabinet, and an overwhelming emptiness encompassed the room.

This was where Nancy had left her daughter.

The windows were shut.

The front door remained locked behind her.

Where was she?

Nancy slowly rotated and took a few small steps back into the hallway and toward the kitchen. The only other room Kaylee could be in.

She tiptoed warily, keeping her eyes glued on the vacant entrance.

Why am I tiptoeing?

She shook her head to herself. Why was she so worried?

It was her daughter she was looking for.

Not some monster.

It was her nine-year-old daughter.

But, as she approached the doorway, an overwhelming chill sent itself coursing through Nancy's body; first through her bones, seizing her muscles, and inflating her lungs.

She peered around the doorway.

She nearly jumped out of her skin.

Kaylee sat at the kitchen table.

Why am I jumping? It's Kaylee...

There was something about the way Kaylee had propped herself up.

There was nothing casual in the way Kaylee was sat. It

wasn't like she was in the middle of an activity, or even in the middle of a thought. She sat at the table, her hands laid down upon the wooden surface with symmetrical precision as she stared back at Nancy with wide eyes and a wide grin.

"Hello, Mummy," Kaylee sang out.

Kaylee never calls me Mummy. It's always 'mum' or nothing.

Nancy's breath caught in her throat.

What was going on? Why was her daughter so different, and why was it freaking her out so much?

Nancy withdrew for a moment, backing up into the hallway.

She paused. Gathered herself. Shook herself back to earth.

It was her daughter. Just her daughter, but a little... off. Unwell. Unusual.

Get a grip, Nancy.

Be strong for my family.

It wasn't unusual for young children to change their dialect. Perhaps she'd heard 'mummy' somewhere else? A television program, or at school perhaps.

Once she had composed herself, shaken her mind back to normality, she returned to the kitchen.

And froze.

What the hell...

The glasses in the cabinet, through the glass door... they were upside down.

The chairs were balanced upside down on the table.

The cereal boxes along the kitchen side.

The kettle.

The handwash.

The egg timer, with its sand rushing wildly downwards.

Every single thing in this room was upside down, except for Kaylee, the chair in which she sat, and the table she rested her arms upon.

And Kaylee was in the exact same position.

Her arms hadn't moved an inch. Her smile was the same, her eyes were the same, and her unfaltering stare remained eerily on Nancy's.

Nancy's eyes scanned back and forth in disbelief.

She had been out of the room for seconds.

She hadn't heard anything but sickening silence.

Chairs, when they had touched the table… surely they would have made some noise. The glasses, to all be turned on their heads at that speed, would have created at least a gentle thudding sound as they were placed downwards.

Being able to precariously balance the kettle on its head.

How…

"Hi Mummy," Kaylee repeated.

"How…" Nancy muttered. "How did you do this?"

"Do what, Mummy?"

Nancy flinched at the way Kaylee said *Mummy*. It was with such a happy bounce, such pride. But not pride at Nancy being her mummy; pride at the kick in the teeth it gave to Nancy that she called her such a name.

"The objects… how did you do this?"

Kaylee showed the first utterance of movement she had shown since Nancy had entered the room. Keeping her body in the exact same position, Kaylee's head turned robotically to the left, then to the right, then resumed her stare.

Nancy awaited an answer.

Kaylee just kept smiling.

Kept smiling that sinister, sordid, sacrilegious smile.

"Who are you…" Nancy whispered, quiet enough that only she could hear it.

"What's the matter, Mummy?"

"I… I'm going to go lie down."

Nancy glanced once more at the room.

Her eyes were not deceiving her. It was a painting of perfectly balanced rotation, everything on its head but Kaylee.

Kaylee was such a sweet, kind girl. A friendly girl who loved her mother.

This was not her Kaylee.

APRIL'S WORDS SPUN AROUND OSCAR'S MIND LIKE A HAMSTER ON a wheel.

Julian had turned to her and announced, "We need to visit, there are things we need to clarify."

"Where is it?" April replied.

"It's in Loughborough. It's around a hundred-mile drive."

April had turned to Oscar with a sexy glint in her eye, a cheeky half-smirk, and announced:

"Let's take Oscar. See if he's ready for the big time."

So there he was. In the back of the car heading up the M42, watching Julian and April having a quiet conversation between them in the front. It took him back to being a kid, an only child stuck in the back, whilst his parents had grown-up conversations in the front that he wasn't privy to.

He ruminated on April's sassy grin and declaration that they should take Oscar. He'd found himself really wanting to impress her, somehow wanting to justify her belief in him. So that she could eventually announce, "Yes, we were right, he *is* ready for the big time!"

Maybe it was because he was lonely. Maybe it was because

it was the first girl he had ever met who gave him an ounce of attention. Or maybe it was just because it was something different that could take him away from the monotony of life.

Tewkesbury wasn't the most exciting place. It was advertised as 'a historic riverside town.' They were close.

History – yes. Everything was old and crumbling down, including the majority of its inhabitants.

Riverside – yes, there was a small river.

Town – well, there was a WHSmith. And a pharmacy. And enough charity shops to make you suspect they were taking over the world.

But as for activities, it hadn't been a particularly thriving place to grow up in, or dwell with his parents.

But now – ghosts, exorcists, demons possessing people; and he had these crazy powers that could do something about it.

Even if all this excursion was accomplishing, was to entertain and encourage April and Julian's joint delusions, at least it meant that he was doing something. Being useful.

As they joined the slip road at junction thirteen, entering a roundabout, Julian peering at his satnav, an overwhelming sense of doom overtook Oscar.

His muscles tensed, his bones stiffened, and his armpits began perspiring.

What was going on?

What was this feeling?

He abruptly choked. His lungs expanded, but it felt like no oxygen was filling them. He was wheezing, coughing, spewing up vague air from his sore throat.

Fear had taken him over.

A certainty that he was going to die overcame his immediate thoughts.

What was going on?

Why?

How?

He reached into his pocket, grasping a packet of pills, and held them out in his hands. He struggled to pop any out, such was the shaking of his hands.

After missing a few times, he finally managed to burst some medication into his palm.

He lifted the pills to his mouth.

April's hand clamped tightly around his arm.

The pills hovered away from his gaping lips, unable to cure his anxiety due to the rigid hand firmly placed around his wrist.

"What are you doing?" Oscar frantically cried.

He was starting to well up, and he really didn't want to cry in front of these people. They would think he was sad, or pathetic, or a loser.

Please don't cry.

But his arms shook, his legs seized, and his neck stiffened.

Every piece of him was consumed with a colossal need to take these pills.

He pulled at his arm, reaching his mouth forward, gaping for the release of his medication.

"Don't!" April barked.

"What?" Oscar wept. "Why?"

"Because you don't need them!"

Don't need them?

Fucking look at me!

"Yes, I do!" Oscar blubbered, reaching his jaw forward as April pulled his arm further away.

"No, you don't!" April insisted. "These feelings are not anxiety, not mental health issues, none of that. These feelings are your gift, having been suppressed for so long."

Before his eyes, a sudden premonition appeared. Of a house. A tranquil, serene, family home. A father. A mother.

A daughter.

The daughter he saw.

Kaylee.

She was laughing. Cackling, even. Sadistic roars of humour.

The girl.

The family was in trouble.

His shaking increased.

"I'm going to collapse, I need them!"

"No. You. Don't!"

April's insistent eyes reached out to him, boring into him, devouring him with her determination.

"Do not suppress your gift," she instructed. "Do not numb it. Embrace it. See what it will tell us."

April jarred his arm and the pills flew into the side of the seats and the crevices of the car's floor.

"No!" Oscar jolted upright.

Then the vision of the daughter left him.

He relaxed.

His muscles calmed, his breathing slowed, and his mind became an ecstasy of tranquillity.

"What did you see?" April asked.

"The family… the girl… they are in trouble."

April glanced at Julian, who grinned back.

"See," April smiled sincerely. "Your gift is of use."

As he stepped out of the car, Oscar's mouth dropped in awe.

It wasn't that the house itself was particularly impressive. It was your standard middle-class-family house; two floors, probably three bedrooms, nice brick, generously sized drive. Beside it was a collection of trees, with a lake just about visible beyond them.

It was the feeling in the pit of Oscar's stomach that perturbed him. A stabbing feeling, as if he had swallowed a hundred knives and they were now swirling around inside his stomach, poking rashly at each and every component of his body.

Something was wrong with this house.

Or with something within it.

"Shall we?" Julian prompted, grabbing a leather bag and marching up the porch. Oscar noticed the edge of a cross poking out of this bag, which struck him as being eerily old-fashioned.

"Come on," April prompted, and Oscar scuttled behind them to the front door.

The sound of Julian and April greeting Nancy Kemple occurred in the background, as if it was on a television with a low volume. Oscar was concentrating on other things. Like the walls.

The hallway was decorated with a light-green coating of paint, leading to a circular flower pattern on the wallpaper in the living room. Flashes of red appeared splashed against the walls, then went, like a hazy static.

A sucker punch landed into his gut, a hard hit of wind that came from nothing, and he fell to the floor.

When he lifted his head once more, the room had faded to black-and-white. He was the only one in it.

Whilst the room was modestly furnished and vacant of any person, there was something in the background. Some kind of screaming, or shouting, or moaning.

Before Oscar could find the source of the sound, he had sunk through the floorboards. In an instant, his arms disappeared and his whole body sank through the wood like quicksand, and he fell upon a solid stone floor.

Clouds of dust floated around him and, even though he had hit a hard surface with excessive velocity, he felt nothing.

The stabbing pain inside him remained, but there was no pain caused by his falling through the floorboards, and into what looked like a basement.

He laid out on his front, slowly lifting his head. The basement was consumed by shadows, coated in darkness except for a single light bulb flickering softly above him.

In the shadows, something moved.

He couldn't make out what it was.

But it was everywhere.

Encompassing the edges of the entire room, up against the walls, cloaked in the protection of the light's absence.

Crying. There was crying.

Oscar squinted.

There was movement. They were bodies. Children.

Lots of them. In rags. Cowering. Covering their heads, shielding themselves.

Oscar rose to his knees, looking to his left, to his right, and over his shoulder. They surrounded him, filling the shadows.

"What's going on?" he whispered, barely audible.

Despite the silence of his whimper, the cowering children all gasped at the sound of his voice.

So he spoke louder.

"Who are you?" he forced, trying to sound assertive, despite his voice breaking in the middle of the sentence.

Whispers echoed him, "Who are you?" being quietly gasped around the room.

"Why are you all here? What is going on?"

One of the children stepped forward, allowing a fraction of light upon her face. This girl's face revealed a deadly, charred burn up her cheek and a pattern of red scratches along the other.

"Oh, God." Oscar flinched away. "Who did this to you?"

The girl looked upwards.

"She did…" she whispered in a timid cry.

"Who's she?"

The girl lowered her head back down, focussing her eyes on Oscar's.

"The girl. She's not who she says she is."

"Which girl? Who is she?"

The child cowered. Another child stepped forward, taking her place. This time a boy, half-stripped, with scars from whiplashes spread across his chest, and a deep wound spread upon his face.

"The young girl who lives here is not that girl," the boy told Oscar.

"Then who is she?"

The boy's eyes searched back and forth, trying to summon the others; but they just cowered further into the shadows.

"She is her," the boy said.

"Her? That doesn't make any sense."

"The one who tortures us. The one who keeps us enslaved."

"The girl is keeping you enslaved?" Oscar repeated, filled with confusion.

"Please... help us..."

An unprecedented bolt jolted through Oscar's body, sending him to the floor, his head smacking against the ground.

This time he felt it.

Only, when he lifted his head, he wasn't in the basement anymore.

He was in the living room.

Everyone was staring.

Henry and Kaylee's wide eyes fixed upon him. Julian watched, intrigued. April knelt by his side, rubbing his back.

"It's okay, Oscar," April assured him.

But it wasn't okay.

Oscar was far from okay.

"Oscar, just calm down, tell us what you saw."

With complete disregard for April, he flung himself to his feet and attempted to charge at the front door. He found himself unable to balance and collapsed against the nearest wall.

Doing all he could to gain his balance, he forced himself back to his feet.

He felt someone's arms around him, trying to help, but he reached out and shoved them off him.

He didn't want help.

He didn't want anyone to touch him.

What the fuck just happened?

Using the door to steady himself, he dragged his feet to the front door and burst out, stumbling onto the lawn.

The sun shone down on him, casting burning rays over his skin, initially blinding him as he dove to the floor, shielding his eyes.

He vomited over a patch of flowers.

19

THE WORLD SPUN LIKE HE WAS DRUNK.

Oscar was on his knees, coughing up that morning's cereal, squinting with pain as his stomach churned, overcome with a painful acidic stab. Any time he tried to look up he'd stay rigidly still, but the lawn would spin to his right, the same patch of grass moving around and around and around.

"Cool it, Oscar," he heard April's voice instruct him.

Cool it?

If she wasn't so fricking hot, I'd have told her to piss off.

He felt her gentle hand rest against his back.

"Don't worry, this will go within a minute," she reassured him, though he didn't quite believe her. "You've just got to control it."

"Control it?" he gasped between sweaty panting and spits of sickly remains. "Are you fucking kidding me?"

"Oscar, man, this is something we're used to seeing in people like you."

"People like me?" he barked. "There is no 'people like me.'"

He closed his eyes for a moment. When he opened them the world still spun, but at a faster pace. April's raised eyebrow came into focus, and he seethed at her as she knelt beside him with a sympathetic smile.

"I have mental health problems," Oscar snapped. "I need my medication. This is what happens when I don't have my medication."

"And what is this, Oscar?" April laughed with a cocky smile that only infuriated Oscar further.

"This?" he echoed, with such tension it came out at a far higher pitch than he'd intended. "This is an episode."

"An episode, huh?" April chuckled.

"Would you stop laughing at me!" Oscar demanded. He tried to get to his feet but found himself unsteady, and fell straight back onto his backside.

"Relax, Oscar."

Oscar's head still pounded, but his vision was finally returning to normal. The front garden became still. Whatever it was, it had ended; but he still felt terrible.

"Would you stop telling me to relax!"

April took a bottle of water from beside her and offered it out to Oscar. She looked at him like you would a child who had gotten something wrong and had just learnt they were being silly. Her eyebrows were raised and her smile was patronisingly wide.

Oscar snatched the water bottle from her and gulped it down, not realising how dehydrated he had become.

"What did you see?" April inquired.

"What do you mean, what did I see?" Oscar frowned, taking another swig from the bottle. "What does it matter, what I saw?"

April let out a big sigh, an exhalation of irritation.

"I'm only just starting to come around to you, Oscar; don't do my nut in now."

"Me do *your* nut in?"

April gazed up at the warm family home, casting her eyes over the loving house of terror.

"Inside that house," she began, "is a mother, a father, and a daughter who are going through something nothing short of atrocious. And it is our duty to help them."

"Our duty?" Oscar sneered. "What do you mean our duty? Why is it *our duty*?"

"Because we can, you fool," she joked, placing a reassuring hand on Oscar's shoulder that made him feel all warm inside.

"I can't help anyone." Oscar's eyes dropped to the floor as he despondently shook his head.

"Stop it with the puppy dog eyes and the weak boy act, it's getting old. What you had is called a *glimpse.*"

"A what?" Oscar lifted his head slightly, hesitantly intrigued.

"A glimpse, Oscar. It's what we call it when you have a vision, when you see something that isn't there, or was there, or will be there."

"What?"

"Many people have had many glimpses. A lot of them don't even know it. And if you truly have the gift, that won't be your last."

"What?!" Oscar screeched.

It was not a pleasant experience. In fact, it was a bloody awful experience, one that Oscar was happy to be medicated for and would thoroughly love to never have again.

"Don't worry," April reassured him. "Once you learn to control them, and harness them, they won't be like that. You just have to get used to them."

"I don't–"

"I have glimpses, too," April interrupted. "Well, kind of glimpses. I don't have fully formed visions like you seem to. I am able to act as a conduit for speaking to the dead, or to the beyond, and I can see visions of their life when I do it."

"Really?"

"Yes. You can see glimpses but, what Julian and I are thinking, is that your glimpses are about people, and the forces hovering around them or controlling them. You can see and feel these entities."

Oscar took a moment for this situation to sink in.

Yesterday, he was a Morrison's checkout boy.

Now I don't have a clue what is going on.

"Which is why you are important to us." She looked him dead in the eyes. "Which is why you are important to me."

He filled with a giddy buzz that sent tingles to the tips of his fingers and the tips of his toes.

"Now, what did you see?" she asked.

"I was in the basement, and there were all these children. And they were, like, I don't know..." He strained to remember, but in a sudden wave, it all came flooding back. "They said the girl is not who she says she is."

"That confirms it then."

"Confirms what?"

"The girl is not who she says she is. That, matched with the demon you saw, I'd say means we have a pretty strong case of possession."

April sprang to her feet and offered her hand out to Oscar.

"Come on, we need to help Julian do his thing."

Oscar didn't want to get up, but the simple act of being able to put his hand in hers, even if it was just to help him stand, was too inviting.

"Can I be honest?" Oscar asked, his hands tentatively twitching.

"Always," April replied.

"I still don't really buy it. I mean, I know you believe it's true, it's just... I'm an atheist. I don't believe in all this. It makes a lot more sense to me that everyone involved is crazy."

"Good," April declared. "If you believed everything, you

would be no good at this job. You need to have a sceptical mind."

She grabbed hold of his hand, which once again made his whole body tickle with teasing excitement.

"Once you have seen Julian do his thing you will believe," she asserted. "I mean, he's going to poke and prod to try and bring this demon out into the open, just to make sure. Once you've seen that happen – there is *no* questioning anything *ever again.*"

And with that, she dragged him back into the house and shut the door behind them.

20

OSCAR TOOK EACH CREAKY STEP WITH A CURIOUS HESITANCY. Part of him was starting to believe, but part of him was also wary about what Julian might do to provoke this demon into revealing itself.

Yes, he could be about to witness the evidence he longed for.

But he could also be about to witness a huge case of child abuse.

Either way, he found his feet unintentionally guiding him toward the bedroom. His lip quivered as April turned back to him and gave him a deep, sincere gaze into his eyes.

"Are you ready for this?" she asked.

Oscar reluctantly nodded.

"Remember – a demon will say and do things to provoke you, and everyone else in the room. You must not respond to it, or listen to it. You understand?"

He nodded once more.

"Oscar, I'm going to need an actual confirmation from you that you understand this."

"Y-yes," he stuttered. "I understand."

"Julian is going to get this thing to say its name. If it admits to being Ardat Lili, or Lilith – we will take that as evidence."

Bracing herself with a deep breath and relaxing her muscles, they entered the bedroom.

As Oscar passed the threshold he was hit with a sudden stab of frozen air. His breath was visible, such was the low temperature of the room. Henry stood in the corner of the room with a tearful Nancy in his arms, shielding her from the potential torment.

Julian stood dominantly over the bed, over Kaylee, whose wrists were fastened to the bed-posts with handcuffs, and her ankles with belts. The girl looked distraught; a face full of fear, tears trickling down her cheeks, no understanding of what was happening.

A sickening feeling of uncertainty filled Oscar. This wasn't right. It felt like a scene from a movie, one that would never realistically happen due to the complete negligence and disregard for the child involved. This child didn't look possessed; she looked devastated. Utterly inconsolable at what her parents and these strangers were doing to her.

"Are we ready?" Julian prompted April with a deadened voice. April nodded and shut the door behind them.

Julian turned to Kaylee on the bed beneath him, glaring at her with a face full of disdain.

This wasn't right.

Whatever these people believed, Oscar couldn't watch this.

This is just wrong.

"April, I can't–" he began, but was abruptly silenced as April shushed him.

Julian made the shape of a cross over his body, then kissed his hands. He dropped his head, closing his eyes, and giving a silent prayer. When his eyes shot open they were full of determined resolution. Full of tenacity; they were the eyes of a man with strong convictions in what he was about to do.

"Kaylee, are you okay?" Julian asked.

The little girl turned her head, eyes full of tears, and gaped wide-eyed at the scary man stood over her.

"Listen to me, Kaylee," Julian began. "I know this is tough, and I know you don't want to do this, but I'm going to need to speak to whatever it is inside you."

She vigorously shook her head, tears streaming down her face, pleading under her breath, "No, no, no, please, no…"

"I need you to be strong," Julian insisted. "If you want us to get this thing out of you, I need you to be really, really strong."

"Please…" she begged, her voice jittering like a scratched disc.

"Just relax, take a back seat, and let us talk to this thing. Can you do that for us? Can you be strong?"

Kaylee briefly closed her eyes and heavily exhaled. She feebly nodded. Her tensed muscles relaxed. Her whole body sank into the bed.

"I am no longer speaking to Kaylee. I speak to the thing within. In the name of God, I command you to reveal yourself."

Kaylee remained still, her eyes staring at the ceiling above, bloodshot and unmoved.

"In the name of the Father, the Son, and the Holy Ghost, I implore you, demon, reveal to us your name."

Oscar backed up against the wall. He glanced at the parents in the corner of the room, the mother with her face plastered against her husband's chest, unable to watch.

"In Jesus' name, I require you to reveal yourself!/"

"Why are you doing this?" Kaylee whimpered, a small, weak voice echoing from her shaking body.

"What is your name?"

Kaylee locked eyes with Oscar.

"Why are you letting them do this to me?" she asked. "Why aren't you stopping them?"

Oscar gazed back, mortified, pinned against the wall.

Why was Oscar letting them do this?

Why wasn't Oscar stopping them?

"April, get me my bag," Julian commanded.

April picked up the tatty, leather bag and took it over to Julian. He withdrew a cross, gently kissed it, and dropped the bag to the floor.

"In the name of the holy angels and archangels, reveal your name."

"Please, stop them!" Kaylee continued to beseech Oscar. "Why won't you stop them?"

Julian grabbed the cross and pressed it up against the young girl's chest. She writhed in pain, struggling under the pressure Julian was putting on her with his wooden weapon.

"Please, make it stop!" the girl moaned. "Why are you hurting me?"

Oscar shook his head. This was assault. This was cruelty. He couldn't do this.

Julian lifted the cross to Kaylee's neck and pressed down hard, and harder still.

"Please!" Kaylee lifted her head back but kept her eyes hellbent on Oscar's. "Please do something!"

Julian pressed the cross again on her neck so hard she stopped breathing. Beneath his firm grip she suffocated, coughing and choking against him – but Julian did not repent.

"You need to stop this," Oscar spoke, so softly no one noticed.

"I can't breathe!" the girl cried, then squinted a glare toward Oscar. "You really are a shitty little loser, aren't you?" she asked mockingly.

She gasped for air that didn't come.

Oscar couldn't take this anymore.

He couldn't be a witness to this.

He couldn't stand by and watch a child die.

Without a moment's hesitation, he burst out of the room and marched down the corridor.

"Where are you going?" demanded April's voice. Oscar froze and turned to see her standing in the doorway of the bedroom.

"This is barbaric!" Oscar claimed.

"Are you fucking kidding me?" April growled, full of aggression Oscar had never seen from her before.

"He's throttling her!"

"He's throttling the demon!"

Oscar turned and strode to the stairs.

"She's right, isn't she?" April asked with a mocking shake of the head.

"What?" Oscar asked, pausing on the top step.

"What Kaylee just said. What the demon just said. You are a shitty little loser."

Oscar shook his head, full of adamant resistance.

"You can't hold that against me," he retorted. "Just because I'm not going to watch a child be tortured."

"You really think a child suffocating would say to a random person in the room that they are a loser, huh?"

Oscar went to reply but had nothing. She was right.

"I'm not going to keep chasing you!" April was shouting now, full of anger, full of frustration. "If every time things get a little rough, if every time you feel it's too stressful, you bail, then go on. Fuck off. We don't need you."

Oscar looked to his feet, shaking his head.

All his life.

All his life, he had run.

"Make the choice, Oscar. Either you're going to man up and help us, or you are going to leave now and never look back. Either way, choose. Because I can't be arsed with you running off no more."

With that, she went back inside the room and slammed the door behind her.

Oscar lingered on that top step.

Thinking deeply.

There was something going on here.

Was he going to admit it? Face it? Fight it?

Or was he going to do what he had always done?

With a reluctant sigh, and a brief moment of contemplation, he found his feet carrying him straight back into that room.

With an approving nod from April, he looked to Julian doing all he could to pin down Kaylee, who was bouncing and seizing, pulling against her restraints.

"Grab her legs!" Julian shouted at Oscar. Oscar didn't waste a moment in complying, grabbing hold of Kaylee's legs and pinning them down, just as April forced down her waist and Julian pinned down her shoulders.

Oscar saw the girl's eyes. They had changed.

They were something else.

Her pupils had fully dilated, with trails of red spiralling in every direction.

Her body rose fractionally off the bed, stiff as a plank.

It laughed, but this laugh was deep, croaky, sinister. Not the kind of voice a little girl would speak.

"For the last time, demon," Julian spoke, clearly and succinctly. "What is your name?"

Kaylee moved her head toward Julian – or rather, the demon moved Kaylee's head toward Julian. Looking him deep in his eyes, Oscar watched her grin grow, witnessing what he thought he would never witness.

"My name is Ardat Lili," it croaked, full of triumphant arrogance. "But you can call me Lilith."

21

JASON UNDERSTOOD WHY SOME OFFICERS NEVER MARRIED.

It was gone 2.00 a.m.

Five hours since his shift had ended.

And there he was. Sat half-shaven, half-awake, with a half-empty paper cup perched on his crotch – his ninth coffee that day.

What was worse, he saw nothing wrong with that.

And he knew his wife would be furious.

It was just… that girl. Something about her was off. At first, it was a trivial curiosity. Since getting hold of the CCTV footage of her interview and playing it over and over, it had become an incessant nagging. A need to understand. Call it the instinct of experience, or call it being a nosy, lifeless prick; it just didn't make any sense.

He rewound the stream and watched Kaylee Kemple once more.

Still, she sat there. Motionless. A sadistic grin.

Yes, it was extreme to call the smile of a nine-year-old girl 'sadistic.' How could a girl that age have any kind of evil temperament? Personality disorders, or even psychopathy, were known to develop in late adolescence. It was just something…

Off.

That was the only way he could describe it, and it was immensely frustrating. Almost twenty years into the job and the best he could come up with was, "She's off."

"Pathetic," he muttered to himself, finishing the last of his cold, grainy coffee he couldn't even remember making.

The girl was from a middle-class family. Her dad was a doctor. Her mother was an incredibly caring woman. There were no nurturing influences to create negative behaviour.

So, what was it?

He crumpled the paper cup and threw it at the bin, missing completely and hitting the wall. Slamming his fist on the table with a heavy hand, he leant forward in his chair, getting as close to the screen as possible.

He rubbed his eyes, shook his head and ran his hands through his hair, doing whatever he could to wake himself up.

His next shift started in a few hours.

May as well just sleep in his office chair. It wouldn't be the first time.

His eyes hovered inches from the screen, staring avidly at the pixelated face.

She didn't blink.

Not once did the damn girl blink.

She stared back at the questioning officer, eyes wide open, a smile spread across her cute little cheeks. Freckles gleaming on a face full of guilty innocence, a mocking smile mocking the useless interrogation.

"My daddy molested me," she would repeat every now and then. It was like she was stuck on repeat. A toy doll that could only say one thing.

And the way she said it… It was so bouncy, so playful. It

was like she was saying, "I'd like a lolly," or, "Would you like to play with me?"

Her hands remained at perfect symmetry to each other at all times, resting on each knee. She wore a spotty t-shirt and a frilly skirt. The skirt rode up her legs, as if intentionally. She sat with legs wide open, a playful glint in her eyes filled with lust.

Which was ridiculous to think. Perverted, even.

It's a nine-year-old girl, for Christ's sake.

He'd met many women who attempted to use their sexuality to distract the man questioning them. Particularly hookers guilty of drugs or theft.

But to accuse a young girl – a *child* – of doing it was preposterous.

Yet, there was something remotely lechorous in the way she sat, peering at the man looking toward her.

There were some ridiculous theories floating around that this girl was possessed.

Maybe.

"Jesus," he growled at himself, leaning back in his chair.

What was wrong with him? Accusing a little girl of not only trying to seduce an officer but being possessed.

It really was time to go home.

His bed was calling him, home to what was likely an angry wife.

As was his half-empty bottle of whiskey stood solitary on his desk.

A dirty tumbler glass waiting to be filled and weakly sipped.

Yet, despite willing himself to get up, get his coat, and get going, he couldn't. He felt compelled to keep watching. Keep thinking. Find the answer.

He paused the video.

And froze.

"What the fuck…"

This time he knew he should go home and go to bed.

Because at the exact moment he had paused it…

On the frozen screen in front of him…

The innocent little girl's eyes flickered red, and a contorted shadow spread across the wall behind her.

THE STARS HUNG GRACEFULLY IN THE STILL NIGHT SKY. THE SUN had long since set, and the tranquillity of the restful dark painted the night sky with harmony.

A run-down hotel stood loosely beside an empty car park. Cars could be heard speeding across the nearby motorway, and the 'o' sign for 'hotel' flickered erratically.

Inside a busy hotel room, April lay casually on the bed. Oscar perched on the end, watching Julian, who paced back and forth agitatedly. Julian continually muttered to himself, and Oscar could only just pick out odd snippets such as, "No no no," "Think, damn it," and, "Why her?"

Oscar glanced over his shoulder at April, who simply played on her phone, not paying any attention. She was evidently used to Julian's frantic pacing back and forth, and Oscar could imagine it being a frequent occurrence whilst they were in the midst of an investigation.

Oscar still couldn't entirely believe what had happened. Had he really seen a girl levitate? How had her eyes become red? And how did she make such an impossibly low-pitched noise?

No longer did he feel foolish in admitting that he was beginning to believe what they were telling him.

"Right!" Julian abruptly declared. "I've got it."

April put her phone away and listened, prompting Oscar to also pay attention.

"I am going to make a phone call to grant consent for an exorcism," he decided. "Then – I am going to bed."

Without a moment's hesitation, he marched out the door and his footsteps grew faint as they disappeared down the corridor.

Oscar turned to April, slightly bemused. An instant decision for quite an extreme solution – an exorcism – then bolting out the door to sleep.

"Don't worry about it," April reassured him, as if reading his mind. "You'll get used to his erratic ways."

"What's his deal?" Oscar asked, turning himself around so he was sitting cross-legged on the bed, leaning comfortably towards April. "I mean, he seems quite intense."

"Yeah, he can be. But he's good at what he does."

Oscar nodded, giving a slight chuckle.

April leant forward, echoing Oscar's body language. His whole body shook. They were so close he could see the various shades of red on her lip. Her welcoming scent clung to the air around him, filling his belly with fluttering butterflies. Her eyes were focussed on his; her wide, big, blue eyes.

"So, Oscar," she began, putting her hands on his legs in a friendly gesture that shot through him in a lightning strike of lust. "What's your deal?"

"What do you mean?" he asked faintly, full of nerves.

"What's your family?"

"Well, I have a mum, a dad, a cat… that's pretty much it. No brothers or sisters or anything."

"What are your mum and dad like?"

"Well, she's horrible, but I think that's just because I've let them down...." He thought about it for a few moments. "They used to be amazing. Supportive, loving. Best I could hope for." He dropped his head. "More than I deserve, I guess. I... I've been a bit of a let-down. I don't know, I just never really had much ambition."

Oscar stopped himself talking, as he realised how much unprompted information he was giving. She didn't need to know this. Why would she even care?

It was at this point he realised just how lonely he was. The first point of human contact and he was spilling his guts. First time being this close to a female, and he was sat there with his hormones raging.

"So I guess working at Morrison's your entire life isn't really your ambition?"

Oscar chuckled.

"No."

"Well, now you're a Sensitive. You'll never have to work there again."

Lifting his head with a genuine smile, he thought about what that would be like. Working with April, day after day, solving people's ghostly problems. It was a dream.

"What about you?" Oscar prompted. "What's your, like, powers?"

"My *gift*," she began, stressing the world gift, "is that I can act as a conduit. I can sense that not of this world, in a similar way to how you can see it."

"What's a conduit?"

"A conduit," she began, edging closer still, smiling at him, "is someone who acts as, like, an empty house, for someone from the other side to stay in when we need to talk."

"So, you have, like, demons and stuff inside of you?"

"In a way, yes."

"What's that like?"

"I don't know, I kind of take a back seat when it happens. They take the house, and I go sit in the garden."

She laughed at her ridiculous analogy. Her laughter was heavenly, a joyous sound Oscar could listen to all day.

"What about your parents, your family?" Oscar asked.

Then the smile went.

Her whole face changed. Her eyes briefly lingered on his, then looked away. Her smile faded to a frown and she anxiously bit her lip. Her body that had only moments before been leant toward him in an upright position, entering his personal space, was now hunched over. Her hands ran over her arms, warming them.

She stood, meandering to the window, away from Oscar. Away from the perfect situation they had just shared.

"I'm sorry, April, I–"

"We have a long day tomorrow," she interrupted. "You should go to your room. Go to sleep."

She didn't avert her solemn gaze from the window. She looked so lonely, a solitary being in need of love.

But Oscar didn't know how to give that to her. It wasn't like he was particularly experienced with girls. It wasn't like he knew how to break down someone's defences and get through to them, to beseech them to share their deepest, darkest secrets, to reveal their ghosts.

So he stood, looked at her one more time, and turned. Shoving his hands in his pockets, and ruing himself for ruining such a perfect moment, he left the room.

Shortly after, he crawled into bed in the room next door.

Though he was sure he could hear a faint sobbing from the other side of the wall.

23

Humidity hung in the morning air. A soft breeze accompanied, but did little to quell the heat.

Oscar didn't mind. This was how he liked it. Warm.

He couldn't stand the cold.

Glancing at his watch, he willed April to hurry up. He was stood beside the car with Julian in awkward silence.

Julian didn't seem perturbed by it. He stood casually, smoothly leant against his car with an air of patience. Like waiting for April was something he was used to.

Oscar was not so relaxed. He shifted his weight from one foot to the other, his legs growing increasingly tired from standing still. He occasionally glanced at Julian but tried not to stare, in fear that Julian would reciprocate his glance and the situation would grow even more uncomfortable.

"Relax," Julian eventually spoke. "You're wasting energy."

Oscar tried to stand still. He would get in the car, but it was too hot to even touch. The metal rims and the car seat needed cooling, and the air conditioning seemed to be doing little about it.

"So…" Oscar attempted, deciding to break the silence. "How long have you known April?"

Julian looked to Oscar with an expression full of irritation. As if he was perturbed to be having his thoughts disrupted by meaningless chatter.

"A while."

"Oh, yeah?" Oscar nodded, trying to think of another question to ask but coming up short.

"Why do you ask?" Julian blankly prompted, his eyes squinting sceptically toward Oscar like he was a mugger asking for the time.

"I don't know, just wondered."

"You're not growing an extra fondness for our April, are you?" Julian folded his arms and raised his eyebrows.

Oscar couldn't lie. He was an awful liar.

"Well, yeah, she's all right, I guess. She's cool. I like her."

Julian took a moment to survey the nearby surroundings, then turned his face to Oscar, focussing dead on his eyes.

"If you so much as touch her, I'll break your legs."

Oscar froze.

Did he just hear that right?

His hands twitched clumsily. An inept stuttering bounced out of his quivering lips.

"What?" Oscar asked, attempting to sound big and confident, but only coming out as a whisper.

"You heard," Julian replied. "I've been with April for years."

"You mean, you're *with* her?"

"No, you dope. As in, we've been doing this for years. I picked her up off the streets when she was fifteen."

Oscar's jaw dropped. He did not know this.

"What happened?"

"She ran away from home at fourteen when she decided she'd rather the streets than her parents."

"Oh my God, I didn't know…"

"I found her a year later, living in a cheap sleeping bag on the porch of a broken-down shop. I could tell there was something about her. See, that's part of my gift – I can see this in others."

"She actually lived on the streets?"

"I helped April to harness her gift, to use it. I've watched her grow into the woman she is today. And I wouldn't stand by as some little dweeb undoes all that."

As if by perfect timing, April appeared from her room and sauntered over to them.

Oscar remained transfixed, rooted to the spot, staring open-mouthed at April as she strutted sexily toward them. He was attracted to her, he couldn't deny that – except, now there was something else. A new found respect. Living on the streets at fourteen.

To have overcome such things…

It was remarkable.

And to think he was complaining to her last night that his parents were too supportive, and wanted him to have ambitions.

I'm such a doofus.

"Here she is," Julian greeted her. "Did you lose your way?"

"Hardy har!" April mockingly retorted, then turned to Oscar and gave him a sneaky wink. "Mornin', squirt."

Julian and April climbed into the front of the car. Oscar had to quickly bring himself back to earth and remind himself to take his seat in the back.

Growing up on the streets? Sleeping on the porch of a broken-down shop?

He didn't take his eyes from her for the entire drive.

No wonder Julian was so protective.

24

OSCAR STOOD ALONE AT THE BACK OF THE ROOM, WATCHING Julian prepare for the exorcism with a perfectionist's precision. It was like watching an obsessive doctor prepare his tools for surgery. Every item was taken out of his bag, held, meticulously contemplated, and laid out in perfect symmetry upon a table next to him.

The final three items were withdrawn with such care it was like Julian was nursing a child.

With gentle hands he lifted a pristine, leather-bound book with nothing but a gold cross indented on it, which glinted in the faint lamplight. He briefly rested it against his forehead, closing his eyes, breathing it in, then placed it perfectly upon the table beside him. He opened it to a specific section, where he ran his hand over the thin pages to ensure there were no creases.

He withdrew a small set of rosary beads. They were like an old, string necklace, with black circles decorating the length of its body. At the end was a small, silver cross. Julian wrapped the string around his right hand a few times until it was firmly in place, and lifted the cross to his mouth. He gently placed a soft, lingering kiss upon it, closing his eyes and taking a deep moment of scrutinising thought.

Following this, he placed the rosary beads around his neck and tucked them beneath his shirt.

Finally, and most mysteriously, he withdrew a picture. Oscar didn't manage to get a decent glance of this picture but was sure it was of a young woman he didn't recognise.

Julian stole a brief glance at this photo and tucked it into his inside pocket.

"Leave me," Julian instructed. "I need to say my final prayers. I will let April know when to bring the girl."

Julian's eyeline didn't falter from the empty bed and the vacant restraints beneath him. Despite giving orders, his demands were gently spoken. His eyes glazed over as if in a translucent state, within a deep, mental preparation.

Oscar complied without hesitation and left the room. He made his way down the hallway to the closed door of the child's bedroom, where April stood.

"How is he?" April asked.

"Fine, I guess," Oscar answered honestly, having no reference of comparison to know whether Julian's preparations were the norm. "Is Kaylee okay?"

"She's in there with her parents now."

Oscar held April's eye contact. They shared a moment of content silence. It felt like they were preparing for battle; as if a solemn, devastating act was about to take place. Everyone was speaking so quietly, acting so serenely. Like it was the calm before the storm.

"Julian said you'd know when to bring the girl."

"Yeah," April confirmed, nodding. "He normally needs a bit of time to prepare."

"He had a photo that he put in his pocket. What was it?"

April's head dropped. She flexed her fingers and curled her hands into fists, doing her best to mask her discomfort. After gathering her thoughts, she lifted her head and fixed her eyes on Oscar's.

"It's of a young woman," April informed him, speaking slowly and softly. An assured solemnness echoed in her voice. "It is the photograph of the first woman he ever performed an exorcism on. He was one of only around ten people the church allowed to perform an exorcism, despite not being an ordained priest. He was taught along with a few other Sensitives by a man called Derek Lansdale. I know you don't know who he is, but if you did, trust me,you'd be impressed."

"That's a bit weird though, isn't it?" Oscar mused. "I mean, why does he need to carry a photo of his first exorcism around?"

April hesitated. She pursed her lips and gave a slight, unconscious shake of the head.

"Because she died, Oscar," April finally admitted. "Julian did his best, but the girl did not survive."

"She died?" Oscar was agape. "I didn't realise someone could die in something like this!"

"Oh, yes, they definitely can. And they have. And Julian never forgets it."

Oscar was lost for words.

Julian had lost a girl to death in an exorcism…

How bad could it have been?

Surely it was just saying a few words, babbling a few prayers, a spray of holy water, and it was done?

"How…" he unintentionally gasped.

"I don't think you quite realise what is about to occur, do you, Oscar?"

"I…"

"An exorcism isn't a wham, bam, thank you ma'am kind of thing. It can take hours. Sometimes days, weeks even. You are fighting something made of pure evil. Something that doesn't give up without a fight."

"I… I don't know what to say…"

"An exorcism changes you, Oscar. Remember that."

The door behind Oscar creaked open, and Julian stepped halfway out.

"I'm ready, April," he spoke gently, and returned to the room.

With a raise of her eyebrows Oscar interpreted as a gesture of "here we go," she knocked on the door behind her.

"It's time," she announced.

A few moments passed and the door opened.

Nancy stepped out, wiping the corners of her eyes with a tissue.

Henry followed, placing an arm around his wife.

This gave Oscar a chance to look at the little girl.

But this was no little girl.

In body, yes. But her face was deathly pale, and her eyes a fully dilated mixture of black and red. Her skin was torn, dirty fingernails were cracked, and the crotch of her ripped pyjamas was stained blood red.

It focussed its eyes on Oscar and grinned a wide, sickening grin.

For the first time Oscar was absolutely, unequivocally sure that he was not in the presence of something human – but of something completely and entirely evil.

25

THERE WERE MANY BAD EXPERIENCES NANCY EXPECTED TO HAVE to endure as a mother.

The pain of watching them leave for the first day at school, for university, for a first date.

When they get bullied at school or get their heart broken for the first time and they come home to you, crying into your arms.

Mental health issues. Illnesses. Anxiety.

All terrible things, but things to be expected.

But Nancy had never expected this.

She still questioned herself. Was this the right thing to do? Or was she sanctioning child abuse on her own daughter?

She had to remind herself.

She *saw* her daughter rise off the bed.

She *heard* her daughter speak in a voice she couldn't possibly speak in.

She *felt* something in her house that had replaced the loving embrace of Kaylee.

Such a happy-go-lucky child, full of curiosity and friendliness. The kind of child who would spark a conversation with a stranger for no apparent reason.

Turned to this.

A shadow of the girl she was.

It took everything she had to hold herself back, to keep herself secluded in her husband's arms. To watch helplessly as her daughter was ripped out of her bed, kicking and screaming, and led to the cold bedroom that had been prepared for her.

She stood with Henry, watching for as long as she could.

They tied her down on the bed, fastening her arms and legs. She resisted. Kicking. Screaming. Punching. Nancy didn't know if that's what she had expected. She had no idea what she had expected.

But not this.

Not witnessing such torture.

She couldn't watch. She turned to her husband's chest and soaked his shirt with her tears. She grew repulsed at the sound of her own weeping. Loud, audible convulsions of tears, crying helplessly.

Because it's all she could do.

Cry.

It's all a mother can ever do.

Just watch as their child wanders alone into the world, hoping that they will return to you. Hoping beyond hope that they know they can.

She couldn't watch the exorcism. It was heart-wrenching.

Though she expected not watching may be just as bad. She'd experienced the noises coming from her room over the past month. The sounds were atrocious. Vile, disgusting, sickening screams, pounding against the walls, destroying their disrupted sleep.

But it was not her daughter's voice.

And she had to remember this.

It was her body, but it was not her.

The voice wailing from the jaw that loudly clicked out of place came in multiple pitches. It was low, it was high, it was croaky, it was painful – but none of it was Kaylee. Her voice was not there. Not even a resemblance of it was etched into the triumphant screams of the demon feigning pain in a ploy to play with the family who cared so much for its victim.

Some prayer was being shouted at her. She tuned it out. They were all words. The Father, the God, the Holy Ghost, all of it was just words.

If there was a god, then he let this happen to her daughter.

When she died, when she came face-to-face with this transient being – she would be having a few strong words.

Where was he?

The exorcist was calling on him to help, but where was he when the demon took her? Huh?

Where was he then?

"Nancy, I think we need to leave them to it," Henry suggested, obviously deciding her crying was getting too loud. That her emotional state was becoming a burden for others to bear.

Maybe it was disrupting what the Sensitives were trying to do.

She didn't care.

She would not leave her daughter.

"Come on, honey, we need to go. We need to leave them to it."

"No!" she cried out, resisting with all her might.

"Nancy, we can't help them like this." Henry turned to Julian, taking hold of his wife. "We'll be just outside, okay?"

He held his arms tightly around her, but she rooted her feet to the floor like two dead weights.

"I can't..." she wept.

"We have to. Come on." He lifted her chin so her red, wet

eyes could see his. "We will sit on the stairs outside. We'll be right there if she needs us. Come on."

She knew it made sense.

She stole a glance over her shoulder at her daughter.

She wailed in pain.

It wailed in pain.

Or in masochistic joy.

She couldn't bear to decide.

Feeling resolute, she allowed her husband to drag her out of the room, placing her on the top step.

She flung her arms around him and squeezed with all her might, holding on and not letting go.

2 6

Watching Oscar made April think back to her first exorcism.

Despite being fifteen when Julian took her in, she was at least seventeen before she had truly begun to master her gift. Julian had still refused to take her to an exorcism until she was eighteen.

This had really annoyed her. How was it she was old enough to be used as a conduit, and to be exposed to this morbid, malevolent life – but she wasn't old enough to witness an exorcism?

She remembered Julian's words clearly: "A conduit is someone who lends their body to the occult. A possessed victim is a person who has had their body stolen. You are not ready to see such lack of control."

April had seen many, many things in her life. From her sleeping bag she had watched women get harassed, men fight, and had even been pissed on by an aggressive drunk. How was it she had been exposed to such evil but wasn't deemed a capable enough witness to the removal of a demon from its victim?

She had thought it was ridiculous.

Then she witnessed her first exorcism.

And she understood the reasons in a way one never can until they experience the thing itself. She'd known little about Julian's experience of being an exorcist. She only knew vaguely of Anna, the girl he had sadly lost a few years before.

But seeing the things she saw... Hearing the things she heard... It was traumatic. But, far worse than the things she saw or heard were the personal taunts. The way each demon seemed to know every little thing about her life, and how it could use that knowledge against her.

What's worse, the demon's verbal tirade was normally bizarrely perceptive and full of painful truths.

She had since become immune. She'd managed to thicken her skin to it.

But now, watching Oscar, she recognised the look of abject fear and paralysing confusion painted across his face. The look that showed he hated having to do this but felt compelled to by some moral duty. He couldn't argue with it, couldn't deny his true calling – but hated having to listen to what the demon said.

He struggled to endure it in exactly the way April struggled to watch it.

And now, she could see Oscar's struggle to endure. And she could see the demon picking up on its advantage over him perfectly.

"Hey, you," it's wicked, deep voice croaked out of the face of a scared little girl. "Yeah, the scrawny one stood at the back who hasn't got a clue what he's doing."

Oscar glanced nervously at April, who held her hand out in a calm, reassuring manner. Some attempt to keep him cool, keep him undeterred. They couldn't let him react to it. A demon feeds off negative energy.

"You want to fuck me, don't you?" the demon taunted.

"What?" Oscar replied, a face full of horror.

"Oscar, don't," April instructed him.

The room was chaos. The window had smashed to bits and fragments of glass were dancing in a tornado of objects. The bed the girl was restrained upon rattled, bashing and banging against the floor and the wall. Its laughter never stopped. Despite how much Julian shouted and screamed his prayers its quiet, subdued laughter still stood out above the noise with an uncomfortable prominence.

"In the name of the Father, the Son, and the Holy Spirit, we demand you, demon Lilith, leave this girl!" Julian repeated his demands repeatedly until they became white noise. They didn't seem to be doing a damn thing.

"No, no, no," the demon sang in a mocking, sinister voice. "It's not me you want to fuck, is it? It's *her*!"

The demon's eyes shot to April, whose stare consequently turned to Oscar. She saw his face full of awkward distress, evidently desperate not to let such information be divulged.

"Every time she touches you, every time she looks at you, you get some big fucking hard-on, don't you?"

"Shut up!" Oscar shouted.

"No, Oscar!" April demanded, moving in front of him, blocking his view of the wretched demon, gripping his shoulders. "You can't react, you will only fuel it. Endure it."

"You like how she's touching you now, don't you? Touch his dick, I bet it's like a rock."

She could see the question written over Oscar's face – how were such words coming from a nine-year-old girl?

She had to let him suffer it. She couldn't allow him to react. He had to learn. If he was going to do this, he had to grow a thick skin to the abuse.

Only he wasn't a particularly confident, thick-skinned person.

"I bet you don't even like her. You're just lonely and pathetic."

She saw Oscar's eyes peering at the demon over her shoulder. Squinting, glaring, full of rage.

"You don't have a chance. You are a fucking nerd with a small dick and no life. You may as well just die."

"Oscar, look at me," she urged him, unsuccessfully. "Don't look at it, look at me."

"You don't have a gift," the demon persisted.

"Oscar, look at me," she pleaded.

"Your life is nothing, and you may as well not live it."

She could see him deciding that the demon was telling the truth.

She could see it winning.

His face was consumed with terror as the realisation dawned upon him that this demon was right.

But the demon wasn't right.

She needed to do something.

"You pathetic, scrawny little maggot. She hates you. Everyone does."

Tears glistened in the corner of his eyes.

Without thinking or comprehending what she was doing, she grabbed the side of his cheeks and pulled his face into hers. She planted a soft but firm kiss upon his lips, lingering for a few seconds, then pulling away, looking him deep in the eyes.

His eyes widened toward her, his open jaw shaking. He looked gleefully apprehensive yet elatedly confused.

"Now stop listening to it, and help us," she demanded.

"Guys, I need your help," Julian announced, urging them closer with the wave of his arm.

Oscar nodded firmly at April.

Together, they stepped toward the end of the bed, ready to do what they could.

THE HANDCUFFS SHATTERED INTO PIECES.

The ankle restraints flew off with ease.

The girl rose from the bed, the demon forcing her to helplessly levitate.

Oscar pushed down upon Kaylee's ankles with what little strength he had. Despite her being such a little girl, it felt like he was pushing against a brick wall.

He could see April across from him struggling to hold down Kaylee's arms. At least it wasn't just him who couldn't pin her down.

The girl's body lingered in the air, her crotch raised up as her arms and legs dangled beneath her like spaghetti.

Oscar gave up trying to hold her down. Not only was he competing with her immense weight, but also with the chaos of the room. The loose furniture bustled, vibrating across the floor. The window smashed in, sending tiny fragments of glass bustling in circles. The floor shook, unsteadying his shaking legs.

"Mother of God!" cried out Julian, "of blessed Michael the

Archangel, of the blessed apostles Peter and Paul and all the saints."

"Give me your fucking worst," the demon insisted, tormenting Julian with its resistance.

Oscar was impressed with how little Julian allowed this thing to faze him. Oscar's whole body convulsed with shakes of fear, flinching every time this thing spoke or settled its sickening eyes upon him. He doubted his eyes, in disbelief of what he saw, but did not doubt his nose nor the temperature; he was repulsed at the foul smell of the room and shivering from the cold. Still, Julian stood defiantly. Throughout the entire ordeal, Julian wore a disobedient snarl that he did not let up.

It was the face of experience.

"Come on, you cunt, is that it?"

"With the holy authority of God, we confidently undertake to repulse the attacks and deceits of the devil."

"I love the deceits of the devil!"

Oscar and April were flung to the floor, like an invisible cannon ball had fired into their bellies, forcing them onto their backs. Oscar slammed into the far wall and April knocked into a nearby lamp.

Groaning in pain, Oscar looked over at April and saw her struggling to get up. Her hand gently dabbed a throbbing red bump on her forehead.

Oscar tried to get up and help her but found himself pushed into the wall once more, pinned down and forced to watch April as she clattered into a wardrobe door.

She did not get up.

Julian grabbed his cross, clutching it tightly, gripping it, holding it toward the demon. This seemed to help, like it was a barrier that stopped him being thrown across the room like the other two, as he was only made to stumble backward a few steps.

Oscar watched with a mixture of astonishment and horror

as the girl continued to rise until she was easily six feet off the ground, hanging helplessly.

"God arises, his enemies are scattered!" Julian persisted.

"I know you, Julian Barth."

Kaylee's deformed, mangled face locked eyes with Julian.

"You know who I am?"

"Smoke is driven away, as wax melts before the fire!"

"You know what I do to men when they sleep?"

"The wicked perish at the presence of God."

"Hey – how's Anna?"

If the reminder of this girl's death upset Julian, he didn't show it. He swiftly produced a small bottle with a cross engraved on it. Unscrewing it as quickly as he could, he splashed it over the floating body. Hisses of burning tinged the girl's skin, causing a wave of smoke to waft upwards. The demon plummeted back to the bumpy mattress.

"Anna says that you were the one who deserved to die."

This was a perfect time for Julian to go all-out attack, to continue his barrage of prayers and flicking his holy water.

But he didn't.

Julian had faltered. Frozen in stupefied trepidation.

His face looked locked onto what the demon had just said.

This Anna girl had affected him deeply.

But he was experienced.

He had to have enough resolve to deal with it.

With an aggressive snarl, he put bad thoughts to the back of his mind and stood strong.

But it was too late.

The demon had already taken advantage of the momentary lapse in concentration.

It dove off the bed, launched itself toward the shattered window and smashed through it, crushing the remaining pieces of glass to pieces like it was powdery ash.

Julian rushed to the window, April following. Oscar

abruptly got to his feet and joined them just in time to see the faint shadow of a girl disappear into the trees.

"Where is she going?" April asked.

Both she and Oscar watched Julian, cautiously expectant. They could not let her get away.

"The lake," Julian replied. "There's a lake through those trees."

Without a moment's hesitation, Julian sprinted out of the room, thudding past Kaylee's parents and down the stairs.

"What do we do?" Oscar asked helplessly to April.

"Whatever we can," she retorted, following Julian out of the door.

Oscar cast his eyes over the now-vacant chaos of the room, torn strips of wallpaper ripped to shreds, shards of glass ingrained in the carpet, and ripped, bloody bedsheets glistening in the moonlight.

Forcing himself forward, he charged to the door of the room and followed the steps of the others.

28

IT TOOK EVERY MUSCLE AND EVERY OUNCE OF ENERGY OSCAR had to keep up with the heavy rustles of April's feet treading on damp leaves. He could see her faint shadow between the trees ahead, most likely following Julian's faint shadow.

His stomach rumbled, pushing a swig of sick to his mouth.

But he needed to be strong.

He willed himself to be strong.

He spat it out and continued.

The trees became sparser and sparser until Oscar found himself coming to an opening. Before him was a peaceful lake, dimly lit beneath a generous moon, surrounded by green plants, red flowers, and other natural beauty.

A few yards down the lake, the water was not so peaceful. He could hear thrashing and shouting and deep-throated, sinister cackles. Oscar instinctively ran in the direction of the voices, stumbling over a loose branch as he lurched himself forward.

Kaylee's wounded, demented body lay scantily clad in a wooden boat, taunting the girl's saviours with greyed hands aggressively grabbing her crotch.

"*I want to fuck!*" she cried.

Julian stood in this boat, towering over the girl's body. The body was swaying side to side with bigger and bigger movements, thrashing the small wooden boat against waves of water, bombarding the lake with a violent battering.

April lurched into the water and waded through. Once she reached the boat, she took a position at the end where Kaylee's head lay, holding it still. She clutched onto her with all her might, but still the boat swung from side to side, causing Julian to fall to his knees.

"Oscar, get over here!" she demanded, looking over her shoulder at him with a frantic glare.

Oscar jumped into the water, wading through, pushing against the resistance, willing himself quickly forward.

He reached the side of the boat by Kaylee's feet and held onto her ankles, gripping tightly until it hurt his fingers, doing all he could to steady it and give Julian the best chance.

Julian stood, balancing precariously, steadying himself with immense difficulty.

The demon was in hysterics. The little girl's mouth howled with echoing, deep, manic laughter. Its crotch rose slightly in the air, feet and arms stiffening like planks, convulsing in a seizure of malevolence.

Julian was not deterred. He withdrew his cross once more, kissing it, clutching it.

"Behold the cross of the Lord, the flee band of enemies," Julian spoke, even more assertively, removing the rosary beads from around his neck.

"The lion of the tribe of Juda," April spoke in response to Julian's words, tightening her grip on Kaylee's head until the veins of her hands stuck out. "The offspring of David hath conquered."

Julian held the cross out to the demon.

"I send you back to where you came from. Foul demon, you

may have taken us to steady water, but it is nothing like the pits of hell to which I will be sending you back, in God's almighty name."

For the first time, Oscar saw a flicker of terror across the demon's face.

"May thy mercy, Lord, descend upon us," Julian spoke, full of venomous confidence.

"As great as our hope in thee," April offered in response.

Julian dropped to his knees, Oscar quickly reacting to grip the boat hard and stop it from capsizing. Julian pressed the cross against Kaylee's heart and the demon cried out in pain, multiple anguished voices resounding from its mouth.

"From the snares of the devil!" Julian screamed out, clutching the cross harder and harder, pushing it further into the demon's face. The more he did this, the more the demon cried out in pain.

"Deliver us, oh Lord!" April answered, angry splashes drenching her chest.

"That thy church may serve thee in peace and liberty – free this girl!"

"Deliver us, oh Lord!"

The girl seized in an uncontrollable fit. A visible struggle entwined her face, dancing between a hateful, angry expression and innocent eyes of a young girl in torment. Oscar and April did all they could to hold the boat still, but it shook with such a mighty rage, swaying uncontrollably from side to side, thrashing water into Oscar's eyes.

"Crush down on all enemies of thy church, and release this girl in the name of God!"

"We beseech thee to hear us!"

The fit grew more and more violent until the girl was practically rising off the boat. April clambered into the wooden vessel, laying on top of her with all her weight to prevent Kaylee from flailing into drowning submission, meaning

Oscar had to put all his strength into holding the boat still by himself.

"I command you demon, in the name of God, to leave this body!"

"We beseech thee to hear us!"

April's eyes widened toward Oscar and she gestured with her eyebrows, encouraging him to join in the chant.

"Leave this girl, in the name of God!"

"We beseech thee to hear us!"

April waved her arm at Oscar to join in. He stood strong, full of assured resolve.

"In the name of God, I command you demon – *leave this girl!*"

Oscar joined in with April, "We beseech thee to hear us."

April mouthed at him, "Louder."

"I command you in the name of God, begone demon – be gone!"

"We beseech thee to hear us!" Oscar screamed out in unison with April.

The girl stiffened into a final contorted convulsion, then… nothing.

Her body lay flat on the boat.

Julian closed his eyes in satisfied exhaustion. April's panting grew still, calmly subsiding until she was knelt in a gently rocking boat, breathing every breath of anxiety out.

The boat's swaying back and forth lessened, tranquillity took over, until a loosely calm steady boat floated on a peaceful lake.

Oscar's mental state gradually changed; from feeling like he had a head full of stressed voices screaming and screaming at him, to a quiet, empty mind of passive equanimity.

"Is it done?" Oscar asked.

Julian gestured for Oscar to go to his side. Slowly, and with an affirmative glance at April who responded with an encouraging nod, Oscar meandered to Julian.

"You have the gift of being able to see these demons, Oscar," Julian told him. "I need you to place a hand on her head. I need you to tell me if it's gone."

"How will I know?"

"You will know if there is a demon there. Trust yourself."

Oscar stretched an arm over the girl, her eyes wide and terrified. They were no longer red, no longer fully dilated; but were two pained, hazy, mortified eyes, full of both relief and sadness.

Lowering his arm cautiously, he gently placed it on the girl's forehead. It was drenched with sweat, uncomfortably hot, and shivering manically. But he saw nothing.

There was no vision like before.

Nothing at all.

"It's gone," he confirmed.

Julian collapsed on the base of the boat beside a teary Kaylee. His shirt was drenched with lake water and perspiration, his face red, and his eyelids heavy.

April leant back, a hand resting on her forehead.

Her eyes turned to his.

She smiled. Nodded to him. And that was all he needed. He understood what it meant. "You did well, kid," or something along those lines.

It had worked.

The girl was safe.

The demon was gone.

Oscar looked down upon Kaylee's face once more. A solemn tear trickled down her cheek. She shook, a face wrapped up in relief and misery. Trauma that she still didn't fully understand.

"I want my mum…" she whispered.

Oscar nodded, and helped drag the boat to the side of the lake so they could take her back to her mother.

29

By the time Kaylee had limped and stumbled up the stairs, Nancy was on her knees.

Oscar struggled to remain unemotional as he stood in the doorway, watching mother and father reunited with their daughter.

Behind him Julian still sat on the floor recovering. April was also resting after what had been a truly remarkably savage and enduring night, gently drying her hair with a kitchen towel.

But for Oscar, he couldn't avoid witnessing this moment.

Perhaps April and Julian were used to it. They were immune to the emotions involved, or they just learnt not to watch this moment occur to save themselves from emotional torment.

Oscar wanted to savour it.

Nancy clung to her daughter with tight, gripping arms wrapped in a desperate embrace. Her crying was loud, but she didn't care – and why should she? She had her daughter back.

Despite being in a cripplingly weakened state, Kaylee hugged tighter and tighter. None of the malevolent stares or sinister scowls remained. The sweet, innocent, extroverted child was back, though admittedly she was considerably wounded.

Oscar wasn't even sure what mental state she would be in. For anyone, enduring possession must be a hard, daunting experience; but for a girl so young, it must have been beyond traumatic.

As Oscar watched mother and daughter continue to cling to each other, to hug, to cry, to console each other's vastly externalised pain, his eyes drifted to Henry, the father.

Henry, who had also endured hard times. Being locked in a jail cell, accused of incredibly devastating allegations. He, too, must have a range of emotions.

Except, he didn't.

He stood still, expressionless. Watching his family reunite. His limp hand vaguely rubbed his wife's back in an attempt at frail reassurance. There was nothing about his face or body language that suggested he was flooded with complex feelings at the sight of this.

Still, people dealt with their emotions in different ways.

Maybe this was his way. Being stern and strong for his family.

Or maybe he was in fact guilty. Now it would come out.

Ridiculous thoughts. Stop it.

There was no doubt to be had.

This was a happy moment of a family sharing their love in their own ways, on what must be an overwhelming sense of relief.

Oscar felt a soft hand upon his back and recognised the touch as April's.

"Come on," she prompted him, walking forward and shaking Henry's hand.

"Thank you so much," Henry said, taking her hand firmly in his.

Maybe he was grateful then. Maybe he was just concealing his true state of mind.

Oscar looked over his shoulder to see if he could help tidy but found that Julian had somehow already packed everything up and was on his way.

Nancy stood and faced the Sensitives, still with her arms draped around her daughter.

"Please, stay," she insisted. "Let me do something for you. Make you tea, get you some wine, anything, I don't know…"

Julian planted a reassuring hand on her shoulder. "Please, you don't owe us anything. Enjoy having your family back. We have a long drive ahead of us."

"But I can't thank you enough…"

"Seeing you reunite with your daughter," Julian spoke sincerely, "is reward enough."

With a warm smile, a comforting nod, and a grateful handshake, he followed April down the stairs and through the front door.

Oscar nodded at Nancy, smiling as she continued to thank them. He then echoed Julian's sentiments in placing a reassuring hand on Henry's shoulder.

Then he paused.

There was something…

Henry smiled back at him.

And Oscar realised he was staying in the moment for too long. It was getting awkward.

So, with a nod, he followed his new companions out the front door and to the car.

"You can drive," Julian informed April, then turned to Oscar, "and you can ride up front. I'm laying down in the back and going to sleep. I am shattered."

"I'm not surprised," responded Oscar honestly.

By the time Oscar had found his seat in the front, watched

April turn the ignition, and looked over his shoulder at Julian – the guy was already asleep.

As April backed down the drive, Oscar watched the house grow smaller. He smiled resolutely as she directed the car to the motorway.

"How are you feeling?" April asked. "Your first exorcism. The first demon you've helped get rid of."

"I'm feeling... pretty good, April. Pretty good."

And for once, he was not lying.

He was feeling good.

He had helped do something worthwhile.

So he buried a deep, unsettling feeling that they were leaving something unfinished, and enjoyed the relaxing ride back down the M42 and onto the M5 toward his hometown of Tewkesbury.

30

The sign for junction 9 of the M5 passed by the window and the return journey was almost at an end.

Yet Oscar couldn't shake his bad feeling.

He glanced at the back seat where Julian was still asleep, then to April, who drove with a yawn. Neither of them seemed perturbed in the same way he was. They were the ones with the experience. The knowledge. Surely, if something wasn't entirely right, they would see it too.

Still, leaving the family's home just hadn't felt right.

It felt incomplete.

"What is it?" prompted April, noticing Oscar's discontent.

"Nothing," he lied. "I don't know. It's just…"

"Shocked?" April guessed. "First time, and you don't know how to react?"

"No, it's not that. I mean, it was shocking. But it's just…"

April signalled to turn off the motorway, taking the slip road toward the roundabout. Once she had slowed down and paused at the traffic lights, she turned an inquisitive stare to Oscar, trying to read him, uncomfortable at his unease.

"What?" she asked, more urgency in her voice. "What is it?"

"It just feels, I don't know, incomplete. Like there's something–"

Then it dawned on him.

A sudden flash.

As he left.

He nodded at Nancy. Smiling at her.

Then he turned to Henry.

Kaylee's father.

He placed a hand on his shoulder.

And then...

"Oh, God..." Oscar stuttered, lip trembling, arms shaking.

"What?" April frantically asked, trying to keep her eyes on the road at the same time as furiously glancing at Oscar. "What is it? What do you see?"

In Henry's eyes...

A flicker of fire faded to red. Henry's shadow engulfed the wall in a menacing shade of black, leering over the entire room, overwhelming their eyes with a black outline of shaded claws.

Behind Henry stood a beast.

Much like the one he had seen behind Kaylee at their first meeting, except this one was far bigger. Its carnivorous eyes and volcanic breath consumed the room in an air of fiery smoke. Oscar had an inexplicable feeling that he could not articulate – but was completely certain of – that he was in the presence of complete evil.

Oscar felt his body slip away. He began convulsing, seizing with large, fevered jolts. He foamed uncontrollably at the mouth, feeling the warm liquid soak his chin. In his vision, he saw a small black dot, a black dot that grew bigger and bigger, closer and closer, until that was all he saw.

Then he was back in the Kemple's house.

Standing before Henry Kemple.

With his reassuring hand on the father's shoulder, just where it had been before saying goodbye.

Except, there was something else. A beast. Guiding his every move with a dominant, snake-like arm, warped around Henry's throat like Henry was just a puppet, and this thing a puppeteer.

Behind this beastly figure were two grand wings ending in two points as sharp as a knife. Its tail spiralled from the rear end of its body, curling into a simmer of flames. Aside from a male torso, there was nothing human about it. Its face was ugly and treacherous, with a large nose, pointed fangs, and a head of hair Oscar first thought were dreadlocks, then realised were snakes. Its legs resembled that of a farm animal, with hairy, thick muscles ending in hooves that were home to three sharp curling, pointed claws.

This beast stood over Henry with a cocky grin, moving into its victim's body until its foul exterior had gone, completely soaked into every orifice and flake of skin of Henry.

Oscar's eyes shot open.

He lay on hard cement that dug into the back of his head. The car sat stationary beside him. April and Julian fussed over him, urging him to come to, repeatedly shouting his name.

As Oscar's vision refocussed, he rotated his head slightly, pulling a muscle in his neck. As he winced in pain, he realised he was on the hard shoulder of the slip road, laid on his back, his whole body aching from a violent fit.

"Relax, Oscar," Julian instructed, putting his arm out to halt April's frantic cries and replace them with his calming, soft voice. "It's okay."

Julian helped Oscar lean up, giving him a minute to take in where he was, to readjust, to come back down to earth.

"You scared us," Julian said.

Then Oscar remembered what he saw.

They didn't have much time.

His eyes opened wide with alarm, his hand clutching onto Julian's shoulders, his eyes shooting between him and April.

"We have to go back!" he cried out. "We have to go back!"

"Why, Oscar?" Julian asked, still keeping his cool. "What is it? What did you see?"

"It's Henry Kemple, her father…"

Julian's eyes grew wide with horror and his calm façade faded away as quickly as it had arrived.

"What about him?"

"The whole thing, the demon in Kaylee, she was just a pawn. Henry…"

"What about Henry?"

Oscar thought about Kaylee. A helpless little girl.

Nancy. A loving mother with no idea what danger she and her daughter were in.

Then Henry.

"Oh, God…"

3 1

Henry sat back in his armchair, allowing the body to rest.

It was an older body than Lilu was used to.

But it was the only choice available.

Lilith had done her task, but unfortunately, she was done. Removed. Failed.

Pathetic, weak little girl.

The woman he loved more than hell itself, but still a disappointment.

Lilu would not be so easy to fight.

Nancy had made Kaylee some tea. Beans on toast. As Kaylee devoured it, Nancy dabbed at her wounds with a wet flannel. A whole medical kit spread out across the living room floor.

Ridiculous human.

She thinks a few little cuts on a face are going to hurt?

She thinks nursing her daughter with love and rainbows and happiness will save her from what was to come?

He grew sick of her. How much longer did he have to endure of this pitiful imbecile?

Kaylee flinched from the pressure on her wound.

"Oh, my baby, I'm so sorry," Nancy spoke.

So weak. So eager to protect.

He stood.

Contemplated.

Watched.

"Where are you going?" Nancy asked, not moving her loving gaze from her wounded daughter.

He ignored her, stepping heavily and precisely out of the room, into the kitchen. He opened drawers, looked in cupboards, searched the sink.

Finally, he grew tired of looking. There was a solid, robust, toaster on the side.

That would do.

He ripped the toaster from the wall, took it into the living room, and stood over Nancy.

Nancy peered up at him from her kneeling position beside her daughter, eyes full of confusion.

"What are you doing with the toaster?" she asked innocently.

He held it above his head.

"Henry?"

With all the force that this body had, with all the muscles available, he brought the toaster soaring downwards and thrust it into her forehead with lethal force.

Kaylee jumped, her beans on toast flinging off her lap, cowering against the wall.

Nancy crawled along the floor. Dizzy. Shocked.

She dabbed her forehead and looked up.

"What are you doing?" she feebly uttered.

Her entire face was covered in trickling blood, accompanied by a beautifully grey bruise.

Lovely.

He lunged the toaster back down, sinking it into her head with excessive force and relative ease.

"Henry!" she wept, struggling to her knees.

He struck her with the toaster again.

This time she didn't move.

He brought it back down and slammed it into her head. Again. Again and again.

And again.

And again.

And again.

He threw the toaster to the side, discarding it like a finished chocolate wrapper. He took hold of a clump of her hair in his sweaty fist and lifted her head up.

Her eyes hazed over with a groggy absence. She gurgled an oozing of blood that went trickling down her chin. Her nose bent to the side, teeth fell past her cracked lip, and most of her pale skin was covered in dark-grey bruising.

He dragged her across the room by the hair, reaching a wooden television stand.

He launched her head into the television, sending her cranium flying into a cracked, sparking mess. Keeping hold of her hair, he lifted her head once more and drove her skull down into the solidity of the wooden surface.

He kept going until her face was elegantly unrecognisable.

He threw her on the floor.

She did not move.

He climbed on top of her and slid his hands around her neck, tightening his grip.

But he didn't need to.

He already felt no pulse.

He dropped her body to the floor like a discarded piece of waste.

With a triumphant smirk, he slowly turned his head to the other side of the room.

Kaylee cowered in the corner. Too scared to move. Her eyes wide in terror.

It was just the two of them.

Alone at last.

32

OSCAR GAGGED OVER THE BUSHES, SPEWING A STRINGY BUT thick mouthful of gunk. This vision was not any more tolerable than the last.

But he needed to get over it.

There was more on the line than his weak stomach.

He limped down the garden path and into the home of April and Julian. Being only minutes from the motorway, they had rushed Oscar into the back seat and sped back as fast as they could.

As he returned to the house, Julian's frantic voice hit Oscar like a bombardment on his ear-drums. He made his way to the kitchen, where April sat at the table. She had dissolved some disprin into a small glass of water that she passed to Oscar, and he gratefully drank.

Julian burst into the kitchen, slamming his mobile phone down on the table.

"There's no answer," he declared, turning around, nervously fidgeting. He paced back and forth, covering every tile of the kitchen floor.

"Shouldn't we go back?" Oscar asked, trying to look away

from Julian, as the pacing was making his fuzzy head even dizzier.

Julian ignored him, stuck between various thoughts, none of which seemed to be offering a solution.

"It's a two-hour drive," April replied, placing a comforting hand on Oscar's. "We won't get there in time."

"Surely we need to try? I mean, we can't just sit here and do nothing."

Julian pulled a laptop out of the drawer and slammed it on the table, hurriedly loading it.

"We will," he assured Oscar. "But we need to get in contact with Nancy first and tell her to get her and Kaylee out of the house. I'm going to have to go online, see if there's any other number or way of contacting her."

"I don't get it," Oscar said, a face full of torturous guilt. "How come I'm only getting this vision now, when I touched his shoulder before we left?"

Julian was too absorbed in his futile attempts at finding more contact information, so April took it upon herself to answer.

"Sometimes really powerful demons can block glimpses about themselves," April took over. "It could be that the block dropped once you got far enough away, or that the demon stopped."

"What I still don't get," Julian venomously announced as he clicked harshly on the mouse, "is who the fuck this demon is."

Oscar let a moment pass before answering. He was new, and didn't want to upset anyone – but he was fairly sure he had the answer.

"Didn't you say Kaylee's demon was part of a pair?"

Julian looked up, irritated. "Yes."

"Maybe the girl was possessed by the lower demon. And Henry was taken by the one in charge, and now we are dealing with something all the more powerful, who has been leading the whole thing all along."

Julian and April shared an embarrassed glance.

"I mean," Oscar continued, "that would explain why the girl dropped the accusation, and the dad went free. That could have been when... you know..."

Oscar's voice faded, feeling a little disconcerted by the humiliated look the other two were sharing. Had he overstepped?

"That was..." April began, looking once more at Julian. "... brilliant, Oscar. I don't know why we didn't think of that..."

She looked to Julian once more, who nodded vaguely, the only admittance Oscar knew he would get from him.

April nodded at him, at first shocked at his progression, then with a playful smile that revealed a new admiration.

In a new sudden burst of anger, Julian slammed the lid.

"Nothing," he declared. "Let's just pray there is no late-night traffic to stand in our way."

33

HENRY'S COARSE FOOT KICKED NANCY'S HEAD FURTHER INTO the cupboard beneath the stairs. A cluttered assortment of useless crap fell on her, remnants of pointless possessions hidden away and never used.

Soon it would all be divided up in a will or thrown into a skip.

Nancy's head would not get inside, so in the end, he resorted to having to lift the corpse by the hair, and push it inside with his foot and shut the door quickly before her dead weight fell back upon it.

She was heavier than she looked.

How could Henry have ever fucked that? She was so... human.

He glanced at the time. The police needed to hurry up. It had been at least half an hour since he had called.

He didn't have much time.

The blocking would have worn off. That scrawny little rag-boy would have had a vision by now. Some kind of glimpse that showed the truth about who was inside Henry's body.

Why did the little shit have to touch him on the shoulder?

The kid was almost gone. Leaving. The deed had been done. He was going to be left to it, nothing to stop what he was about to do with this family.

Then the fucking prick touched his shoulder.

A loud, authoritative knock resounded three times against the front door.

Right.

Time to be Henry the father.

I'm upset.

He forced tears out of this mortal, weak body. He bounced on the spot, getting red to his cheeks, forcing himself to be out of breath.

Fucking humans.

He flung open the door.

"Oh, thank God you're here!" he declared through Henry's subordinate mouth, ushering the police officer in.

"My name is Detective Inspector Jason Lyle," the man told him, showing a badge. "I was at your daughter's interrogation."

"Yes, yes, I remember you!" Henry declared, weeping eyes and distraught frown displaying a manner of distress that clearly irritated Jason.

Good.

That would mean it was convincing.

"You told me someone abused your daughter," Jason prompted.

"Yes, yes I did. They came here claiming they were going to help her do all this voodoo stuff. We thought they were good people. At first…"

Henry's hand quickly withdrew his phone and held it out to Jason, a video ready to play.

Lilu watched, surveying the reaction of the officer. He didn't need to see the video to know what images accompanied the vile sounds. So, instead, he studied the detective's reactions. Making sure the shocking images recorded were having their effect.

He watched as Jason Lyle viewed the video of Julian performing an exorcism on Kaylee.

A video that, out of context, looked very bad.

A girl being pinned down on a bed, where she lay in restraints. Jason flinging holy water on her, crosses pressed against her, doing nothing to avert the agonising screams of the poor little girl.

"Once I saw what they were doing," he whimpered, "I tried to stop them. But they just wouldn't. They said they had to make her pure again, then they just kept saying it over and over."

The video ended, and Jason lifted his perturbed visage to Henry.

"And this happened tonight?" Jason asked.

"Yes, it did."

"Have you got a name for this man?"

"Yes. His name is Julian Barth. He claims to be part of some paranormal investigation team from Gloucestershire, calling themselves Sensitives, or something."

"That's the people your lawyers called, was it not?"

"Yes, yes it was, and that was why we trusted them! Oh, we trusted them!"

He considered for a moment whether the last "oh, we trusted them" was too much, but Jason seemed to buy it.

"I'm going to need you and your family to come down to the station and give a statement."

"Kaylee has just gone to sleep; can it wait until the morning?"

"Not really. If we are to arrest this man, we are going to need to take a statement as quickly as we can – time is important, you see."

"I know, but it's been such an ordeal. We'll wake her up in an hour, please, just give us that."

Jason peered peculiarly at Henry.

"In an hour, then, I really must insist."

"We will be there."

"In the meantime, I will contact Gloucestershire about this man. I will need to take this phone, Mr. Kemple."

"Oh, please do."

A creak echoed in the hallway.

Jason peered past Henry at the door to the cupboard under the stairs that had opened very slightly.

"Is everything else okay, Mr. Kemple?" he asked.

"Oh yes, fine, yes."

"I will see you in an hour then."

With another glance down the corridor, Jason turned and walked away, closing the door behind him.

He watched through the window as the police car drove away.

Then he turned. Walked upstairs. Into the little girl's room.

There, Kaylee sat helplessly bound to a chair, duct tape wrapped multiple times around her mouth and body. Her wide, terrified eyes peered up at the face of her loving father, so vastly changed from the man she knew.

"You let them take my Lilith from me," he declared

He bent over, placing his hands on his knees in a way that was so patronising it became mortifyingly sadistic.

"She was what they call a succubus. Do you remember?"

Her eyes flinched.

"I'm not sure if you do. Do you know what succubus means?"

He placed a gentle hand on the side of her face.

A pleasurably sordid grin spread wide across his face, pushing his cheeks into an unsettling leer.

"How about I show you?"

THE HOUSE BUSTLED WITH HASTE. JULIAN'S EXORCISM essentials were restocked and flung back into his leather-bound bag. April clutched the car keys tight and had her trainers back on before Oscar even acknowledged they were moving.

Oscar tried to keep up. Tried to maintain the urgency set by the other two.

A family's lives were at stake.

A mother. A daughter. Both who could already be dead.

As April nodded in confirmation that she was ready and Julian turned his expectant stare to Oscar – the doorbell rang.

They looked at each other, confused.

Julian opened the door and cast his eyes upon two tall, muscular police officers.

"Julian Barth?" one of them prompted in a thick country accent.

"Yes…" he answered, glancing back at April, a look of hesitant terror on his face. "Can I help you?"

"We are going to need you to come with us."

"Is this really necessary? As we have somewhere to be quite urgently."

The two police officers shot each other a look as if they were confirming something, making a silent decision.

"Julian Barth, you are under arrest on suspicion of causing significant harm to an underage child under the Children Act 1989," one of them stated matter-of-factly.

"For *what?*"

"You do not have to say anything, but it may harm your defence if you do not mention when questioned something which you later rely on in court. Anything you do say may be given in evidence."

The officer went to take hold of Julian's arm, but he flinched it away.

"Listen, lad," the officer began, "it's up to you whether you come with us willingly, or whether you come in the handcuffs."

Julian froze, the conundrum of his perilous decision of whether to submit or defy these officers presented clearly upon his face.

But what was he going to do?

He had no way out of this. No way to get to the Kemples without the police interfering and halting the whole process.

He turned to April and whispered a sudden thought of stark realisation.

"It's the dad," he gasped. "He knows we know."

"Come on, son," the policeman demanded, grabbing hold of Julian's arm and dragging him out.

April and Oscar stood helplessly watching, faces like a child saying goodbye to their parents on the first day of school.

"What are we going to do?" Oscar asked April.

April had no answer.

She simply bowed her head and shook it.

"What can we do? He's the exorcist. He's the one who knows how to do this stuff."

"But we can't just let–"

"We can't do anything about it!" she snapped.

After she watched the police car disappear down the street and turn the corner, she shut the door with a ferocious, agitated slam.

Oscar searched for an answer, but he didn't have one.

"They are on their own," April declared.

THIS IS WHAT YOU GET WHEN YOU TRY TO DO SOMETHING GREAT
in a world that people don't understand.

You get burnt at the stake for it.

And it's infuriating.

And April was so, so fed up.

Just because the world hadn't seen what they'd seen.
Because the world wasn't open-minded enough to believe
what they must. Because the world was infantile and cruel and
pathetic and–

"Fuck," April muttered within a sickened sigh.

She sat on the stairs, her head rested against the wall,
vacantly watching the door that Julian had departed through
not too long ago.

These ignorant people had no idea what they were doing.

But what was she meant to do without Julian?

Julian was the one who'd taken her off the streets. Given
her a home. Shown her what to do. Led her.

Without his skill set, she was useless.

She was a conduit and a glimpser – not an exorcist.

"Hey," came Oscar's soft voice.

April moved only her eyes, choosing to remain slumped miserably against the wall. She looked at Oscar edging into view, leaning against the wall of the hallway.

Now really wasn't the time.

She didn't have the patience for his inexperience and ridiculously low self-esteem.

She wished he would go away.

"How you doing?" he asked, a face full of concern.

"How do you think I'm doing?" she snapped.

She knew she should be nicer to him. He was trying to make sure she was okay. But she didn't care.

She wanted to be alone.

"There was nothing you could have done," he reassured her.

"Piss off, Oscar," April instructed. "Not in the mood."

Oscar's head dropped. His hands went into his pockets and his whole body slouched into a hunched posture, curling over into his easily intimidated, withdrawn stance.

He retracted back into the other room.

He looked downbeat and downtrodden, but April didn't care.

April didn't care about anything.

An innocent family was likely about to die.

Without Julian, she was nothing. She couldn't attempt an exorcism. God knows Oscar couldn't.

It was useless.

April jumped as a bag was thrown to the ground before her. Scowling irritably at the leather-bound bag that contained all of Julian's items, she turned her anger to Oscar who had re-entered the hallway, and now stood over it.

"What are you doing?" April demanded through clenched teeth and stiffened jaw.

"I'm going to Loughborough," he announced. "Are you coming with me?"

April shook her head.

Pathetic.

"You're not going to Loughborough," she replied.

"Oh yes, I am!" Oscar declared, grinning wildly. "I'm going to go do everything I can to save that family."

"We are nothing without Julian, don't be ridiculous."

"Yes," Oscar confirmed, nodding as he took a moment to think about his choice of words. "But I'm still going to try."

"Oscar, as lovely as this whole thing is, we wouldn't survive it. Without Julian there to help–"

"Yeah, well, Julian isn't there to help, is he?"

April tilted her head back and sighed.

"So we're going to have to do it without him," Oscar decided.

"Get a grip man, you can't do this–"

"Can't do this?" Oscar repeated, waving his arms in astonishment. "Five days ago, I thought I couldn't survive without my medication. Five days ago, I thought ghosts or demons didn't exist, never mind that I could fight them. And five days ago, I thought no woman would ever talk to me."

April looked away, blushing.

"And then you came along," Oscar continued, crouching before April, beseeching her with his eyes. "And you showed me that I can do those things."

"Oscar–"

"And now it's time for me to show you what you can do."

Her eyes met his and she felt truly warm inside. Yes, he was young, and stupid, and scruffy, and immensely irritating. But he had kind eyes, a warm smile, and the best of intentions.

"So I'm going, with or without you. But I'd rather it was with you. So what do you say, April? Are you coming?"

Beneath the ridiculous boyish exterior, he was a sweet man. And he made her feel like she could do anything.

And she could do anything.

"Yes," she answered. "But I'm driving."

OSCAR'S HANDS GRIPPED THE SIDES OF THE PASSENGER SEAT, flinching his eyes away from the sight before him. He had never been in a car going so fast. Every car in the other lanes of the M5 were just blurs.

Oscar glanced at the speedometer beside the steering wheel that April was clutching with eager alarm.

I didn't even know a car could go that fast...

"So how long since you passed your test?" Oscar inquired, trying to find something that could reassure his dangerously high blood pressure.

"I'm taking it next week."

"What?"

Oscar decided the best thing to do would be to close his eyes really tightly and pretend he was somewhere else.

But he couldn't do that.

Because every time he closed his eyes, he saw it again.

The father. The demon. Standing over him.

Then, just as April recklessly merged the car across three lanes and onto the M42, the visions hit him once more.

They took his breath away like he'd been sucker punched.

He gasped for breath as he fought the invasive thoughts that just kept coming and coming.

The horns. The serpentine snake-ish legs. The cackling grimace of the mouldy, cracked lips upon its ugly face.

Then he came to. Sweating and panting, he could once more see the road before him.

"Hold on, Oscar," April urged him. "Come on, stay with me."

He turned toward her, but before he could register the concern on her face, he was gone again.

This time he was looking up at Henry.

Henry was bringing a toaster.

Why was he bringing a toaster?

He looked to his side. Kaylee sat beneath him, devouring a plate of baked beans on toast.

Then he realised.

I'm Nancy. This is what Nancy saw.

He fell to the floor with a sudden blow, his entire body jolting.

His eyes flung open and he was back in the car, but he was seizing, his body uncontrollably convulsing.

"I need my medication!" Oscar screamed. "Only my medication can stop this!"

"No!" April defied. "You cannot have it. You have to do this yourself."

"But I can't!" Oscar wailed, his arms helplessly reaching out.

He slipped back again.

He was looking up. In a living room. Henry was above him.

Blood was trickling into his eyes. He could feel it oozing, dripping in a gulp of thick mess.

But he didn't have time to wipe it.

Henry brought the toaster down onto his head once more.

His eyes jerked open.

April was frantically switching her gaze between the road and Oscar. Looking back and forth, back and forth.

"Nancy…" Oscar whimpered. "She's dead… He's killed her…"

"What?"

"I saw it… He's killed her…"

"What about Kaylee? Is Kaylee okay?"

He was back in the living room, being dragged by a large mound of hair toward a television.

Kaylee was at the end of the room, cowering in a ball. Crying. Weeping. Desperately abandoned.

His head went into the television.

A smash and a set of sparks fluttered over his vision.

"My medication, please…"

"No, Oscar, control it!"

His head smashed into the wooden table.

Everything went dark. Hazy.

Nothing but the sound of a skull being bludgeoned into wood.

Then it occurred to him.

If I die in a vision – do I die in real life?

"I'm about to die…" Oscar cried out.

"Stop it! Get a grip!"

The smell of freshly polished wood.

The sound of bones cracking into pieces.

The taste of thick blood trickling down his throat, choking him, coughing on loose teeth.

"Oscar – you are in control. You are the master of these glimpses."

His eyes opened briefly.

April's worried face looked down upon him.

He was in a heap on the floor of the car.

"Come on, Oscar."

The pain of a smashed cranium consumed him. His nervous system shattered.

"Oscar – I believe you can do this."

April.

April believes.

April believes I can do this.

His fists turned to a tight grip. Clenching for war. Readying his body for the fight.

Everything was no longer blank.

He stood up.

He left Nancy's body, backed away.

Watching as Henry continued to pummel her head into the wooden surface.

Watched as Kaylee continued to cower in the corner.

April.

April believes.

April knows I can do this. She's said it all along.

No more.

I am in control.

Oscar closed his eyes, scrunching his face, screaming so hard it felt like razor blades dragging through his throat.

Enough.

Enough being a loser.

Enough medication.

Enough being some going-nowhere, jacking off, pathetic little piece of shit.

A boy backs down and lets these things control him.

April.

A man stands up and takes control.

April believes.

Thank you, April.

His eyes flung open.

Manically sweating, blood rushing to his head.

He sat up. Looked around himself.

He was in a car, going one hundred miles per hour.

His panting subsided.

He wiped the sweat from his brow.

He turned to April.

"Thank you," he spoke.

April smiled, then turned her attention to driving.

Finally, he was in control.

37

JASON STOOD SOLEMNLY OUTSIDE THE POLICE STATION, SOAKING up the peaceful night sky. The stars were shining brightly. There was a slight breeze lingering in the air, and there was minimal activity around the station. It was rare to have such a quiet night, and he wasn't sure whether he liked it. As an officer, you live for the busy nights but pray for the quiet ones.

He checked his watch.

It had been two hours.

Henry Kemple should have brought his family to the station by now.

A police car turned into the station car park and interrupted his trail of thought. He recognised instantly the face in the back as being the one from the video and gazed at him with morose curiosity.

Wanting to make sure this guy knew who was the boss, he stood tall, stiffening his posture, ensuring his feet were shoulder-width apart and his arms were sturdily folded.

The driver's window wound down and the officer turned to Jason.

"You Detective Inspector Jason Lyle?"

"I am," Jason nodded. "This my suspect?"

"Yeah. Where do you want him?" the officer asked as if he was delivering a parcel.

"Bring him out, I'll take him in."

The two officers stood out from the car, opened the back door, and brought the suspect out.

Julian Barth was a tidy man, mid-20s, completely unsuspicious.

But then again, they all are, aren't they?

No one can truly predict an abuser by looking at them.

"Thank you." Jason directed the officers as he took hold of Julian by the arm. "Much appreciated."

Jason led Julian into the station and booked him in. All the time, watching him. Studying him. He liked to do this with all his suspects, and had done so for fifteen years. Making sure he knew what to expect. If they were heavy, could they use their weight against him? If they were short, could they be nimble?

But as he directed Julian through to the cells, he saw nothing from him that would indicate a threat. If anything, the man seemed to be seething under his breath the entire time, as if muttering in angst.

Then, just as he was about to shut the door, Julian spoke.

"Do you have any idea what you're doing?"

Jason paused. He didn't normally waste time listening to the angry ramblings of perpetrators once he had locked them in the cell.

But it was something about this case.

About the girl.

Something had unsettled him...

He remained blank, strong in his body language, hovering in the doorway. Julian now sat on the bed, his head in his hands, his legs bouncing agitatedly.

"That girl is in serious danger," Julian claimed.

"Not anymore," Jason spoke, softly yet assertively.

"Her father is not what you think he is."

Jason folded his arms and leant against the side of the doorway, lifting an eyebrow.

"From what I've seen of the cruelty you've committed—"

"I gave her an exorcism!" Julian shouted, immediately giving Jason the balance of control. "I don't have time to sit here and argue with you about whether or not ghosts and demons exist, but they do – and they were in her. And now they are in her dad. And he is going to *kill* her if I don't do anything."

"See, what gets me – is I can't figure out whether you've made this all up, or whether you actually believe it yourself."

"For God's sake, you don't understand!"

Julian stood as if to lurch himself forward and plead. Jason abruptly held his arm out and went to shut the door, as if preparing for an attack, prompting Julian to instantly put his hands in the air and stand back.

"I'm not going to attack you," Julian promised.

"Damn right you're not."

"I just need you to understand."

Jason nodded patronisingly.

"I think I understand all right."

Jason went to shut the door.

"Wait!"

Jason didn't speak, but hovered the door slightly ajar, so he could just see Julian within the crack.

"You've worked this case, right?"

Jason didn't answer.

"I'm taking that as a yes. So, I'm assuming you spoke to this girl when she was arrested. That you interrogated her, and her dad."

Jason raised his eyebrows.

"Well, did you not think there was something off about

her? Was she acting in the way you would expect a sweet little middle-class girl to do?"

Jason considered this.

She wasn't.

But that meant nothing.

"Was she?" Julian repeated, his hands stretched out in desperation. He looked like he thought he was getting somewhere.

True, this girl was strange.

But at no point did that mean demons suddenly existed.

As Jason backed away, he just about heard Julian shout one more thing.

"Play it backwards! Play it–"

Jason closed the door and locked the cell.

THE PEACEFUL NIGHT CAST A TRANSLUCENT GLOW OVER THE tranquil evening.

Oscar and April didn't give a shit.

As April haphazardly swung the car onto the Kemple's drive, an overwhelming sense of dread filled Oscar like a bucket of poison filtering through his body.

It was one thing to persuade April they should drive up to Loughborough and fight this thing. It was another thing entirely to step out of the car and face an evil entity from hell that could very well kill you.

Glimpses filled Oscar's head, and he was finally starting to get a loose grip over these crushing visions. So long as he retained his calm head and kept his breathing slow, he was in control.

As he stepped out of the car and stood beside April, the house flashed red. A splatter of blood appeared on the inside of the living room window, vanishing as quickly as it appeared.

An omen of what may have already happened, or so Oscar assumed.

"I don't like this," April admitted.

"You kidding?" Oscar scoffed, turning to her. "You're the one I'm relying on."

"It's just too quiet."

She was right.

An eerie stillness lingered around the house. A silence that screamed too loudly. There were no lights, no flickers of shadows, no sign of life whatsoever. Just a feeling of destitution, as if something bad had either happened or was about to happen. Or both.

April began the cautious steps forward, prompting Oscar to follow. His legs wobbled, buckling weakly under the anxiety that filled his gut.

Everything about this was wrong.

Everything about this told Oscar to back away.

But he couldn't. He had come this far.

"Should we knock?" Oscar asked April, realising he hadn't thought this far ahead.

April shook her head.

He tried opening the door, but it opened about an inch until it stopped suddenly.

"I think it's on a latch," Oscar decided.

"Well, you're a strong man."

Oscar frowned at the ridiculous assertion. Just an excuse for him to do his shoulder in, rather than her.

Still, it made him gush, and he couldn't let her down.

He took a step back and barged against the door. It buckled slightly but did not falter. So he leant back and barged against it once more, forcing the door to swing back against the inside wall.

Oscar glanced at April, feeling smug, to see if she was impressed. Her eyes remained focussed as she stepped inside, Oscar following and shutting the door behind them.

It was pitch-black, except for the clock on the oven in the

far kitchen and the moonlight through the windows of the nearby living room.

It took a few moments for Oscar's eyes to adjust. He scanned the vacant rooms. The stairs to his right, the living room to his left, the kitchen ahead of him.

There were too many places for something to jump out.

Too many places for them to get caught.

"Where to?" Oscar whispered to April.

"We need to find Nancy and Kaylee, get them out," April urged.

Taking a wary step forward, Oscar jumped at the sound of a creak. Not looking behind him to avoid the humiliation of seeing April's face at his immense fear, he looked for the source of the creak.

The downstairs cupboard, beneath the stairs.

The door was slightly open, something resting upon it from the inside, forcing it to buckle marginally beneath the pressure.

Oscar looked at April, who nodded toward it, urging him to open it.

Summoning all the courage he could, he placed his sweaty palm on the handle and swung it open.

The dead body of Nancy fell to their feet, her bludgeoned head covered in dried blood. One of her eyes could be made out beneath the smashed skull, staring rigidly up at Oscar.

FOR THE SECOND NIGHT RUNNING, JASON SAT IN HIS OFFICE, HIS mind dwelling on the chilling case of Kaylee Kemple.

For the second night running, a half-empty cup sat on his desk, home to cold coffee and broken biscuit. The night birds hooted and tweeted outside the open window of his stuffy office, accompanying his deep contemplation with a gentle background noise to a station that was otherwise silent.

Something Julian Barth had said to him was severely troubling.

"Did you not think there was something off about her?"

Well, honestly, yes. Jason did. But that didn't mean holding a girl down and disguising child abuse with aged religious concepts was a valid excuse.

He picked up his phone and dialled the Kemple's number.

"Hello, you have reached Henry Kemple. I'm not able to get to the phone right now, so please leave a message at the beep."

Irritated, Jason clutched the phone with exasperation.

"Yes, hello, this is Detective Inspector Jason Lyle. Mr. Kemple, you were meant to come down the station an hour after we spoke. This was over two hours ago now. Please, can you let me know what is taking so long? If you don't come down, this may mean we will have to let the suspect go without charge. Get back to me."

He hung up, slamming the phone on the desk.

It was strange. Really, really strange.

That Henry Kemple called Jason to his house to show him this video, prompting him to arrest Julian, then does not show to give his statement.

Why would he do that?

Julian kept insinuating there was something Jason did not know about.

So what was it?

Once again, he opened his laptop and loaded the CCTV video of the interrogation with Kaylee.

Again, she sat there, so still. Her body so perfectly symmetrical, all her joints entwined within a rigid position. Her legs beneath her arms that lay neatly on the table. So innocently deprived. So haphazardly sweet and evil.

"My daddy molested me," she announced in a sickening voice that seemed so... fakely sweet.

What was she doing?

Then it happened.

A brief flicker, where it looked like a cloud appeared on the screen. In less than a second, it was gone.

What was that?

Why hadn't he seen it before?

Jason stopped the video and dragged the bar back to the beginning, playing it once more.

"My daddy molested me."

Sure enough, it happened again. So quickly it would be missed in a blink. Half a second looking away, one would never realise it was there.

He scrolled the video back once more, but this time went

frame by frame. Clicking the mouse then waiting, seeing if it showed up.

Nothing.

Then…

Jason practically fell off his chair. He clambered backward, backing away from the screen in horror.

He stood.

Paced back and forth a few times.

Opened out the window. Had some fresh air. Drank the rest of his cold coffee.

"What the fuck…"

Then, once he was mentally ready, he turned back to the screen once more.

There, behind the girl, was a form of smoke, appearing for a single frame. But it wasn't just any smoke; it was in the shape of a figure, with horns, a baby, the tail of a snake.

It was just a cloud of smoke.

A cloud of smoke taking the elusive shape of… What? A ghost? A demon?

He was seeing things.

It was nothing.

A blip on the recording. A coincidence.

Then he recalled the last thing Julian had said as he shut the cell door.

"Play it backward!"

Play it backward… Could he have meant the interview?

He hit the reverse button.

And there, in clear, audible words, he heard it. The words that had said "my daddy molested me" in a detestable, freakish voice, now said something different:

"Please help me."

No. It can't be. I'm going crazy.

Maybe he should show this to someone?

"Please help me. Please help me," it repeated again and again and again.

He hit stop.

He had to show this to someone. He had to.

No. They would think I am crazy. This is ridiculous.

He thought about playing it again but didn't need to.

In a fit of dizziness, he stumbled out the door, knocking a stack of papers off his desk as he did. He barged through the empty corridors to the cell block, marching toward Julian's cell.

He banged on the cell door to get Julian's attention. Julian stood up from his bed, approaching Jason, who leered haphazardly through the window.

"What is going on?" Jason cried out.

"That girl was possessed, and we freed her. Now the father is possessed, and is likely going to kill her as a result."

Jason backed away.

What was going on?

Was he really doing this?

Oh, God...

"Can she still be saved?" Jason urgently demanded. "If I get us there with blue lights, can she still be saved?"

Julian shrugged. "She may well already be dead, but it's worth a shot."

Jason nodded and tripped on his way to get the keys, trying to keep himself steady, in disbelief at what he was doing.

4 0

It took everything Oscar had to fight his gag reflex.

It was the first time he had ever seen a dead body, and the emasculated part of him wished he could say he handled it better. Something he may have been able to do if the body hadn't been such a deformed, mangled, distorted corpse.

"Pull yourself together," April urged him.

He nodded vacantly, unaware he was even responding. His eyes remained transfixed on the lifeless eyes staring vacantly back at him.

April nudged him and pulled his face toward hers.

"I need you, Oscar. Don't flake out on me now."

She needs me?

Not caring that he was probably taking that the completely opposite way to which it was intended, he decided she was right. He was acting how the old Oscar would have acted.

No more.

This was the new Oscar.

A clang of heavily falling furniture thudded against the ceiling above, vibrating a cloud of dust off the wooden beams.

Oscar and April exchanged a silent glance of confirmation. They were heading upstairs.

Reaching into the bag April had brought in, Oscar withdrew a cross and clutched onto it.

So silly, really. A week ago he refused to even set foot in a church, what with how ridiculous a concept religion was.

Now here he was, clutching onto a cross in the hope it was going to keep him alive.

Step by step, he crept. Placing one gentle foot above the other, placing them down with enough care so as to avoid the creak of the old wooden floorboards beneath the faded carpet.

As he approached the landing, he peered across the dark hallway. The girl's room, at the far end of the corridor, gifted them a tiny crack, with a minuscule shaft of light shining out.

Oscar hesitated.

Exhaled deeply.

April took hold of his hand and grasped it, squeezing it tightly in comfort.

Oscar appreciated it.

It wasn't just about how being able to hold her hand filled his body with excited tingles, but the reassurance it gave him to feel her soft skin against his.

It gave him the strength to take the final few steps.

With a deep breath he gathered himself, filling his mind with calm thoughts to quell the rabid anxiety coursing through him.

He lunged himself forward and barged through the door, holding his cross out, gripping it so tightly the edges splintered painfully into his palm.

Fuck the pain.

It was time to step up.

It took a moment of repulsion for him to ignore the sight before him. Willing it to fade into the background, he urged himself to overcome it.

The girl was laid in a bloody heap upon the bed. Oscar could see her chest rising up and down, slowly taking in what air she could – a sign that she was still alive, at least. But her face was badly bruised, her body cut, her clothes ripped and torn.

Henry turned his head toward Oscar and April with a devious growl. It was inhuman – like an alerted wild animal turning toward its prey. From the position Henry held over Kaylee, Oscar dreaded to think about what the poor girl's father was doing.

The guy was almost unrecognisable.

What had been neatly groomed, gelled hair was now a sweaty mess mixed with patches of blood. His eyes were large circles of red. His skin was barely present, faded to a dark-pale scar, wrinkled with wounds. His mouth was black, with blood seeping through the cracks of his teeth, and his torn lips lifted uncomfortably at a skewed angle across his face. White blotches of scar tissue decorated his eyelids.

But what freaked Oscar out most was Henry's body. Every joint was distorted, bent in a way that was unnatural for a human's bones to bend, turning in every direction he shouldn't.

His growl was merciless. A mixture of various carnivorous animals, a scream that sent Oscar against the back of the wall.

But Oscar was not letting this thing win.

The poor girl looked to have been tortured to the edge of her life, and it was up to him to provide her salvation.

"Back away, you foul beast!" Oscar demanded, holding his cross out.

April joined him, clutching rosary beads toward the demonic creature before them.

Oscar did his best to remember the prayer Julian had used.

"In the name of the Father, the Son, and the Holy Spirit, leave this being!"

A sinister smirk grew across Henry's crooked face.

"The angels in heaven command you!"

The angels in heaven? That wasn't it, was it?

The grin turned into a malevolent chuckle.

"The power of Christ demands you to let this man go!"

In an effortless swipe, Henry's claw swung over the cross and rosary beads, knocking them to the floor.

It stood facing them.

Oscar cowered. Glanced at April. Lip quivering.

Was this it?

Was this how he was about to die?

The first time he ever tried doing the right thing in his entire life was going to be the last thing he ever did?

That was when, in a huge stroke of good fortune, the door swung open.

In stormed a police officer named Jason Lyle, followed by the strong march of Julian, holding his own cross, demanding the demon away.

JASON DOVE ON HENRY, TAKING HIM TO THE GROUND, PINNING him down with all of his weight.

Jason's jaw dropped at the sight of Henry's face. It was an animalistic mess – its glare intensified like a rabid beast, snarling and snapping its jaw at Jason, excessive saliva dripping down his chin in bloody gunks.

Julian held his cross toward Henry.

"Dear heavenly Father," Julian began.

But it wasn't enough.

Henry soared into the air and, before Jason could understand what was happening, he had been smacked into the ceiling. He cried with pain as he was held there for a moment, the bump of the lamp digging into his back as it gave off sparks that sent violent shivers up and down his body. Henry then plummeted back to the floor, shaking like a dog drying itself so as to knock Jason away from him.

Jason's groaning body rolled onto the floor.

Everything hurt. Every bone, every muscle.

He lifted his head slowly, dragging his hazy vision upwards. He saw what was on the bed.

Kaylee.

Tied to the bed by each wrist and ankle.

Her clothes were bloody and ripped.

Her eyes were closed. Jason wasn't entirely sure she was breathing.

He forced every last piece of energy he had to his muscles, relying on adrenaline to force him to his feet.

Henry climbed to all fours, turning toward Jason and hissing. His eyeballs were succumbed by a complete bloody red, his hands wrapped around into claws, and its body curled up and tensing. It walked forward like an untamed beast, glaring at Julian, waiting for its turn to pounce.

The possessed body of Henry leapt forward, diving toward Julian, but Jason sent it on its side with a large swing of his fist, landing his knuckles in the side of the possessed man's face.

Jason managed to get himself back to his feet in time to thwack his asp around the back of Henry's head. Henry's body lay absently on the floor, eyelids flickering, losing consciousness.

Henry's body wriggled on the floor like a beast struggling to find its legs.

Jason swung his asp once more into Henry's head, knocking him out cold.

"We need to get him restrained, and now," Julian instructed. "We aren't going to do this without him still."

Jason withdrew his handcuffs and handed them to Julian.

"Use this," he instructed, then ran to Kaylee's side. He removed the restraints from the girl and held her dead weight in his arms, shaking her, willing her to come around.

The poor, wretched girl coughed, dribbling blood down her cheek. Then her coughing turned to desperate breaths, which turned to vacant wheezing.

She wasn't breathing.

He lay her down, wiping the trickling blood off her cheeks.

"No, come on…" he whispered, pleading with her to live, pleading even though it did nothing.

He thought back to his first aid training.

What should he do?

Don't panic.

That was the first thing. Don't panic.

Clear the airway. That was the next thing he remembered.

Taking a screwed-up piece of tissue from his pocket, he wiped away all the blood, patting her back to ensure everything came up.

He laid her firmly on her back and knelt beside her neck, opening her mouth.

He pinched the nostrils.

Took a deep breath.

Leant down, breathed oxygen into the little girl's lungs.

Looked at her chest.

It didn't rise.

The oxygen wasn't even going into her lungs.

What am I doing wrong?

He pinched her nose.

Why did I tell them to meet me at the station in an hour? How could I miss what that arsehole was doing to his daughter?

No time to think about that now.

Stop it.

Covering her mouth with his, pinching the nose, ensuring there was no way air could escape – he breathed out once more.

Her chest laid flat.

It did not rise.

The blood. She was choking up blood.

It must be clogging up her throat.

He resumed CPR.

He pumped her chest with his hands.

He gave her as much oxygen as he was able to give.

Again.

And again.

And again.

Nothing.

Absolutely nothing.

Jason turned and looked to Julian watching expectantly. He'd managed to handcuff Henry and find some rope that he was wrapping around him but he, just like Oscar and April, watched on helplessly, waiting to see if Kaylee lived or died.

"She's not breathing," Jason muttered, having to tell himself as much as the others.

As if with a protesting response, Kaylee spluttered a quick movement of her chest.

Jason's head shot back to her, watching her intently, the whole room holding a collective breath.

She spluttered some more.

Her chest rose.

He could feel her breath brushing against his cheek.

He turned back to the rest of the room.

"She needs to go to a hospital," Jason told them.

Julian looked from Jason, to Oscar and April.

"I'll take her," Oscar reluctantly decided. Out of everyone there he was evidently the most useless, and the one they could do without.

He stepped forward and began picking the girl up.

"No," Julian decided. Oscar turned back to him, bemused. "We need you, Oscar."

Oscar looked to April, then back to Julian. A flicker of happiness adorned his face, an emotion he tried to conceal; a young girl's life hung in the balance and this wasn't the time for him to be pleased that they needed him.

"Jason, could you?" Julian asked.

Jason nodded. "I'm going to need to call this in. How long do you need?"

"An hour."

"Okay."

Jason picked Kaylee up and swiftly took her away.

42

A CALM TRANQUILLITY DESCENDED OVER THE DINING TABLE OF
the Kemple residence.

Henry, with his hands restrained in handcuffs through the
back of his chair and an uncomfortable rope wrapped around
his chest, opened his bloody eyes, surveying the scene with
disgust.

The demon that dwelled within looked around itself, then
grunted a sneer of amusement.

Julian sat directly opposite, with Oscar and April to his left
and right. Sage sat on the table burning slowly, sending a small
slither of smoke trailing into the air, surrounded by three lit
candles. They held hands around the table, Oscar and April's
hands crossing over Henry's body.

He leant his head back and guffawed. The demon's laugh
rang out of Henry's helpless mouth, shaking the loose scabs
poking off his face.

"You fucking idiots," it declared. "You're doing a séance,
aren't you? Or is it a cleansing? Or a fucked-up kind of
exorcism?"

"Please remember," Julian spoke to the other two, holding

eye contact with Henry's evil eyes. "To do exactly as I say, and do not break the circle."

Julian bowed his head and closed his eyes.

Henry grinned wildly, a sadistic curve smeared across his face. His laugh continued, high-pitched like a hyena, then low like a thunderous rumble in a distant jungle.

"Spirits, hear us," Julian began, slowly and calmly. "We have amongst us an unclean spirit."

"Hah!" Henry blurted out. "Unclean!"

"We need help casting this demon out of our brother's body."

Henry leant his head forward, turning to Oscar. "Hey," he whispered. "Hey, you."

Oscar opened his eyes, then turned away as Julian pulled on his arm, a prompt to ignore any taunts.

"Yo, Oscar, mate," Henry continued to whisper, as if he was talking to a naughty friend at the back of a class. "Wanna hear what I did to Kaylee?"

"If there are any spirits with us right now," Julian persisted, trying to ignore the demon's tease, "please help us cleanse this house of evil."

"Hey," Henry continued his sneaky whispers. "I practically broke her in two."

Oscar scrunched up his face, doing all he could to ignore the demon, refusing to give in to its sickening words.

"I fucked her in places you should never be fucked."

Oscar turned to Henry. He knew he shouldn't, he couldn't help it.

But he didn't see Henry sat beside him.

There, in its true form, was the demon Lilu. Its scarred body was decorated in a coat of armour, decorated like a war hero. But its face... its face sent shivers seizing up and down Oscar's chest. It was curved like that of a ravenous goat, twisted horns raising out of a contorted head, bloody fangs overlapping the edge of its mouth. Attached to its back were two large wings, almost as big as its body.

Then Oscar looked closer.

Its face... it wasn't just scrunched up out of a terrifying contortion of evil. It was upset. It was crying.

This thing was crying.

This gave Oscar an idea.

"You are pathetic," Oscar spoke.

"Oscar, what are you doing?" Julian demanded. They had forewarned Oscar not to interact with it and not to interrupt the process, yet there he was.

"A crying demon," Oscar continued. "How ridiculous."

"Oscar, what the hell are you–"

"Julian," April interjected, sensing that Oscar was onto something.

Julian calmed down and, despite being overcome by confusion, turned to Oscar and watched.

"Did you cry while you were raping her?" Oscar asked the demon, shocking himself momentarily at the words coming out of his mouth.

"How – how dare you!" the demon stuttered. "I will kill you!"

"Oh yeah, you gonna cry while you do that too?"

The demon roared, causing the candle flames to flicker manically, the table shaking.

Oscar shook his head, undeterred.

This demon's weakness was his weakness.

It was a loser. It got upset about pathetic, trivial things. It needed to be a man instead of some idiot weeping over a woman.

"Yeah, that would have been a lot more convincing if you weren't crying like a bitch."

"I – am not – crying!"

Oscar had never let anyone see him cry. He had taken medication to numb emotions so he didn't have to cry.

Because that would mean he cared.

He had never had a reason to care.

But now, looking around himself, he found his purpose. Julian, watching expectantly. April, astounded at his progress.

Beautiful, lovely, punky April.

Oscar was not like this sack-of-shit demon anymore.

And that was why he was going to win.

"You miss Ardat Lili, don't you?"

The demon's eyes narrowed, squinting into a devastated glare, fury depicted over its face. At least, it looked as if it was attempting fury. In truth, its menace grew less, its helpless eyes giving it away.

"You know what we did to Ardat Lili?"

The demon growled.

"We removed her from that body like a little bitch."

The demon released another deafening roar.

Oscar smiled. He was enjoying this.

"Oh yeah, go ahead and roar, that's so scary. At least I'm man enough to admit I'm a dipshit loser who can't get a girl. What are you?"

The table shook, vibrating uncontrollably. The sage quivered across it, the contents of the room trembling and shaking.

Who do you think you are? the demon screamed.

Oscar stood over Henry, looming over him like an uncontrollable shadow.

"Me?" Oscar stood, gyrating his finger at the demon, seeing its hold on Henry growing weaker. "I'm a loser who lives with his parents, works in a supermarket, needs meds to handle life, can't get a girl, gets looked down on by every person I see, gets intimidated easily, spends my days looking forward to my nightly masturbation session and is likely to never amount to shit!"

Oscar dropped his head closer to Henry's, until he was within inches, staring intensely into the demon's weakened eyes.

He felt the demon's tepid breath against his.

He didn't care.

He was not scared anymore.

This thing may have hooves.

It may be bloody.

It may be bigger, be evil, be far scarier than Oscar ever would be.

But it couldn't beat Oscar. Couldn't even mount a challenge.

Oscar had a gift.

He had friends.

There was a girl in the world willing to talk to him.

But, most of all, Oscar had grown something this crying-baby-demon didn't have.

A set of balls.

"So, you tell me," he spoke coolly and particularly, with an aggressive calmness. "Who's the real loser?"

The demon's final roar shook the house, causing glassware to fall off shelves and smash, photo frames to go sailing across the room, the table to fly into the far wall.

Then it all dropped.

Henry's body collapsed to the floor.

Oscar watched in awe as he saw the translucent figure of the demon rise into the air, out of Henry's mouth, then, with a scowl in Oscar's direction, dive hastily into the floor below.

Julian leapt forward, putting his hands on Henry's neck, feeling a pulse.

"He's alive," Julian observed, then glanced at his watch. "We need to go."

"But–"

"No, Oscar. You've done great, but the police will be here soon, let them deal with it."

Julian gathered up his things and, within minutes, was rushing out of the house.

Oscar and April followed.

And, as they did, her hand crept into his.

"Well done," she whispered. Then, with a cheeky grin, "Loser."

Three months later

43

Jason entered the interrogation room, taking his time. He glanced at Henry sitting there helplessly, hands restrained to the table, an unflattering prison outfit looking just as glum as his face.

Jason sat opposite him, undoing Henry's restraints and handing him a coffee. He leant back in his chair, sipping on his hot drink.

"How are you?" Jason asked.

Henry shook his head and snorted.

"How do you think?"

"What did your lawyers say?"

"They said I could possibly get away with temporary insanity. But they think it's unlikely."

Jason reluctantly nodded in agreement.

"Yes, it is. It's worth going for, but with the prolonged torture of Kaylee, and the death of…" Jason drifted off, seeing Henry's face flinch at the mention of his wife's suffering. "Out of curiosity, how much do you actually remember?"

Henry shrugged.

"It comes back in glimpses. Mostly in my dreams."

Jason took a sip of his coffee.

"The good news is that Kaylee is alive, and she's doing well. Doctors expect her to make a full recovery. I mean, physically, anyway."

Henry nodded, forcing a smile, telling himself this was good news.

"What about the Sensitives?" he asked, leaning forward.

"What about them?"

"Couldn't they testify? Tell people what really happened? If they were seen as experts, and they explained it, then surely…"

"And say what?" Jason asked.

A moment of silence passed as the question hung in the air.

"Unfortunately," Jason began, "you're not the first guy to come through here saying that voices made you do it."

Henry bowed his head. "So long as Kaylee is safe."

"I promise you, we will do all we can to make sure she goes to a good home, you can be sure of that."

Henry nodded.

I guess I'll have to settle with that.

"Thank you," he spoke, staring at a coffee stain on the floor. "I appreciate that."

* * *

"So, when are you going to take him to meet Derek?" April asked Julian. "I know he'd be dying to meet him."

Julian just smiled, keeping his answer to himself, watching Oscar across the hallway in the kitchen, in deep conversation on the phone.

"He always spoke about searching out other people like them," April insisted.

"You haven't even met him yet. Why would I take him?"

"Well, why not? He's evidently powerful, isn't he? Probably more so than he realises."

Julian didn't answer. He just stared intently at the young man having an animated discussion. It was true, Oscar was not the person they had first discovered. He had grown into his role, displaying confidence and gifts they could never have predicted.

Maybe it was worth putting more faith in him.

* * *

OSCAR FINISHED HIS PHONE CALL, placed his phone in his pocket and paused.

How great was this?

Something worth investing in. Something with purpose. Something that took him away from the monotony of his previous pointless existence.

He sauntered into the living room, glowing with the radiance of a happy smile.

"We have a poltergeist in Edinburgh," Oscar announced. "Or so they claim."

"Edinburgh?" April repeated, turning to Julian. "That's a hell of a trip."

"Is it worth investigating?" Julian asked.

Oscar paused.

Was it worth investigating?

Well, the woman sounded hysterical. Possibly a religious nutjob. A whacko desperate for attention.

But she was offering £3,000 for investigating.

"Yeah, I'd say so," Oscar decided.

"Well, Jason's just called," Julian pointed out, "says he has a job in Nottingham for a couple who keep hearing things in their attic. Wants us to take a look."

"Could we do it on the way?" Oscar offered.

"Road trip!" April declared. "And maybe we could pay your friend a visit on the way…"

"What friend?" Oscar quizzically inquired.

Julian just smiled knowingly. Oscar wondered who they were referring to, but didn't have a chance to ask. Julian stood, grabbed the car keys from the window-sill and chucked them in April's direction.

"Shotgun!" he declared.

And with that, they prepared their bags and left.

Julian leading the way.

April following behind, joking with Oscar.

Oscar, smiling.

Finally finding somewhere he belonged.

THE SENSITIVES BOOK TWO: MY EXORCISM KILLED ME

BOOK TWO IN THE SENSITIVES SERIES

MY EXORCISM
KILLED ME

RICK WOOD

THEN

Wiltshire, England

1

A WHIRLWIND OF CHAOS ENCOMPASSED THE ROOM WITH SAVAGE intensity.

Fragments of glass.

Rough edges of wrecked pieces of wooden furniture.

Torn paper. Ripped clothes. Shattered light bulbs.

All discarded through the air with no consideration of the disorder it created.

There was nowhere you could step without stabbing a foot or pricking a finger. What had been an ordinary bedroom was now a mess of broken items. Some items lay still and unattended. Some items flapped on the floor like a dying fish. Most items clashed in the air in a hurricane of anarchy.

Derek Lansdale gripped his cross, securing his rigid fingers tightly around its base. He held it out firmly. Pointed it downwards at the helpless girl beneath him.

This hadn't been his toughest exorcism.

This hadn't even been his toughest night.

He had once endured war; but that was a long time ago. The rise of The Sensitives had changed things. Hell had struggled to pose a threat that Derek would deem substantial.

That considered, he still could not underplay how tough this exorcism had been. He had been at it for days, and was running on very little sleep. His aching muscles were growing weary and his head pounded with a fierce migraine.

He was mentally drained. But he had been here plenty of times before.

He had his young apprentice at his side – a Sensitive with an extraordinary power to banish demons from their victims. His wasn't the strongest power he'd ever witnessed, but what he lacked in ability, he made up for in passion.

His name was Julian Barth.

"Julian, I need your help!" Derek bellowed above the crashes and smashes of the room. A chair flew into the far wall, exploding into sharp shards of wood that blasted back into the room, causing Derek to duck.

Julian glanced to the only other people besides him, Derek and the girl, both of whom looked petrified.

One was a priest and the other, a doctor.

The priest, Derek had understood; but the doctor, Derek had raged about for days. This wasn't something he used to have to put up with, but with the church growing more and more concerned about society's lack of understanding toward what occurred during his exorcisms, it was now required. Following a few injuries, the Church had requested a higher level of risk management. Exorcism was yet to successfully merge with modern times.

Julian stood forward, his arms shaking, his lip quivering. This was his first. Derek had told him it would be tough, had forewarned him as to what he would witness. But Julian had expected a few shaking pieces of furniture, a few floating objects – not this. Not a scene of frenzied, torturous mania.

Julian took Derek's side, looking upon the vulnerable girl helplessly restrained to the bed.

Her face was that of Anna Bennett. She was an innocent,

playful, yet shy twelve-year-old girl. She worked hard at school, picked flowers for her teachers, and was always polite to everyone she met.

Except, what they were looking at was not Anna.

In body, yes. It was Anna's skin. Her fingers, her toes. But not her eyes.

It was in her eyes that you couldn't escape an undeniable presence of evil.

It was in her cracked lips, stained skin, and writhing body that the demon lived, causing the girl constant, excruciating agony.

Blood soaked from her crotch, mixing with the urine stains on the bed sheets. Julian had been rendered speechless upon first meeting Anna and witnessing the morbid fascination the demon had with focussing its violent attacks on her crotch. It was a second between her innocent smile and her dinner fork being thrust inside of herself.

"Julian, damn it, I need you to focus!" Derek demanded.

Julian realised he had been in a daydream, thinking about his hesitance, his trepidation, to the point that he had ended up neglecting his responsibilities.

"What do you want me to do, Derek?" he asked, flinching at the fragile wobble of his voice.

"Where is your cross, boy?"

Julian raised his hand, holding his cross out.

"Hold it firmly, like you bloody-well mean it!" Derek prompted.

Julian grasped the cross, pointing it at the demon with forced, disingenuous confidence.

"Now repeat after me. Be gone, demon!"

"Be gone, demon."

"Louder! *Be gone, demon!*"

"Be gone, demon!"

Anna's mouth opened, black saliva trickling down her chin,

and she projectile vomited bloody lumps that splashed down her legs and the bed sheets, flicking onto Julian's shoes.

"Er, Mr Lansdale," came a shy voice from the doctor behind. "I'm concerned."

"About what?" snapped Derek. He'd done enough of these rituals without doctors; he wasn't particularly open to listening to what they had to say just because the Church wanted to afford their exorcists more protection.

Protection from what? The law?

There were far harsher things out there worth protecting themselves from.

"That's the fifth time she's been sick. I'm worried she may not be hydrated. When was the last time you allowed her a glass of water?"

A glass of water?

Derek turned his bemused face to the doctor, full of disdain for his ridiculous contribution.

"Shut up, you stuffy old man," Derek replied, then realised how hypocritical his words were; he was hardly the spritely, energetic young man he used to be.

"You're hurting me..." came an innocent young girl's voice from the face of the wretched demon. It was playing on the doctor's insecurities, but the doctor would not have the experience that Derek had that allowed him to identify the demon's tactics.

"Ignore it," Derek told Julian, ignoring the doctor. "It will imitate the host, try to get a rise from us."

"I need water... I need food... Please..."

"Derek," Julian offered, concerned about the girl's wellbeing.

"Enough!" Derek interrupted, full of irritation. "You need to learn to be tough. A demon will exploit any weakness. Show it nothing but strength."

Julian nodded obediently.

"Behold the cross of the Lord; flee bands of enemies," Derek continued, spitting his prayer with utter detest. "May thy mercy, Lord, descend upon us. Be gone, demon!"

Julian could only watch as the demon stopped writhing and grew still, collapsing into a heap.

Every object in the room that had been firing around in circles fell to the floor with a heavy thud. Furniture, glass, torn clothes – everything came hurtling down to the surface.

A calm tranquility descended upon the room. Like the morning after a heavy night.

At first, they thought the exorcism had been successful.

With decades of experience working against him, Derek was tempted to believe that this was a success also. But he knew enough to know that this may just have been the eye of the storm.

Derek fell against the wall, slumping to the floor, breathing quickly, panting, relishing the opportunity for a break. The older he got, the tougher this became. He could feel his bones growing weaker, his muscles stiff, and his body removed of energy.

Julian was the next generation now. Derek needed to be able to pass his knowledge along and retire. Somewhere in the country, maybe. A nice cottage with a view.

Julian didn't rest. There was something about Anna's state that desperately concerned him.

He took a few cautious steps toward the girl. The closer he tiptoed forward, the more his mind filled with dread.

It all went into slow motion. He reached the girl's side, watching her lying motionless. Her eyes were wide open, but they didn't move. Her chest didn't rise.

He placed two fingers on the side of her neck.

He couldn't feel a pulse.

"Doctor!" Julian exclaimed, turning toward the doctor, who came rushing forward.

The doctor felt for the girl's pulse, then turned back to Derek with terror.

"What?" Derek asked, standing, growing uneasy. "What is it?"

The doctor dragged the girl from the bed and onto the floor, ensuring she was on a hard surface. Without hesitation, he began CPR. He pushed down on the girl's chest repeatedly, doing all he could to restart her heart. He sucked up air and breathed out into her mouth, multiple times, again and again, persisting.

Julian stood next to Derek for what felt like an age, shaking his head, his eyes fighting back tears. He didn't want to look weak in front of Derek.

He looked at Derek's face, looking to see if this was normal, looking for an indication as to how Julian should be acting.

Derek's wide eyes continued to stare at the helpless body of the girl lying on the floor. A flicker of vulnerability passed over his face, but he did his best to conceal it.

This was going to change everything, and he knew it.

"I got cocky," Derek whispered to himself.

No one responded. No one answered. No one confirmed that he had or he hadn't. Everyone just stared.

Stared at the doctor persevering in his attempt to save the girl's life.

Eventually, the doctor stopped. Out of breath, his head turned. Slowly. Looking over the faces waiting for his conclusion.

The doctor just stared at the wide eyes gazing back at him.

"Well?" Julian prompted.

"She's…" the doctor began, pausing, unable to find the words. "She's… dead."

Derek fell to his knees.

Julian watched as Derek shook his head, again and again, rapidly twisting back and forth in denial.

"No..." Derek muttered. "No, no, no, no..."

Julian backed up, covering his face, closing his eyes, bowing his head. He tried looking elsewhere. Away from the girl, away from Derek, endeavouring to find a point in the room he could look where he wouldn't be having to face what had just happened.

What would their excuse to the authorities be?

A demon possessed her?

They would lock them away in a padded cell.

And the girl...

Her mother was waiting downstairs, full of worry, expecting them to have the solution. To rid the horrid entity from her daughter's body.

Soon, they would have to go downstairs and give her the news. Deliver the awful news of her daughter's death.

The mother had been so hopeful. Derek had told her, "No demon has beaten me yet."

She had thought that Derek was her saviour.

And now...

Julian wanted to punch something. To turn the furniture upside down, to kick a chair across the room, to smash a window.

But he didn't.

He didn't even move.

He couldn't.

He just stared absently at the corpse lying on the bed in its own urine, sick, and blood.

NOW

4 years later

Tewkesbury, Gloucestershire

2

JULIAN'S HEAVY SLEEP ENDED ABRUPTLY AS HE BOLTED UPRIGHT like a plank.

For a few minutes he sat. Still. Panting and sweating as his awareness gradually readjusted. His body remained motionless but for his chest, which rapidly expanded and retracted with the heaviness of his breathing.

He tried to prop himself up, but his arms wobbled, as unsteady as his mind. He endeavoured to push himself to a state of balance, but his elbows continued to give way.

That dream.

Again.

That same damn dream.

Anna dies like she does every night.

Her face looks back at him. Her eyes held wide open as if pulled apart by pins. Her pupils fixed on his, full of horror yet absent of life. Chills run down his spine. He is left rooted to the spot in terror.

His mouth won't form words.

His mind won't form thoughts.

It was the same face he saw in every victim of demonic possession he helped. Any time he started the first prayer of an exorcism. Any time he held that cross in his trembling hands and recited that same prayer.

Sure, it was another person, and another helpless soul he was determined to help. But, whenever he looked into their eyes – as in, really looked into their eyes – it was Anna, all over again.

The night fogged his room with darkness. Yet, in his dreams, he saw her as clear as day. What had been the life of an enthusiastic, bubbly twelve-year-old morphed into the stiffened face of a corpse revealing the onset of rigor mortis.

His breath calmed. It was still furious, with a pace to his panting that almost suffocated him, but he was gradually regaining control. As he took that control and allowed his breathing to slow, to continue to calm, his mind finally reached the point where he could focus his blurry vision on the shadows around him.

He was topless. Sweating profusely on a cold autumn night.

The clock read 3.40 a.m.

The same hour.

No need to explain why. Derek had taught him about the witching hour, and what it was.

It was the hour of the demonic. The hour when hell was at its strongest, and committing the foulest acts.

But Julian did not believe it was hell that was haunting him. He believed it was himself. And he would not allow himself to let his mind dwell on other possibilities, just because of the things he had seen.

He hung his head. He felt weak. He needed help.

"Derek…" he whispered, unsure why. The word came out as cold breath that lingered in a haze before him, then protruded into vague smoke.

He rotated his body and placed his bare feet on the carpet. He buried his head in his hands, running his fingers through his soaking hair, sticky with perspiration.

Anna.

She was still there, imprinted on the forefront of his mind. Her cold, dead face, still haunting him.

He wondered if it still haunted Derek.

He switched on a lamp light and grimaced at its brightness, squinting as his eyes adapted to its mild luminosity. He picked up his phone, scrolled through his address book, then put it to his ear.

Waited a few moments.

"Hello?" came a voice at the end.

"Hi, I would like to speak to Derek Lansdale, please."

"Do you know what time this is?" came the irritated voice at the other end of the phone.

"Erm… yeah, I do. Is it possible for me to speak to him?"

"No!" replied the ill-tempered recipient of his late call. "You can call during normal hours like everyone else."

The line went dead.

The one man he counted on. Unable to talk.

It wasn't fair. Derek didn't deserve the fate he had been bestowed. The predicament he was in for trying to help a young girl.

Julian closed his eyes. Considered trying to fall back to sleep, but knew he would not be successful. The constant reoccurrence of these late-night awakenings was making him sluggish in the day, but now he felt wide awake.

His dried sweat was growing cold as it stuck to his skin in the cool night air and he slid a loose t-shirt over his chest. He left his room and trudged across his flat to the kitchen. He opened the fridge, took out a pint of milk, and poured himself a glass.

He leant against the side, absentmindedly sipping, his mind elsewhere. His mind still with Derek. With Anna.

He had to get himself together.

He could never let April see him like this. Or Oscar. No one could see his weaknesses. He was meant to lead them, meant to guide them. Not burden them.

Derek was the only one who could see this side of him. Except, Derek couldn't be there for him anymore. Not like he used to be.

He gulped down the rest of his milk, placed the glass in the sink, and walked back to his room.

He froze.

A whisper carried across the room, as if coming from outside, sailing across the shuffle of the night air. It was a windy night, and he was sure it was just his tired mind forming patterns out of sounds. Chances are, what he thought he heard was just the wind beating against branches or soaring through the cracks of the windows.

Still, it sounded specific.

It sounded as if someone had whispered his name.

He shook his head to himself.

He was a paranormal investigator. He knew what constituted paranoia and what constituted genuine supernatural phenomena.

"Julian…" it whispered once more, ever so faintly, with the rustle of a tree branch tapping against the window.

It was the weather.

Grow up.

He had no inkling or awareness of a feeling of the supernatural in his flat. It was just his tired sub-conscious haunting him. Not a ghost. He was a strong, experienced Sensitive – he would know.

Still.

It was odd.

Shaking his head to himself, he returned to his bedroom and opened a political thriller on his Kindle, trying to keep his mind away from thoughts of demons and ghosts.

He read until he fell back to sleep.

3

Oscar absently stirred his coffee, staring at the milk mixing with the water.

"You know you're meant to drink coffee, right? Not just stir it," teased April, smirking playfully as she sipped her hot chocolate.

Oscar took a big, deep breath, got ready to speak, found the words, urged them to his mouth, and...

"Yeah," was all he could muster.

You absolute wuss. You complete and utter loser. Get a grip! You've battled demons, and you can't even tell a girl how you feel!

It was the ninth time he and April had been together like this. In a situation, alone, with intimate conversation. It was another occasion that left Oscar racking his mind with the question: *is this a date?*

It felt like a date. It was just those two, no Julian. Alone. Together. Talking and smiling at each other. Getting dressed up.

Only for it to amount to nothing.

Oscar was pretty sure he was close to being friend-zoned now, if he hadn't been already.

He should have gone in for the kiss on that first date. Looking back, it was obvious. She'd held his eye contact, fiddled with her keys at the door, then, at the last minute, his belly had filled with a swarm of butterflies. He overthought it, and he backed out.

Now, here they were. Alone. Again. Together. He was wearing a shirt.

He never wore shirts.

Surely, she knew from his shirt that this was a serious occasion?

Or, maybe she's normal, and she doesn't pay attention to everything I wear and keep track of how I attribute the formality of my clothes relative to the occasion.

He could have shown up in a tuxedo, top hat, and tails, and she would have had no idea.

"So…" Oscar began, trying not to let the silence last too long. If it lasted too long, then she would decide she felt uncomfortable with him, decide she no longer liked him, and it wasn't going to happen – that is, if she had actually liked him in the first place.

Here I go, overthinking it again.

"So…?" April repeated, awaiting the thought Oscar was readying himself to verbalise.

"So… how long have we known each other?"

April let out a sigh, thinking carefully before returning her beautiful hazel eyes back to Oscar's reddening face.

"Nine months?" April asked.

She was close.

It's actually eight months, twenty-three days, four hours, and around fifteen minutes.

"Yeah, nine months, something like that," Oscar confirmed. "See, over that time…"

Oscar went to speak, then found his tongue twisting into a fattened obstruction. Her purple hair was tied into a long ponytail beneath a red bandana, and flung loosely over her shoulder. She had a spiky collar on, flared jeans, and a hoodie from some band Oscar had never heard of, with her sleeves pulled up enough to reveal her funky Tim Burton tattoos and multiple music festival bracelets.

"Over that time... what?" April replied, raising her eyebrows and sticking out her bottom lip, as if waiting for Oscar to finish that sentence.

"Well..." Oscar attempted to resume. "We've fought a lot of demons. A lot of ghosts."

"A few."

Sixteen demons, three poltergeists, one banshee, two frauds, and eight seances.

"Yeah, a few."

Oscar took a large sip of his coffee, found that it was too hot and it scalded his tongue, yet held it painfully in his mouth. He paused, not wanting to swallow and burn his throat, but not wanting to spit it back out into his cup in front of April.

April grew confused, watching him in limbo, halted, with the liquid held behind his lips.

"Are you okay?" she asked, stifling a giggle at his expense.

"Mmhm," he lied.

I'm going to have to swallow. It's the only way.

He closed his eyes, readied himself, and gulped down the hot liquid that stung the back of his throat. He attempted to conceal his pain, wincing and flinching in restraint.

"You're an odd creature," April spiritedly observed.

An odd creature?

Is that a good thing? Should I say thank you? Does that mean she likes me? Is odd good? Is being a creature good? Is any of this good?

"Er... cheers."

"You're welcome," April chuckled, taking a sip of her hot chocolate that she seemed to manage to drink without worrying about it burning her whatsoever.

"So, we've known each other long enough to be, like, good friends, yeah?"

April appeared bemused. "…Yeah."

"Good. Good."

This was it.

Come on, Oscar.

Suck it up.

It's time.

"Well, in that time, I've grown quite fond of you," he blurted out, on a roll, not about to stop. "And I actually really quite like–"

April's phone blared out, interrupting Oscar dead in his tracks.

She picked it up and looked at it.

"Sorry, it's Julian," she spoke, then read her text.

Bloody Julian. That sodding guy. I was about to say it…

"Oh my God!" April exclaimed as she read her message, her eyebrows raised. "Jeeze. I can't believe this."

"What? What is it?"

April leant toward Oscar.

"He says it's time for you to meet Derek."

4

DETECTIVE INSPECTOR JASON LYLE STRODE INTO THE HOSPITAL, stroking his trimmed beard with one hand as the other nestled comfortably in his pocket. He was used to unusual crime scenes, and he had been told that this was no exception.

"So, what have we got?" he demanded of his colleague.

"We have a body, and… well… you'd better come see."

Jason followed the officer up the stairs until they reached the children's ward on the fourth floor.

He glanced at the sick children in the beds as he paced past, feeling a sense of morbidity. Pale children weakly prodding at hospital food, attached to machines barely keeping them alive. It made him picture his child in that position and considered how devastating an experience that would be.

No wonder someone snapped in this place if tragically ill children surround them every day.

As they approached the office of the deceased doctor, he paused beside the door and signed in. After stepping into his white suit, he stepped inside.

The body of a middle-aged man lay on the floor. His wide eyes were still open, and his hands were stuck rigidly upwards with his fingers spread out. He looked like he died stuck in a state of shock. Rigor mortis held him rigidly in place, but how? It would have taken at least two hours to set in – so how had his body remained in this position following death, instead of collapsing on the floor?

Jason instantly understood why he had been called. No one could answer this question, and that was why they had resorted to phoning him. He had grown a distinct reputation as a detective with a penchant for unusual cases.

"Talk me through it," he instructed his colleague.

"Well, if you have a look at the lacerations on his throat, there are marks against his oesophagus, showing that he was clearly strangled. And he is stuck in a position of shock, which is puzzling, to say the least. But that's not the strange part."

"Well, what is the strange part?" Jason replied, growing impatient.

"He was shown to have been strangled to death, but the way that he is propped, he – he was petrified in his final moments. He saw something that stuck him like this. It totally contrasts with the notion of a slow death from strangulation, compared to a death of sudden shock, and – well, he appears to have died from both. It's just, well, how is that possible when both take such a vastly different amount of time to kill a guy?"

Jason crouched beside the body, scrutinising it with his searching eyes.

True, the victim had been strangled to death. Something that could easily have taken ten minutes.

Yet it was also true that the victim appeared to have been shocked to death within seconds.

The victim must have seen something. Something when he was close to death, something that terrified him.

But what?

"There's more," Jason's colleague told him.

"More?"

"We've already run DNA. There's no one's DNA on his throat but his. It's as if no one else was in here with him. Similarly, there are no footprints to the door that we can find with either UV or forensic testing. There's no sign of a break-in on the windows. It's as if he did it to himself."

"That's not possible."

"Absolutely, it's not possible. You can't asphyxiate yourself; you'd pass out and relieve the pressure before you could finish. But he absolutely finished."

"Curious."

Jason knew why his scatterbrained subordinate couldn't figure out what had happened.

Because he hadn't seen the things Jason had.

He hadn't witnessed what Jason had witnessed.

This was another case that went down as 'not of this world.' It was not one that would be solved with ordinary methods.

Luckily, Jason knew exactly whom to talk to.

5

Oscar fidgeted nervously in the backseat, gazing at the fields darting quickly past the window.

Wherever Derek lived, it appeared to be in the middle of nowhere. Oscar wasn't sure if he'd seen an actual building for miles.

Maybe he's one of those crazy old men who live in the middle of nowhere, but are geniuses despite being so crazy...

He concluded that he'd watched too many movies, and willed himself to think rationally. He knew very little about Derek, just that he was a war hero. What war, exactly, Oscar wasn't sure.

But from the way Julian spoke about him with such admiration, Oscar knew he must be a great man. It took a lot for Julian to pay someone a compliment, never mind place them on the pedestal he had so done with Derek.

"So, who is Derek, exactly?" Oscar blurted out, then wished he'd thought of a more tactful way to ask the question.

April looked to Julian beside her in the driver's seat. The way Julian's eyes lit up when he spoke about Derek always made her smile.

"Imagine we are all children of the paranormal," Julian answered philosophically. "He would be the father."

"I don't understand. You said he fought in wars?"

"I did. He fought in a war you will never know about because the Church is very good at covering it up. Even if it did involve demons climbing out of the pit of hell and angels coming down from the sky."

Oscar raised his eyebrows and lifted his nose. Church cover-up? Demons climbing out of hell? Angels?

It all seemed a bit far-fetched.

"I don't think you could ever believe how far our battle against hell went until you go to the depths Derek has," Julian spoke ardently, irritated about the scepticism toward his mentor. "This entire world would be non-existent if it weren't for him."

"What exactly did Derek do in this war?"

"He performed an exorcism on the antichrist. At one point, he even faced the devil itself."

Oscar raised his eyebrows in astonishment. He had witnessed exorcisms on children and teenagers that took vast amounts of energy and respite. To actually perform it on an heir to the devil's throne...

Derek Lansdale must have some incredible stories.

"Don't ask him about it," Julian told Oscar, as if reading his mind.

"What?" Oscar retorted. "Why not?"

"You can never comprehend the sacrifices Derek had to make in that war. It took a lot out of him."

I bet.

Oscar understood. It sounded like Derek had been through a lot, and maybe he wouldn't want to talk about it if he'd had to endure such arduous trials. Such things rarely came without sacrifice.

The thought of this only made his nerves worse. He had

seen a lot in his short stint as a paranormal investigator. Still, compared to Julian and April, his experience was small; but compared to Derek, his experience was tiny.

His hands fidgeted, his stomach fluttered, his knees shook. His eyes darted back and forth, not knowing where to look.

"Calm down," came April's ever-soothing voice. Oscar noticed her glancing at him in the mirror. "You can't go in to face a man like this in that state."

"In what state?" Oscar asked, trying to keep his leg still and his hands non-fidgety.

"I know you well enough by now, Oscar," April replied playfully, "to know when you are nervous and overthinking. Just be cool."

'Just be cool.'

Pah!

Easy for April to say, she *was* cool. If Oscar tried to pull off purple hair or Tim Burton tattoos he'd look like a dork. She pulled them off with ease. She was the epitome of cool. Oscar was the epitome of...

I don't know if I really want to finish that sentence.

He looked out the window, watching more fields go by. The road transformed into a one-lane country road, but Julian didn't have to stop too many times for other cars to get past.

"Jeeze, he must live in the middle of nowhere," Oscar declared, then noted Julian's knowing grin in the mirror.

"Yes." Julian nodded cockily. "He does."

Oscar grew confused. Why was Julian being so ominous? Where were they going? Under a bridge? A magical hut? *South bloody Africa?*

"So where exactly does he live?"

"You'll see now, we're here."

They entered a car park, where Julian stopped the car.

Oscar stood out of the car, looking at the building before him with dropped jaw.

Of all the places they were going to end up, this was the last place Oscar had expected.

He glanced at Julian, who nodded confirmation that they were at the right place, then turned his gaze to the exterior of Gloucester Prison.

6

A PRISON.

Of all the places Oscar had expected to end up, this was bottom of the list.

He was a mess of nerves and apprehension. He'd never even considered what it would be like to enter a prison before.

He looked to Julian to see how to behave, and felt a brief sting of resentment for how cool and together he appeared. He wondered if Julian had felt like he did the first time he entered the prison – awkward and anxious.

He looked to April instead, desperate for some indication of how to act. As far as Oscar was aware, April had been here once a few months ago, and this was her second time. Yet she still seemed to walk the path with gumption and confidence, without an ounce of trepidation.

Oscar knew her better than that.

Her face was steely, resolute. It was a stony, expressionless piece of art; it was the face of someone forcing themselves to portray no anxiety.

But why should they feel anxiety? They were entering as visitors, not as prisoners. Oscar had nothing to worry about.

Oscar imagined how he would fare in prison. He'd likely be beaten up by some butch murderous inmate boasting about their victims, before going back to his cell and having to deal with the stench of the commode after his hostile cellmate had used it.

I would not survive in a prison.

They approached a large, dark-blue door with a semicircle atop covered with square bars. It was surrounded by cream bricks, large slabs of stone separating the inside from the out.

Julian opened the door and went into a room where he had a brief conversation with someone Oscar couldn't see. Moments later, a prison officer walked out, waving them to follow. It struck Oscar how the prison officer had nothing to protect himself with; just a chain with keys attached, a white shirt with black locks on the shoulders and smart black trousers. Then again, it made sense – if officers were to carry a weapon there was a chance that a prisoner could take it.

Oscar had once heard a statistic that ninety percent of prison inmates have a weapon on them at any time; which made him even more terrified to be setting foot inside.

"Wait here," the prison officer instructed with a thick Scottish accent. The man walked over to a female prison officer, who approached April.

Oscar watched as the male and female officers searched Julian and April respectively. He watched with bemusement as he wondered how a female prison officer would survive in a male prison, then wondered if it was sexist for him to think that.

Once they had finished, the man stood before Oscar, looking at him expectantly.

"Hi," Oscar offered.

"Open your mouth," the prison officer instructed with a face like lead.

Feeling a little stupid for his weak, sensitive *hi,* and

knowing that Julian was stood with his hand on his hips and rolling his eyes, Oscar reluctantly opened his mouth. The officer searched under his tongue with something that felt like prickly cardboard.

"Open your arms."

Oscar did as he was told and waited as the man patted him down with excruciating thoroughness, searching every pocket, and feeling every inch of his legs.

"Your shoes."

Oscar looked back blankly, then abruptly realised that he was meant to take them off. He removed his daps, giving them to the prison officer and feeling slightly bad for how stinky they must smell. He watched as they were inspected, then returned them to his feet.

"This way," the officer told Julian, who followed him to another room. April followed also, prompting Oscar to suddenly wake up and trail behind them. Oscar, still in the middle of fastening his laces, finished a double knot and stumbled after them.

He looked down as he walked over a circular print on the marble floor that read *H.M. Prison Gloucester*, with a picture of gates with two keys over the top and chains on the side.

Wonder why they bother with art on a prison floor...

Oscar followed the others, running slightly to keep up, as they were taken through a few twisting corridors with cream-coloured walls and dark-blue bars.

Strange, Oscar had always imagined prison bars to be grey and rusty, whereas these appeared fresh, with only occasional cracks in the paint.

They were led to a large hall. In the far corner was a tuck shop, next to a children's play area. Throughout the hall were circular tables screwed to the ground, with four chairs around each, also fastened to the floor.

Various families sat waiting. Oscar was surprised at the

appearance of these families. They all seemed so… normal. Children were well-kept and tidy, women were well-groomed, and men looked soft and friendly.

It struck Oscar how many generalisations and assumptions he had carried with him that were naïvely untrue.

They were directed to a table, where they sat and waited. Over the course of fifteen to twenty minutes, various prisoners came through, each being finger printed and given a bib they were made to wear as they entered. Emotions ran high as they greeted their families and friends.

It made Oscar wonder how he was supposed to act when he met Derek.

Then, as if answering his question, April and Julian suddenly rose. Oscar joined in, wanting to be respectful to the man he was about to meet. He had seen a picture of this man in Julian's home, with a much younger-looking Julian. Derek had been dressed impeccably in a suit, a neatly trimmed beard, and parted grey hair. He had looked like a university professor would stereotypically look – smart, friendly, and approachable. The picture had presented Derek Lansdale as someone wizened with age and experience.

But when Oscar saw the man approaching, he saw nothing of the man in the picture, and he was instantly taken aback. As Derek smiled weakly at Julian, Oscar did his best to conceal his shock.

The man was unhealthily thin; Oscar could practically see ribs through the guy's t-shirt. His beard was long and unkempt, and he hobbled forward, leaning over a walking stick he relied heavily upon. It took an age for him to approach, and as he did, his bony facial features turned into delight. Oscar had initially guessed that this man was in his fifties, but he looked far older and bedraggled.

"Julian," Derek warmly greeted, an aged weakness in his voice. "It is so good to see you."

"And you, Derek." Julian took Derek's hand and held it in both of his, greeting him warmly. "You remember April."

"Of course," Derek answered, his grin spreading from cheek to cheek. "It is a delight to see you again, my dear."

"It's an honour," April answered, taking his hand in hers and shaking it firmly. Oscar wondered how firmly he was going to be able to shake Derek's hand without breaking him.

"And this is Oscar," Julian introduced.

Derek's face lit up. He looked overcome with joy, nodding vigorously, practically beaming.

"It is a privilege to meet you, my friend," Derek offered so kindly that Oscar wondered how on earth someone so caring could end up in prison.

"The privilege is mine," Oscar returned, feeling proud for not messing up his response. He took Derek's hand and shook it warmly, smiling back at him as politely as he could.

Derek backed into his seat slowly, using a hand on his walking stick to lower himself down.

"Oh, God, I forgot to get you anything from the tuck shop," Julian suddenly remembered, and it surprised Oscar to see Julian so flustered in someone else's presence, having been the one who always had it together. "Let me go get you something."

"Nonsense, nonsense." Derek waved Julian's concerns away with his hand. "Snacks would only distract me from meeting our marvellous new Sensitive."

Oscar blushed.

He's talking about me.

"Tell me about yourself, Oscar," Derek prompted in a slow but friendly manner. "Where do you come from?"

"I come from Tewkesbury, down the road."

"Ah, Tewkesbury. I've been there many a time. Have you been in the Olde Black Bull?"

"You mean that rackety old pub?"

"Oh, it's no rackety old pub, my friend. It is one of the most haunted buildings in the country."

Oscar stuck his bottom lip out. He didn't know that. He'd always assumed there could be nothing interesting about his hometown.

"And how are you finding your gift? April tells me you've been supremely helpful so far."

"Well, I hope I have," Oscar spoke, trying to remain focused and polite at all times, desperate not to come off as rude, impolite, or even worse – naïve. "It's been quite the experience so far."

"Oh, it will be. It will be."

A moment of awkward silence settled upon them, and Oscar racked his mind for something to say, finding himself craving Derek's approval.

"Derek," Julian interrupted. "I wondered if we might have a word in private."

"Of course, of course."

"We'll be right outside," April announced, and stood up.

Oscar was staring so gormlessly at Derek with eyes of fascination that he didn't realise it was his cue to leave, and ended up being prodded on the shoulder quite forcefully by April.

"It was lovely to see you again, April," Derek told her.

"It was lovely to see you too."

"And it was an honour to meet you, Oscar." Derek gave him a subtle wink that made Oscar fill with childlike excitement.

"You too," he answered, and followed April out of the room.

As they left, a prison officer met them to guide them to the exit.

"What a lovely man," Oscar spoke.

"Derek is the best," April confirmed as they were guided through the final exit doors and into the car park. "We owe him so much."

"What do you mean?"

"You really have no idea what Derek did for us, do you?"

She smiled knowingly as she unlocked the car, leaving Oscar desperately longing to know what she meant.

7

"HE SEEMS LIKE A NICE BOY," DEREK COMMENTED.

Julian shrugged.

"He's nice enough," Julian answered with a blase attitude. "But he seems more determined on getting into April's pants than he does the job."

"Give him time."

"Time? He's young, pathetic, and seems to not have a clue what he's doing."

"I remember someone who was like that once." Derek smiled and peered knowingly at Julian.

Julian forced a chuckle. Derek was right. Julian had been incredibly hormonal and arrogant when they had first met. Not to mention impatient. And innocent. And annoying.

Julian sighed a sigh of hesitation. He tapped his hands on the table a few times, let out a final huff, then turned to Derek, deciding to broach the subject.

"How have things been?" he asked.

"Fine," Derek answered, being purposefully obtuse.

"You know what I mean. Has anything else been going on in the prison?"

Derek looked over his shoulder. The nearest prison officer was wandering past a family a few tables away.

"Yes," Derek answered. "And no. Yes, the same things have been happening, and no, you needn't concern yourself."

"Derek–"

"I am perfectly capable of taking care of myself against whatever entity is in here," Derek insisted. "Don't you know who I am?"

Julian laughed. Only he could recognise the joke in Derek's question – the man was far too humble to ever really say anything like that.

Then Julian's laughter died, recognising Derek's throw-away question as a clear avoidance technique, and refused to let the subject go.

"You need my help, Derek. If there is something here, and it's harming prisoners, or *you*, then…"

Julian sighed despondently. How do you tell someone with Derek's vast experience that they need to let someone help them? Derek was not only a war hero, but he was a better man and a better mentor than Julian could ever put into words.

But he hobbled around with a walking stick! His muscles ached after a short walk. His mind was weary and tired and slow to respond – how was Julian meant to tell him that?

"Like I said, Julian. I am quite capable of fighting the demonic and the ghostly."

"Once, you were," Julian blurted out honestly. "A long time ago, you would have shown everyone how it's done. You would have put your Sensitives-in-training to shame; you would have put us in our place and proven that arrogance is our downfall. But not now."

"Why not now?"

"Because look at you, Derek. You're thin. You're weak. You tell me nothing's wrong, and I believe you, but…"

"Say it," Derek demanded.

Derek had always appreciated direct, blunt honesty, rather than what he called, "fannying about around the subject."

"You're old. You're not the man you once were."

"I'm fifty-four."

"Yes. You are fifty-four. And in those fifty-four years, you have done more than most people could hope to do in hundreds – and it has quite clearly worn you down."

Derek fell silent. Julian watched as he dropped his head in quiet contemplation, feeling a sudden pang of guilt. Derek had done so much for him...

Well then, maybe this was his way of repaying him! After all, life is just one big circle. You're born and you rely on others, then you grow up, then you grow old, and rely on others again. Derek just needed to realise...

No. Who am I to tell a man like Derek he needs help?

"I'm sorry, Derek, I–"

"Never apologise for something that you mean, otherwise you're being insincere."

Derek spoke without looking up. A few minutes of silence hung over the table like a black cloud. Julian did his best to think of something to say, but he knew that in this situation, it was best to let Derek find the first word.

"Yes, Julian, I get it," Derek reluctantly admitted. "But, as far as we are aware, this is not a demon, and probably just some petty poltergeist. Until we know anything more, I can still handle some little poltergeist."

"Time's up!" called out the prison officer.

Julian looked up. They were the last left in the room. Everyone else was gone.

That was odd. He didn't see them go.

"I keep having dreams," Julian softly revealed. "About..."

"About what?"

"About Anna."

Derek looked back at him with an eerie curiosity.

A prison officer appeared behind him. "Time to go."

Julian tried to gauge the look on Derek's face, but couldn't. It was as if Derek's expression had fallen into a cold lucidity. Deep thoughts burdening a heavy mind behind those ageing eyes – but what? What were those thoughts? What was he thinking?

Julian needed guidance. He needed Derek to say something.

"All the best, Julian," Derek finally spoke, before turning and being led away.

Julian was completely alone, left to sit amongst a room of unanswered questions.

THEN

8

_____

AMAZEMENT OVERCAME JULIAN'S EYES, GROWING UPON HIM LIKE a sunrise. His energetic mind could hardly conceive of the information Derek was bestowing upon his youthful shoulders.

"A Sensitive?" Julian remarked. "Why the hell are they called Sensitives?"

"Not they, you," Derek pointed out, "are termed a Sensitive, and aptly so. It refers to how you have a sensitivity to the paranormal that others do not. You can see, feel, or even do things that others would not believe are real."

Julian looked around himself in astonishment. This guy had walked into his place of work, claimed to know who he was, then spent three weeks taking him on a whirlwind of education. He had since learnt what was truly possible in both this life, and beyond it. He'd seen things he hadn't dreamt of being able to see, and been taught things he would never have possibly thought true.

"Why, though?" Julian's inexperienced mind wondered. "Why am I a Sensitive? Why *me?*"

"Because heaven conceived *you.* There is something within

you, something you can use. We can't be entirely sure of what your gift is, but from what I've seen, I would imagine you to be a talented exorcist."

"An exorcist?"

Now Derek was having him on.

An exorcist?

Such a thing only exists in movies, and not the kind that Julian would normally watch. He had always found the whole concept too far-fetched, and avoided horrors. He was far more at home with an Academy-Award winning drama; far more realistic.

How little he knew.

"I am an accomplished exorcist myself," Derek humbly asserted. "And have banished many demons from the bodies of many victims."

"But how can you be sure it's a demon, and not just, you know, a nutter?"

Derek smirked. Julian was asking the right questions.

"Julian, I would be annoyed if you didn't ask me such a thing."

Julian smiled, chuffed to have been delivered a compliment by this man who seemed to have such vast life experience.

"We do rigorous testing to ensure the person involved is a victim, and not one with severe mental health issues," Derek told Julian. "And I'll be honest with you – ninety-nine percent of the time it proves to be the latter."

"So how do you know for sure?"

"Tell me, Julian – have you ever seen a mentally ill person levitate six feet high off a bed? Speak in Latin when they don't even know what Latin is? Have objects fly around the room of their own accord whenever you recite a prayer?"

"I guess not."

"Julian, I admire your gumption – I too was an atheist before I understood how things were. Which is good, so you should be – no proof, no belief, that's what I've always said." He knelt against the table and leant toward Julian. "Being honest, I'm not entirely sure if I am on board with the whole concept of God, even after what I've seen. But I know what I've seen. And I know what you will see too."

Julian was in awe, totally overcome with wonder. This man had shown him so many things, had opened his eyes to a whole world he didn't even know was possible.

Derek opened his bag and placed several objects upon the table.

"This is a cross, as I'm sure you recognise." Derek pointed to his first item. "Then these are rosary beads, this is holy water. These are essential items you need to defeat a demon in an exorcism."

Julian looked over the items with bemusement, then back to Derek.

"But, Derek, how do you defeat something as powerful as a demon?"

"The demon is the easy part. Trust me. It's their taunts you have to resist."

"What do you mean?"

Derek looked to his young apprentice with a knowing smile.

"The biggest obstacle you will ever have to overcome, my friend, is yourself."

NOW

9

APRIL LAUGHED AND GAVE OSCAR A FRIENDLY PUSH.

"No, it's my turn," she insisted.

"Fine!" Oscar responded, smiling warmly at the woman of his dreams occupying the passenger seat in front of him.

"Right, would you rather..." April took a moment's thought. "I got it. Would you rather – watch your parents have sex, or have your parents watch you have sex?"

Oscar blurted out a stream of awkward laughter.

"And I can't pick neither?"

"No!" April grinned. "It's the game, you have to pick one."

"Okay, I guess... oh man. I'd rather watch them..."

Oscar pulled a face of disgust. April raised her eyebrows, playing at being perturbed.

"All right, here's one for you," Oscar took over. "Would you rather have hair that always stank of pee, or have breasts that could talk, but constantly argue with each other?"

"Oh man, that one's easy. Talking breasts all the way."

"Really?"

"Yeah! I always wondered what they'd say if they could talk."

Oscar chuckled. He looked into her eyes, and she looked back. They held their eye contact in a moment of electricity, watching each other intently.

"I got one," Oscar spoke, coming up with an idea. "Would you rather date me, or date no one?"

April smiled so wide she practically glowed.

"I would rather date–"

The door to the driver's seat swung open and Julian threw himself into the car, scowling, not looking at anyone else. His bad mood was immediately apparent and an uncomfortable, tense silence took over the car.

With a regretful glance at Oscar, April turned around to face the front and put her seat belt on.

Cursing his luck, Oscar stared out the window. Julian turned the ignition and drove away, swinging them around the corner to the car park's exit. Oscar watched as the prison faded from view, and they were travelling between absent fields once more.

"What's up?" April quietly asked, looking to Julian.

"I don't want to talk about it," Julian snapped.

"But you're never in a bad mood after we've seen Derek. I don't get it."

"I said I don't want to talk about it!"

The next ten minutes passed without so much as grunt or a cough from anyone. Julian's eyes remained intently glaring at the road before him.

Oscar watched Julian, wondering what could have troubled him so much. Julian was always so excited to see Derek, it was hard to understand why he would be so irrefutably angry.

Maybe he'd had some bad news.

Maybe Derek had said something sad.

Or, maybe, this was just Julian being Julian. He was always so ill-tempered whenever he was around Oscar, to the point Oscar wasn't entirely sure if Julian had another range of emotions, or whether it was just Oscar that the problem was with.

Oscar had been meaning to enquire about Derek's incarceration on the ride home, but found himself wondering whether it was the right time. He needed to know why Derek was in there, what had happened, and about Derek's history.

But he dare not speak.

But then again, maybe, talking about Derek in a positive light would take Julian's mind off whatever he was ruminating about.

Oscar decided he was going to try to converse with Julian, figuring whatever he said or did seemed to annoy the guy anyway, so he didn't really have anything to lose.

"Hey, Julian," Oscar spoke, watching Julian's scowl turn to him in the rear-view mirror. "You know you said Derek is a war hero."

"He is," grunted Julian defensively.

"What war? What happened?"

Julian sighed with exasperation. He ran a hand over his face, frustrated at having to engage in what would likely turn into a long, embellished conversation. At that moment, he just wanted to remain in furious silence.

April gave him a wary glance.

"He has a right to know, Julian," she urged him.

"Fine," Julian mumbled.

Oscar waited a moment for Julian to gather his thoughts, watching and waiting with intrigue.

"He had a very close friend," Julian began. "This friend was a great exorcist, the greatest there has ever been. But he also had something evil within him. Derek trained him, then had to fight him."

"Evil? Like a demon?"

"Worse than a demon."

Oscar watched the fields go by the window, considering

this. To think – that weak, dishevelled man fought something as powerful as a prince of hell.

"But I don't get it. For such a great man, why is he in prison?" Oscar asked.

Julian took in a big, deep breath. His mouth moved as if he was trying to find the words, but was unable to force them out of his lips.

Oscar had never seen Julian stumped for words before.

"Derek took Julian to his first exorcism" – April took over, watching Julian breathe a sigh of relief that he didn't have to recollect this memory – "where they exorcised a young girl called Anna."

Oscar remembered April mentioning this girl before he witnessed Julian perform an exorcism for the first time. He remembered April telling him what happened.

"Oh," Oscar confirmed, understanding what Julian was finding so difficult to say.

"Derek was arrested for the girl's death," April continued. "The prosecution claimed that he let this girl, in his care, die. They said he didn't give her food or water, or rest. He was eventually charged with manslaughter by negligence, and sent to prison."

"And that's where he is now," Julian angrily interjected. "The man who saved this entire world from an apocalypse, stuck in jail to rot because the law doesn't take into account the reality of–"

Julian cut himself off. His fists were gripping the steering wheel and his leg was shaking. He willed himself to calm down.

Oscar nodded, and let them continue the rest of the journey in silence.

1 0

ANOTHER NIGHT, MORE LONG, RESTLESS HOURS OF CONSTANT shifting. Derek knew that the prison experience was intentionally uncomfortable, but surely giving them beds like this was against their human rights?

He could feel every square set of wires digging into his back, pressing against his bones. He tried sleeping on his side, but every morning he woke up in agony. It didn't help that he wasn't particularly in the best physical condition he'd ever been in.

Once, he'd even tried getting rid of the bumpy mattress altogether, but the indents of the solid metal frame were even worse. Some mornings he'd find himself waking up on the floor, having had a far better sleep because of it.

He tried listening carefully. It's what he'd always told those he taught – stop, listen to the elements, take them in. Allow them to relax your state of mind.

In the distance, he could hear an owl, roaming free, liberated to make noise and fly away at will.

The smell of stale urine accompanied the distant wails of someone in the midst of a mental breakdown.

No, paying attention to the elements did not help him here.

Eventually, he found himself drifting into a restless slumber, still unable to find peace in his sleep. His mind searched his unconscious for ways to torment his aching brain. Images of Anna taunted him; as if his incarceration wasn't enough, his guilt was even worse.

The thought of her still made him sick. A churning in his stomach twisted and turned every time he saw her face.

Like most nights, he watched as she died in the doctor's arms. Watched as she...

"Derek."

His eyes sprung open.

He bolted upright, sweating, looking back and forth.

No one was there. Just darkness.

It was his dream.

It must have been in his dream.

He couldn't let himself be paranoid, just because of what he knew about this world.

I've seen too much.

With knowledge like he had, he needed to be careful not to attribute ghosts to nothing.

But there was something. A scratching. Something from outside his cell.

Speaking.

Low, eerie speaking.

Derek twisted himself out of his bed and hoisted himself to his feet via the nearby sink. Grabbing his walking stick, he hobbled to the edge of his cell and peered into the corridor.

He occupied cell twenty-five of A Wing. Opposite him, and to his left and right, were at least forty cells. The wing carried on above him into three more floors, home to a similar number of prisoners. It was a category B prison, meaning most of the inmates were in for violent offences, and he often had to ensure he remained withdrawn from conflict and bullying that occurred. Each cell had a narrow single bed, a television with a small screen, a metal sink, and a metal toilet with no seat. It was the minimum they were allowed.

The bars to the cells were dark blue, the floor a dark brown, and the walls a light cream colour. The walls of the wing and the cells caused every movement to echo, meaning Derek could clearly hear any scuffle occurring along the corridor, however small or insignificant. The scuttle of a rat could sound like the feet of a giant, if he let it.

Peering as far as he could through the bars, Derek saw a few figures beside the entrance to a cell a few down from his, at what was known as the segregation cells. These were the cells where prisoners were sent to be separated and watched, either for their protection or someone else's.

"Get on your feet, old man," came a gruff voice. Derek recognised it as that of the prison governor, Jackson Kullins.

On his feet before the governor was one of Derek's very few acquaintances, Sully. Sully and Derek often shared silent lunches, becoming friendly on the basis that they were the two eldest on the wing. Sully was still Derek's senior by a long way, Derek estimating Sully to be in his late seventies. He had never asked, nor had he ever asked what Sully was in for, a gesture that was unspoken and mutual.

"I said get on your feet," Kullins barked in a snarling whisper.

Sully struggled to his feet, his weak bones and soft hands unable to support his weight. As soon as his wobbling knees had taken him to his feet, Kullins kicked them out again, sending Sully slamming onto his back.

Kullins spat at Sully.

"That's what you are," Kullins told the poor old man. He watched as two prison officers dragged him back into his cell, grunting another obscenity that Derek couldn't make out.

Kullins's face suddenly shot in Derek's direction, and

Derek retracted back into his cell with a gasp. He struggled to his bed as quick as his aching legs could take him, hearing the governor's footsteps growing nearer.

He returned to his bed, laying on his side and facing the wall as he heard the footsteps pause beside his cell. They stopped, hovered for a moment, then left. Derek kept his eyes closed until he heard the door to the wing shut.

"Derek."

His head spun around once more.

Something whispered his name again.

"Derek."

He searched his cell with his weary eyes, looking in every dark corner, every which way he could.

"You are in danger, you need to leave."

He spun to his feet, looking around.

Nothing.

"Who's there?" he whispered.

He listened intently.

Waited for a response in the eerie silence.

Nothing.

Probably the hallucination of an ageing mind.

Or, something trying to warn him. Maybe someone he used to know, giving him an omen, suggesting that he find a way to escape.

Either way, it could wait until morning.

He wasn't going anywhere.

He lay down and closed his eyes, hoping that Sully was okay.

11

ANOTHER COFFEE, ANOTHER CAFÉ, ANOTHER AWKWARD conversation.

Oscar couldn't understand what was causing him so much stress.

It's just a girl, right?

Men have been admitting their affections for girls since the dawn of time.

Well, technically, man didn't evolve at the dawn of time, dinosaurs did. And, actually, when man originally evolved into cavemen, they didn't admit their affection, they just clobbered the girl they fancied over the head and dragged them into a cave.

It was a much simpler time.

Not that Oscar intended to clobber April over the head and drag her into a cave. In fact, having thought about it, the whole concept was actually quite wrong.

What the hell is wrong with me? I'm sitting here opposite the woman I fancy in silence as I daydream about bloody cavemen...

"So," Oscar began, before abruptly realising he hadn't thought through how he was going to complete that sentence.

"So," April repeated in anticipation, taking a sip of hot chocolate, then wiping a bit of cream off her nose.

Ooh, what I'd give to be that bit of cream.

Hang on.

What? I'd like to be wiped off her nose?

Oscar hung his head in a mixture of confused shame and anxious apprehension.

"So, how long have we known each other?" he blurted out, louder and quicker than he had intended.

"Didn't you ask me this the other day?"

"Yeah, yeah, I did..." Oscar nodded, unsure how to respond. "But, er... I didn't get a chance to finish it."

He took a big deep breath, let it out, then took a large sip of his coffee. He held the coffee by his mouth and took a longer sip than he wanted, anything to avoid having to confront the chaotic words that were pushing against the inside of his lips.

"What's up, Oscar?" April asked. "You look nervous."

"Nervous? Look nervous? I'm not nervous. Who's nervous? Are you nervous?"

"Oscar, you're being a little weird."

He went to speak, nodded, held his breath, and took another large, drawn-out sip of coffee.

"You're really cool, aren't you? I mean, you're not going to say you're cool, but you are. Cool, I mean."

"Okay. So we've established I'm cool..."

"Yeah, yeah, we have. I'm glad we've established that."

He took another elongated sip of coffee, to find that he was out of coffee, and panicked.

"I wanted to talk about us. As in, you and me."

"Okay," April urged him, smiling, wanting him to continue.

"Well." Oscar took another big, deep breath. Went to drink his coffee again, forgetting that the cup was empty, and ended up poising the cup by his mouth to disguise the fact that the coffee was gone.

"Isn't your cup empty?"

Oscar froze, dropped his coffee cup to the table, and looked in it.

"Oh, yeah. That explains why no coffee was coming out."

"So, you were saying?" April prompted him, raising her eyebrows expectantly, willing him to finish.

"Well. I think you're cool, as you know."

"Yes, we have confirmed this."

"Good, I – I'm glad. Now, I just, ghosts and stuff, they are scary, but what I'm feeling in my gut, is, also, erm, scary. I mean, not in the same way, just…"

He paused.

Stared at his empty coffee cup.

Looked at April, her wide, beautiful eyes gazing back at him, her long, flowing hair brushing down her shoulders like the wind down a mountain. Her skin was perfect, her fashion sense was perfect, her personality was perfect, she…

She's too perfect for me.

He shook his head.

He was kidding himself.

A woman like this would never go for a guy like him.

"Never mind," he muttered, staring into the black abyss of his mug.

"Never mind?" April asked, disappointment in her voice.

"Yeah… Never mind…"

Oscar only saw April's crestfallen face out the corner of his eye. She finished her drink and stood.

"I guess I'd better get going then," she told him, evidently dejected. She was out of her seat and through the door before he could muster any form of objection.

Oscar, you complete and utter arse.

He hung his head and mentally scolded himself.

Was he ever going to get a grip?

12

THE CEILING ABOVE JULIAN'S BED HAD BECOME A FAMILIAR SIGHT. He lay sleepily and with vague thoughts, in the midst of another sleepless night, enduring hours and hours of staring until its dark cream colour morphed into an indefinite blur. He traced the familiar indents with his eyes, following the same cracks, to the same cobwebs hanging loosely in the corner, absent of an owner. He was fairly sure that, should he ever be required, he would be able to draw an accurate picture of its various bumps and indentations, and the various shades cast upon it by the moon peering through a narrow crack in the curtains.

He would kill to fall asleep, yet, at the same time, he dreaded it.

Staying awake meant his mind dwelled on the eyes of that same young girl being drained of life; but falling asleep meant her pale face plagued his nightmares.

It was affecting him, and even worse, it was affecting his work.

Derek had taught him to be a thorough professional. To be presentable, courteous, and do the best job you can. Yet, more recently, he had found himself growing snappy and irritable. He was aware he already had some instinctive impatience, and so dreaded to consider how he must inevitably be coming across.

He closed his eyes. Willed the bad thoughts away.

Why now?

Why was it, after four years, the memories of Anna were only now surfacing so severely?

That night had attacked his memory numerous times since, but it had been a black cloud he could control. It gave him resilience, whilst reminding him what was at stake. Before every exorcism, every cleansing, every supernatural ritual, he would remember her. She would remind him of what he could lose – and that knowledge had made him a thorough, scrupulous, professional paranormal investigator.

He had never let a situation get to the point that Anna's exorcism did.

He opened his eyes.

Glanced at the clock.

3.05 a.m.

Was it really that late?

Have I really been lying here, dozing in and out of consciousness, constantly thinking, for four hours?

He swivelled himself around and leant on the edge of the bed.

There were sleeping tablets in the drawer of the kitchen.

They were the last resort. It was never good to rely on pills to get you to sleep, and Julian hated having to do it. But it was the only way.

I need sleep... Desperately...

He stood, wiping sweat from his brow. The bedroom was sticky hot, to the point that the duvet was sticking to his bare torso.

He opened the bedroom door and stepped into the living room of his flat.

A wave of frozen air hit him.

His high temperature instantly plummeted. His skin grew goose pimples, his shoulders shuddered, and his hands shivered, overwhelmed by a sudden and unexpected change from extreme humidity to unbearable cold.

He made his way across the living room and to the kitchen, shivering, rubbing his arms, trying to generate heat.

That's when he realised.

If he was investigating somewhere...

If he was looking for signs of an entity in a home...

Then a sudden drop in temperature would be a major factor he'd be looking to consider.

No.

Don't be ridiculous.

Yes, sudden changes in temperature, rooms that have an unexpected cold compared to the rest of the location – that is a sign of an entity dwelling within.

But the sign was one of many. It would take numerous indications to confirm anything. Julian prided himself on being obsessively scientific when it came to confirming whether a location was home to a dangerous presence. A change in temperature was a sure sign, yes, but would not be enough as an isolated symptom.

He couldn't let his mind run away from him just because of what he knew and what he'd seen.

He opened the cupboard beneath the sink and sifted through a bunch of medicine boxes. He found a pack of sleeping aids, popped two, and placed them in his mouth.

He took a small glass out of the cupboard, filled it with water, looked up, and–

He dropped the glass, smashing it on the floor beside his bare feet.

He looked away, shook his head, looked back.

It was nothing.

Nothing was there.

But I swear I saw...

In the reflection of the kitchen window, his own face looked back at him.

But he had seen...

Anna...

Her face...

The still, dead eyes of her corpse...

No. Stop it.

It was a tired mind playing tired tricks. All that stared back at him in that reflection was his own pair of eyes and horrified face. He had seen nothing. It was a passing trick of his feeble state of mind; that was all.

And now there was broken glass on his feet.

"Shit," he muttered angrily.

He found a dustpan and brush from the drawer, swept the glass, and put it in the bin. He bypassed the glass and took a mouthful of water straight from the tap, then swallowed the pills.

Shaking his head to himself, he returned to the bedroom, having one last glance over his shoulder at the window.

Nothing was there.

It was just a painful memory.

Tricks of the mind.

There was nothing strong enough to indicate anything untoward occurring.

Be scientific.

He returned to the sweltering heat of his bedroom, climbed into bed and closed his eyes, waiting for the tablets to take effect.

THEN

13

JULIAN GAZED AROUND DEREK'S STUDY IN ASTONISHMENT. THE vast collection of books demonstrated physically Derek's immense resources and incredible knowledge. Everything you could ever want to know about the paranormal was in a large shelving unit against a wall in his study.

"This" – Derek began, opening a hefty, worn-out, leather-bound book, forcing a hundred particles of dust to float into the air – "is called *The Rites of Exorcism.* This has everything you need to know."

Julian peered over Derek's shoulder.

"Is this what you will be using on that girl?" Julian asked. "Anna, I think her name was?"

"Yes, these are the prayers I will recite. They are the prayers I have recited for years. Before you were even born, I imagine."

Julian raised his eyebrows in bewilderment. He never ceased to be amazed.

"Care to take a look?"

Derek smiled at Julian, standing back so he could see.

Julian placed his hand on the page. It had a brown tint, and the paper was thin from age. The act of an exorcism was an ancient art, he knew that – but he had never contemplated how ancient the book would have been.

He slowly traced his forefinger over the first line of a prayer written in an old font, immaculately preserved.

IN THE NAME *of Jesus Christ, our God and Lord, strengthened by the intercession of the Immaculate Virgin Mary, Mother of God, of Blessed Michael the Archangel, so the wicked perish at the presence of God.*

"Wow," Julian unknowingly whispered.

"Why 'wow'?" Derek asked, prompting Julian to abruptly realise he had spoken.

"It's just, it's so… preachy. Religious. I've never really gone in for this kind of stuff."

"Neither have I. And despite having seen what I have seen, I question those who do."

"You mean, you fight in God's name, but judge those who believe in God? How does that make sense?"

A warm grin spread across Derek from cheek to cheek, pleased that Julian was asking the right questions.

"You still need to approach this with a scientific mind – you believe something once you can't prove otherwise. I have seen angels, demons, even the devil himself. I have seen enough to know for certain. But people who follow this stuff blindly without having seen a shred of true, undeniable evidence?" Derek shrugged his shoulders. "Ninety-nine percent of the potential possessions I visit are mental health issues interpreted by a highly religious family. So rarely is it ever the real thing. I believe people could use a tad more scrutiny with their thinking."

Julian nodded. It was a lot to take in, though it made a lot of sense. It must be frustrating to visit continual claims of hauntings that turn out to be nothing.

Or so he'd find out when he took on the role of exorcist himself someday.

"Let me show you another chapter," Derek decided. He bent over the book and began sifting through pages.

As he did that, Julian wandered over to the impressive book collection, looking across the titles. There was everything from mediumship, telling the difference between psychosis and genuine possession, seances, exorcism through the ages – any topic that could be covered was there.

Then something caught his eye.

A small book hidden behind two larger books. He reached between them and pulled it out, surveying the spine with his curious eyes.

The author was Derek Lansdale.

How peculiar, Derek never mentioned writing a book...

He pulled it out and looked at the cover, reading the title quietly to himself.

My Journal of The Edward King War.

"Hey, Derek?" Julian spoke, turning toward his mentor.

"Yes?" Derek replied, lifting his eyes up.

"What's this? What's the Edward King war?" Julian asked, lifting the book.

Derek's face instantly dropped. It turned cold, melancholy, petrified even. A wash of terror swept over his face.

"Where did you find that?" Derek gasped.

"It was wedged between two bigger books. I just thought–"

Julian had no time to finish the sentence. Derek snatched the book out of his hands and cradled it in his arms, hugging it tightly so there was no way Julian could get to it.

"Sorry, Derek, I didn't mean..."

"It's fine," Derek lied. "Just – look at the book I told you to look at."

Derek scurried out of the room and pounded up the stairs.

Julian was left standing there, wondering what he had just witnessed.

NOW

14

A BRUSH AGAINST DEREK'S FACE MADE HIM INSTINCTIVELY WAVE his hand to waft it away.

He turned onto his other side, groaning, irritated at being awakened. He allowed his mind to sink further into his unconscious, returning to the emptiness of a heavy slumber

It came again. Something brushing. Sweeping past his cheek.

It was the same, but different.

Before, it had felt like a faint touch, barely pricking his skin. Like a feather softly caressing him.

The second time, he could feel something. Something stronger, something definite, pressing with a gentle but sinister force. Something fleetingly placed against his cheek with four soft indents.

Something that felt like...

His eyes flickered. His mind stirred.

Something that felt like fingers.

"Go away," he grunted, his sleepy state not fully acknowledging the occurrence. Whoever was trying to wake him could return in the morning.

He allowed his heavy eyelids to remain shut, pressing together with the desperate ease of a tired mind.

Hang on.

His eyes shot open.

He was in a locked cell.

Someone had touched his cheek.

He was in a locked cell, and someone had touched his cheek.

He sat up, looking around.

The full moon was high in the sky, casting little light through the narrow window at the top of his cell. He cast his eyes around the narrow room, peering across the small, confined space.

He was alone.

Alone in his cell, as he had been when he'd settled down to sleep.

Had he really felt that?

Had it just been part of his sleep? A trick of the mind?

He shook his head.

No.

I've seen enough to know when something is just a trick of the mind.

Too much was happening. And it was all too convenient that it was happening to him.

"Who's there?" he asked. It had been a while since he had tried to contact something not of this world. Years, even. His voice sounded a lot older and weaker than it had the last time he'd attempted to open communication with the dead or the demonic.

But he was not afraid.

He had been to hell.

Twice.

He'd seen enough to know how to battle these things.

Except, that was before. That was when he was full of

energy, youthful exuberance, and fighting at the side of a friend who had enough powers to return him back to earth.

That was nothing like now.

He was an incarcerated inmate who required a walking stick just to be able to plod the short but long journey from his cell to the medical wing.

He wasn't in the best condition of his life, and he knew it.

A soft brush pressed against the back of his top; an easy breeze fixed against his clothes.

He didn't move.

He waited. Listened.

Remained desperately immobile.

It came again, pushing his back, turning from a slight press of air to something definite, pushing against him.

It pushed hard, growing more forceful until he could feel the indentations of each specific finger pressing against his shoulder blade.

He leapt to his feet and spun around, ready to confront whatever was there.

But nothing was there.

Nothing.

Something moved in the corner of his eye. Something outside the cell. Something dark and silhouetted.

"I repeat, who is there?" he asked the silence, his voice echoing with adamant gumption.

Nothing happened.

"Of all the people you can haunt, trust me, I am the last man you want to mess with," he declared with the confidence of someone who could back his statement up.

Something flickered once again out the corner of his eye.

A figure moved past his cell, so fast that if he had blinked, he would have missed it. He wasn't looking directly at it, so couldn't be sure of what he had seen, but he could vaguely recall a large, looming, shadowy figure, with long fingers and a thin, contorted head.

He strode the few paces it took to get to the bars of his cell, ignoring the pain in his limp as he dragged his heavy leg.

"Who's there?" he whispered, careful not to wake the other prisoners – he was cautious as to what they would do to him in the morning if he interrupted their rest.

He strained to look across the walls of the wing. The place was in complete darkness, and his view was restricted by the wall of his cell.

It can't hurt me.

He repeated it to himself again and again.

It can't hurt me. It can't hurt me.

He wondered whether he was reassuring himself of the truth, or trying to convince himself of a lie.

As if providing him with his answer, he was launched across the cell, through the air, hitting the far wall with a painful thud. His back cracked against the solid stone and he fell into a helpless slump on the floor.

His bad leg throbbed. Even though it was his back that had made the worst contact with the wall, it was his leg that pulsated with agonising intensity.

A delayed ache in his back shortly joined it.

It felt like he had more bones than he had before, each of them hurting, excruciating from the impact.

It can hurt me.

He remained where he was, frightened that if he were to try and get to his feet he would either fail, or the entity would force him onto his back once more.

So he stayed in a messy ball on the floor, staring at the end of the cell. Watching. Waiting.

Waiting for something, or someone, to appear, and to confront him.

Whatever it was.

Whatever it could be.

The ghost of a murdered ex-prisoner?

The dead child of a prison birth?

Or a demon seeking vengeance against Derek. Something that wanted revenge for being exorcised, and knew that Derek was trapped with nowhere to go.

There would be plenty of them.

But nothing came.

His mind was full of loose speculations that did not materialise as he stared at the dark, empty void of A Wing.

He remained fixed in his position, glaring at the doors to the cell, waiting for something to reveal itself. To show him what he was up against. To fill him with dread.

He awoke in the morning when the prison officer came to open his cell.

15

OSCAR WAS STARTING TO GET THE HANG OF THIS.

It was another house savaged by another spirit that refused to move on.

Which makes sense, really. I mean, if you were dead, would you want to move on? Or would you do everything you could to stay on this earth?

Denial is the most common human trait, yet the most counterproductive.

And here he was, at another routine cleansing, in a previously tranquil family home, with an angry, uneasy spirit. April had placed burning sage in the middle of the living room, Julian had cast a circle of salt around the outside of the house, and Oscar was stood, prepared for what he counted as his twelfth cleansing, going over his words in his mind.

The room was dark and empty. Furniture had been moved elsewhere so that it couldn't shake and cause damage. Photo frames had been removed, as faces provided access to the evil spirits they fought. And any loose items that could be picked up or thrown were in a few boxes in the hallway. The residents of the house waited patiently in the dining room.

Oscar, April, and Julian were alone – well, alone in the sense that they were the only people who were alive in the room.

April closed her eyes and bowed her head, sitting cross-legged on the floor.

This was the part that put lumps in Oscar's belly. He knew April was an expert conduit and had done this many, many times – but he still worried that she wouldn't return. That when she allowed her body to be used as a vessel, the entity that entered her would refuse to let her body go. He had to remind himself that she was in control. Just so long as he did his prayers and recited the incantations correctly, she would remain the one in control.

He hadn't failed her yet, and he did not intend to.

Julian watched April, waiting as she fell into a deep trance.

"We call on the spirit within this house." Julian spoke calmly and assertively, standing opposite April, the burning sage between them. "I ask you to use this woman as your vessel, to allow us to speak to you."

He waited.

It rarely happened the first time.

Spirits were normally hesitant to engage in direct conversation with the residents of the house they were reluctant to leave, but Oscar had seen this numerous times – they always surfaced eventually.

"I repeat, the spirit within this house, use April as a vessel to speak to us."

Oscar looked around himself.

Julian paused.

Nothing.

"I repeat, spirit in this house–"

A gust of wind burst past Oscar, past Julian, and against April's chest. She seized a few times, shook, then allowed her head to lift, her eyes still closed.

"Spirit, my name is Julian. Please tell me yours."

They waited a few moments in eerie silence, staring at April, awaiting the spirit's response.

"My name" – she spoke in a voice distinctly not hers; it was that of an old, grumpy man, the kind of cynical old man who was impatient and hated everything – "my name is none of your business."

"Spirit, I have given you mine. It is only fair you give me yours."

"Leave this house," came the blunt response.

"I'm afraid I cannot do that."

Oscar readied himself.

It was nearly his part.

As soon as they had the spirit in a vulnerable state, as soon as it realised it was no longer alive, that it needed to move on, that's when he would say the prayers. The prayers that would cleanse April of the host, and the house of its spirit.

April could keep the entity within her long enough for Oscar to expel it.

"Spirit, I have some bad news for you."

An angry groan escaped April.

"You are dead," Julian spoke.

April's lips remained sealed.

"I repeat, spirit, you are dead. Surely you must realise this."

"You lie."

"I do not lie, I promise you. You are dead, and you need to move on."

"This is my home!"

"Not anymore. In life, yes, but in death… You no longer belong in this world, spirit."

"No!"

Julian gave a nod to Oscar.

"It is time for you to leave."

"No! I will never leave!"

Julian lifted his cross toward April.

"No! No! Get it away!"

Oscar stood forward.

"I know my transgressions, and my sin is ever before me," Oscar began, full of confidence. This was his part and he loved it. Loved being able to expel something from someone's body. He knew a demon would be way too powerful for him – that's what a trained exorcist like Julian was for – but a dead person refusing to leave this world; that was something he could deal with. "Against you, you alone, I have sinned. Indeed, I was born guilty, but I hide my face from your sins, and blot out all my iniquities."

"No! No! What are you doing?" cried the old man.

Julian smiled. It was working.

"Create in me a clean heart, oh God, and put a new and right spirit within this woman."

"No! Stop it!"

"In the name, power and authority of Jesus Christ, Lord and Saviour God, Holy Ghost, do the work I need right now, as I make these proclamations."

"Stop!"

"I renounce and reject all sins, and I–"

He stuttered.

"And I–"

Shit.

The words escaped Oscar. Fell out of his mind like water through fingers.

"And I – I…"

The old man cackled.

"You foolish boy…"

Julian shot Oscar a look of lividity, pure anger surging from his eyes.

"And I… shit…"

"Oscar, say the prayer."

"I… I've forgotten it…"

"Say the damn prayer!"

"I can't! I forgot!"

"I will never leave!" declared the old man.

"He's going to take April, say the prayer!"

"I can't!"

"Say the fucking prayer, Oscar!"

"…"

Julian shoved Oscar out of the way and stood over April's body, pressing the cross against her head.

"I renounce and reject any sinful items kept here," Julian took over.

The old man writhed in pain.

"I renounce and reject any sinful things broadcast within this house, and within this body," Julian continued.

"No!"

"I renounce and reject sinful evil within this host!"

April stiffened like a plank for a few moments, then flopped onto the floor.

Julian dove to her side, shaking her, willing her eyes to open. Eventually, they did.

Oscar rushed to their side.

"Is she okay?"

"Fuck off, Oscar!" Julian shouted, a venomous glare of detest aimed in his direction.

Oscar backed away.

"April, are you okay?" Julian shook her once more.

Her eyes feebly blinked, and Julian helped her sit up, leaning her against the sofa. She rubbed her face, coming around, and finally readjusted to the room.

Julian stood and faced Oscar.

Oscar was stuck to the spot, looking wide-eyed and terrified from April to Julian, to April, to Julian.

"April, I'm so sorry," Oscar genuinely lamented.

"Don't you dare, you complete, bloody imbecile," Julian snapped.

"Julian, don't," April pleaded. "It's fine."

"No, it's not!" Julian shouted, not removing his glare from a desperately anxious Oscar. "Do you know what you could have done?"

"I didn't mean to–"

"Of course you didn't, but that's the worst part, isn't it? You didn't mean to, you just happen to be a fucking moron."

"Julian!" April cried out, taken aback at the words pouring out of Julian's mouth.

"You are not worth my time, and you will never amount to shit, you complete and utter fucking liability!" Julian was now screaming.

"I'm sorry!" Oscar cried, covering his face.

"Julian, that's enough!" April demanded.

No one moved. They remained in angry, stone-cold silence.

"I'm going to go tell the woman who lives here we've been successful," Julian decided, finally breaking the absence of noise and leaving the room. "I daren't give you another job you might fuck up."

Oscar and April shared a look. A look in which Oscar could tell he had let her down.

"I'll wait in the car," he told her and left, hanging his head in shame, wondering if there would ever be anything he could do that he would not screw up.

16

JULIAN CHARGED OUT OF THE HOUSE, CLENCHED FISTS, MAKING A beeline to the car.

Oscar shamefully followed. April watched him as he dragged his feet out of the house, head hung, eyes low, like a puppy who's lost their owner. She knew Oscar well enough to know that this wasn't him making a scene; if anything, this was him doing his best not to. He didn't want anyone to know how much he had let himself down.

It had been an unpleasant experience, but he did not deserve Julian's ill-tempered rant.

He was young. He was new. Yes, he'd had a fair bit of field experience, but he was still learning at a faster rate than either she or Julian had.

It wasn't fair.

"Oscar, just wait here," she told him, pausing him outside the front door.

He faked a smile, unable to look her in the eyes.

She took hold of his hand, knowing how much her touch meant to him, and he met her eyes.

"I'm fine, Oscar. Honestly," she reassured him. "Just – hang on."

He hesitantly nodded, his wounded look still fixed to his face. He was trying to conceal it, trying to put a brave mask on – but she knew him well enough by now.

Having persuaded Oscar to remain put, she stormed down the driveway toward the car, where Julian was opening the car door. April intercepted it and slammed it shut, glaring at his eyes, those eyes that had previously been so caring. Something had changed in him over the last few days, and she did not know what it was, but it did not excuse him talking to Oscar like that. She had to stand up to him.

Even if it was the first time in her life she'd ever had to stand up to such a close, faithful friend.

"What the hell is wrong with you?" she barked.

"What do you mean?" he demanded, bending down to meet her glare with his, a venom in his voice she had never heard before.

"He's just a kid!"

"Yes, he is just a kid. It's time he grew up. He could have done some serious damage to you in there."

"But he didn't!"

"But he could have!"

She shook her head and folded her arms, pursing her lips, doing her best to contain her fury.

"Don't you dare try and pretend that was for my benefit. Not a single bit of that was for my protection. It was for your own ego, against someone who so blatantly looks up to you. You love him feeding out of your hand, don't you?"

"Oh, sorry, am I going to offend your useless little boyfriend?"

He barged her out the way with his shoulder, opened the car door, and threw himself into the driver's seat. As he started the engine, he went to close the door, to find April stood in the way once more, her arms still folded and her scowl intensifying.

"Move out of the way, April."

"No." She shook her head.

He huffed. She knew he would not shove her completely out of the way. There would be no way he could apologise for pushing her.

"Do you know what? You deserve him!" he exclaimed. "Both of you are little kids, who have no idea what it's like to live in this real world. I cannot stop dreaming about Anna. Do you have any idea what that is like? What it's like to see that every night? No, because you've never had to deal with the real repercussions of what these things can do to people!"

"Shut up, Julian. I've been channelling enough evil things to know the reality of this world."

"Yeah? Try having a kid die on you."

Tense silence ensued.

Was that what this was about?

Because she hadn't had a kid like Anna die on her?

And it was her fault she hadn't had that experience? That meant she knew nothing?

No.

It couldn't be.

She knew Julian. She knew this wasn't about her, or Oscar – it was about him. Something was going on.

Normally, she could read him so well. But now...

He was panting. His eyes were breaking. He would consider himself too manly to cry openly in front of her, she knew that, but she could see it in his eyes. That little boy inside breaking, shattering to pieces and fading away like smoke.

"This isn't you," April told him, lowering her voice, trying to be soothing and calm, rather than heated and angry. "You're direct, that's what you're like; that's fine. But you've never been this bad."

He shook his head. Slammed his hands on the steering wheel. His face was breaking, and he was desperate to leave the situation, April could see that. But she wasn't letting him go anywhere.

"Get out of the way, April," he instructed, putting his hand on the door handle.

"No."

He sighed.

"Do you know what Derek once told me?"

"What?"

"The biggest obstacle you ever have to overcome is yourself."

And with that, he shoved her, closed the door, and drove away.

Within seconds, Oscar was at her side.

"How are we going to get home now?" he innocently mused.

Julian had taken her off the street when she was a teenager. Taught her everything she knew. She couldn't bear to have him upset or mad at her.

She turned and pushed herself into Oscar's arms, covering her face, feeling his warm embrace wrap around her.

THEN

17

A CALM BREEZE FLUTTERED THROUGH THE OPEN WINDOW, filling the room with a summer glow. The sound of birds singing to each other, children laughing as they cycled past, a postman whistling a jaunty tune – it all sauntered so eagerly through Julian's mind.

But Julian's mind was nothing like the scene outside.

Inside his head it was a tsunami. Angry faces bickering, turning to green and red, phasing away into horned beasts and wicked grins. Storms plunged from grey clouds, peeking from the corners of his mind into his melancholy solace.

His hand absently fiddled with a two-pence coin, turning it around between his thumb and his forefinger, spinning it, then tapping it against the desk.

His tired eyes lingered outside the window, scalding the happy scenes, willing the mothers to take their kids away and hide them from the dark recesses of this world.

Demons existed.

Ghosts existed.

The devil existed.

Everything he had thought untrue. Everything he had

argued against. Everything those irrational religious minds had sworn to him. Everything he had deplored through various statuses on social media about the ridiculous wars caused by religion.

It was real. And he felt foolish.

How they would laugh at him now!

How they would mock him and ridicule him, sneer at him for his upturned nose, shake their heads at his ignorant, uneducated mind.

And to them, he would sneer right back.

Because they praise their God. They worship him.

They have no idea what God can do.

He could remove a demon from a child. Once the exorcist had tested their faith, and proven their devotion, and God willingly lent his hand in removing the entity, then that child would be saved.

And what happened should God not be willing? Should God not approve the test of dedication?

Anna.

That's what happened.

He slammed the coin down on the table and shifted position, as if he was about to get up and do something. Make a stand. Volunteer a contribution to society. Do something that would make a difference; that would change what happened.

Yet he remained static. The bones of his rear end shifting uncomfortably against the solid wooden seat of his kitchen. Mentally deploring the world parading by his window.

Because there was nothing he could do.

He could stand and try, but so what?

She was dead.

Dead.

Dead, dead, dead.

A young girl robbed of the right to grow old. A young girl's future taken away, her innocence ravaged, her sparkling smile replaced with a pale, vacant, stone-cold face.

Her eyes.

Those bloody eyes.

Those bloody, shitty, fucking eyes.

They stared at him.

And he did nothing but stare back.

Stare into their nothingness. Because there was nothing he could do.

He could make a stand against the rest of the demons. Against anything else that tried to take a child's life. Anything else that ever tried to consume one of God's children.

God.

He grunted a sarcastic laugh.

He would plead for His strength. He would beg for His mercy. He would pray to Him, beg for Him to take victims from their demons.

But Julian would never respect Him.

Because He did nothing.

Because God did not deem Derek's words faithful enough. Because Derek, a man who had literally fought and killed in His name for decades, did not pass the test.

Fuck him.

There was nothing more to think. Nothing more to say.

Anna was dead.

And with it, the soul of his mentor left too.

NOW

18

THE DEAD OF NIGHT ENCAPSULATED THE PRISON IN A CLOAK OF darkness. The half-moon barely shone through the window of Derek's cell, meaning he had a large shadow to work in.

Good. Darkness works better.

He sat on the floor, keeping himself calm, readying himself for what was to come. He was strong enough at contacting the paranormal elements that it wouldn't take him much, but it would take its toll on his weary body. His injuries, added to his aching bones and stiffened muscles, made him less responsive. But he was still determined to do this.

He lit a small tealight candle he'd acquired through paying another prisoner to smuggle it in for him. It wasn't the burning sage, the circle of salt, or the large candles he would normally require for a cleansing, but it would be enough for someone of his abilities.

At least, he hoped it would be.

He bowed his head and opened his lips into a barely audible whisper. If he was to do this, he needed to remain undisturbed, as an interruption would not only get him in trouble, but it would break his focus and ultimately the process.

"Holy Spirit," he began, "Thou make me see everything, and show me which way to reach my ideal. Thou who give me the divine gift to forgive and forget the wrong that is done to me and who is in all instances of my life with me. I pray, Holy Spirit, please show me the unclean spirits that haunt this cell."

He waited.

Nothing.

He bowed his head and closed his eyes, ensuring he remained calm, focussed, and completely at peace.

"Holy Spirit," he continued in his hushed voice, "with thy mercy, allow me to see what it is that dwells within this prison."

He opened his eyes.

This often took a while, he told himself. Just need to be patient.

Just need to remain calm.

"Holy Spirit, I–"

A swift brush of air against his face interrupted him. Slowly, he raised his head, opening his eyes.

Even after all this time, he still looked upon responsive spirits in disbelief that they answered his call.

"Hello, my name is Derek," he introduced himself. "What's yours?"

"Elizabeth," answered an apparition forming before him from a mixture of mist and smoke. It was a young woman, dressed in attire from before the prison was built. Her brown hair hung over her shoulders. She had an innocent smile and a long, dark-orange gown. Derek estimated the fifteenth century, based on the images of history he had studied.

"Elizabeth, thank you for responding to me," Derek spoke.

Elizabeth did not say a word. She hovered in the cell before him, a translucent figure hanging with the freedom of death.

"Elizabeth, why are you here?" Derek asked. "I don't imagine you were in this prison at any point, were you?"

"No."

"I would predict that you died before this prison was built, am I correct?"

"Yes."

"Were you murdered?"

"Yes."

"Elizabeth, I appreciate your answers, but can you tell me anything else? Anything about this prison? About why you haunt it?"

The apparition hung her head. Derek thought he saw a gentle sob, but couldn't be sure. After an extended period of thinking time, she raised her head again. Derek willed himself to be patient, to see what she had to say.

"You are in danger," she told him bluntly.

"Me?"

"Yes."

"What about the other prisoners here? Are they in danger too?"

She hung her head once more.

"Are they in danger from you, Elizabeth?" he asked.

She didn't respond. She simply continued to hang her head in subdued silence.

"Are you going to hurt them?"

After a moment's hesitation, she shook her head, and lifted it once more to look Derek in the eyes.

"It is Jackson Kullins, the prison governor, that you need to fear."

"The governor? Why?"

She forced a solemn smile as she began to fade.

"No, please, Elizabeth, don't go. I need to ask you–"

But it was too late.

The spirit had faded into the darkness.

The tealight flickered before him, burning out and turning into a string of smoke fading into the air and mixing with the moisture of his cell.

Derek didn't move.

He stared into the darkness where she had manifested herself, watching the shadows rest still in the cell before him.

19

Yet another sleepless night sent Julian's mind into a swirl of chaotic memories that clashed and spun until it was a storm he could no longer make sense of.

Julian lay on his back, staring at the ceiling, feeling the hours go by. He willed himself to close his eyes, to get some rest, to fall asleep, but they wouldn't shut. No matter how much he urged himself to sleep, his mind would not rest.

The covers lay in a crumpled mess around his knees, his bare torso sweating in the heat of the room. It was just this one room, just the bedroom that was this hot. The rest of the flat was so cold he could see his breath in the air. No matter what he did with the heating, no matter how he adjusted the radiators, nothing would fix the drastic change in temperature.

He tried closing his eyes. They were so heavy, so ready for sleep, but his mind wasn't. His thoughts bounced from manic recollections to parasitic images – that first exorcism projected onto the cinema screen of his mind, repeating itself as if the film reel was broken.

"Julian."

He lifted his head. Looked around the room.

The vague light from the moon seeped through a crack in the curtains, allowing him enough light to see that the room was empty. The corners were coated in still shadows, fixed and unfazed.

"Julian."

It came again.

A whisper so faint he wasn't entirely sure if he had heard it.

Tired minds cause tired hallucinations.

His thoughts were so incessant. Every night, the same damn images. The same twist in his gut, the same retching feeling crawling up the inside of his throat, the same sound of silence that pounded his eardrums with incessant ferocity. His concentration dwelled so exclusively on this one girl, that he was bound to start conjuring up sounds and images in his unconscious.

Still, he was curious.

The voice was so hushed he couldn't be sure who it belonged to. It was a vague whisper, barely audible, so much so it could easily have been the wind or a brush of his leg against the duvet.

He sat up, turning his legs out of bed and placing his bare feet on the warm carpet.

He took the glass of water from beside him, taking a big sip, drinking gulp, after gulp, after gulp.

The time read 3.08 a.m.

He placed the empty glass on his bedside table and paused. Resting. Listening. Waiting to hear something conclusive, something definite, something he could incontrovertibly attribute to something not of this world.

Nothing.

Just the silence of an empty flat.

Now I need the bloody toilet.

He stood, treading lightly out of his room, and taking the few slow steps across the living room to the bathroom.

He paused as he did, watching, waiting. The room was as he'd left it. A book placed on the sofa in a way that would preserve his page. His hoodie on the floor. His shoes beside the front door.

Nothing was there besides him.

He shook his head to himself. Reminding himself he was being silly. Turned his back to the room and opened the bathroom door.

"You killed me."

He halted.

He slowly rotated back around so he had the entire open flat in his vision.

The rooms were covered in darkness. No movement. Nothing out of place.

It's my mind.

The only explanation.

Stop it.

He couldn't let people see him like this.

Get it together.

In a sudden jolt that overcame him like an electric shock, he grew colder. The temperature around him plummeted, and he could not only see a hint of his breath in the air, but could see it fully forming into a messy cloud.

He stepped into the room, getting colder still, placing his feet on the frosty, solid floor. The lower temperature beneath his feet hurt like a sharp ice prick. He couldn't keep them on the floor for too long, otherwise the pain would spread up his ankles, to his shins, causing an ache he couldn't deny.

"Who's there?" he asked.

His eyes darted back and forth, surveying every floor, wall, and piece of furniture with precise scrutiny.

The more he stepped into the room, the more he was forced to shiver. It was as if the temperature was dropping further still with each step. He wrapped his arms around his chest, rubbing his arms, doing all he could to stay warm. At this rate, he was going to catch a cold.

"Hello?" he tried once more.

Then he had a thought.

A thought he wouldn't normally have entertained, but with all that was happening, he decided he had to.

It took him a few moments to conjure the confidence to say it. His whole body stiffened, his lip trembling, his arms shaking.

"Is that..." he tried, failing to finish the question.

He closed his eyes.

Come on.

His body shuddered as he opened his eyes once more.

In a spurt of self-assurance, he blurted it out.

"Is that Anna?"

Almost immediately he was launched off his feet, against the door of the bathroom, forced to fall into a mess on the floor.

"You killed me!" the voice repeated, this time in an aggressive scream, filling the room with ear-piercing noise. *"You killed me! You killed me!"*

Then it stopped.

The cold slunk away like a thief in the night, and he could no longer see his breath on the air.

He was left in a painful heap, huddled in a ball, denying what had just happened, willing himself to have the guts to get up.

He tried to explain it with rational thought, with other ideas of what it could be, but every flash of logical thinking escaped him as he realised his deepest fears could potentially be being carried out in his own home.

No.
These things didn't happen to him.
It had to be his mind.
It had to be.
It had to.

20

A DOZEN PAPERS AND OPEN BOOKS LAY ON THE FLOOR AROUND Oscar. He read and read and read the same words over and over again, forcing them to sink in, ensuring he remembered them.

He had really screwed up, and he knew it.

April was nice to him about it, even defending him against Julian's outburst, but deep down, Oscar had felt the scalding words were justified. He had one role in that cleansing, and it was the same role he had repeated multiple times now – say the words that ensured the bad spirit leaves April's host body.

If they waited too long to rid her body of the entity, they could end up with an unprecedented possession to deal with. A possession of someone both he and Julian cared deeply about. And it would have been Oscar at fault.

It wasn't so much that he cared about Julian's words – though he did; that's just what he told himself. It was the fact that they were right. He could have severely let April down.

So he re-read the words, again and again, repeating them out loud.

"In the name, power, and authority of Jesus Christ, Lord

and Saviour God, Holy Ghost, do the work I need right now, as I make these proclamations. In the name, power, and authority of Jesus Christ, Lord and Saviour God, Holy Ghost, do the work I need right now, as I make these proclamations."

He knew them already. He knew them so, so well. He could recite them in his sleep.

But it was like lines in a play – you could learn them until you were blue in the face, yet when it came to actually saying them in front of a crowd and remembering them under pressure, that's when you truly falter.

A knock on the door roused him from his persistent studying. It was a rhythmic knocking he recognised as April's. He leapt to his feet with a bounce, then practically dove out of the room and toward the front door, stumbling over a stray pair of shoes as he did.

"Hey, April," he said happily, opening the door to her.

His face fell as he saw her expression.

"Hey," she responded glumly.

She walked into the house and through to the living room, where she found numerous books and papers scattered around.

"Oh, Oscar." She shook her head. "You don't need to do this."

"Yes, I do. It's important. I can't get this wrong."

"It was a stumble; you are still learning. Julian was a dick. Honestly, you don't need to worry so much."

A warm glow spread through him. It was ridiculous how any time she paid him the littlest of compliments it sent him into a state of childish joy, but it did.

"I looked at our emails earlier," April began, sitting on the edge of a seat. Oscar sat opposite her. "They haven't been checked in days."

"Who should have checked them?" Oscar asked, momentarily worried this was another thing he had screwed up.

"Julian does it. We have job offers worth thousands, and no one has replied to them."

"How strange."

It was strange. Julian was the epitome of professionalism. And especially after Julian had reacted so negatively to Oscar's screw-up, it was bizarre that he wouldn't do something as routinely important as checking the company's emails and responding to new clients.

"I'm worried, Oscar," April confessed, and Oscar could see that worry in her eyes.

"Have you tried talking to him?"

"No."

"Try it. FaceTime him now. I'll be here."

"Will you hold my hand?"

Oscar's heart raced. His belly tingled.

"Of course."

April took out her phone and opened FaceTime. She held Oscar's hand tightly as she waited for Julian's response to her call.

Even though he knew it was for comfort rather than romance – or so he assumed – it still brought him great pleasure to have her skin resting against his. It occurred to him how besotted he actually was with this woman, that a simple touch of her hand could send him wild.

After an extensive wait, the call was finally answered. A few shuffles came out of the phone's speaker, rustles against a set of dirty bed sheets. Eventually, Julian's face appeared on the screen. His eyeballs were bloodshot, with pronounced bags under his eyes. His eyelids rested heavily, his face was pale, and his lips were cracked and bleeding.

April had to stifle a gasp at his appearance. Oscar had never seen him like this, and was sure she hadn't either.

"April?" Julian grunted sleepily. "What do you want?"

"What are you doing in bed, Julian? It's the middle of the afternoon."

Julian turned his head groggily toward a crack in the curtains, noticing a bright light shining through. He turned his head back, slowly and with much effort.

"What do you want, April?" he repeated.

"No one's checked the company email."

Julian sighed, running a grubby hand through his sweaty hair.

"Right. I'll do it. Is there anything else?"

Oscar knew April was trying to disguise her upset, but it was clear for him to see. Julian had taken care of her for so long, he was like an older brother – and here he was, being short and ill-tempered with her, and it was clearly breaking her heart.

"What is going on, Julian?" she persisted. "This isn't like you."

"What's not like me?"

"Have you looked in a mirror? You look like hell."

"Thanks, April," he sarcastically retorted. "Is there anything else?"

She closed her eyes and took a moment to gather herself.

"Yes. I'm worried about you."

"Well, you don't need to be."

"Really? Julian, I've never seen you like this, I–"

"Is that all, April? Because I really don't have time for this."

Her eyes watered, but she did all she could to keep it together.

"You don't have time for me?"

With an exasperated huff, Julian's face disappeared off-screen as the call ended.

April turned to Oscar, stumped, her mouth wide open in shock, fumbling for the words.

"I–" was all that she managed.

She closed her eyes and rested her head against Oscar's chest.

Oscar put a hand on the back of her head and gently stroked her hair. He tried to think of something to say, but couldn't.

So he did his best to be there for her, however little that may matter.

21

THE FLAT HAD NEVER BEEN SUCH A MESS.

Julian didn't care.

He lay on the floor of the living room, staring at the ceiling above, motionless, unmoved. If he stayed still, maybe it would leave him alone.

Please.

Maybe *she* would leave him alone.

Was it Anna? Was it her ghost? Or was it someone with knowledge of Anna tormenting him?

Was it even paranormal?

It was more likely to be the ravings of a tired, paranoid mind. The abyss he was sinking into was consuming him into a rabid psychosis. Fragments of his mind breaking like pieces of glass entwined with painful memories he couldn't escape.

Fragments.

This is how it starts, after all. The descent into madness.

Voices. Delusions. Obsession.

Stop it.

He coughed at the stench of his own body odour. His trousers were becoming crunchy, stuck to his legs with dry sweat. Papers, magazines, and unopened mail were scattered across various parts of the floor. His furniture was out of place, his Wi-Fi box was flickering red, and his curtains kept the overpowering light out.

He closed his eyes, watching the imprint of a strip of light visible through a crack in his curtains turn into a splodge upon his retina, circling and fading into nothing.

He stretched his arms out.

Damn, my muscles ache.

His biceps felt stretched and unused.

His hand felt...

What's that?

Something was in his hand.

Something.

His hand.

It was in...

Something soft. Something bumpy yet smooth. Something small.

What could...

He lifted his hand up and squinted at the object before him.

A scrunchie.

A little girl's scrunchie. It was a reddish pink, small enough to fit at the top of a pony tail in the hair of a twelve-year-old girl.

"How did that get here..." he muttered.

He stared at it, turning it in his hands.

Unless...

Was this Anna's?

Not possible.

This is ridiculous.

Ridiculous.

She's dead.

How could she...

He leapt to his feet, determined not to believe it, focusing on channelling his thoughts into the rational.

Maybe it was April's.

Yeah, that's right. It could be April's.

Except that, in the entire time Julian had known April, he had never seen her hair tied back with a scrunchie.

No.

It's April's.

Not Anna's.

Not Anna's.

Please, not Anna's.

His head shook, flickering splashes of grease against the wall.

Please.

He refused to believe it.

No. Not real.

I can't let this be true.

He traipsed toward the kitchen, finding his throat parched and dry, desperate for water. He flung open the cupboard and clumsily withdrew a glass, hitting it against all the other glasses in the cupboard, then turned the tap on too fast and overflowed the glass.

He turned, leant against the sink, and drank the water.

He stared at the fridge.

There was something else.

The fridge...

Something on the fridge.

There was something.

What?

He placed the glass heavily on the side and approached.

Something...

A picture. Attached with a magnet to the door of his fridge.

A picture.

A picture of...

He recoiled in horror. He couldn't deny this, he couldn't.

He couldn't explain it. He couldn't...

He screamed.

It wasn't her. It wasn't her. It couldn't be her.

He grabbed the picture from the front of the fridge, gawping at it.

Anna and her mother. Arms around each other. Smiling wildly, in some sunny climate, likely on holiday. Happy. Together.

Alive.

"What the fuck..."

No.

No, no, no. This is crazy. Bloody crazy.

He ripped the picture up, vigorously shaking his head, refusing.

"No, not a chance, not real, you can't, no..."

Anna.

It wasn't.

She wasn't...

He threw it in the bin and charged through the living room, back and forth, back and forth, hands in his hair, pacing back and forth, back and forth, shaking his head, refusing to believe, back and forth.

"No, no, no, it's not real, it's–"

He stopped.

The wall.

No.

He fell to his knees. Tears streamed down his cheeks like tumultuous waves.

The wall.

He couldn't deny this.

"No!" he bellowed, turning away, then looking back.

The whole of the wall was taken up with three clear words written in red.

You did this.

22

A FRANTIC COMMOTION AWOKE DEREK FROM HIS RESTLESS sleep. The bright light through the cell window told him it was morning.

He leant up, wearily rubbing his eyes, slowly readjusting after another night of disturbed sleep.

Cries and shouts sounded throughout the wing. At first, Derek thought a riot was underway, but as he listened to the shouts, he concluded that it must be something more.

"Leave him alone!"

"Dirty fucking warden!"

"You're next, prick!"

Derek dragged himself to his feet and edged toward the door to his cell. Normally by now, he would have been awoken by the prison officer. His cell door would have been opened, and people would be roaming freely throughout the wing.

No such thing had happened.

As he peered out of his door and down the narrow angle of the wall of cells, he couldn't see anyone else at their cell door.

So what was all the uproar about?

He turned, edging toward the window of the cell, and stood on the rim of the toilet so he could peer out of it. Climbing onto it took a few attempts, such was the pain in his bad leg, but he managed. And as the view out of his cell window became clear, shock overcame him.

Below was the courtyard of the prison, a solid cement floor surrounded by dark-red, mossy bricks. In the middle of the courtyard stood Jackson Kullins, the prison governor, feet shoulder-width apart, a stubborn frown over a piercing set of sadistic eyes.

But that wasn't what everyone was shouting at.

At the far side of the courtyard, a small set of stairs were placed against a wall; a wall as faded, graffitied, and weathered as every other wall of the courtyard. Beside this stood a masked man, fixing a rope to an arched wooden frame before him.

Derek's heart raced and his muscles stiffened.

It was the gallows.

And the man with the mask was the executioner.

Two other prison officers carried a handcuffed man, kicking and screaming toward the set of stairs. They forcibly fixed a brown bag around his head, tying it with a tight piece of string.

"Leave him alone, you piece of shit!"

"Do this, you'll be next!"

"Leave him the fuck alone!"

Helpless shouts of aggressive jeers continued to pour out of cell windows, from each floor of Derek's wing and the cells on the other sides of the courtyard. Yet, however much the abuse continued to rain down upon the scene below, it did nothing to deter the resolve upon the face of Kullins, the executioner, or the officers wrestling the man up the small set of stairs.

They placed the flailing man's head through the noose.

"Prisoner," the governor bellowed, leering at the man. "Do you have anything to say?"

The man stopped fighting. He remained still, heavy breathing causing the bag to retract.

"Very well," Kullins continued. "Hang him!"

The man was pushed off the stairs and forced to hang helplessly on the rope.

Derek watched in horror as the man's body powerlessly struggled against the suffocation of his throat. The man thrashed out his legs, pulled against his restrained hands, even tried to swing the rope back and forth with such despairing aggression Derek thought the gallows would collapse.

Then the man stopped struggling.

He just convulsed. Spasmed, his body throbbing as it struggled for oxygen.

Finally, it went limp.

It just hung there.

Dangling helplessly. The swinging to and fro calming until the empty body hung still.

Derek couldn't understand.

This was modern Britain. This was 2017.

They didn't hang people anymore.

Not for over half a century, at least.

So how was this happening? How was the governor getting away with this?

"*Silence!*" Kullins's strong voice bellowed, reverberating against the walls of the courtyard.

Every jeer and heckle ceased with instant obedience.

Every murderer, attacker, torturer – every dangerous prisoner's mouth shut firmly and abruptly. There must have been hundreds of heckling voices that instantly terminated. Their terrified eyes gazed upon the governor standing beside the loose body of the deceased.

"You see this?" the governor shouted. His voice was so

powerful it carried through the courtyard to every wing without a hint of breakage or quiver. "You continue to be miscreants, you continue to shout and holler with the audacity you have just shown, this will be *your* fate."

Derek peered at the faces at the windows of the other cells. These hardened men turned to little boys, gawking vulnerably at the man shouting from beneath them.

"I will not tolerate disobedience in my prison. Go back to your cells!"

He strode across the courtyard and disappeared past the wall.

Every face watched in ear-splitting silence as the executioner presented a pair of sheers and used it to cut the rope, forcing the dead man's body to fall into a heavy lump.

The two prison officers took an arm each and dragged the man away, disappearing out of sight, assumingly to bury the corpse in an unmarked grave.

Derek slipped from his precarious perch upon the toilet and collapsed on the floor. He winced in agony at the pounding of the solid floor against his troubled leg, but daren't make any sound.

He held the leg tightly in his arms, scrunching his face, enduring it, waiting for the pain to pass.

He did not want to make a noise.

He did not want to attract attention.

He did not want to face that man's fate.

As he sat, rocking back and forth, gripping his leg between his hands, he thought about what the apparition had told him yesterday.

The prison governor was the one they needed to look out for. Which was strange, as he appeared to be a brutal psychopath, yet had shown no supernatural element to him that Derek had seen.

The thoughts escaped as an incurable pain in his bad leg took over, but he willed himself to keep wincing in silence.

He could not let anyone hear him.

He could not risk suffering the same fate as that man.

For if the other inmates didn't kill him, if a paranormal attack didn't kill him – then there was still a far more dangerous threat looming within these prison walls.

THEN

23

SHIFTING UNCOMFORTABLY ON THE WOODEN SEAT, JULIAN peered into the distance to see if he could spot Derek. Through the crowds of people, he could just about make out the back of a tidy parted haircut, obscured by dozens of heads.

Anna's family was in there somewhere – but most of the people sat between him and Derek were nothing more than voyeurs. Vultures. Courtroom drama enthusiasts. Either the press or people who are too nosy for their own good.

Julian had intentionally taken a seat at the back, as he didn't want Derek to see him. Derek wouldn't have wanted him there. Derek was a strong man, and the most common flaw of a strong man was that they never wanted people to see them in their darkest moments.

But sometimes, the strongest people we know can be so because we see them at their most vulnerable.

Derek had always taught Julian that if you want to measure where a man is, you need to see how far they've come.

"The biggest obstacle you ever have to overcome, is yourself," Derek had once told him. Those were ten words that had been permanently engrained in his thoughts ever since.

Julian wondered, for a fleeting moment, whether he should have sat closer to the front; that way, when Derek did glance back, he would see a supportive face amongst the crowd of people who had already assumed his guilt. Maybe, in his darkest moment, Derek would wish that he had asked his dearest friend to attend.

But then again, Derek never glanced back.

He never gave his audience the pleasure of seeing his eyes break.

Julian had endured the whole ordeal with a visage of utter disdain. He'd barely been able to listen as the prosecution had ripped Derek to shreds, exposed his many heroic acts from the 1980s onwards as ravings of a dangerous, deluded fool. Each time Derek had disposed of a demon from a helpless victim, it had been turned into a disgusting, volatile, neglectful act of a delusional man.

It was a shame people made such strong assumptions about what they didn't understand.

As a result, Julian's faith in the judicial system had severely wavered, to the point where he no longer had any faith in society's ability to act with fair justice. He'd always thought of the United Kingdom as a developed country, a country of tolerance. Yet he had sat for weeks as overpaid hypocrites tore Derek's character apart in front of twelve supposedly impartial jurors.

What gave those twelve people the right to judge?

They had no special qualifications. No educated ability to scrutinise the situation with clarity.

They were being fed facts in a biased way, intended to cloud their minds until the innocent man doesn't prevail, but the best-made argument wins.

Derek was an educated man of a modest estate. His representation wasn't equal to that of the deceased girl's rich family.

The one thing Julian couldn't understand is how anyone,

whatever their beliefs, could judge Derek Lansdale as ever having anything but that girl's best interests at heart.

Her death was a tragedy, but if it weren't for Derek, it would have happened sooner and with far more violent means.

"Derek Lansdale, please rise," commanded the judge.

Derek obeyed, as did his lawyer.

Now Julian could see him.

Now Julian could see Derek's face from the side on, staring across the courtroom at the jurors. Everyone else would see his expression as assured and resilient. Julian knew him well enough to recognise the look in his eyes as a performance.

It was a look of pure fear masked by self-assurance.

Maybe Derek didn't realise how judgemental these people were. Derek probably still had faith in the system. Julian did not.

That was one thing Julian admired in Derek, whilst also resenting – the ability to see the good in everything and everyone, no matter what the situation.

"Have you reached a verdict?" the judge asked the jury's representative, who was also standing.

"Yes, we have, Your Honour," the man in a cheap grey suit replied.

"And what say you?"

"We, the jury, find the defendant – guilty – of manslaughter by gross negligence."

Derek's face didn't falter. A flicker of his cheek signalled to Julian a weakness in his eyes, like he was fighting tears, but to everyone else, he was stone cold.

Anna's mother turned to her husband, burying her head in his shoulder and weeping.

Fool.

You never want to insult a grieving mother, but Julian couldn't help but place blame on her. She approved the exorcism on her daughter. In fact, she had decided to seek Derek out and specifically request that he perform it. If Derek was responsible for the girl's death – which Julian unequivocally believed he wasn't – then she should be equally guilty.

"Mr Lansdale, have you anything to say?" the judge requested.

Derek's face slowly turned to the voyeurs watching him from the gallery, and his eyes fixed on Julian.

Julian froze.

Derek knew Julian was there.

He'd probably known all along. Of course he had. Derek misses nothing.

They held eye contact for a moment, a look of painful resolve shared between them. Derek shook his head with a fractional movement – something Julian took as an indication that they weren't to fight this; that they were to accept it and move on with their lives.

"My client does not wish to say anything," Derek's lawyer announced, "but I wish to remind you that, at the beginning of the trial, my client requested that if he was found guilty, that he be sentenced immediately."

The judge took a moment to contemplate this.

"Very well," he decided. "Derek Lansdale, you are sentenced to a minimum of fourteen years for the death of Anna Bennett through manslaughter by gross negligence. The court is adjourned."

Derek stood sternly, allowing his hands to be restrained behind his back.

Julian couldn't fight back his tears as he watched the spectators from the galleries cheering at Derek's sentence – clapping and whooping as he was unfairly found guilty of the neglectful death of a little girl under his protection.

Derek had done everything he could to save that girl from the demon.

Julian had watched, learnt, and soaked up every piece of wisdom he could from this man. Now he was forced to watch as an officer restrained him and took him out of the courtroom to cheers and jeers.

He remained the only person sitting. Frantically immobile. Manically unsure. Devastation soaking his thoughts.

His arms shook.

His lip trembled.

Derek had disappeared behind the crowd of mocking celebrations.

He was left to sit there and think about what it all meant.

NOW

24

Jason had delayed and delayed this visit as much as possible. Over the past few days, he had exhausted the various possibilities for the doctor's death.

Suicide.

A killer who was slick enough to remove his DNA.

And leave no footprints.

And not be seen on CCTV, neither entering nor leaving the office.

He hated it, but it was time to start entertaining other options. He hated it, as he knew how others saw him. They saw him as the man who sought out the strange cases, the ones that would lead him down a path the other officers either saw as too dangerous, or, in most cases, too silly.

Being honest with himself, a year or so ago he'd have thought the exact same thing. He'd have demanded he left the station and seek psychiatric help, accompanied by a suspension.

But he had found results. Or, more pertinently, the Sensitives had found results, and he had taken credit for it. And that was the only reason he hadn't been completely dismissed. The few times he'd used the Sensitives over the last few months, he had managed to give the families involved the closure other officers couldn't.

Now he was going one step further. This wasn't just a phone call that the other officers could pretend to ignore. This was him going to Julian, asking for his help, and inviting him to come aboard a complicated murder case.

To say he felt nervous would be an understatement. He felt apprehensive, self-critical, and worried about what others were going to say about him, whether it be to his face or behind his back.

He already heard the whispers.

His colleagues thought he didn't, but he did.

He went to place a firm knock on Julian's door to find that it was already slightly ajar.

He nudged it with his hand, allowing it to creak open, and took in the dark, chaotically messy flat displayed before him.

Writing decorated the wall in red ink, ripped paper was strewn all over the floor, and the stench of body odour and expired food overwhelmed his sense of smell.

"Julian?" he asked.

A sudden gasp drew his attention.

The eyes of a man appeared from behind the sofa. It was Julian all right, but not as he had seen him before. His hair was a greasy mess, his eyes were wide and bloodshot, and he wore nothing but stained, ripped pyjama trousers. And the way Julian looked at Jason was like that of a startled wild animal.

"Julian, what the hell?" Jason asked, remaining in the doorway, wary about entering further.

"Have you come for her?" Julian asked in a quick whisper.

"Come for who, Julian? What is going on?"

Julian's eyes darted back and forth. He jumped across the floor like a demented deer, as if he had heard something, alerted to danger, hiding behind a torn armchair.

"Julian?" Jason prompted. "What are you doing?"

"You need to leave!"

"Funnily enough, I actually came to you for help."

"Help?" Julian answered with a mild roar coming from his throat. "You need to go."

"Julian, I–"

"Go!"

Jason shook his head. It was no good. He wasn't about to wait around for this.

He shut the door behind him and left.

25

ANOTHER CAFÉ. ANOTHER AWKWARD SILENCE AS OSCAR LOOSELY stirred his tea and April sat opposite him, waiting for him to say what they were both waiting for him to say.

Except, she seemed to be growing increasingly unsure with every attempt Oscar made at broaching the subject of his feelings for her.

He watched her for a few moments. Her eyes glazed over as she stared at the hot chocolate before her.

Normally, she would be scooping the marshmallows with her spoon, slurping on the cream, then relishing the taste of the warmth sliding down her throat.

But she wasn't.

Her mind was elsewhere.

"April, I–" Oscar tried, willing himself to tell her how he felt.

But she didn't look up, didn't respond, didn't look with waiting eyes for him to finally confess his adoration for her.

Her eyes remained down, a glum expression taking over her face.

"April, what's up?" Oscar asked, deciding that he needed to figure out her mood first.

She shrugged.

"Seriously, what is it?"

April gave a big, heavy sigh, and shrugged her shoulders again.

"You can shrug all you want, I can tell there's something on your mind."

She glanced up at him, held his eye contact for a moment, then dropped her gaze back toward her hot chocolate, watching the cream slowly melt.

"I don't know," she exhaled.

"Yeah, you do," Oscar insisted. "What is it?"

"It's just..." She opened her mouth, struggling for the words, moving her lips to form a sentence that didn't come out.

"It's Julian, isn't it?"

Oscar knew her well enough by now to read such things. He recognised the slight twitch of her nose that indicated her feeling perturbed, and he could see the tilt in her smile that indicated a troubled mind.

He hadn't even realised he knew her that well.

It was almost as if they were already a couple.

Almost.

"April, talk to me."

She lifted her head but did not fix her gaze onto Oscar, instead choosing to stare out of the window. She watched people pass by with no idea of the true reality that lurked in the darkness of their world.

"I just... I've never seen Julian like this."

Oscar nodded.

He tried to think of what to say, what words he could possibly use that would be of some comfort. He had never particularly been the one that people would go to for advice or words of reassurance. He hadn't particularly been the person people would go to for anything. He so wanted to make everything better, to wrap his arms around her and show how much she meant to him, to exorcise the demons of her mind, to will the bad thoughts away.

But he didn't know how.

"Like what?" Oscar asked, knowing it was a stupid question, but feeling he had to say something.

"Crazy. Just – crazy. He looked a state."

"Have you ever seen him like that before?"

"No, God no. I don't think I've ever even seen him without gelled hair before." She finally turned her gaze to Oscar. "I'm scared, Oscar."

"Scared? Of what?"

"Of whatever it is going on with him. What if it's something he can't overcome? What if it's something he can't fight?"

Oscar nodded. These were all relevant questions. He just didn't have the answers. He watched her, continually struggling to find a way to quell her concerns.

"I guess all you can really do is just be there for him."

Oscar concealed a smile, pleased at the wonderful advice he had just given.

"I guess, but… what if that's not enough?"

His face dropped again. He didn't know what to say.

"Look, you saw him on FaceTime. We don't know, we haven't seen him in person."

"You're right. We should go see him."

Oscar frowned. That was not what he meant, but he could hardly argue with it now.

In truth, Julian had been an arse toward him since the day they'd met. Yet he was clearly important to April, and he knew he needed to be supportive.

"Okay, let's go," Oscar decided.

"Are you coming?"

Oscar hesitated.

"But what do we do if we can't get in?"

"I have a spare key in my car."

Oscar sighed. There was no way out of this.

"Of course."

"Oh, Oscar, you are the best!"

She took his hand in hers and stroked it, sending more tingles racing up and down his body. He dropped his head to avoid revealing a blush.

"Let's go."

"Aren't you going to finish your hot chocolate?"

April shrugged and led Oscar out. The whole way out of the café and down the street, she did not let go of his hand.

APRIL EDGED TOWARD JULIAN'S FRONT DOOR FULL OF trepidation, taking each unsure step one at a time. Oscar remained by her side, her hand in his, holding tightly. She didn't know whether it was for reassurance or closeness, but she was happy to have Oscar nearby.

She let go as they approached the door, fearing that implications of romantic involvement with Oscar may just push Julian further over the edge. She wondered why she was so worried about Julian's reaction to the possibility of her being romantically involved with Oscar, but pushed the thought aside as she knocked four audible, clear knocks upon the door.

Nothing.

She glanced at Oscar, who looked equally as unnerved as she did. She awaited an answer, a queasy feeling churning in the pit of her stomach.

She put her ear to the door. Listened.

Movement. There was movement. She was sure of it.

Scurrying, maybe; a persistent, vigorous scuffle.

She pressed down on the door handle and the door creaked

open into the flat. It both surprised her and scared her to find it open.

"He never leaves his door unlocked," she whispered to Oscar, growing increasingly cautious.

She entered, followed by Oscar, and instantly halted. Her jaw dropped at what she saw. Her hands covered her mouth to quell a distinct gasp.

"Oh, dear God," she whispered.

Julian was on his hands and knees, wearing nothing but stained pyjama trousers, fervently scrubbing the walls with a dirty sponge and a filthy tub of water. Smeared across the wall was a large red smudge, dripping downwards.

Her first thoughts were that the red smeared across the wall was blood, but as she apprehensively edged forward, it became clear that it was ink. Julian barely acknowledged her, continuously scrubbing, only to make the ink more and more smudged.

"Julian?" she spoke, quieter than she'd intended, still stuck in a mixture of shock and worry.

"Got to scrub it off," Julian muttered. "Got to keep scrubbing, can't talk."

"Julian?"

"Scrubbing. Anna. Got to – got to scrub."

"Julian, what are you on?" April asked, this time with a lot more force.

Julian shook his head with a few uneven shakes, his arms nervously quivering. His head continued to shake with a stuttering vibration as he persistently and aggressively scoured the wall.

"Julian, please stop!" April pleaded, trying to force a confidence to her voice, but finding it quivering with nothing but shaken anxiety.

"Can't stop…" Julian whispered.

In a spurt of frustration, April stepped forward and

grabbed onto Julian's wrists, holding him still and looking him in the eyes.

The man who looked back faintly resembled Julian. His eyes were wide, bloodshot, above pronounced grey bags. They were Julian's eyes, but like she had never seen before – they were like a startled, famished creature who had no idea what was happening.

"Julian, what are you doing?"

He shook his hands, trying to release them from her grasp, but she held on more tightly.

"Julian, I'm really worried," she persisted, tears appearing in the corners of her eyes. "Please, please tell me what is happening."

"April…" he whispered, putting a pinch of hope in her mind as he recognised her. His eyes remained wide, as if in a state of permanent perplexity. "You need to go."

"Julian, please, would you–"

"Get off me!" he screamed in her face and shoved her away.

Oscar quickly intervened to catch her as she fell. She remained on the floor in his arms, watching Julian in disbelief.

He'd pushed her.

He actually pushed me…

Julian continued scrubbing, undeterred.

"Anna. Got to… Scrub. Anna. Scrub."

He didn't even register what he had done.

"Julian, what – please, tell me what to do."

"I'm fine!" he barked.

"Julian, please…"

Julian rose to his feet and turned around with a menacing glare, jabbing his finger antagonistically toward April.

"Go!" he demanded with unsettling force in his furiously shaking voice. "I got to – I got to do this – you go!"

"Let me help–"

"*Now!*"

He turned back to the wall, unsuccessfully washing away the red stains that would not fade. He scrubbed, and scrubbed, and scrubbed. Repetitively scouring at the wall with vigorous swipes, having no success of being rid of the red, but relentlessly persisting nonetheless.

"Come on, April," Oscar's soft voice spoke into her ear. "We need to go."

"I can't..." April muttered, her eyes fixed on her dearest friend in his catatonic, demented state.

"We aren't needed here," Oscar told her.

He kept his arms around her as he helped her to her feet and, with her eyes remaining on Julian, he guided her out of the flat.

Julian didn't even notice.

He barely even blinked.

OSCAR WATCHED APRIL CAREFULLY THROUGHOUT THE SOLEMN walk home, desperately wishing he could think of the right words to say.

What could you say?

Oscar already knew that he was socially awkward and rarely said the right thing at the right time, and was very much aware that whatever came out of his mouth would likely do more harm than good.

So he remained quiet, just trying to be there for her. He plucked up the courage to put an arm around her, and she not only allowed it, but rested her head in the curve of his shoulder. He pulled her closer and they walked home in comfortable silence, both relishing the closeness.

Eventually, they arrived at April's front door.

"I don't suppose you want me to come in?" he asked.

"Not today," she replied, fiddling with her keys, staring at the ground.

"I figured. Probably not the best time..." his voice drifted off into a mumble as he shifted his weight from leg to leg, unsure why he was delaying leaving.

"Thank you," she sombrely spoke.

"For what?"

"For being there for me today. You're a good friend."

A friend.

Right.

That's all he was. A good friend.

Stop it, this isn't about me. I just need to be there for her right now, it isn't the right time.

With a sad but heart-meltingly sweet smile, she leant forward and placed a delicate kiss on his cheek. Before he could respond or react, she had opened the door, said good-bye, and locked it behind her.

He stood there, staring at the door, not wanting to leave but knowing that he must.

"You're welcome, April," he spoke irritably to himself. "You're welcome, and you are oh, so perfect, and I am such a loser. I..."

She couldn't hear him. Why not now?

"I adore you. I'm crazy about you. I think you're the best person I've ever met. You make me tingle, make me nervous, and I..."

He bowed his head.

Let out a large breath of frustration.

"And I'm a loser who can't even tell you the truth about how I feel."

He turned, folded his arms, and trod heavily away. He looked over his shoulder as he left and saw April watching him from between the curtains in the front window.

He paused.

Looked at her.

She looked back.

Time to grow up.

He broke eye contact and trudged away.

Grey clouds travelled overhead and a fine rain began to

pour. Oscar let it. Allowed it to soak him from head to toe with its heavy droplets.

Julian.

What does she see in him?

He's good at what he does, but Oscar had never seen the guy crack a joke, or even smile. From day one he had been the thorn in Oscar's side, spoiling everything.

Maybe it was time Oscar gave him a piece of his mind.

If something is going on, get a grip. Get medication, get therapy, get a lobotomy if it helps – but stop April from feeling like utter shit because of it.

Yes.

That's what I'll do.

In that moment, he decided – he would confront Julian. Return to his flat and see what he could do to talk some sense into him.

Either he could help him, or tell him to get a grip and stop hurting those who care about him.

Man to man.

Or quivering boy to having-a-mental-breakdown-man.

Either way, this couldn't continue.

THEN

28

THE STREETS WERE A COLD PLACE, EVEN IN WINTER. WHEN
night set in, April was repeatedly forced to huddle in that
doorway, wrapping her arms around herself, cuddling her
body for warmth. The more she rubbed her hands up and
down her chest, the more it became bearable.

Not that it was, in any way, the least bit bearable.

But there were two options. The streets, or her mum's
house.

She knew which one she'd prefer.

Not that she wasn't tempted. Nights of being abused by
drunks, urinated on by drug addicts, and propositioned for
prostitution by perverts who thought she was that desperate –
those were the nights she thought about how warm the room
back at her mum's house was.

But that room had probably been the only warmth in that
house.

They had probably turned it into a home gym by now. Or,
in all likelihood, a bar, with shelves of spirits and fridges of
beer they could use to get themselves nicely drunk and aptly
abusive.

She leant her head back and closed her eyes. Tried to sleep. She never slept properly, not on the streets – you always had to be ready and alert. Some scumbag may come to rob you or touch you up, and you had to be ready to react, however tired you may be.

"April," came a voice nearby.

She promptly turned her head to find a large figure silhouetted by the lamppost behind it, standing over her.

This person knew her name.

Oh, God, was it her mum? Was it her mum's boyfriend? Had they found her?

"April, it's okay," the voice repeated. It wasn't a voice she recognised. It was well spoken, like the lead in a romantic comedy.

She didn't know anyone who spoke like that.

"How do you know my name?" she demanded.

The figure crouched beside her. As his face came into view, it surprised her how young this man looked. He couldn't be any more than late twenties. He was clean-shaven, with dark-blond hair swept to the side, and wearing smart trousers with a shirt and an open collar.

"Because I've seen you," he answered with an air of obtrusive charm about his voice.

"How have you seen me? You been following me?"

"No, no," he chuckled. "I've never met you before tonight. I meant that I've seen you in my mind."

Oh great, another drug addict.

She clenched her fists, ready to defend herself.

"Back off, arsehole, before I break your jaw," she threatened.

"Whoa, April, I'm not here to hurt you," he insisted. "Quite the opposite. My name is Julian."

Julian?

Was this some toffy private school boy come to taunt her?

Well, she was having none of it.

"Fuck off, Julian. I mean it."

"I have a gift," he told her, ignoring her protests. "A special gift. A gift that means I can sense other people like me. They are called Sensitives. That's what you are, April. You are a Sensitive."

What was this guy on?

"I don't know what you want from me, mate – but you ain't getting it!"

"Tell me, April, have you ever seen something you knew was there but couldn't be? Have you ever made something happen that you couldn't make happen, yet still did? Have you had a feeling that something was with you, but something you couldn't explain in words?"

She paused, peering at him, curiously cautious. Every word he said made sense, and she knew exactly what he was talking about. But it was too close, too bizarrely accurate. How could he know about these things?

"I know because I am the same," he told her, immediately answering her thoughts. "And this isn't a curse you've been given. Quite the opposite, in fact. And I'm here to show you how to use it, how to harness it."

Could she harness it?

All these things she saw, she did, she felt – he could teach her to use it?

To give it a purpose?

"Who are you?" she asked, her layer of thick skin thinning.

"Like I said, my name is Julian, and I am a Sensitive, like you, ready to show you the way."

He stood and held out his hand.

"What do you say, April? Want to come with me? Want to find out what you can do?" He looked over his shoulder, and up and down the street. "Or do you want to stay here, eating scraps and sleeping with one eye open every night?"

She took his hand.

She knew exactly which option she wanted.

NOW

29

Derek sat on the edge of the bed, surveying the medical room with curiosity. It was, without a doubt, the most cheerful room of the prison, with charts and posters about the human body decorating its light-blue walls.

Jane, the prison's doctor, sat before him, nursing his leg in her delicate hands. She was in her early thirties, with long, blond hair, and a smile that was always eager to welcome him. She was also the only person he'd found within the prison that could engage him in intellectual conversation, and visiting her had often been a welcome relief, despite it being for his deteriorating health.

"Just stretch it for me," she instructed him. He attempted to follow her instructions but winced at the pain before he could fully straighten his knee.

"That's okay," she reassured him, allowing him to move his leg back as she made a few notes on a pad. "Lift up your shirt for me."

She placed the end of her stethoscope against Derek's chest, prompting him to flinch from the cold of the metal against his skin.

"Been reading much more Hawkins recently?" she asked.

"Just finished *The Grand Design*. Found it fascinating."

"Really?"

She paused as she listened through her stethoscope, as though stopping at a moment of concern. She placed it back around her neck before making a few more notes.

"What's the matter, Doctor?" Derek inquired. "You don't look happy."

"I'm concerned, Derek, if I'm to be honest with you."

"Why?"

She hesitated, fiddling with the pen in her mouth, brushing her long, blond hair back over her shoulder. Derek wondered how tough it must be being an attractive woman working in a prison, and that she must get many taunts and comments from the more hormonal convicts. She seemed a strong person, and if it deterred her, you couldn't tell.

"Your heart rate is down, your blood pressure is down, and you can't straighten your leg."

"Is that bad?"

"Well, you could straighten it a few weeks ago. And if I was to put your heart rate over the past few months into a graph, it would have a negative correlation."

"Oh."

She sighed. Derek watched her as she puzzled something through her mind, her thoughts entwining as she struggled to verbalise the sad repercussions of Derek's deteriorating health.

"Just tell me straight," Derek requested. "Just be honest with me."

"Okay, Derek." She nodded and turned to him, forcing a sad, sympathetic smile. "You aren't in a good way. And I think you know that. And I think you know why."

Derek's eyes dropped.

At this rate, he would never see the outside of the prison again.

At this rate, those prison walls would be the last thing he saw.

"I understand."

"I'm going to see you again in a few days, I think, maybe prepare a few tests, see where we can go from here. Get you some treatment. Okay?"

"Thank you, Doctor."

"Take care of yourself, Derek."

Derek stood, resting his weight on his good leg, reaching for his walking stick. He used it to hobble forward, taking far longer to reach the door to the doctor's office than he had done a month, or even a week ago.

He placed a hand on the door handle and turned it.

It wouldn't turn.

He tried again, forcing his feeble strength against it. It must be locked.

"The door's locked," Derek announced, and turned back to the room.

Jane was gone.

She wasn't there.

In fact, no one was there.

"What's with the–"

There was nothing.

Not even equipment. The room was empty.

What on earth...

He tried the door again. It wouldn't open. It was definitely locked.

He turned back to the empty room.

There was no bed, no equipment, no Jane. It was empty, as if it was a vacant storage room, absent of life.

Derek couldn't understand it. He frantically shook his head, his arms shaking in fear.

Had he just imagined it?

Had he just hallucinated the entire events of the last ten

minutes?

It wasn't possible.

It wasn't.

It...

"Jane?" Derek whispered.

An eerie wind brushed against him, stinking of rotten meat.

He turned and pushed down on the door handle with all his force. It opened, forcing him to barge through.

As he steadied himself, he looked up. He filled with dread. Shaking, as he cast his eyes over the stern, hostile face of the prison governor.

"What are you doing?" Kullins demanded.

"The door was locked. Thank you for opening it."

"What are you on about, you fool? There is no lock."

Derek's eyes shot to the door handle.

There was no place for a key. No latch. Nothing.

How could that be?

What is happening?

The governor stepped into Derek's personal space, looming over him with a severe advantage in build and height, narrowing his eyes into a menacing glare.

"Are we going to have a problem?" the governor asked in a slow, hushed voice.

"No, sir," Derek answered, his lip trembling, his weak bones shaking, his feeble knees battering against each other.

"Get back to your cell."

"Yes, sir."

Derek turned as swiftly as his frail body would allow and stumbled forward, shuffling as quickly as he could, but nowhere near as quick as he once was.

He did not look back; but for the entirety of his long walk back to A Wing, he could still feel the governor's dirty breath breathing down his collar.

30

Oscar charged up the path to the door of Julian's flat, full of fury, full of all the words he planned to hurl Julian's way.

How dare he upset April like this!

You need to get a grip!

What do you think you are doing?

Each of those words fell away once he actually placed his hand on the handle and realised it was time to say them all.

It was Julian. He was like an older brother who bullied you, yet you still craved his approval. Oscar hovered, feeling a wave of nerves overcome him, nearly succumbing to the cowardice he had become most acquainted with.

Come on, man. For once in your life, just... have some guts!

Willing himself on, he leant on the door and barged into the flat.

"Julian, I don't know what you think you are doing–"

Julian wasn't there.

Oscar scanned the room, searching for him.

The ink still covered the wall in a light-red coating, like a thin layer of watercolour paint.

But Julian...

Oscar stepped forward, looking in the bedroom, the kitchen, then, as he stepped into the living room, he tripped over something heavy, sprawled across the floor.

Julian was laid flat out on his back, his eyes open, staring wide-eyed with a fixed gaze upon the ceiling above.

"Julian?" Oscar asked, surprised by Julian's catatonic state.

Julian didn't reply. His eyes rigidly open. His mouth agape.

His face not showing a flinch of reaction.

"Julian, come on, we're getting sick of this, man."

Julian still didn't reply.

He just stared at the nothingness floating above him. Alert, wide eyes, fixed upon a stationary head upon a solidly immobile body. He was like a plank, stiff and unmoving, laid stubbornly on the floorboards.

"Julian, I think it's time—"

Julian muttered something. Something so quiet Oscar couldn't make it out. Julian's lips only budged a fraction, as the rest of his body remained immobile.

"Julian—"

"She never leaves..." Julian uttered once more.

"Who, Julian?" Oscar asked. "Who never leaves?"

"She's here... She's always here..."

Oscar knelt beside Julian. His anger had been replaced by pity. He was unsure whether to tell him to get a grip, or to get him help.

"Who, Julian? What's going on?"

"Anna..."

Anna?

She was the girl who died... The one in Julian's first exorcism...

Is that what this was all about?

"Anna's dead, Julian," Oscar told him, then instantly regretted being so direct.

"That doesn't stop her..." Julian spoke in another quiet utterance.

"Doesn't stop her what, Julian? What is she doing?"

Julian's head finally moved, but Oscar wished that it hadn't. It rotated so slowly and so sinisterly toward him that it sent chills firing up his body. Julian's chilling gaze was no longer pointed at the ceiling, but at Oscar's terrified eyes.

"She's torturing me... She won't let me go..."

"Won't let you go?"

"It has Derek, too..."

Derek? How does it have Derek? Derek was in prison. Surely if there was a haunting in prison, then Derek would know?

Unless that's what Julian and Derek had spoken about in the prison after Julian had requested a solitary audience with Derek's company.

"Julian, you need to let me understand–"

Oscar placed his hand on Julian's shoulder.

Like a bolt of lightning, he was taken off his feet and hurled across the room. He smacked into the far wall, hitting his head.

Flashes. Glimpses. They battered against his vision like blinding, white light.

He had no time to rub or nurse his injury. A devastating vision abruptly preoccupied his mind.

It felt as if his brain was pounding against his skull. A migraine overtook him, as a sense of clarity descended upon him in a deafeningly apparent glimpse.

The prison.

Gloucester Prison. Derek's home.

Crumbling.

Empty.

Vacant for years.

No one was there.

The walls were empty.

The car park was empty.

The vacant visitor's room, the solemn cells within, the corridors leading to the cells.

It was empty.

The entire prison was...

How was it empty?

Oscar looked to Julian, who remained on the floor.

Touching him had given Oscar a glimpse.

The mask had fallen.

The prison.

It was...

"Oh, shit," he gasped.

Derek was in terrible danger.

OSCAR URGED THE TAXI DRIVER TO GO FASTER AS HE SCROLLED to April's number in his phone's address book.

She had implied that he shouldn't contact her, that she wished to be left alone. But that didn't matter now. He needed to talk to her with a severe urgency, and this taxi driver was tediously sticking to the speed limits.

He put the phone to his ear, listening to the ring, waiting for her to pick up.

"Hi, this is April, I can't answer the phone right now but–"

"Damn it, April."

Oscar hung up, then selected her name once more, placing the phone to his ear.

It rang and rang and rang and rang until eventually…

"Hi, this is April, I can't answer the–"

"Christ's sake, come on!" Oscar growled, unable to avoid his frustration from pouring out.

He selected her name once more. He knew she was there. If he just kept persisting and persisting, eventually she would get fed up and answer.

Surely.

"Hi?" came an irritated voice.

"April, thank God!"

"Oscar, I thought I told you I wanted to be left alone."

"Yes, I know, but – just listen, April!"

"Oscar, now's not the time."

"Would you just listen for fuck's sake!"

The line remained silent as Oscar huffed, surprising himself with his dramatic outburst.

"I had a glimpse. The prison we went to, it had a block on it, I couldn't see it. Then I touched Julian and it's the same thing that's haunting the prison that's haunting him, so that meant the block dropped, then I could see it, I could see it, April, in its true form."

"What are you on about, Oscar? See what in its true form?"

"The prison!"

Oscar realised he was stumbling over his words, being unclear, but he couldn't help it. His desperate concern was becoming stronger and stronger, growing more and more pertinent, filling his mind with terror.

"What about the prison?"

"April, I had a vision that it was empty, that it was crumbling down."

"That it was empty?"

"Yes. Then I looked it up. I looked the prison up on my phone, April."

"And what? What happened?"

Oscar ran his hand over his head, through his hair, trying to find the words, trying to force a coherent sentence to his lips.

"I looked it up, and I looked up its history, and I saw, April, I saw…"

"Saw what, Oscar?"

He knew she was getting frustrated.

He tried to calm himself down. Tried to force himself to see sense, to avoid the nonsensical ramblings.

"The prison, April – it shut in 2013. It was open, then it shut in 2013."

"What do you mean it shut in 2013?"

"April, it hasn't been a prison for four years. It's closed."

THEN

3 2

DEREK'S WRISTS BURNT. HE'D NEVER THOUGHT ABOUT HOW painful handcuffs would be.

He'd never really given thought to this experience whatsoever, if he was being honest with himself.

It was so surreal.

It felt as if it didn't exist. As if the police van he sat in the back of wasn't real. As if the voices of the police talking in the front were in a distant dream.

He knew that he would have to face his reality soon enough.

Because within an hour, he would be in a prison cell. Alone. In uniform. Staring at a bed and toilet in a cell smaller than a child's bedroom. With nothing but him and his guilt to fill the walls around him.

Prison. That's where they said he was being taken.

Prison.

It was actually happening.

Just as the thought entered his mind, the police van stopped.

Then... nothing.

Nothing happened.

The voices of the officers were no longer there. In fact, he could no longer see their shadows against the blackened glass that separated him from them. He wished he had a window he could peer out of; that he could use to gain some clarity over what was happening, but he had to settle for patience.

Eventually, the answers would reveal themselves.

He was left to his thoughts. Left with frantic worries spinning around and around.

What if he was attacked?

What if a prisoner took offence to him?

What if...

No.

He bowed his head and allowed the truth to settle over him.

I deserve to be here.

A girl died in his presence. Because he couldn't save her. Because he didn't do enough.

He was getting off lightly.

Her young, sweet face implanted itself in the forefront of his thoughts. He closed his eyes and allowed his troubled mind to dwell on her delicate eyes. He saw her not as she was when she died, or when she had a demon pounding against the inside of her flesh. No, he saw her in the early days of possession. When she still had her young, beautiful, smiling face. When she beamed up at him. When she greeted him with thorough politeness, eager to interact, eager to allow him into her family's home. Eager to show him around, to show him her favourite toy, her favourite song, her favourite...

No.

He was getting off lightly.

A girl was dead.

And it was his fault.

"Derek."

His eyes shot open.

His head spun around. Scanned the van.

He was alone.

His sight contested as much.

But his other senses…

The reek of rotting meat hit him with sudden impact.

He knew what that meant.

It was a smell he had grown familiar with when fighting the demonic.

"Derek," the voice boomed out once more.

"What?" Derek snarled.

"This is what God gives you now."

He frowned. He was not fooled.

"You are no God," Derek defied.

"And where is he?"

Derek did not respond. He knew better than to communicate with something attempting to enter his mind, something attempting to poison his thoughts.

"You killed her."

He ignored it.

It was right, but he ignored it.

"You may as well have put a knife to her throat and cut it yourself."

He held back tears.

He would not let it enter his head.

He would not.

He could not.

"You could have torn her scrawny face from her meek body."

"Stop it."

He grew angry with himself for responding.

"You may as well have punched yourself up her cunt like I did."

"Shut up!"

He bowed his head. Scrunched up his eyes.

He could not let it enter his head.

Because then it would involve him in whatever it wished to do.

He was guilty. He felt guilty. But the power of that guilt...

It wanted to play on his—

He closed his head, scrunched up his eyes, did all he could to block it out.

"You may as well have eaten her from the inside like I did."

"Go away!" he cried out.

Years of serving, of being an expert, of telling others to ignore the taunts, and he could not follow his own advice.

Because it was right.

He could not accept it, but it was.

He may as well have just killed her himself.

"Yes. That's it. That's right."

It was his fault.

"That's right, it is your fault."

And he had to pay.

"And you will. You will not only pay for her death, but for the hundreds of demons you have defeated, for all the times you have fought me. You will suffer."

"No!"

The backdoors to the van swung open.

And he forgot everything. Everything he had learnt about fighting the demonic. Everything he had taught others.

He couldn't think. It felt like fingers digging into his skull, taking over his mind until he couldn't think of anything but the pain.

Reality slipped away.

His mind was going elsewhere.

Somewhere else. Somewhere he would not be able to fight.

Something put a block on his mind. Stopped him from resisting. Stopped him from fighting

And he let it.

Let it wash over him.

He fell still. Silent. Submissive.

It entered him. Entered his mind like a poisonous gas penetrating his nostrils, his ears, his mouth.

It consumed him. Took to every part of his lungs, his cells, his thoughts – until it was as much a part of his veins as his blood.

A man stood in front of Derek, a cloud of smoke settling behind him. His menacing glare fixed intently on Derek's eyes.

Derek fell to the floor, cowering, his mind racked with guilt.

"My name is Kullins," the man told him – a sick, wide grin spreading across his pale face. "And it's time to come home."

NOW

33

Derek stood cautiously on the wing, looking back and forth, back and forth.

Some prisoners were playing cards around a table, and further down the corridors, some were playing pool. He noticed a group of prisoners picking on a younger, timid inmate, surrounding their victim and bullying him into submission.

To Derek's far right was the prison officer on duty.

Doing nothing about the poor lad being bullied.

As always.

Normally, this would concern Derek. He feared what would happen if another prisoner chose to kick out his cane and show him who's boss. He tended to keep himself to himself, and that had served him well so far, but there was only so much he could do until they chose to turn their ill treatment toward him.

But today this was a relief, as Derek did not want to be noticed. And if the prison officer was not distracted by a group of thugs surrounding and pounding on an intimidated youngster, he would be unlikely to notice what Derek was doing.

He stepped back into his cell, looking around himself cautiously, remaining unnoticed.

The haunting had been stepping up its attacks more recently; that was clear.

It meant Derek had to step up his defence.

He withdrew a few pieces of wood from beneath his bed, retreating to the corner of his cell and turning his back to the door so the items were shielded from any prying eyes passing by.

Getting a few loose pieces of wood hadn't been easy. It was bizarre, really, how if he claimed he smoked, they would hand him a lighter, or if he wanted a coffee, he would be allowed a kettle. But items such as wooden blocks that would not set alight an officer or burn another prisoner with boiling water were deemed as a banned, offensive weapon.

Maybe it's because there was no context as to why someone would want wood within a prison, therefore, it could only be used as a weapon.

Well, I am using it as a damn weapon.

Just not the same kind of weapons other prisoners may wield...

He pulled out a large piece of frayed rope, well used and worn down from parcels and transporting various items, but the best he could get.

And it would do.

It hadn't taken much to fool the corrupt system within these walls. A few packets of cigarettes to the right inmate on C Wing and he had the items he desired.

In all honesty, the prison officers likely turned away and pretended they didn't know. After all, if they came into a wing and decided to notice, it would be more trouble than it was worth. If they decided to stand up to a prisoner, they were vastly outnumbered.

He held out the two small planks of wood. The corners

were sharp, and splinters poked off the wooden slabs like a porcupine's back, but it would do.

A few small cuts from a few splinters was nothing compared to the obtrusive aggression a malevolent force could wager against him.

He laid the longer plank on the floor and placed the smaller plank sideways a third of the way down.

It made a rustic, rough, homemade cross.

He had no holy water. No rosary beads. No Bible, no prayer book, nothing else he could use to perform an exorcism or a cleansing. But he would rather be with this makeshift weapon than be left defenceless against the violent paranormal elements he could feel roaming the prison wings.

He wrapped the rope around the two shards of wood, placing it diagonally one way, then the other, then around a few more times, tightening it repeatedly until the two pieces of wood were fixed in place.

After wrapping numerous circles at various angles, he checked the security of the cross, ensuring that the two pieces of wood were firmly fastened.

They didn't budge.

He finished the cross with a final knot.

This was it.

No turning back.

This night, once everyone was asleep, once darkness had descended on these dirty, worn-out walls, he would put up his fight.

He would exorcise these demons from this prison.

He just had to put the cross somewhere.

Suddenly, it struck him.

Something had happened.

The wing. It had fallen into a dead silence.

The general ambience of prisoners talking and interacting had ceased. An uncomfortable hush had descended.

Eerie absence floated into Derek's cell. There was no idle chatter, no competitive gloats of inmates winning at cards, no leers from intimidating, aggressive bullies. Never had silent thugs made him more worried.

A few heavy footsteps grew closer, then ceased.

Derek slowly turned over his shoulder.

The dark, shadow-encased face of the prison governor stood in the doorway of his cell, his narrow-eyed glare intensifying into a brutal grimace.

"What have you got there?" Kullins asked.

34

Oscar's and April's eyes flickered with disbelief as they stared dumbfounded at the computer screen.

"We really need Julian for this," Oscar regretfully admitted.

"Julian is not of any help to us," April hesitantly responded. "For now, we are on our own."

"I just – I can't…" Oscar ran his hands through his hair, searching for the words. "We can't do this on our own."

"We either do it on our own, or Derek…" April trailed off.

"Derek is a powerful exorcist; surely he can manage."

"Did you see the state of him?" April closed her eyes and shook her head, wishing she could think of a better solution. "Besides, Derek has no idea how big this thing is. He probably thinks it's just a small haunting, not… a total mirage. Whatever it is has taken him over completely. He is as good as possessed."

April stood, pacing the room, racking her thoughts for a solution that was logical and unlikely to put either of them in fatal danger. Unfortunately, such ideas were not forthcoming.

Oscar sat at the computer, taking over the research, re-looking over what they had found. He willed the words he had already read numerous times to somehow change. Maybe, if he looked again, with his own eyes, his full attention on the screen, he would find that the words said something else.

He was kidding himself.

"Do you know which cell he's in?" Oscar asked.

"No, why?"

"Can you find out?"

April paused for a moment, searching the room, looking for something that would indicate Derek's cell number. There was paper work Julian had left on the side so she started sifting through it, finding a few pages with the prison's watermark on.

Reading back the opening paragraph, Oscar read what it had told them about the history of the prison.

PARANORMAL RESEARCHERS HAD FOUND *multiple occurrences of supernatural phenomena in A Wing, Cell 25. The spirit of a girl called Elizabeth, murdered in the fifteenth century on the land where the prison was later built, has been seen by prisoners and guards throughout the prison's open years. One prisoner claimed to see Elizabeth's disembodied hand pointing at him.*

"I'VE GOT IT," April exclaimed.

It can't be. It can't be. It can't be.

"What is it?" Oscar hesitantly asked.

"He's on A Wing, in Cell 25."

Shit.

"Of course he bloody is."

Oscar continued to scroll downwards, reading about an infamous prison governor who had owned the prison in the late 1800s. The man had executed over a hundred prisoners and buried them in unmarked graves. What's more, this governor was thought to have possessed another prison governor in the 1990s.

"Have you read this about the governor?" Oscar asked.

"No, what does it say?"

"It says that a governor, named Jackson Kullins, marched over a hundred prisoners to the gallows and watched them being executed. Apparently, another prison governor in the 1990s marched numerous prisoners there for petty misbehaviour and tried to hang them, just as Kullins had done before. He was stopped at the last minute, at which point he couldn't remember what he had done. April, if this prison governor is still there…"

"What's the governor's name again?" April asked, lifting an old letter from Derek that she found to have mention of the prison governor.

"His name was Jackson Kullins," Oscar read.

April dropped the letter.

Oscar didn't need to ask her why.

He stood, unable to sit anymore, anxious energy in his legs forcing him to pace.

"But why?" Oscar mused. "Why would Derek allow this thing to take him?"

April sank into deep thought, then turned to Oscar with an abrupt click of her fingers.

"Guilt!"

"What?"

"The block on you dropped when you touched Julian, right?"

"Yes, but I don't get what that—"

"Don't you see? Derek was there when Anna died. His guilt… Entities thrive on negative energy. Derek must feel so bad that it's powering an entire prison!"

Oscar shook his head, at first in disbelief, then in vigorous denial.

"How the hell are we supposed to do this?" he asked, a pained expression entwining his face. "This isn't an entity. This is something powerful enough to create a whole prison full of apparitions. I can't do this. I can't even get a sodding incantation right!"

"We don't have a choice," April told him.

"This is too big an obstacle–"

April stepped forward, ceasing Oscar's nervous pacing by placing her hands on the side of his face. She brought his head in close to hers and leant her forehead against his. She was so close he could feel her breath against him. His lips were almost touching hers.

Almost.

"A good man once said," she told him, "that the biggest obstacle you have to overcome is yourself."

"Who said that?"

April smiled. Once they had gathered their things, she took his hand, and together they left.

35

Kullins's hardened eyes glared upon Derek with a sickening intensity. He seemed to be forever in shadow, walking around with lengthy, effortless strides, looming over his victims whatever their size. His face looked incapable of smiling. His presence alone filled a room with a negative ambience that sent fear trickling down your forehead in drops of desperate perspiration.

"Er…" Derek stuttered.

"I said," the governor repeated with a slow, quiet intensity that allowed him to pronounce each and every syllable, "what have you got there?"

Derek looked down upon the wooden cross he had so slickly fashioned moments ago. It had offered him a feeling of salvation. Now he held it in his quivering hands with an immediate feeling of dread.

"It's…" Derek thought about what excuses he could give, but found none presenting themselves. "It's a cross. It gives me comfort. It–"

Derek's voice cut off as soon as the governor took a large

stride into the cell, encompassing Derek in his shadow as he peered at the item.

"It looks like a weapon."

"It – it's not, I swear, it's just a crucifix. It gives me comfort. I needed one."

The governor held out his large hand with his thick fingers protruding from his dirty palm.

Derek didn't hesitate, understanding what this meant, handing over the cross, his hands shaking so vigorously they made the cross bounce from side to side.

The governor took the supposed weapon, scrutinising it with his eyes. He ran a finger over it, feeling the edge of the splinters without a wince of pain. He glanced at Derek, his fleeting stare indicating that the splinters were not holding Derek in good stead. Kullins's hand continued to trace the edge until they reached the end of the cross, and felt the large spike.

"Are you telling me," he directed at Derek, "that this sharp point could not do someone damage?"

"I suppose it could, but–"

"So you are about to tell me that you were not intending to use it to attack another prisoner, an officer, or even me, the governor himself?"

"No! Not at all! I swear, I never meant anyone any harm!"

The governor lowered himself to Derek's level with an unhurried, measured descent, and gave him a deadly, prolonged glare.

"Do you think I'm a fool?" he asked, in such a husky whisper only Derek could have heard him.

"No. No, I don't."

The governor nodded, as if deciding something in his mind, a dreaded conclusion being drawn without any other choice.

He stood, turned to the prison officers standing obediently

behind him, and gave a nod. They entered the cell, grabbed Derek by his arms, and dragged him out.

"What? Where am I going?" Derek desperately asked.

He tried thrashing, struggling, but it did nothing. His leg wouldn't lift without pain, and his muscles were far too decrepit for him to muster the energy required.

"You have made a big mistake," the governor told Derek, then turned to the officers. "This way."

"What?" Derek panicked, overcome with fear and dread.

Where were they taking him?

The gallows?

Surely not.

They wouldn't be allowed to hang him for this. He had human rights. This was 2017; you couldn't treat people like this, not anymore. Executions hadn't been done in this country for a long, long time. Even if they had, Kullins couldn't legally execute him for forging a weapon.

It was not possible.

Yet there he was, being dragged through the wing, watched helplessly by the passing, solemn faces of the other prisoners, all lined up outside their cells.

The governor was one man. There were easily seventy prisoners on that wing. Why weren't they doing anything?

The governor told the prisoners to line up and they did it. This was just one man. One man whom, if they worked as a unit, they could all easily overthrow.

But they didn't. The remained static. Terrified.

How did one man create so much fear?

This didn't make sense.

None of this made sense.

What was going on? Was this something playing a trick? A mirage? A hallucination? The onset of psychosis? Or maybe all these people were possessed?

No. Derek had never known such a thing to happen. Even

when fighting in the harshest war known to man, he had never encountered a mass possession before.

So what, then?

What was happening?

The prisoners' regretful faces faded from view as he was dragged through the corridor, forced to watch the crumbling ceilings pass.

It was strange... The prison had been in such great shape. Not perfect, but liveable. And now...

Now it was crumbling. Peeling. Falling to pieces.

The paint was cracking, dropping from the walls. The cell bars were growing rust, the ceiling plaster falling apart.

What is going on?

He found himself dragged into the courtyard, feeling the harsh bumps of the pavement digging into the back of his legs as he was pulled across the rough ground, forcing him to cry out in anguish.

The officers dumped him onto the dry gravel.

Derek looked up and saw the executioner preparing a noose in the exact place he had seen a man hang only days ago.

ONCE AGAIN, APRIL MANAGED TO FRIGHTEN OSCAR WITH WHAT she claimed were 'impeccable' driving skills. She swung around every corner, sped through every traffic light, and overtook every car she could.

Oscar's hands gripped the side of his seat until they hurt.

"Jesus, April, let's try and be alive when we get there."

Eventually, they reached the country roads that occupied the final bulk of the journey. Oscar could see the concentration on April's face. She was intently focused as she swung around the corners, ensuring they reached the prison in one piece and in record time.

When she finally reached the prison car park, Oscar's jaw dropped.

He opened the door and edged out, taking small steps toward the prison, looking upon it with amazement.

This was nothing like the prison he had previously been to. It was the same prison. But it was...

"What?" April asked. "What is it you see?"

Oscar placed a hand on her shoulder. Being a conduit, she could then use his ability to glimpse in order to see the prison in its true form. And as the veil lifted, she too was stupefied to the spot, struck with astonishment.

The prison's sign that had once displayed itself proudly above its entrance with perfect, clean and clear lettering, was now a faded image. Its print was covered in moss, and its proud symbol speckled in mould of various shades of green and brown.

Trees leant at crooked angles, overhanging the car park. Leaves flaked from curving twigs, prickling out from corrupt, contorted roots. The ominously lavish spiralling of branches blocked out the late evening light, leaving the prison in darkness.

The thick stones that had made up the sturdy wall still stood, but were covered in blemishes and divots. Weeds entwined weeds, travelling up and around the space between the slabs. The windows had large, twisting cracks, and the path leading up to the prison was stained with tufts of overgrown grass.

"What the..." April gasped.

"How did we not see this before?"

"Oscar, for something to be able to do this... It has to be really powerful. I mean – Derek is stuck in a full spiritual realm, strong enough to create a whole delusion for both him and us as visitors."

Her lip trembled.

"And he has absolutely no idea..."

Oscar vaguely nodded, not a clue what to say. There was no verbal acknowledgement he could give that would display his anxiety at the task ahead.

"Oh my God..." April suddenly realised something. "But if this is being powered by both Derek *and* Julian's guilt, then..."

"What? What is it?"

"Julian... That's how it's this powerful..."

Oscar frowned, confused, unable to make sense of what she was saying.

"What is it, April?"

Her mouth widened even further. A sense of understanding overcame her, prompting her to shake with dread.

"Both Derek and Julian were there when Anna died. They were there when this started. They are both going to be there when it ends."

April's eyes dropped for a moment, then weakly rose to meet Oscar's.

He knew what she was about to say. And he really, truly, did not want her to say it.

"No, April, no," he refuted. "You can't."

"I have to."

"No..."

"We have to defeat it at both of them, at the same time – or it won't work."

Oscar shook his head intently. There was no way he could do this on his own. This prison was being overpowered by a presence with the ability to concoct an entire world and present it to Derek, not just in images, but by interacting with him. This was a savage, eager, powerful malevolent force.

And I'm just a shitty little boy.

"Please, April..."

April stepped forward, placing her hands once more on the side of Oscar's face, pulling him in close, meeting his eyes with hers, inches away.

Whilst the same rush of excitement filled him, he was also overcome with the hard-hitting feeling of dread.

"If this thing has Julian, then he's also in incredible danger. I have to help him."

"Then we'll do it afterwards! We'll free Derek, then he can help!"

"No, Oscar, you don't get it. This thing is haunting them

both. We need to fight it at both places, otherwise it will be no good. Otherwise, we don't stand a chance."

As Oscar realised there was nothing he could do to change her mind, he savoured the moment of closeness. He put his arms around her, holding her near. He could feel her body against his, could feel her arms beneath his soft touch. He wished he could never let her out of his embrace.

He was no longer just mortified for his own safety, but for hers too.

"You'll be fine, Oscar."

"But what happened before, when I forgot the–"

"What happened before was a temporary glitch. It happens. You are stronger and more powerful than you could possibly realise. Once you realise your full strength, these things will fear you."

"Well, I'd say that day is pretty far off because right now, I'm pissing my pants."

She giggled, forcing a mystified smile in return.

"By the way," April softly spoke. "The answer is yes."

"What do you mean?"

"Yes. I do feel the same way."

With that revelation, she pulled his forehead down and placed a soft, tender kiss upon it.

She wrenched herself away without looking back, ran back to the car, and sped out of the car park.

Oscar turned and looked upon the prison.

He felt sick.

"Right," he told himself. "Time to get it together."

Feeling a surge of forced self-confidence, he charged toward the door. As soon as he reached the threshold, a largely invisible force punched him in the gut with an unforgiving gust of wind, sending him flying backwards, landing on the harsh cement of the car park surface.

This was not going to be easy.

Derek's gut churned, rolling and entwining, an acidic feeling of nausea battling his stomach.

His eyes stuck open as he stared agape at the gallows being mounted and the noose being hung atop it. A man with a covered face – a cowardly man Derek knew was just a regular prison officer being forced into being an executioner – attached the rope securely to the wooden beam, ensuring it was fixed well enough that there was no possibility of it giving way.

So there was no way, should Derek's neck fail to snap, that he would not subsequently choke to death.

Derek looked around himself, searching for an escape, pleading for salvation.

He was trapped inside a large group of prison officers forming a perfect rectangle, creating an invisible box from which he could not escape. They stood in perfect symmetry and of equal distance to one another. Their hands were behind their backs and their heads were partially dropped, each of their faces echoing the same blank, solemn expression.

They were almost too unified. Too perfectly coordinated. Mirroring each other too flawlessly.

It was unnatural.

Derek leapt to his feet and attempted to run, but fell onto his front. An officer went to stop him, but found they needn't, as he lay pathetically upon the floor writhing in agony from his weak body and his rotting leg.

A mouthful of sick lurched up his throat, forcing him to spew blood and lumps over the crooked cement.

A few raindrops stuttered upon the ground, falling loosely, as if an omen of things to come.

He looked up from his place on the floor, watching as Kullins climbed the stairs of the gallows to check the strength of the noose.

The man lifted out an arm and placed a rough fist around the rope. With a sadistic smile he tested it, confirming its secure rigidity. There was no way that rope would break.

Kullins deliberately twisted until his eyes met Derek's, and he took a moment of vast, vile pleasure at Derek's helpless devastation.

Derek's mind was a mess of manic thoughts and helpless struggles. Hectic and fleeting thoughts of important moments in his life flashed before his eyes.

He was engaged once. To a woman who betrayed him; who saw his pursuit against the paranormal as a joke.

He had taken on a prodigy who fell to hell, and a prodigy who stood against him.

He taught students in a lecture theatre. University students willing to entertain the notion of demons and ghosts.

This was all for other people.

He never did anything that could help himself.

So this is what it's like to die...

Thoughts swirled around his head like locusts, his insecurities highlighting that he had done everything wrong. His final thoughts acting as a final attack of furious anxieties, telling him that redemption was something he would not be afforded.

The executioner descended the steps. His eyes peered through his mask, looking upon Derek's.

They weren't the eyes of a killer. They were the eyes of a man who was too afraid not to kill. A man petrified that he would be next, should he not carry out his orders.

Those were the eyes of weakness.

Derek attempted to drag himself away, to pull himself along the bumpy ground. The bumps of the cement ripped his trousers and cut his knees, leaving a trail of red across the damp surface.

The worst part of it all was that Derek knew these few yards he gained would do nothing. That thought was imprinted pertinently against the front of his mind, high-lighting his pathetically helpless state.

But he couldn't do nothing. He had to try, however feeble an attempt it may be.

He could have minutes left.

It depended on how merciful the governor would be.

Would he be asked to give his final words?

What would his final words be?

In abandoned desperation, he tried to think of something wise, something that would say "screw you" to the whole establishment.

But he came up with nothing. He knew that if he gave himself another hour, he would. It was something the French called l'esprit de l'escalier, literally translated as 'the wit of the staircase.' It was a phrase for those moments when you thought of something to say after the retort was relevant.

Such pathetic, unhelpful thoughts were appearing to him in a time of grave need.

What good was his useless knowledge to him now?

He could recite every exorcism prayer, conduct a successful séance, or banish an unclean spirit from your home.

But he could not save himself from being dragged across a prison courtyard to his death.

The executioner's hefty boots stood firmly before him, halting his useless attempt to escape.

Derek rolled onto his back and peered up at the cowardly eyes staring down at him.

"You don't want to do this, do you?" he asked.

The executioner's eye narrowed into a glare.

"You don't have to. You know it's wrong. You know you can say no."

The executioner bent over Derek and took the scruff of his collar in a small, scrawny fist.

"You'll shut the hell up if you know what's good for you," came the voice of a little man trying his best to sound tough.

Derek had no choice but to allow himself to be dragged helplessly across the courtyard, toward the gallows, watching his fate grow ever closer.

38

THIS WAS MORE THAN OSCAR HAD EVER BEEN PREPARED FOR.

But he wasn't just fighting for himself anymore.

Or Derek.

Or even Julian.

He remembered what April had said.

This thing was attacking both Julian and Derek. They needed to be rid of it at the prison, and at Julian's home. The entity needed to be defeated on all fronts.

Only, this meant the logical conclusion was that if Oscar couldn't defeat it...

Then April couldn't either.

Meaning that she would perish too.

She was relying on him.

He let those words sink in.

She is relying. On me.

For a fleeting moment, Oscar missed when his life was as simple as working at Morrison's, then going home, touching himself, and playing on the Xbox until he fell asleep.

That was the old Oscar. He was gone now.

It was time to be solid. To be confident. To be fierce.

No more forgetting silly incantations.

No more wussing out every time he went to tell April how he felt.

No more allowing Julian to speak to him like a petulant child.

It was time to stand strong. Stand sturdy. Stand tall.

Time to be firmly defiant in the face of evil.

Or something along those lines...

Oscar withdrew the crucifix from his pocket. He pointed it authoritatively toward the prison entrance. The entry point looked vacant, but something with the power to take him clean off his feet and into the air was strong, visible or not.

"Back off, unclean spirit!" Oscar screamed, feeling a tinge of embarrassment as his voice broke. He pushed any feelings of embarrassment to the back of his mind and persevered forward. "I demand you allow me passage into this prison!"

He edged closer and closer, holding his cross firmly, staring intently at the prison doors.

As he approached the door he felt a strong surge of wind fight against him, but he wrapped his unyielding fingers around his cross and stood strong.

"I come to you today, bowing in my heart, asking for protection from the evil one!" Oscar shouted at the malevolent force battering against him. He could feel his hair waving against frequent surges of wind, but he was not deterred. He pushed against the gust with all his might. "We are assailed moment by moment with evil images that leave us vulnerable to every sin of every kind. Against this sin, I beg your salvation!"

The force pushed harder still against Oscar as he approached the threshold, but Oscar forced his heavy legs forward, his cross before him, bellowing his prayers against the wind.

He skidded backwards but refuted the force, treading with all his might.

"Surround me!" he continued, raising his voice higher. "Surround me! Encompass me with Your strength and Your might! Let all that take refuge be glad, let them ever sing for joy! Let my voice sing for joy, let your love be ever present, surround me with your good graces – surround me!"

His foot stepped over the threshold. The door went to slam against him, but he held out his cross and remained strong.

"Surround me!"

As if he was being afforded an extra layer of protection, the door stuck mid-swipe. It flapped back and forth, the evil from within fighting against the good forces from outside, and it was no one's guess who was going to win.

Oscar strode further forward, trying to force his way in, pushing against the resistance.

"You may shelter us, Your name may exult you, for it is You that blesses the righteous man, and call me righteous as I fight in Your name, O Lord!"

Another step.

He managed another step.

The door wafted, beating against itself with fever and ferocity.

"Surround me with your favour – surround me with your shield! Allow me safe passage to this house of evil!"

With a surge of strength, Oscar forced himself into the prison, diving upon the floor.

The door slammed behind him.

Oscar remained on his knees in the middle of a corridor, feeling the wind rushing around him in a vigorous tornado, an aggressive swirling of evil gusts encompassing him in a malicious, powerful force.

Screams echoed along the corridor and assaulted his ears.

Wails of pain and torture blasted against him.

Cries of the suffering, begs of the tormented, racing across the echoes of the chaotic wind until it became deafening.

Oscar covered his ears, unable to take the battering of his eardrums. It was louder than any music concert he had ever been to; it was as if loudspeakers were pinned against his head, forcing manic vibrations to pound through his ears and fill his mind with disorder.

He couldn't let it beat him.

He couldn't.

He had to continue.

"Strengthen us in the power of Your might!" he shouted, unable to hear his own voice above the noise. "Dress us in Your armour, fill my blood and bones, against the spiritual forces of wickedness and evil!"

The screams bellowed louder still.

Everyone who had ever suffered, died, been tortured, disembowelled, hurt, left to go crazy; all of them reached inside Oscar's head and pulverised his cranium. His head throbbed with the power of a hundred shrieks, trying to make him crazy, trying to take his sanity from him in one desperate act of servitude.

"Surround me!" he persisted, his voice fading in the ear-splitting racket. His ears were pounding, hurting, burning as if they were about to burst.

"You are our keeper! And I beg you – surround me with your protection!"

Screaming. Crying. Twisting his mind.

"Surround me!"

Forcing his head into a manic haze of thrashing suffering.

"Surround me!"

Suddenly, it stopped.

The wind. The voices. The noise.

Silence.

Assuming it was a trick, he did not move. He kept his hands

over his ears, kept his crouched knees still. His heart beat against his chest, his hands pushing against his ears.

He opened an eyelid.

Then the other.

He peered around himself.

He waited, as if expecting something to pounce at him.

Nothing did.

He removed his hands.

The walls crumbled. The bars at the end of the corridor rusted. The floor he knelt upon ripped his jeans with bumps and broken fragments.

But there was silence.

Nothing fought against him.

It had worked.

He was in.

3 9

Thoughts of doubt and fear forced April to contemplate her decision.

Had she done the right thing?

She had basically just left Oscar to deal with an incredibly powerful, furious malevolent force.

I'm an idiot. What have I done?

He was talented, yes – but inexperienced.

But so was she once. She had to be left to make her own mistakes and learn from them. Only after that did she seize her talent and become the force she had become.

But she'd left him there.

On his own. Helpless.

I had no choice.

They didn't have Derek or Julian, which was going to make this so much tougher. And, what's more, the spirit that was battling against them was clearly battling at both the prison and Julian's home. If she had stayed with him and defeated the prison's entity, it would have just reformed. Both sides of this thing needed to be destroyed.

So she had gotten in her car and sped away, regretfully

watching him grow smaller in her rear-view mirror. Watching as he stood, readying himself, then disappearing from view.

If only she could know how he was doing.

No.

Stop it.

This is no time for reservations.

She had faith in him.

With all that she had seen, she had come to believe in the impossible.

It was time to stand tall, stand strong, and above all else, focus.

She wasn't going to have it any easier at her end.

She brought the car to a stop against the side of the road, ignoring the double yellow lines. She didn't have time to find an appropriate parking space and, being honest, she didn't give a damn whether they chose to give her a ticket at that particular moment.

She rushed out of the car and sprinted up the path to Julian's flat.

"Julian!" she shouted, banging her fists against the door. "Julian, open up!"

There was no response, but there was definite noise.

A frantic clatter, followed by a shattering smash.

The door rattled, battling against its hinges, the wickedness within berating her, fuelling her fear.

She put her ear closer to the door and listened.

The sound of objects clattering against walls, furniture smashing, accompanied by hysterical shouting.

Multiple voices of hysterical shouting.

None of them Julian's.

She tried the door handle, on the off-chance that, maybe, it was unlocked – but she had no such luck.

She stood back, took a few paces run-up, and launched her shoulder into the door.

It did nothing. It barely even shook. It hurt her shoulder more than it hurt the door.

What next?

She ran to the kitchen window and tried to peer inside. Flickers of shadows bounced around, but she was at too much of an angle to see the main commotion.

I could smash the glass...

But what with?

Then it hit her.

The spare key. She had a spare key.

But where was it? She didn't have time to go home and get it – she had no assurances that Julian was still alive, and the chances were decreasing by the minute.

Then she realised.

"You idiot," she muttered to herself as she turned back to her car, where she kept the spare key in the glove compartment.

A traffic warden was already writing out a ticket.

They don't waste a moment, do they...

"Did you know you're on double yellow lines?"

"Couldn't care less, mate."

She opened the car, reached inside the glove compartment, grabbed the key, and sprinted back toward the door.

She went to shove the key in but, with her desperation to get inside and with the struggle to fit them in the trembling lock, she fumbled it and dropped it on the floor.

"Crap!"

She picked it up, willed herself to concentrate, and placed it into the lock. She had to be of sound mind if she was going to do anything, and she was already letting this thing get the better of her.

She opened the door and stepped inside.

The room was a crazed chaos. A tornado of broken objects

battered the walls, spinning in a ferocious circle so quick and so violent April could not get anywhere near it.

She edged forward, holding a hand out, guiding her way through the anarchy that masked her vision.

Through the pandemonium, she saw him.

Julian.

In the centre of the violently spinning broken glass and his destroyed possessions.

Lying on the floor amongst a mess of ripped paper, his eyes closed.

He wore nothing but pyjama trousers, which were rags, ripped and torn to shreds. His torso was covered in cuts and bruises, and numerous marks decorated the flaking skin of his pale face.

Most of the cuts engrained upon his body were in the shape of an upside-down crucifix. A symbol that represented Satanism – as a mocking of the Holy Trinity, and a representation of the unholy trinity; removing the Father, the Son and the Holy Spirit, and replacing them with the devil, the antichrist, and the false prophet.

If such marks were being cut into his body, then it was a sure, unequivocal sign that something deadly and of pure evil was at work here, and they were in grave danger.

"Julian!" April screamed.

In an immediate response, she was launched off her feet and thrown out of the flat, forced to land harshly on her back. As she groaned with pain, the front door slammed shut.

THE CORRIDORS OF THE PRISON SEEMED TO HAVE GROWN INTO A vast maze. They were no longer the clean, sterile corridors Oscar had previously walked down – they were now mossy, rusting, broken-down corridors of a building that had been left uncared for.

And they seemed to lead to nowhere.

The route had turned into a perplexing labyrinth, entwining like weeds around a tree, growing obscurely in each direction.

Oscar was in severe danger of getting lost.

He searched for a sign, searched for something that would indicate where he needed to go.

Finally, he found it. A sign that read *A Wing.*

That was Derek's wing, he was sure of it – he recalled discovering that Derek was in the 'haunted' cell, which was A Wing Cell 25.

He followed the sign, stepping carefully and cautiously through the darkness. Night had fully descended upon the prison and there were no lamps to guide Oscar's way.

He took out his iPhone, selected the flashlight option and

directed it forward, peering into the distance just to find a vague nothingness. Darkness led him further into the endless corridor but, with no other indication of where to go other than the signage, he kept his hand against the wall to help him guide his way, and slowly stepped forward.

His faint footsteps echoed lightly against the stony floor. His hand ran over the cracks and bumps of the walls, giving him a small amount of reassurance that he was safe.

Safe.

"Hah."

He couldn't help but grunt at the ridiculousness of the concept. Safety was an illusion that had been painted for him by naiveté. Just a year ago he would have thought he was safe; now he knew better. True safety never really wraps its comforting arms around you – there is always something lurking, ready to rip it away.

And such a statement was truer now more than ever.

He realised he was shivering. The prison grew colder the further he made it in. He knew enough to know that this was a sure sign that the evil dwelling within these halls was growing stronger.

But that wasn't the real reason he was shaking.

His lunch turned over in the pit of his stomach and he did all he could to not bring it up. He was terrified. This thing had managed to launch him off his feet before he even made it into the prison. Now, he was nearing the dead centre, and he knew it was just a matter of time until he came to a face-to-face confrontation.

With a spark of luck, he found himself next to the door with a big, clear sign upon it: *A Wing*.

He put his hand against the door to open it.

Paused.

This was too easy.

Luck would not be on his side. This thing had taken over a whole prison; it was too powerful.

He had found A Wing through reordered corridors that appeared to be leading nowhere. It just didn't make sense.

Was it a trick?

The corridors had twisted and contorted, changed and messed up his path. The prison could have kept him searching for days, kept him trapped and lost in the depths of the hell-hole permanently if it wished.

So why had the prison allowed him to find this wing?

What were its intentions?

With an extra level of caution, he pushed the door open, elongating its squeak as he opened it slowly.

He edged in, pointing his light into the wing, moving it from left to right, up and down, inspecting every crevasse and every corner.

The wing appeared as he expected. Rusting cell doors, mould on the walls, and a strong smell of damp. It was an ageing, decrepit, pit of decay that looked as if it had been unin-habited for years.

As he made it into the wing, he rotated in full circles, aware that something could jump out onto his back at any moment. He shone his light all around, listening to every sound, inspecting every wall, every floor, and the bars to every cell.

A smell of rotting meat hit him in the face, forcing him to choke. It was overwhelming. A repugnant smell pushing against him.

It could only mean one thing.

It was the indication that something was in there with him.

"Hello?" Oscar offered, his voice reverberating against the walls.

He edged forward, and the smell just continued getting stronger.

"I know you're there," Oscar spoke, more confidently than he felt. "Show yourself."

He turned around once more, shining his light across every wall and into every cell. There were so many cells; three floors of them. Something could easily be waiting, ready to pounce.

"I'm not scared of you," he lied. "You may as well come out and face me."

Clap. Clap. Clap.

Oscar froze. His breath caught in his throat.

He daren't move.

Clap. Clap. Clap.

He shone the light into every cell, to the floors above, behind him, before him.

Clap. Clap. Clap.

"You don't scare me. Show yourself."

The clapping grew louder.

Clap. Clap. Clap.

It came from a cell to the right.

Oscar immediately turned his light to the nearest cell and watched with astonishment as a figure emerged, lit only by the light from his phone. As the silhouette came into the vague luminescence, Oscar scrutinised its appearance. It was a man, wearing a prison officer's uniform; the same uniform as the man who had led them into the prison on his first visit.

The man continued to clap sarcastically, a large grin beneath his moustache, his greying hair swept to one side.

Oscar's light flickered against the cell number the man had just walked out of.

Cell 25.

"Who are you?" Oscar demanded, rooted to the spot.

The man halted a few yards away from Oscar, ceasing his clapping, and giving a mocking bow.

"Well done, my boy," the man spoke. "Well done."

"Who are you?"

"I am a prison officer. And I believe you are... Oscar? Is that right? One of *his* friends?"

"You are not a prison officer here. This prison hasn't been used in four years."

"Okay, I will correct myself, my dear fellow – I *used* to be a prison officer here. Now I am dead."

Oscar kept his light shining on this man's face, staring at him intently, mentally preparing himself for any sudden move.

This was too easy. Too simple.

The entity had directed him to Derek's cell and had just revealed itself. Entered polite conversation, instead of furiously attacking Oscar with everything it had.

It didn't make any sense.

"Where's Derek?" Oscar commanded.

"Derek? Remind me..."

"Give it a rest, I know you have him. Where is he? Is he in Cell 25?"

The prison officer's grin extended, growing into a vicious smirk.

"Answer me this, my boy. What do you plan to do should you find him?"

Oscar didn't respond. He didn't want to bite. He knew what it wanted.

"A young lad like you. Do you *really* think you could save him?"

Why did it matter?

Why did the entity care about whether or not he thought he could save Derek?

Why was it just talking to him, making idle conversation?

"He is safe with us now. Part of the prison. Where he will stay."

Then he realised.

This was all for show.

It was a distraction. Keeping Oscar occupied.

The entity didn't care about him, it was Derek it was after – and this apparition was just doing its best to keep Oscar away from whatever they were doing.

"What have you done with him?"

Oscar ran past the entity, into Cell 25.

The prison officer instantly manifested itself into a large demonic creature, ravenous fangs exuding from its bloody jaws.

Oscar held out his cross and sprinted past, finding himself alone in what used to be Derek's home.

It was empty.

Oscar ran to the cell window and looked out upon the courtyard.

That's when he saw Derek.

Being led up a set of stairs to the gallows, where an empty noose awaited him.

41

APRIL LEAPT DEFIANTLY TO HER FEET, HER FISTS CLENCHED, blood firing through her veins. She had battled enough evil things in her time to know the typical tactics of intimidation. This didn't scare her.

She charged at the door, leading with her shoulder, putting all her weight behind it, and barged open the door, falling to her feet amongst the mess of Julian's ill-kept living room.

"Julian!" she yelped, having to squint to be able to see him inside the hysterically gushing wind, isolated by thrashing objects that created a circular force around him.

She needed to get in there with him, inside of the spinning anarchy. That way she could get through to him, beseech him, help him battle from the inside.

She dragged herself to her feet, resisting the force that attempted to repel her, refusing to be pushed back down. She put all her weight behind her, pressing her feet down against the stained, cracked floor, forcing herself forward.

It was like wading through water. She did all she could to resist the entity's force, relying solely on will and determination.

She reached out toward the objects circling Julian, reaching her hand toward the revolving mayhem, until she just about poked a hand inside the edge of the spinning force.

"Ow!"

She instinctively withdrew her hand.

Something had cut her. A slit along her palm throbbed with pain, blood seeping down her wrist.

Broken pieces of furniture, splinters, sharp objects, kitchen knives, ripped paper – everything that had been in that flat was part of that forcefield separating her from Julian. What had cut her could have been anything.

Luckily, she had slowly edged her hand in. She knew that if she'd tried jumping through, she would have more than an injured palm.

She held her wrist for a few moments, staring intently at her gushing open wound, her incoherent thoughts racing to produce a way that she could stop the bleeding.

There was nothing she could use. She was going to have to endure it.

Julian was the priority.

She looked around, searching for some way to get to him.

"Julian!" she tried again. "Julian, wake up!"

It was no good.

His body remained still, entwined with the disorder of the room. Ravaged by whatever was tormenting him.

"Julian, please!"

She was sure she could hear a chuckle echo throughout the room, mocking her helplessness.

She sighed.

She needed to think of something.

Maybe if I could create some kind of shield...

She turned back to the room, searching it, looking for anything that could help her.

Some of the remains of Julian's desk rested against the far

wall, nudging ever so slightly back and forth on the outskirts of the wind. She seized a plank and placed it cautiously into the mess surging through the air.

She withdrew it, looking upon its resulting state – a piece of shaved and shattered mess.

"Shit!"

She took a deep inward breath and let it out. Stayed calm. Told herself not to panic. Told herself to ride out this storm.

"Julian, wake up, it's me!" she tried once more, fearing that the only way to get to him would be to appeal to his strength, and hope that he heard her through the howling gale. It was his guilt that was controlling this, that was fuelling this – that negative energy was powering this entity.

"Julian, come on!"

He stirred, groaned, but only to shift in his unconscious state.

"Damn it, Julian, you listen to me now!"

His nose twitched. His hands flexed.

"Julian, I know you can hear me!"

His eyelids fluttered.

She knew he could hear her.

But she needed a break. A momentary weakness in the spirit that could allow her to jump through the mess, to get closer to him so he could hear her loud and clear.

But how?

She couldn't create a shield. She couldn't protect herself from it. There was nothing she could do.

Then she thought – maybe she didn't have to.

Oscar could create that weakness.

Any success he had at the prison would surely impact on the strength of the entity this end.

She had to continue to have faith.

Once again, she was reliant on the two men in her life.

42

THE DEMONIC APPARITION HOVERED IN THE DOORWAY TO THE cell, its deformed mouth now distorted into an even larger grin. Horns twisted from its head, blood dribbled from its chin, and a sharp tail thrashed against the walls of the cell.

Oscar shook his head.

He could not be afraid.

He could not let himself be deterred through even the slightest tinge of dread.

This thing was powering itself on fear. Oscar could not give it that.

"You're going to kill him?" Oscar asked defiantly. "And for what?"

"This man has tormented Hell for decades," a large, booming voice bashed against the cell walls. "This will be our final revenge."

"I won't let you take him."

"There is nothing you can do about it."

Oscar held out his cross and charged forward. As long as he had this crucifix in his hand, he knew that he–

The demon's snapping red tail cracked the cross out of

Oscar's hands so quickly he barely noticed, sending it soaring to the far wall, smashing into pieces.

Oscar's eyes looked to this creature, feigning defiance, his heart thudding against his chest.

"Cover my mind with the helmet of Your salvation," Oscar spoke the prayer, unable to force the shaking out of his voice. "Surround me constantly, as I am Your child. Fix my thoughts with—"

Oscar rose into the air by his chest, continuing to rise, the rest of his body hanging loosely like a rag doll.

He felt his arms fixing in place, growing rigidly behind his back. An invisible force was constraining him, holding him still, pulling him tighter.

"Keep the enemy at bay," he persevered, his voice coming out as a dim croak. "Calm my emotions with the peace of Your presence. Help me follow Your command and—"

Something constricted tightly around his neck. He could feel thick fingers around his throat, tightening. Long fingers, with sharp claws, wrapping themselves around his oesophagus. He tried to speak, but it was too tight, and barely a whimper could escape his lips.

He couldn't speak his prayer.

That was my only chance.

He struggled for breath. He thrashed for it, but his body was held so firmly in place not a single muscle could move.

He was suffocating.

I'm going to die.

His eyes remained wide open, staring with terror at the face of the true form of this thing glaring back at him, searing into his eyes. Enjoying his helpless asphyxiation. Enjoying the look of terror as an acknowledgement that this could be the end spread across his fearful face.

It was big. It was vile. And its demonic features were petrifying.

Its cackles turned to hysterics.

"You fool!" its voice echoed with a dirty gust of wind against Oscar's face. "You really thought you stood a chance..."

Blots of light obscured his vision.

He could feel his body going. Life draining.

Soon he would be unconscious.

Then he would die.

Without ever telling April how he felt. Without ever proving Julian wrong. Without ever meaning a damn thing to this world.

Something brushed against his hand.

Something else, like a gentle breeze, enclosing it, holding it. It was small, like a child's hand.

There was something else in there with them.

The entity's triumphant grin turned to an aggressive snarl, glaring at something behind Oscar's back.

"Let – him – go!" cried a young girl's voice, a girl who couldn't be more than a child.

He felt the grip around his throat loosen, and he managed to gasp a gulp of air. He breathed whilst he still could, taking in all the oxygen he was able.

The firm hold on his body loosened. He was still held in place, but he could wiggle his toes and flex his arms.

"Leave him be!" the young girl's voice repeated.

The entity growled.

Oscar dropped to the floor, landing heavily on his elbow. He grabbed it, at first willing the pain away, then feeling grateful that the only pain he felt was a sore elbow.

"You will not take him!" the entity bellowed, then disappeared into the air.

Oscar rolled onto his back, searching for whatever it was that had appeared behind him.

It was a young girl, dressed in clothing from a long time ago. From at least five centuries in the past.

"Who are you?" Oscar gasped.

"My name is Elizabeth," the spirit told him. "Derek's in danger. I tried to warn him. You need to save your friend."

"I need to get to the courtyard. How can I do this?"

"I will grant you safe passage, but you need to go now."

He clambered to his feet, nodding gratefully at the girl.

"Thank you."

"Go!"

He turned, stumbling to his feet, sprinting as fast as he could out of the cell and through the wing.

Numerous faces screamed at him as he passed them, claws swiping, jaws snapping. Trying to grab him. Trying to swipe him away.

But none of them reached him, thanks to Elizabeth.

The entity had been momentarily weakened, if only for a few fleeting seconds.

Within minutes he had reached the edge of the courtyard, and Derek was in sight.

But Derek could not see Oscar.

Because Derek had a bag over his head, a noose around his neck, and the executioner was just about to push him off the steps.

43

THE TWIRLING OBJECTS AROUND JULIAN SLOWED DOWN.

Yes!

Oscar had done something.

But she knew it wouldn't last long.

Jumping over that barrier was a risk. It could start again any second. It could still hurt her.

But she had no time to second guess herself.

She had to take the opportunity, and do it hastily.

She closed her eyes, pressing her eyelids together as firmly as she could, and took a large leap forward.

She opened her eyes.

Julian lay below her.

The chaotic mess resumed its manic spinning, encasing both her and Julian within it.

"Julian," she pleaded, shaking him. "Come on."

He groaned. But it was something.

"Julian!"

He began to stir, his eyes flickering open, closed, open, closed.

"Julian, wake up, it's me!"

His eyes hazily opened, peering upwards, squinting at April, his vision attempting to refocus.

"Thank God, Julian. It's me!"

"…April?" he asked feebly, his eyes closing once again.

She shook him.

"No, do not go back to sleep!"

His eyes opened.

"Listen to me, Julian, you are under attack!"

"What?" he mumbled. "Where is Anna?"

"Anna is *dead*, Julian; she has been for years. And it's *not* your fault."

Julian groggily rotated his head, peering at his surroundings, watching their prison spin around them.

The room fell silent. Everything still spun, but as if going into slow motion. April watched Julian intently, hoping he would come back, praying for him to return.

"Julian, you need to destroy this."

"Destroy what?"

"It's your guilt that's doing this. You're a wreck. It's some kind of entity and it is feeding off you. You and Derek. You need to stop feeding it."

He groaned and turned onto his side, closing his eyes.

"Go away, April, and leave me alone."

"No!" she refuted, and shook him more aggressively.

He turned to her with a scowl.

"What the fuck are you doing?"

"Saving your life!" she shouted, her eyes filling with tears, her face breaking, her heart beating. "You took me off the streets, remember? You taught me how to harness my powers. You did that!"

"I know who you are…" He tried to turn back over again.

"Then stop looking away from me, you arsehole!"

He turned his face back to her, his eyes widening, growing angry.

Emotions overcame her. Every piece of her cried for him, longed for him to understand, to return to her. For years and years, she had been under his wing, and now he was falling into the dark abyss and she could not take it.

"Who the hell do you think–"

"You did *not* kill Anna! Nor did Derek. You both did all you could for her, it just was *not* enough. You *need* to understand that right now."

"You don't know anything about it."

"I know that your shitty reaction is shitty enough to create this mess. You need to be strong, Julian. You need to be strong, or we're all dead. Me, you, Oscar, Derek – we are all goners."

Julian's eyes met hers. For the first time, she saw his vulnerability. His weakness. He looked back at her, full of dismay, full of pain.

"You don't understand..." he whispered.

"Yes, I do."

"I watched her die..."

"And she would have died sooner, and far more violently, if you two hadn't stepped in!"

Tears trickled down his cheeks.

This was good.

He was facing it.

He was finally facing his demons.

"You need to be strong!"

"I can't, April. I can't keep being the strong one, the one who can never do any wrong, that's not who I am..."

"I'm not asking you to be who you are not. I'm just asking you to be..."

"To be what?"

Her eyes broke.

"To be the man who took me off the streets and gave me a home," she beseeched him, peering sincerely into his blood-shot, fading eyes, her cheeks soaked with tears. "The man who taught me how to harness my power. The man who saved me from the gutter."

"April…"

"To be the man who taught me my greatest lesson."

"Which is?"

She grabbed the back of his sweaty hair, turning his face toward hers with full aggression, forcing him to look in her eyes, forcing him to see the pain she was having to endure.

"That the biggest obstacle you will ever have to overcome is yourself."

He watched her intently.

Watched as Derek's wise words escaped her lips.

Watched as those words washed over him, cleansing him with a clear mind.

She was right.

"Help me to my feet," he told her.

She helped him gain balance, helping him to stand upright and assuredly before the sickening state his flat had been left in.

No more.

"Leave!" he bellowed. "Leave my flat, you bastard of hell!"

Screeches entwined with screams, and shouts filled the air, accompanied by an ominous grey smoke.

"You don't scare me," he boldly revealed, narrowing his eyes.

The force grew weaker. Objects flew into the wall, out of the entwining circle. Glasses exploded. Heavier pieces of furniture fell upon the floor, the entity no longer with the strength to be able to hold them afloat.

"Go back to hell where you belong."

The noise grew less.

The chaos dullened.

April had done their part.

It was up to Oscar now.

44

OSCAR LAUNCHED HIMSELF FORWARD, SPRINTING ACROSS THE courtyard as fast as his aching legs would take him.

Prison officers stood vacantly, watching with absent eyes. As he ran amongst them, each of them turned and transformed into a transparent apparition, launching themselves toward Oscar.

Oscar raised his arms and shielded his face, saving himself from the surge of wind that each demonic force thrust against him.

Each one unsteadied his balance, pushing against him, forcing him to stumble.

But he would not be discouraged.

The executioner saw Oscar coming and decided it was time.

With a forceful kick, the man pushed Derek off the steps.

Derek, a bag over his head and a noose tied tightly around his neck, dangled helplessly. He tried kicking, but his legs – his legs weren't what they used to be. The dreaded sound of him choking carried across the courtyard. It was all that could be heard.

Oscar decided it was time to stop shielding himself.

He stood tall, his arms to his side, his fists clenched, his face a snarling visage of determination.

He strode forward. Another prison officer launched a demonic attack at him, but he screamed in its face, refuting its power, sending it away.

Derek didn't have long.

Minutes.

Oscar couldn't waste a moment.

He charged forward, the gallows growing closer.

A man stepped in front of him. A man who towered over him with a sadistic glare. His unsettling presence alone sent waves of malicious sin charging in every direction like volts of electricity.

He terrified Oscar. Out of everything he had faced so far, this was what mortified him.

Oscar knew who this man was.

This was Kullins.

This was the prison governor.

"Get out of my way," Oscar instructed, not faltering in his confident strides forward.

The governor's mouth opened and extended. In an aggressive gust of wind, Oscar was sent onto his back.

He stood back up straight away, refusing to be pushed down.

"You'll need to do better than that!" he claimed.

The governor smirked, a glint in his eye, as if to say, "Challenge accepted." He transformed, and he was the governor no more.

His arms extended into large claws, his teeth manifesting into vile fangs dripping with blood, his eyes turning a mixture of dark yellow and red.

Oscar felt goose bumps prick. His heart thudding. He fell to his back beneath the snarling, ravenous creature that presented itself before him. It was like the fierce beast he had faced on A Wing, but bigger, bloodier, and full of infinite evil. A demon of the underworld, looming over the courtyard, sinful eyes and piercing claws that elongated into large, sharp points.

"Okay, you did better..." Oscar conceded.

He glanced at Derek.

His body was thrashing.

He was still alive. But not for long.

The prayers he had been using so far wouldn't be good enough. He knew what he'd have to use.

The incantation.

The one he had previously forgotten.

As soon as he realised which prayer he would have to use his anxiety took over, and every word he knew slipped out of his mind like water through fingers.

The demon's claw struck against the ground. Oscar rolled to his side, narrowly missing the strike, but the force of its fist shook the ground enough to make Oscar rise into the air then collapse harshly back against the bumpy gravel.

"Shit, come on!" he willed himself.

He closed his eyes.

Calmed his mind.

He could feel the demon's claw swipe through the air toward him.

He thought back to that book he had reread again and again, desperate not to make the same mistake.

He had it.

God damn, I have it!

"I know my transgressions," he began, "and my sin is ever before me."

He opened his eyes.

The demon's claw halted above him.

"Against you, you alone, I have sinned," Oscar continued, rising to his feet. "Indeed, I was born guilty, but I hide my face from your sins, and blot out all my iniquities."

The demon growled, a force of dirty wind spewing in Oscar's direction.

But Oscar knew it was a feeble attempt at intimidating him. The demon recognised the prayer, and knew it had nowhere to go.

"Create in me a clean heart, oh God, and put a new and right spirit within this place."

He stepped forward, edging toward the beast, his eyes focussed intently on his deadliest enemy.

Out of the corner of his eyes, he could see Derek's body struggling less. A state of unconsciousness descended upon him.

"In the name, power and authority of Jesus Christ, Lord and Saviour God, Holy Ghost, do the work I need right now, as I make these proclamations."

The demon howled in agony, curling up into a helpless ball upon the floor.

The executioner that stood beside the gallows looked to Oscar with terrified eyes, transformed into a puff of air, and disappeared into the night sky.

"I renounce and reject sins, and I–"

Shit.

He froze.

This is where I messed up before.

He looked upon the demon.

"I renounce and reject sins, and I–"

The demon ceased its writhing and looked back at Oscar.

"I renounce and reject sins, and I…"

The demon grinned.

As did Oscar.

"I renounce and reject sins – *and any sinful items kept here!*"

Fooled you.

The demon howled in a final shriek of anguish, its skin tingeing, smoke rising from its body.

"Be gone, beast! Be banished from the place you once resided! *Be gone!*"

The demon burst into a ball of flames, and with one final, high-pitched screech, plunged downwards into the ground, sailing back to hell where it belonged.

Oscar rushed up the stairs and dove onto the top of the gallows. He swung it with all his force, coercing the wooden beams to unbalance, swinging and swinging until, eventually, the contraption collapsed onto the floor and broke into a few shards of wood.

Oscar leapt to Derek's side, removed the bag, and untied the noose.

Derek's eyes were closed.

Oscar rested his ear against Derek's chest, listening for breath, listening for a heartbeat.

At first, nothing.

Then, there it was.

A faint boom. Slow and soft, but there nonetheless.

Derek's chest rose up and down, slowly, weakly.

Derek's eyes opened.

But he wasn't all there. He was groggy, behind the eyes somewhere, his mind a hazy mess.

But he was alive.

I did it.

He helped Derek to his feet and dragged him back to the car park.

He felt silly phoning for a taxi after all that happened, but it arrived within half an hour, and the driver helped carry Derek into the backseat.

"What the hell have you been doing 'ere?" the taxi driver inquired. "This ain't been open for years."

"You know," Oscar replied as they drove away from the prison and toward Julian's flat, "you've told me that just a tad too late."

Oscar was out of the taxi like a bullet, running toward Julian's flat with everything he had.

The taxi driver helped Derek out of the car, tutting at Oscar's lack of empathy. Oscar didn't care.

He had to check on April.

The door was open.

Oscar ran through it and came to a skidding halt.

The room was a huge mess. Broken objects lay across the floor with such frequency he had to walk precariously from the sparse gaps on the floor, trying not to step on anything sharp.

Julian sat beside April on the sofa, with a warm blanket around him.

As soon as Oscar entered the room, April stood.

They stared.

April smiled, walking toward Oscar, tiptoeing through the mess of the floor until she finally reached him.

Derek entered behind them and made his way to the sofa beside Julian, but Oscar only cared about one thing.

April smiled. Oscar smiled back. Their arms flung around each other in a warm, tight, loving embrace.

"You clever, clever boy," she told him. "You are so clever. I'm so proud of you!"

"Well…"

"Really!" She pulled back and looked him in the eyes, keeping her arms firmly and gratefully around him. "You did amazingly. You took on the entire place by yourself. I just…"

Her smile said it all.

"I know," he answered, pretending to be modest, but was already blushing from all the delightful praise she was endowing on him. "It was tough, but I got there in the end."

With a surge of confidence, he held her tight.

He was going to say it.

How he felt.

Everything he had kept inside.

"April, listen, I have something to tell you. I feel–"

"Oh, shut up!"

She pulled his face toward hers and planted a soft, delicate, earth-shattering kiss upon his lips. The whole room spun, his whole body tingling, every piece of him filling with innocent joy.

He closed his eyes and sank into it, allowing the kiss to get more and more passionate, tying his arms around her, pulling her in close. He could feel her body against him, he could feel her breasts pressing against his chest, could feel her soft, warm lips pressing firmly against his. Butterflies swarmed around his chest, fluttering free at last.

Eventually, their lips parted, and they stood in an embrace with their foreheads rested against each other, gazing happily into each other's eyes.

"Wow," was all he could say.

"I know."

She smiled back with that sweet smile that made his legs go weak.

"You could have just done this to begin with," he playfully told her.

"I know, but then I'd have missed out on watching you squirm, you idiot."

"You mean, you knew all along?"

"Of course I bloody knew!"

She chuckled as she pulled him in closer once more, pushing her lips against his, holding him close. All their emotions, their stress, their longing, everything came out in that kiss.

It was Oscar's favourite moment of his life so far, and one he wished never ended.

THREE WEEKS LATER

46

Jason sat at his desk, pictures of the case strewn across the table.

A weak knock tapped against his door. Jason was taken aback to see Julian cautiously hovering. He looked far better than he had when Jason last saw him. His hair was well-groomed, he was dressed tidily, and the vile odour was no longer following him around.

"Julian?" Jason asked apprehensively.

"I've come to apologise," Julian announced. "You saw me in a pretty bad state. Stuff was happening. That wasn't me."

Jason leant back in his seat.

"Really?"

"Yes, really."

"But I'm fine now. Really, I am. You said you had a case for me?"

Jason chewed on the end of his pen.

Could he really still trust Julian? After the state he'd seen him in?

"I did."

"You did?"

"The case has gotten far, far worse. At first, it was just a deceased doctor. Now it's…"

"What?" Julian asked, stepping forward, taking the seat opposite Jason. "What is it?"

"Now it's the entire children's ward of the hospital. Something is happening to them. Something no one can explain."

Julian smiled. He was glad to be back to work.

"Tell me about it, I want to help," he told Jason assuredly.

* * *

DEREK SHUFFLED THE NEWSPAPER, rereading the headline, still in disbelief.

MAN FOUND Guilty of Murder Gone Missing on Route to Prison

"REMARKABLE," he whispered. He checked the date. 29th October 2013.

Four years ago.

"I don't suppose you knew about this?" Derek asked, feeling foolish for asking such an obvious question.

"I found it in the library archives," Julian answered. "Took me four hours to find – it was pretty well hidden. It says two officers and a transported inmate completely disappeared from the vehicle in transit. They don't give a name. I imagine that's thanks to our friends in Rome."

Derek folded the newspaper up. "Curious."

"Of course, I never gave much thought to it at the time. I can't even remember seeing the story reported. And I would never give thought to it, considering I visited you shortly after in Gloucester prison." Julian sighed, rubbing his sinus. "I feel so stupid."

"Don't. Have you contacted–"

Julian knew what he was going to ask. "Yes. I know you told me the church was good at covering stuff up, but I never…"

"What did they say?"

"They said that they assumed hell had taken you. They assumed that was the reason to the empty van. They used their power to move the police onto other ventures – their words."

Derek snorted a huff of amusement. It was typical of his experience that those less aware of the supernatural never realise how much authority the church has in concealing conspiracies.

"They've covered up bigger problems before."

Julian sat across from Derek, watching him intently, loosely stirring his coffee with his teaspoon, allowing the ambience of the café to fade into the background and people to walk by unnoticed.

"How does it feel?" Julian asked. "You know, being out of prison?"

Derek smiled into his coffee, giving a slight chuckle.

"Well, I was never really in, was I?" he responded.

"You know what I mean."

Derek sighed, turning his gaze to the window. Julian studied him carefully, wondering what he was thinking. He knew that Derek often liked to philosophise and scrutinise the passing world, contemplating people innocently going about their lives, happily unaware of what dwelled beneath them.

Sometimes, Julian thought, Derek probably envied them. Wished he could have lived his life in ignorance.

"I feel foolish, Julian," Derek finally answered, keeping his gaze focussed on passersby. "That a man of my knowledge and experience could be convinced by such a thing."

"It could have happened to any of us; you can't blame yourself. No one could have predicted something that big taking an entire prison." He took a precarious sip of his coffee. "I certainly didn't."

"Yes, but I should have. Which leads me onto the reason that I believe such a thing was able to happen to me in the first place..."

Derek took in a big, deep breath, holding it for a few seconds, then letting it out. What for, Julian didn't know, but he watched his former mentor intently, awaiting what he was about to say as he took a few moments of mental preparation.

"What do you mean?" Julian prompted.

"That Oscar is a good catch," Derek declared, instantly changing the conversation. "Not only did he manage to take on this entity, he managed to fight his way into a prison of evil, and do it without me, or you, probably never really realising the extent of what he was taking on."

"Yeah, he did well."

"Did well? What the boy achieved was remarkable."

"I guess."

Derek smiled.

Julian knew Derek saw a lot of his younger self in him, and this was another moment of familiarity. Julian remembered what Derek was like when they first began his training. He was cocky, and Derek was not forthcoming with his praise. It brought him down to earth, but also destroyed his self-belief.

Now, Julian was doing the same thing with Oscar. Maybe it was time to give the praise where it was due.

"You need to watch him," Derek continued. "Harness him. You need to teach him the way."

"Why do you keep saying that *I* need to do this? Surely you're still going to be there? Not hanging up the cross yet, are you?"

Derek sighed. Placed his coffee down. Sat back in his chair and looked deeply upon Julian's face with his ageing eyes.

"I'm dying, Julian."

Julian froze.

"Oh."

DEREK LANSDALE HAD BEEN THE BANE OF HELL'S EXISTENCE since his endless tirade began.

The wrath of the devil fuelled the furious pits of hell, and the fires lashed out harsher than they ever had. This man... He was the sharp, prickly thorn in his harsh, thick side.

But death was coming for Derek Lansdale.

It was coming slowly, but he wasn't the man he was.

He could not oppose them any longer.

Hell had taken him from the humans, preyed on his guilt and made him weaker day by day.

Four years was enough to destroy him.

Now his illness would do the rest.

But there were more.

The devil roared a deafening roar at the thought, a scream that pounded through the hot air of the underworld.

The Sensitives.

Heaven's children. Carrying on the battle.

They had to be destroyed.

Not just killed, not just removed – but completely and totally ripped apart and thrown to the flames.

A sinister cackle rang out through the burning amber glow of the underworld.

An idea sparked.

Hell would pick them off one by one.

It was to be so simple.

And they would start with the girl.

April.

Yes.

They would start with her.

THE SENSITIVES BOOK THREE: CLOSE TO DEATH

CLOSE TO DEATH

RICK WOOD

THEN

Edinburgh, Scotland
2008

1

As Derek's placed his tense foot into the sparse gaps of empty floor, his thoughts could barely process what he was witnessing.

It was a slaughter. Practically genocide. So many children, so many young lives lost. Some of them would have only just learnt to talk. Just learnt to read. To write.

Now their remains were only vaguely recognisable as features of mutilated bodies.

As his feet absentmindedly carried him through the various rooms of the house, it was all the same. Fresh blood trickling down ripped wallpaper. Limbs left askew across various ornaments. Bodies left inside out.

And their faces. Their wretched, wide eyes. Their innocent pale skin. Their mouths twisted to a frown or contorted to a scream.

Deadly still.

Never to move again. Never to breathe a flicker of hair out of their faces. Never to tell an adoptive parent they loved them. Never to be given the luxury of growing old.

This couldn't have been her. It couldn't have been.

Just as the thought hit him, he saw a flutter of a dress outside the window. Beyond the trees, beyond the twisting path, directed to the edge of the nearby hill.

Was that her?

"So," came the furious Scottish accent of a police officer appearing in the doorway. "You still telling me that this was the wee work of a demon?"

Derek said nothing. He knew there were no words he could give that would appease the tragic, unspeakable events that had occurred in this formerly warm abode.

So he just stared. Looked into the eyes of the furious man glaring back into his.

"Pathetic. You come here with your religious nonsense, telling us we can rely on you. That we need to be patient."

"Which you weren't," Derek spoke, against his better judgement. "You weren't patient. And you didn't rely on me. That's why this has happened."

"*Get out!*" screamed the officer, his skin a shade of red similar to that of the splattered walls.

It was not a good decision to stay. Derek had seen what he needed to see and said what he wished to say. Without meeting the man's eyes, he stepped lightly down the stairs and out of the house.

He pursued the path, leaving the chaos of the crime scene behind him. He followed it between the twisting trees until he came to an opening. The opening was beside a steep hillside, which he followed. The vertical drop below his feet made his legs quiver, but he had to rely on his resolve.

Because this is where he found her.

Alone. Torn. Unable to cope.

Close up, he could see the destruction on her face. A formerly happy-go-lucky, spritely nineteen-year-old girl now stood solemnly, with the crust of dried blood weighing down her filthy dress and her mouth bathed in red that still trickled from her lips.

"Madelina," Derek spoke, softly and reassuringly. He did his best to show by his voice that he was not judging her, that he was not blaming her. He knew that, whilst her hands were covered in guilt, it was not her mind that had commanded them to commit the actions she had committed. "Please. Don't move."

Her head slowly twisted toward him. Her cheeks were stained with tears. Her hair was contorted into a scraggly mess. Bags sat so prominently under her bloodshot eyes it looked like a permanent shadow. She stood feebly, her knees trembling, on the edge of the sharp drop.

She was a wreck, no doubt about it. And Derek could completely understand why.

"Madelina, please. Don't."

"Don't?" she whispered back at him. "Did you see what I did?"

Her acknowledgement of what had occurred forced more tears to her eyes. They erupted down her face, dripping onto her collar, her body convulsing in mortified guilt.

"But you didn't do it," Derek said. "Did you?"

"Look at me."

"Yes, but–"

"*Look at me!*" her whisper turned to a scream, her voice breaking under the strain of her shout.

Derek glanced over his shoulder, hoping that no one had heard.

"I am. I am looking at you."

"Does it not look like I did this?" she asserted. "Does it not look like it was by my hands? By my... my teeth."

Her head dropped. Her eyelids pushed together. She could not look at him any longer.

"Madelina, listen to me–"

"I ate them, Derek," she continued, her voice quivering, convulsing, returning to a low whisper that almost got carried away on the breeze. "I ripped them apart. They are in me. Right now, I can feel them, turning in my stomach. I can feel my body digesting them."

"It wasn't you, Madelina."

"Look at me–"

"I *am* looking at you, Madelina. But we've talked about this. It's what's inside you. It's what's controlling you."

"What's controlling me?"

"She is. Lamia. You know this, I've told you this. Please, let me help you, I can get rid of it."

"And what if you do? Huh? What if you do?"

Derek's voice faltered.

"They are hardly going to forgive me, are they? The evidence won't work in court. I'll be in the press as – as the girl who ate... *babies...* and claimed she was possessed. How would that look?"

"You have to believe in people, Madelina. It's the only way."

Madelina shook her head with such adamant refusal that Derek began to feel her slip away. She was out of arm's reach, and he knew that if he edged toward her, it would only make things worse. He was relying entirely on his words, in hope that he could string a sentence together that would convince her against what she so stubbornly believed was the truth.

"People are good. You are good. You *have* to believe that. Or... or then, well – then you are lost."

"I wish I could believe in people the way you do, Derek."

Her eyes turned toward the heavy drop. She was inches away. Just inches.

"All you need to do is see it. It's there. You just need to look at people, and–"

Derek did not have time to finish his sentence.

She threw herself with all the force she could, and she fell hard, into the abyss of the sudden, deep drop.

By the time Derek reached the hillside, retracted the arms he'd flung toward her and peered below, she was already dead.

Her upturned body and broken neck were just visible in the small lines that surrounded her body.

2

Martin's feet could barely find a space void of blood or mayhem.

He had barely made his way through the open doorway before he toppled back, collapsed on the front porch and vomited his morning's healthy portion of Weetabix over the welcome mat.

He couldn't turn his head back. But he knew that he must. He had to see it. If there was any way he could have gotten away without seeing it, he would have. If there was some way he could have let his legs carry him away through the fields, away from the house, full of blissful ignorance, he would have done.

But this was his and Derek's doing. This girl was their responsibility. And she had – no, that *thing* inside of her womb had – ripped apart a building full of vulnerable, helpless, young children.

His eyes traced the floor, his head lolling as he forced it to rotate just a little more, until finally, the inside of the house came into his vision.

Dear God.

Eaten. So many of them, eaten. But only partially. Why?

Why only partially?

Were they still alive when she did this?

He couldn't. He couldn't look. It was not something he could bear to comprehend.

Not yet.

Not ever.

He pushed himself to his feet and staggered to the driveway as he attempted to walk away, unable to keep his balance. After falling onto his open palms, he brushed the gravel onto his jeans and traipsed back to the car. He used it for support as he collapsed upon it, burying his face in his arms.

He had told Derek.

Dammit, why had he told Derek?

Because Derek normally knows best.

Normally.

But, no. Not this time. Derek had insisted. This heavily pregnant woman was too weak for an exorcism. She wouldn't survive it. They had to wait until the child was born and hope for the best.

"Believe in hope," Derek had told Martin, his ever-wise words endowing their worldly knowledge upon him. "Believe in good. It's what we pray to when we exorcise a demon, but we don't always need an exorcism for it to help us."

That was Derek's solution to everything.

A positive outlook.

Martin had served by his side during The Edward King War. He had learnt so much from him. He had been plucked out of his youth at just fifteen years old and coerced into a battle that was far bigger than he was.

Why? Because heaven had conceived him. As a backup plan. As the solution to their mess of trusting hell. Of hoping for the best.

He was the first Sensitive.

He was heaven's solution for hoping for the best.

But he hadn't been Derek's.

Derek, who had taught him everything he knew.

Derek, who had not only let Martin down, but Madelina, and the entire orphanage that lay in shreds behind him.

From a distance, Derek's figure approached, cast in a smooth silhouette from the evening sun. As he grew closer, Martin could see that his head was down and he was in a deep, contemplative trance.

Martin didn't care.

"You!" he spat, as soon as Derek came close enough to hear.

Derek waved away the hostility, unwilling to engage.

"Don't wave me away!" Martin growled. "Have you seen what she has done?"

Derek paused by the car. Not looking at Martin. Not looking anywhere but down. A fallen face. A body bereft, void of energy.

"Don't ignore me," Martin insisted. "Have you seen–"

"Yes!" Derek interrupted with a hasty annoyance. "Yes, I have bloody well seen what she has done."

"And? And what are you–"

"She's dead."

Martin's words fell short.

He didn't know what to think. Anger at Derek? Sadness at her death? Relief that her suffering was over?

"How?" Martin demanded.

"She wouldn't listen to reason, she – she threw herself off."

"And what do you have to say about that?"

Derek frowned.

"What the hell do you mean, what do I have to say about that?"

"Because I told you! *I* told *you*! She needed an exorcism, she needed–"

"She was eight months bloody gone, Martin."

"So?"

"We needed to trust in hope."

"Yeah? You seen what hope has done? Have you?" Martin's fists clenched, his whole body tensed, lurching forward, ready to unleash. "Go have a look why don't you?"

"I have."

"And have you seen the guts? The blood? The pieces of children?"

"Go to hell, Martin."

Derek opened the car door.

"No, Derek, you can't–"

"Martin, stop."

Martin watched Derek. He could see Derek's pain. Could see the look on his face. Could see how much this mistake was eating him up inside, in a way that Derek probably hadn't completely come to terms with yet.

How could you?

How could you ever come to terms with–

Martin's head dropped.

He had said it. Insisted they should exorcise her, pregnant or not, that she could take it. Derek hadn't listened to him. This could have been avoided, if only Derek had listened to him. If he had *listened*. But he hadn't. He hadn't listened, and now–

"No," Martin decided. "Tell you what, Derek. *You* go to hell."

Martin turned and walked away.

That was the last time they ever saw each other alive.

Worcester, England
2014

3

A CONDUIT.

When April had first been introduced to the word, she had looked it up in the dictionary. It told her that she was either:

1. *A channel for conveying water or other fluid.*
2. *A tube or trough for protecting electric wiring.*

Being fairly sure that she was neither a water carrier nor an electrical conductor, she had decided that she would have to relearn everything she knew.

A drastic conclusion to come to, but one that undoubtedly proved true throughout the subsequent years.

"Right, so, erm – what?" April asked.

"A conduit," Julian repeated for the nth time that hour. "That is what you are. A conduit."

"I thought I was a Sensitive?"

"Yes, you are, but different Sensitives have different gifts. All right? I am good at exorcisms and detecting other Sensitives. You are a–"

"Yeah, a conduit, I get that." She nodded, her youthful

exuberance beginning to wear down Julian's patience. "But what is a conduit? I mean, what do I do?"

"A conduit acts as a host for whatever spirit, demon, or undead we are trying to contact."

"A host? What, like, for a party?"

Julian rubbed his sinus. Took a few breaths. Lifted his head again.

"No," he answered with clear pronunciation. "You are a host, as in, you let them use your body."

"I let a dead person use my body?" April repeated, her face scrunched into repulsion. "That's icky! I don't want a dead dude in me!"

"Technically, it's the undead spirit. It allows us to speak to them."

"And what do I do while you are speaking to them, and all that?"

"You feel them."

April's repulsed face grew more extreme.

"I don't mean like that!" Julian said with exasperation. "As in, whilst you are host to their spirit, you will be able to feel that dead person's feelings. Maybe even see their memories. They will show you who they are."

"I still don't get how I'm supposed to do that."

Julian allowed an irritated smile to spread itself across his reddening cheeks.

"Do you trust me?" he asked.

"What?"

"I said, do you trust me?"

"Well, yeah, I guess."

"Then you will allow me to show you."

Julian lit the three candles placed carefully around April. He turned off the lights, meaning the living room was lit by nothing but a flickering amber glow.

"We came to this house because of a spirit that won't leave

it. I need you to see what its memories are. See what happened. Why it's still here."

"How do I do that?"

"You close your eyes and concentrate. Erase all thought. Go blank as I recite my prayer."

April huffed.

"Fine."

She closed her eyes. Wiped her thoughts. Concentrated.

Thought about that turkey sandwich waiting for her in the fridge back home.

No! No thoughts!

She compelled the turkey sandwich from her mind and focused on her breathing.

Nothing but her breathing.

In. Out. Deep breaths.

Her mind grew blissfully clear.

Calm.

Tranquil.

In. Out.

Deep breaths.

"The spirit of the Lord be with me," Julian's voice spoke clearly and articulately. "He hath anointed me to preach to the unwilling, to those that remain. In the name of the Lord, as we pray that he will forgive our sins, we pray that he reveals yours."

She felt her mind slip into a steady absence.

She was there. Aware. But in the way that you can see through the windscreen of a car from the backseat.

Her arms became loose. Her legs grew hollow. Her mind faded to blank.

"To the Saviour, show us the unclean spirit. Allow them to reveal themselves, so we can help them move on."

Deeper and deeper into the trance.

Sinking further.

"Spirit in this room, I call on you now. Use this vessel to show us your past, and show us your purpose."

A flicker of thought pounced itself like the fire in a lighter, then evaporated just as clearly.

April could see it in her mind, as clear as her own thoughts. But they weren't her thoughts.

They didn't feel anything like her thoughts.

"Show us."

A living room.

The living room she was in, but older. The furniture was different. More... retro. Flowery. Furniture like a grandparent would have.

Her hands were wrinkly. Old. Veins stuck out like exposed wiring in a faulty cable.

Before her was a little girl.

Anger.

She felt anger. A little sadness, but mostly anger.

"I don't feel like speaking," she said, but not in her voice. It was old and croaky, like that of an old man. She could feel her mouth moving, but her voice remained dormant.

That child. That girl. Beneath her greying hands.

The girl screamed.

"This is my home," the old man's voice exclaimed through her unwilling lips.

Those hands. They wrapped themselves around the child's throat.

Hostility.

They squeezed.

Rage.

They tightened until her breath pushed itself out of her throat and she could breathe no more.

"My home!"

Fury.

Scorn.

Wrath.

Every form of anger flowed through her, like a painful ache after running too fast. They pulled on her muscles like weights, filled her thoughts with rabid desire to kill, to hate, to maim this child, to rip her apart.

She looked down.

The child's body was limp.

"My home!"

Her body convulsed upwards, stiffening into a plank, held rigidly for a few moments.

She heard Julian uttering a few desperate prayers, holding a cross against her chest. She was held there until his prayers finished and her body could fall limp again, at which point she flopped like a discarded puppet on the ground.

Julian rushed to her side.

"We heard his voice," he told her. "He spoke through you. Did you hear it?"

She nodded frenziedly, her thoughts trying to make sense of what she had seen.

"I saw…"

"What? What did you see?"

"I saw…"

"What, April, what?"

She closed her eyes. Willed her panting to stop. Gathered her rambles into coherent thoughts that made sense.

Everything changed in that moment.

Her knowledge. Her worldview. Her purpose.

Everything became new.

"I saw him. I saw him strangle a child. A girl."

"Good, April. You saw what he had done."

She cried. Tears poured. She covered her face, not wanting to seem weak, but unable to control the frantic despair that she had been made to feel.

"What is it, April? What is it?"

"I felt anger… I wanted to kill her… I wanted to…"

"*You* didn't want to, April. *He* did."

It made sense. Those final few words from Julian made it all fit in place.

She was a conduit.

She felt the feelings of the dead. Of others.

She hated it. It had hurt her, scarred her mind with feelings she would never be able to forget.

Yet she had a feeling it was only the first of many.

NOW

Gloucester, England
2018

(8 MONTHS)

4

THE DUVET COCOONED TOMMY IN A SHIELD OF SILENCE, trapped alone with the smell of sweat and sickness.

His arms shook – out of fear or illness, he could not tell. Possibly both. The small amount of blood left in his body raced through his hollow veins. Tears formed in the corner of his eyes, causing a half-moon crescent blur across his vision, masking the darkness he had encompassed himself within.

He closed his eyes. Tight. As much as he could. As if it would change anything. As if closing his eyes and refusing to listen would mean that nothing was there.

For a moment, his erratic breathing was the only thing disturbing the slumber throughout the children's ward of the hospital, and he wished he was at home. He wished he had his mummy's arms to envelop him in safety. He had begged her not to go, pleaded for her to stay after visiting times were over, but she had to be wrenched away by the nurses, insisting it was time for the children on the ward to sleep, insisting she would just have to come back in the morning.

Insisting that Tommy had to face this night alone.

Another night. Another absent sleep. Another terrified

darkness, counting down the minutes, the hours, until the curtains would be opened and sunlight would bathe him in relief once more.

For it was only at night it came. Only night.

The night was still in its infancy, almost as young as his eight-year-old self, yet to grow into the full, ferocious force that the night's adolescence would bring.

At school they had told him to pray to God. When he was scared, afraid, or worried, to put his hands together and pray. That vicar that came to visit him, who made him laugh, he tried to help him believe in such a notion.

But prayer did nothing for those other boys. Prayer did nothing for that girl who died of her cancer two days ago. The girl he used to play with, laugh with, until he awoke one morning to find an empty bed.

Prayer did nothing for the boy who woke with a large scar down his chest. The police officer told them not to be worried, that nothing was going to get them, that this was a one-off.

But there was still that look in his eye. That look where his lips spoke of reassurance, but his eyes spoke of confusion. How something could sneak in and tear a child apart in the middle of a children's ward without being noticed was beyond him.

It was beyond any of them.

Tommy looked at his watch. Pressed the light button and illuminated the Purple Power Ranger behind the clock hands.

It had been minutes. A few minutes down of so many.

He held his breath.

There it was.

That sound of a trickling, greasy tail sliding along solid floor. Like the squelch a wet slap against the side of a swimming pool, continuous in its hasty yet silent movement.

Tommy was tempted to look. Tempted to pull down the duvet to see what the monster looked like, to get an impression of what it was that tormented the ward every single mortifying night.

But he daren't.

If he looked at it, it would be real.

He kept his arms wrapped over his head, padding at the outside of his skull where his hair once was.

"Tommy…"

His eyes sprung open to the sound of his name, so subtle it could be mistaken for a breeze.

"Tommy…"

One could be forgiven for attributing the sound to other things. To the breathing of another child, the rustle of the bedsheets, the sudden gulp in his breath. But Tommy knew what he'd heard.

He knew.

It was a woman's voice. A sultry voice. It almost sounded human.

"Tommy… where are you…"

He shook his head. Put his hands over his eyes and furiously shook. The hairs on his arms stood on end, his spine turned to ice, but he refused.

No.

No, it can't be.

A faint shadow fell over the side of his duvet. He could see something.

A figure, but not. A face with too many features to be real. Fingers, but elongated into piercing claws. Large, exposed breasts contorted into skewwhiff directions. And a long, thick serpent tail flailing behind it.

"Tommy… I know you're there…"

"Go away!" he tried to shout, but it just came out as a croak. His voice had gone, disappeared with his courage.

How does no one else see it?

Why is it the nurses, the doctors, the parents, the visitors, the vicars, the patients, why – why is it only him and the really, really sick ever heard its crooked joints as they moved closer, breaking the stiffness of its bones with every flex?

They never heard its laughter, left under its breath, so quiet yet pounding against the inside of his skull.

They never heard its speaking. Its slow utterances, quivering with the fever of its joyous loathing.

The shadow stopped. Halted. Tommy buried his head in his lap, covered his ears, covered his eyes.

Just a few more hours till morning.

Just a few more hours till morning.

Just a few more hours till morning.

"I can... hear you... breathing..."

"Go away!"

"It's... your... turn..."

"Leave me alone!"

The duvet slid slowly along his skin. Lifting his head slightly, he saw the shadow of its claw twisting it away, pulling it off.

Tommy's hands reached out and clamped onto the duvet.

It did nothing.

It still slithered away, slithered like a wet snake, slipping between his fingers. He reached for it, grabbed it, did everything he could not to let it go.

It still did nothing.

The duvet was swept straight off.

He didn't look. He didn't let himself. He covered his face once more, burying his head between his legs, his hands over his ears, his eyes shut tight. Refusing. Refusing to let this thing into his life, to let it live, to let it get him. Refusing to be party to its games. Refusing to...

He shivered. He was cold. It was as if a frost had suddenly thrown itself like an icy cloth over his body. He had never felt so cold before.

His hands seized in convulsions of terror.

"Leave me alone…"

"Tommy… you know I can't…"

"No!"

Tommy screamed. A high-pitched, deafening, ear-piercing, shrill scream.

And just as he did that, he finally allowed his head to look up and stare into the eyes of his murderer.

The nurses did not find his corpse until morning.

5

April's Primark panties slipped down around her ankles, squeezed open by the pressure of the widening space between her Converses. She thrust the least expensive pregnancy test she had found in the pharmacy between her legs, and peered at the ceiling as she tried not to splash any urine on her hands.

Once she'd finished, she held the stick out in one hand, and her watch in the other.

A tuneless hum escaped her lips, quiet enough so as not to escape the sanctity of her cubicle. Anything to pass the long two minutes she had to wait, with partially sprinkled fingers, just to witness whether one line would turn into two.

The bustle of the toilet door opened and closed, and the high-heeled shoes of two girls with upper-middle-class accents entered, obviously put on – let's be fair, they were in the bathroom of a Wetherspoons – chatting about some girl who had put weight on.

My God. Am I going to put weight on?
No.
Stop it.

It hasn't even come back positive yet.

She glanced at her watch. Ninety-six seconds and counting.

"She totally, like, ballooned, and I was totally grossed out. I mean, like, a whale would have been thinner than her," came the uppity voice, with an upper inflexion rising at the end of the sentence as if her statement were a question.

Please, just sod off...

Seventy-two seconds.

"I totally cannot believe Dave ploughed her."

Ploughed?

Oh, wow. Jeeze. Classy bitches then.

April looked over the cubicle wall, scanning the graffiti with her dormant eyes. Apparently, Alison hearts Simon 4eva. Good for her.

There was also a random girl's phone number, the declaration that Jade is a slut, and the following quote: 'War doesn't say who is right, only who is left.'

That's just what I want in the middle of a pregnancy scare – ethics on war.

Her mind escaped the graffiti and turned to Oscar. Such a lovely young man, a perfect boyfriend. Geeky, yes. A little dweeby, absolutely – but a heart of gold. He adored April – probably because she was the first woman who ever looked at him for longer than three seconds without saying, "Excuse me, but why are you staring?"

April decided she was being cynical. Probably just pregnancy hormones.

Stop it! I don't know if I'm pregnant yet!

Fifty-four seconds.

Even though their relationship was still in its infancy, Oscar had been a devoted, faithful, loving boyfriend. He'd said the words *I love you* far before April had expected, and she'd taken him to bed probably far quicker than he expected, but they worked. They read each other's minds, finished each other's sentences, and could not bear spending a moment away from each other.

But he was still young. As was she.

Were they really ready to be parents?

How would he even react?

He'd probably go running for the hills.

No.

That's not true.

Not Oscar. He was a kind soul. He would never do anything to hurt her, and she knew it.

"Like, oh my God, Suzie, why are you wearing that shade? It totally clashes with my top."

Oh, dear God. Do people like this actually exist?

She pulled off some toilet paper and dabbed at her hands. The urine sprinkles as she'd held the test in place had gone. She lifted her fingers curiously to her nose, pulling back with repulsion at the smell.

Great. Dried piss stuck to fingers. *Just what I wanted.*

She scanned the other wall.

Apparently, Alison had also hearted Jack, Keith, and Andrew, but each of their names had been scribbled out.

How often does Alison use this cubicle anyway?

She checked her phone.

Thirty-six seconds.

She let out a large sigh, prompting her lips to vibrate in a long raspberry. This was the longest two minutes of her life. How could two minutes last so long?

Thirty-two seconds.

Uuuuurrrrrgggggghhhhhh.

"Like, Suzie, you are totally splashing me with your water. Like, what the heck? Could you watch it?"

April felt sorry for Suzie.

She wondered what the faceless voices looked like. Suzie was probably incredibly normal, and her friend probably wore so much makeup she had a face like plaster. Maybe she worked in the makeup aisle in Boots, had a really bad fake tan, and wore every product she sold on her crusty, fading skin.

Twenty seconds.

Oh God.

No.

I'm not ready for the answer.

Got to chill out.

Fifteen seconds.

"Oh my God, Alison just texted me; the beast is coming out. Suzie, you totally cannot speak to her. I forbid it."

Jeeze, Suzie, grow a pair.

Ten seconds.

She began hyperventilating. She pushed the stick away from her, turning her head away, pushing the truth as far away from her eyes as she could.

Five seconds.

Tick-tock.

"Suzie, my life is, like, falling apart right now."

Three.

Two.

One.

April looked at the stick.

With a scream, she burst out of the cubicle and vomited over the sink, splashing Suzie's Armani makeup bag in the process.

She pulled her jeans up from around her ankles, fastened them, then threw up another mouthful of Weetabix.

"Oh my God, like, what are you doing?"

"Piss off, Suzie."

April looked at herself in the mirror. Her static hair waving in obscure directions, her skin pale, and her lip quivering beneath a splatter of sick.

In her mind, she could only think the same two words over, and over, and over again:

I'm pregnant.

(7 MONTHS)

6

_____

THE COLD, STERILE WALLS OF THE HOSPITAL CORRIDOR CAUSED A rejected feeling of morbidity to settle in Julian's gut. What is it about these solid floors reflecting the long strips of white light, plain, pale walls vacant of decoration, and constant consecutive perfectly aligned rooms – what is it about them that always makes a person feel a tinge of longing sadness in their gut?

It's because this is where everything bad happens to you, Julian decided.

Every dying grandparent ends up there. Every painful broken arm, every helpless surgery, and every sick child. This is where they go.

The faces of the nurses were colder than the corridors; no eye contact and no smiles. This was where they worked, and where they witnessed death on a daily basis. To an extent, Julian understood it. He hardly showed up to an exorcism full of positivity and an eagerness to get to work. He showed up with his game face on, aware that death is a very real possibility lurking behind any poor decision.

He followed Jason Lyle into the lift. Jason was a police

officer known to have a penchant for bizarre and baffling cases, ones that he normally brought the Sensitives into. It hadn't always been like that – in fact, Jason had solicited Julian's arrest over a year ago. But, having witnessed the truth of the supernatural forces attacking this world, he now sought their advice on a regular basis.

Julian held his hand out as the lift doors went to close, waiting for Derek to catch up. He took far longer than he did weeks ago – or even days ago. He looked to be deteriorating by the minute. His hair was growing back in a small mound after his last dose of chemotherapy, but his energy was not growing back as fast. He turned pale and out of breath, hobbling along on his walking stick, desperate not to be a burden in his unsuccessful attempt to catch up with the other two.

As Derek entered the lift and Julian allowed the doors to close, he studied Derek for a few moments. The sad truth was that Julian knew there was going to come a time when Derek would not be able to help him anymore and, whilst it had never been verbalised, he was fairly sure that Derek understood this too. But, until that day, Derek insisted that he was still an integral part of the paranormal hunting process – saying, "If anything's going to kill me, it'll be a demon, not a damn illness!"

As ever, Julian's mentor's words could not have been any closer to the truth.

With a sullen ping the lift doors parted and they stepped into the children's ward. At first, they walked through what seemed to be an inflated corridor – a passageway to the main ward, wide enough that it contained a row of beds on either side. This led them to a larger, square room with a succession of beds around the edges and a few lines of beds through the middle. Happy clowns and playful pictures of colourful fields adorned the curtains draped around the overcrowded succession of beds, but they only added a sense of irony to the morose and sombre mood of the wing. Julian imagined that this ward wouldn't have felt much different to Derek than the prison he had previously been trapped inside. People walked sombrely, without eye contact, desperate not to share their sorrow, helplessly confined to the sanctity of their beds and their cubicles.

That, Julian imagined, was why Derek was so adamant in not occupying the hospital bed he so sorely needed.

"Detective Inspector Jason Lyle," Jason introduced himself to a nearby nurse. "We're here investigating the death of Tommy Rowe."

The nurse's grim expression fell even lower.

"Right this way."

She led them to the corner of the larger room, where the far bed had been cordoned off by police tape and been further hidden by the drawn curtain. The beds around this police tape had recently been filled on Jason's confirmation that they were nearly done with the crime scene; he just wanted the thoughts of another set of people before it was completely cleared.

As they approached the crime scene, Jason tore down a strip of the tape and opened the curtain, allowing Julian and Derek inside. They stood and stared for a few moments.

The sheets themselves were a crusty red. The floor still held the remnants of the attack, and one would struggle to read the screens on the nearby machines, such was the mass of blood stains.

"Jesus," Julian unknowingly gasped.

"Yeah," Jason acknowledged.

"How many is that now?"

"We have the doctor, and this is the second child. Both with the same circumstance. The same problem."

"Remind me," Derek requested, his voice slow and weak.

"No evidence of an intruder, neither on CCTV nor by

forensic analysis. No evidence of DNA but the boy's. But an attack that undoubtedly went on beyond the point of death – not one that could be attributed to suicide."

Derek feebly nodded. Every word seemed to fall on his ears at a slower pace. It took him a few minutes to fully comprehend and process the answer to his question, in which time Julian grew guiltily impatient.

"Why would a kid that young commit suicide anyway?" Julian pointed out. "It's... Wow. It's unusual."

"Yes, it is unusual; that's why I've recruited you."

"No, that's not what I mean. It's – the whole situation is unusual. We have no doubt from what we've seen so far that there is strong evidence to attribute this to something... more. It's just that this isn't typical of the type of assailant we are speaking of."

"What do you mean?"

Julian sighed, raising his hand to his cheek, which he stroked curiously.

"Just hypothesising here – but those who are close to death, such as a seriously sick child, are more vulnerable to seeing elements that exist beyond death. That suggests that a demon, or spirit – an entity, shall we say – is at play. It's just, demons aren't serial killers, so much as manipulators."

"It's a demon. Surely it would do whatever?"

"Yes, that would be true – but its capabilities would not extend to physical interaction as much as physical manipulation. A demon would normally guide a host to carry out its actions, which would leave the DNA of said host, or one would have thought. This... it's curious."

Jason's phone rang. He looked at it, and an expression of irritation swept over his face.

"I'll be right back," he said, and left.

Julian turned to Derek, who was lowering himself slowly

into a chair in the corner of the room. He closed his eyes for a moment, gathering his energy.

"You all right?" Julian inquired.

"Fine," Derek replied.

"You know, you really need to check into a–"

"I'm not having this same argument again."

Julian sighed to keep cool, and decided to return focus to the scene at hand.

"So, what do you think?" Julian asked.

"This does appear to be some kind of entity."

"Well, there we have it. Just another day at the office. Playing with all the evil in the world."

Derek stared with a half-smile at Julian. Julian thought for a moment that this was his delayed reaction, then noticed the glint in his eye Derek always had when he was having a deep thought.

"What?"

"Such a cynic," Derek observed. "Always so desperate to attribute everything to evil."

"Well, don't you? What with everything we've seen, the true horrors, how can you not dwell on all the shittiness in this world? This world is crap. Stinking. And overfilled with evil and misery."

Derek leant his head back and closed his eyes, but did not lose the smile from his face.

"If I have one dying wish, before I go," he announced. "It's that I prove you wrong."

"Prove me wrong?"

"It's easy, when all you are exposed to is the sadness in the world, to believe that's all there is. You just have to remember sometimes to push that aside and see all the good it is concealing."

"Out of everyone I know, surely you have the most reason not to believe that."

Derek's grin widened. His eyes opened and fell on Julian's.

"And that, my good friend, is why I choose to."

Julian dropped his head.

As good as Derek's intentions were, he struggled to believe him. Yes, Julian was sure there was good in the world.

It's just that the child's bloodstains on the sheets before him suggested otherwise.

7

OSCAR BURST THROUGH THE DOOR WITH A JOVIAL SMILE GLUED upon his bright face. He had spent the day hunting for the perfect six-month anniversary/moving in together present for April, and had returned with a bracelet he was, at first, incredibly confident she would like. The journey home, however, had left him profusely doubtful, and he was desperate to get the moment of exchange over and done with.

He closed the door behind him and kicked his shoes off, calling hastily for her.

"April! April!"

Silence.

Having been caught up in his eager happiness, he had failed to notice the absence of light. Not a lamp was lit in the house, and it left him with a sense of foreboding building in the pit of his stomach, like a set of locusts setting up a wrestling match inside his belly.

Maybe she wasn't home?

But the door wasn't locked.

"April? Are you there?"

He warily edged through to the kitchen, looking around, switching the light on as he entered.

Nothing.

"April? Please answer me."

He edged through to the living room, and the sight of an ominous silhouette in the corner made him jump. After the initial shock he saw it was April, and turned the light on.

"April, what are you doing?"

He rushed over to her and put his hands on her arms. That's when he saw her face. Her wet eyes, her red cheeks, and her solemn expression pointed at the floor. Her body wasn't in the confident posture she normally sauntered through these rooms with, but instead had a morose slant, like a wilted flower or an expired piece of fruit.

"What is it?" Oscar insisted. He tried lifting her face, but she wouldn't budge. "Hey, come on. Happy six-month anniversary. Yeah? I got you something."

He took a big breath, readied himself for rejection, and withdrew the bracelet from his bag, presenting it to her. She greeted it with an immediate gasp, grabbing it off him, and lifting it to her eyes. She studied its gold plate and decorative indentations.

"You like it?"

"I – I love it."

Her hands dropped and her sombreness returned, as if she had just remembered something awful that meant the bracelet's charm wouldn't last.

Oscar grew abruptly fearful. Why was she so sad? He'd never seen her this sad before.

Then it struck him.

Is she going to break up with me?

His breathing quickened pace and his head rushed around a hundred responses, none of them good.

No. Don't be so pessimistic.

But in truth, he had already decided that she was not only going to break up with him, but for a man with far more muscles, intelligence, and a more generous penis size.

"April…"

"Oscar, I'm pregnant," she blurted out.

Oscar breathed a sigh of relief. His body untensed and his muscles relaxed.

She wasn't cheating.

She wasn't breaking up with him.

Everything was okay.

"Oh, phew," he unknowingly spoke.

"What?" April retorted, a face full of fury.

"Oh, no, I mean–"

Then it suddenly sunk over him, what she had just said.

Pregnant.

April.

Pregnant April.

Baby.

April pregnant baby.

"So…"

His first question was, *is it mine?* But his instinct told him that this was not the correct response.

He fought against words in his mind to form a coherent phrase. Finally, he relaxed, and allowed his true feelings to rise to the surface.

"That's… brilliant!"

"What?"

"That's… amazing. I mean, I know it's not planned, but… wow. I mean, I – I'm happy!"

"You're happy? Honestly?"

"Yes."

Oscar threw his hands around April and lifted her up – making sure not to groan as he did, as that made her insecure (he'd learnt that before) – and spun her around. It put a strain on his muscles that he didn't expect, despite her small, dainty disposition – but he didn't care. He regretted nothing. He was elated.

"Why?"

"What?"

"Why are you so happy, Oscar?"

"Because you – you are the love of my life. And I always dreamt of this eventually. Sure, it may be a little sooner than we thought–"

"A *lot* sooner."

"–but, you know what, screw it. I love you. I love us. And if this gives me something else to love, well then, I guess I'll just have to find the room."

April smiled quizzically at him. It was as if he'd just reminded her of all the millions of reasons that she loved him. She flung her arms around his neck and pushed a passionate, heartfelt kiss against his lips.

"I love you, Oscar."

"I love you, April."

He held her tight as those words sank through his thoughts like a hand brushing through a gentle wave: *I'm going to be a daddy. I'm going to have a baby with April.*

And he knew, in that precious moment, that nothing could take away that fiery spark he felt pumping through him that told him this was the woman his life had been created for.

8

'Beat those Holiday Blues.'

'Five Fun Fat-Burning Facts.'

'Organise Your Clear-out Like a Pro.'

As Oscar thumbed through the pages of the *Good House-keeping* magazine, he decided it was not for him. He didn't find that he particularly had any post-Christmas blues, nor did he find a longing desire to burn lots of fat. If anything, he was a bit thin and scrawny, and he could do with adding some. Any t-shirt he wore was either too baggy or, if tight, only outlined his strange boniness.

He threw the magazine back onto the pile and sifted through the rest of the reading material available in the waiting room of the obstetrician's office – a word he had learnt the previous day. When April had requested he go with her to the obstetrician's, he assumed it was some ridiculous magic show at the local theatre. After April had appeared extremely disappointed and overly-sensitive at his detest of the idea, he googled it on his phone, and returned to the room to make a swift and much needed apology.

So there he sat, in the waiting room. Reading the women's monthlies piled upon the table next to him.

Cosmopolitan. Red. Prime. OK! InStyle.

Why are all these magazines for women?

He sighed and turned away. Honestly, did they not think men ever sat in a waiting room? Yet he could not think of a single waiting room he'd been in that had a copy of *Empire* or *Sci-Fi Now*. It was as if there was some giant conspiracy where the magazine suppliers of waiting rooms were trying to prohibit men from the whole waiting experience.

"What are you thinking about?" April asked him, with a cheeky smile on her face.

Oscar wondered whether to be honest or not.

"I was thinking about how much I'm looking forward to our first scan," he replied, prompting a loving smile from April's beaming face. He pushed the thoughts of magazine conspiracies from his mind and took her hand firmly in his.

"Do you have any idea how far along you actually are?" Oscar asked. "I mean, I know we're bound to find out, I just wondered."

"I don't know."

Oscar nodded. He looked around the waiting room. They were, without doubt, the youngest couple there. Not only that, but the only couple without a rounded pregnant belly. There were four other women, three of which had a man next to them, and a few who had toddlers playing with some waiting room toys, having found something evidently far more interesting than the collection of women's monthlies. Some of the men had facial hair; Oscar could barely grow a substantial amount of whiskers to resemble a moustache. One man sat in a suit, looking very business-like. The other had hair that was partially grey.

I'm twenty. I'm not that old...

"Hey, April," Oscar subtly whispered, "I feel, like, really…"

"Young?"

"Yeah."

"Totally. It's freaking me out."

Oscar held her hand tighter.

"It's fine. We're adults. It's cool."

Adults.

Yeah, I'm an adult. As if.

Oscar wasn't sure he knew of many other parents who bought tickets for the midnight showing of the new *Star Wars* movie, or who had an impressive comic book collection that took up two bookcases.

April's hand suddenly seized. As Oscar turned to her, he could see her face grimacing.

"What's the matter?" he asked.

"Nothing," April insisted. A rumble of thunder echoed outside the window. "Nothing, I just–"

She abruptly convulsed, grabbing hold of her belly with both hands as she did. Oscar instinctively put his arm around her, but became distracted by the ensuing moans that then came from each of the other pregnant women in the room. Seconds after April's pain, each mother-to-be grabbed hold of their belly, with the same grimace on their face.

April's tension relieved slightly and her arms loosened.

"God, April, are you–"

Before he could say another word, she grabbed onto her belly again, moaning and writhing in agony. Seconds after, the rest of the women followed in perfect unison. A room full of women clutching onto pregnant bellies, and their partners checking if they were okay.

Oscar found it strange. But he thought nothing further of it, and put his arm around April.

Her body loosened once more, and she relaxed.

"Are you all right?" he asked.

"Yeah. Yeah, I'm fine. Just a bit of pain."

"April Cristine?" came the sound of the obstetrician.

April stood up, grabbed her bags, and Oscar had to hurry to follow her into the room.

"Hello, I'm Doctor Janet Stave," the woman introduced herself. She was a portly black woman with a kind face and piercing green eyes. A long, white coat hung open, and she had more jewellery on her arms than needed. Beside her dangling earrings was a comforting, reassuring smile, and the friendliness one would hope for in the situation. "You must be April, which means you must be Oscar."

She shook their hands, and allowed April sit upright on the bed. Oscar took the seat next to April, still keeping hold of her hand.

"Is everything okay then?"

"Yeah, I've just had a few pains in the waiting room, but beside that, fine."

"Okay, well it's perfectly normal to feel a bit of discomfort, but we'll check you out and make sure everything's okay. Are you all right to lean back for me and we'll do your scan?"

April reluctantly laid back, allowing Doctor Stave to lift April's top over her belly and rub some jelly over her navel. It was cold at first, and made April shudder, but she kept hold of Oscar's hand and did her best to quell her nerves.

"Okay, are you ready?"

April nodded, though her eyes screamed terror. Oscar wondered what it was she was worried about. The pregnancy had been unprecedented, yes, but surely she couldn't be letting that cast a negative mindset over the whole process.

"It's okay," Oscar told April. "We're going to see the baby on the screen, and you'll see, it's going to be great."

April nodded again, without any conviction or certainty.

Doctor Stave turned the screen toward them.

"Right, if you just have a look at the screen," she instructed. "You will be able to see—"

Just as Oscar turned his attention toward the monitor to see the image of his child the screen flickered, and the image became a series of wavy lines.

"Oh," Doctor Stave said. "I don't really know what's happening."

She gave the screen a tap and waited. It continued to disrupt, showing squiggly absent lines, as if it was a very old television unable to get a reception.

"This has never happened before," Doctor Stave told them. "I'll tell you what, I'll see if I can get it to print."

She tapped a few keys on the keyboard and switched off the flickering screen. She reached for the printer, which came to life. The whirs of the rolling paper sounded without issue. Then, as soon as it came to ink being placed upon the paper, the printer began to wheeze and cough. The paper jammed, causing a screech that only grew louder and more painful, as if someone had grabbed hold of a cat and squeezed it until it squealed.

"This is really strange," Doctor Stave admitted. "Please just give me a minute. I'll go and see if someone can help."

As she left, April turned her wounded expression toward Oscar. He could see a disguised tear sticking to the corner of her eye.

"Do you think it's a sign?" she asked, her voice weak and worried.

"A sign of what? Don't be silly, equipment malfunctions sometimes. It's all going to be okay."

"But, what if—"

"No," Oscar insisted, placing his hands firmly around hers and forcing her eyes to look into his. "I need you to stop this right now. Stop the worrying about nothing. This is all going to be okay."

"You think?"

"I think? April, I promise." He loosened a hand and ran it affectionately down her cheek. "Everything is going to be perfect."

9

Years ago – hell, maybe even months ago – Derek would have remained by that empty, blood-stained bed and debated with Jason and Julian until his voice grew hoarse.

He knew, however, and very much against his own reluctance, that his time for such contributions was at an end. He did not have the energy to provide the tenacity needed for a hearty debate. It wasn't just the illness, it was in his bones. His heart felt weaker, and he felt tired at such stressful jobs. He wouldn't have been able to join in the conversation for long without falling asleep during the most poignant part of the debate.

No, he knew when he wasn't needed. So he found himself using his sturdy walking stick to guide his aching bones away from the hypothesising and discussing and wondering that Jason and Julian were engaging in to find a place to rest elsewhere in the children's ward whilst he waited.

Maybe he could even get a head start back to the car. He chuckled to himself, as he imagined himself getting a half-hour advantage that they overtook within minutes.

He paused by the water fountain, reaching out for a paper

cup. Even the action of leaning his walking stick against the wall and reaching out his feeble arm took him more energy than he could expend without finding an ache engraining into his bones with a prominence he couldn't ignore.

He hated feeling useless. But the one thing he hated more was feeling like a burden.

"What are you talking about?" came an inquisitive voice.

Derek slowly rotated his head toward a nearby bed, where a young boy's face stared at him.

"Excuse me?" Derek said.

"You were muttering something. What is it?"

"Ah." Derek smiled. The approach of a child was always so direct and without embarrassment. If only we could all be so bold. "I was thinking about something that made me sad."

"What was it?"

"Well. That would take a while to explain."

"I'm not going anywhere."

Derek grinned. He admired the boy's tenacity.

"Okay," Derek decided. "Do you mind if I sit?"

The boy shrugged.

Derek finished his water, retrieved his walking stick, and made the long walk of a few metres to the chair beside the boy's bed.

"You haven't much hair, like me," the boy pointed out, staring at Derek's post-treatment prickles perching atop his scalp. The boy, too, had an absence of hair, only he looked to be more in the midst of it. The only break from the paleness of his face were the prominent black bags beneath his eyes.

"I do. That's because I'm ill, as well."

"Are you really?"

"Yes. My name is Derek, by the way. What is yours?"

"Charlie."

"Charlie. Wonderful name. How old are you, Charlie?"

"Ten."

"Ten. What a lovely age. And do you have a close friend, Charlie? Like a best friend."

The boy pointed at a girl asleep in the bed next to his.

"Her name is Joanna."

"Joanna. A lovely name too." Derek paused to take a moment to gather his thoughts. "Well, Charlie, to answer your question. I had a best friend once, but he died many, many years ago. Since then I have been doing the best I can to pay respect to his memory. To help people. Only now, I can't."

"Why not?"

"Well, because I'm either too old, or too ill. Or both."

Charlie looked down at his fidgeting hands, nodding.

"I understand how you feel. I wish I could have helped Tommy. But I couldn't."

"Who's Tommy?"

Charlie looked confused at the question.

"You know who Tommy is."

"Sorry, Charlie, but I don't."

"You came in with those two other men, didn't you? The ones who have gone to see Tommy's bed?"

Ah.

Derek dropped his head in a moment of understanding.

"I see. And were you and Tommy close?"

Charlie eagerly nodded.

"I'm sorry, Charlie. It's never nice to lose someone we care about. Especially when they are ill."

"He didn't die because he was ill."

"What makes you say that?"

"Because I saw it."

Derek leant forward.

"What did you see, Charlie?"

"The thing that killed him. We've all seen it. Well, all of us who have been here long enough to see it."

"And what does it look like, Charlie?"

Charlie looked fearfully into Derek's eyes. His lips remained tightly sealed, and his eyes widened into a worried stare.

"Charlie, I can help you. What did it look like?"

Charlie shook his head, keeping his lips closed as tight as he could.

"Charlie, what does it–"

"Derek."

Derek turned and saw Jason and Julian waiting behind him, indicating that it was time to leave. He turned back to Charlie and gave him a sincere, heartfelt smile.

"It was nice to meet you, Charlie. I hope to see you again soon."

He nodded at the child and followed the other two out of the building. As he struggled to even remain in the shadow of the other two's hefty pace, ignored as they engaged in heated discussion, his mind remained on Charlie, and what the boy had witnessed.

10

IT WAS A FAMILIAR SIGHT TO JULIAN. MANY BOOKS WITH MANY dusty covers laid open upon a desk, sending powdery clouds into his twitching nose. They were sporadically placed but precisely opened on marked pages that referred to demons with a focus on children.

Julian glanced at Jason with a sly smirk. To him, opening these ancient books, reading their overbearing language, and sifting through their hefty pages was a normal part of the process of identifying who he, or the other Sensitives, were going to have to do battle with. To Jason, this was the first time sifting through these books about demons and the occult. Jason gave the same perplexed looks at the browned pages he thumbed through as Julian had when Derek had first introduced him to them.

"Any ideas?" Julian prompted, standing behind Jason with a knowing expression.

"I – this is – well…"

"You can say no."

Jason returned Julian's grin.

"These books are beyond what I imagined. Does all this

stuff really exist? I mean, these many demons, these many types of ghosts, it all, just, seems…"

"A bit farfetched?"

Jason nodded.

"Tell me about it."

The front door opened and within moments, Oscar and April had burst into the room. Happy smiles spread across their faces, their hands entwined with each other's, barely able to rip their eyes from each other. It made Julian want to gag. It was like seeing a younger sister with an irritating boyfriend.

"Great," Julian said. "Now the happy couple are here, we can get some input."

"Sorry we're late," Oscar offered. The grin stuck to his face spoke nothing of apology whatsoever.

"Well, if you're done touching each other up and giggling like toddlers, a child has died."

April's smile ceased. She bit her lip. She looked up at Julian with those eyes of vulnerability he saw whenever she was scared or worried about something. Those same eyes he had seen when he first approached her when she was living on the streets.

"We kind of have some news," April announced. "I mean, I know this is important, so we'll be really quick."

"What?" Julian barked.

"I'm – well, see…"

"She's pregnant!" Oscar interjected.

Julian felt as if he'd just been smacked in the face with a large metal rod. At first, he couldn't believe it. He thought it was part of some ridiculous, ill-timed joke. Then, as he saw their awaiting expressions peering back it him, the realisation that this news was true washed over him like a bucket of ice.

April? Pregnant?

Oscar? A dad.

It was ridiculous.

They are just kids.

"Well?" April prompted. "Aren't you going to say anything?"

Julian could see it in her eyes. The need for his approval. The need for his reassuring words to tell her it was going to be okay. She needed him to say something to comfort her, to calm her on this inevitable path of destruction she had set herself upon.

But he couldn't.

He had no words.

"It's marvellous news," came a voice from the doorway. As the owner of the soft declaration of joy hobbled further, he managed to reach the nearest chair, planting himself upon it and breathing a sigh of relief. "I told you good would still prevail."

"Derek." Oscar smiled widely. "It's great to see you."

"It's great to see you, too," Derek said. "This is wonderful. A child! You must tell us all the news. How far along are you?"

"Actually, if you lot don't mind," Julian interrupted, "We have two dead kids and a dead doctor on our hands, with a likely imminent death pretty soon. So maybe we can save all this for later."

"Julian?" April said. "Why are you being like this?"

"Like what?" Julian snapped. "What do you want from me? My blessing? Good luck. To the pair of you. It's going to be lovely."

He turned his grimace back to the numerous open books awaiting his attention.

"Julian–"

"Look – if you are quite done, we do actually have a job to do. Like finding out who this demon is."

"You don't need to," came Derek's meek voice. "I can tell you."

"What?" Julian scoffed, bowed his head and rubbed his

sinus, doing all he could to avoid the frustration pent up inside from bursting out.

"I have fought this thing before."

"How could you possibly know that?"

"Oh, I know. Trust me."

"Right." Julian slammed closed all the books, swivelled to Derek, and lurched his body forward with his hands on his hips. "Do go on. Please. Save us the hours we have already pissed away researching."

"The demon's name is Lamia."

"Lamia?"

"Yes. Lamia. A demon of Greek origin, said to be the mistress of a god, once a beautiful queen of Libya. She possessed a young girl from Portugal I once knew. In Scotland."

"It possessed a Portuguese girl in Scotland?" Julian scathingly repeated. "And what is it about this demon that makes you think it's her?"

Derek stroked his chin, studying Julian's defiant face.

"Because this girl killed, and ate, twelve children. Just before I watched her throw herself off a cliff."

"...Oh."

THEN

11

THE CRUNCH OF LEAVES FOUGHT AGAINST THE SOLES OF Martin's feet. The further he walked the sparser they became, replaced by wet soil. Eventually, the wetness mixed with speckles of blood, and Martin ceased his searching.

Beside his feet were two eyes, wide and still, upon the pale face of Madelina's corpse. The hair brushed over her mouth didn't blow outwards from her breath, nor did her chest rise or her fingers flinch. The moonlight barely even reflected in her pupils, such was the lack of life that consumed her.

Martin knelt beside her. Reached a hand out. Brushed the hair off her face. Traced his fingers down her neck, which had grown so stiff, and so cold. They travelled further downwards, gently running down her chest until they landed upon her belly, home to a child that was a month off being born.

He rested his hand there.

He felt nothing.

No bumps. No movement. Not even a gurgle.

Not a single recognition from the baby of its father.

Martin bowed his head. Allowed his eyes to rest shut.

He made the decision never to tell Derek that it was his

child. He'd introduced Madelina as a friend in trouble, believing that his mentor would know the best thing to do. Her symptoms were terrifying – with the lust for meat and bizarre behaviour she was exhibiting, it was as if the demon had targeted Martin personally.

He shook his head. Forced tears from his eyes.

Who was he kidding?

Of course it was a personal attack.

After the wars he and Derek had waged, the demons they had defeated, the lengths they had gone to so they could keep hell quiet and banish evil from the earth. Had they really expected no retaliation?

He allowed his eyes to flutter open, fixing them on hers. They looked back, but they didn't. It was a strange feeling. To see someone staring at him, knowing there was nothing behind that stare.

Even in death, her eyes retained the unmistakable vulnerability they'd held in life. She was so strong, a dominative force, someone who would not take shit off anyone. But beneath that, behind the exterior of her strong feminine character, was a scared voice. He could see it. No one else could, but he could.

He hated Derek. In that moment, he hated him. Despised him. It was his fault. It was all his fault.

Derek had insisted. No exorcism. She was too weak. Too pregnant.

That was his child.

Derek was not to know, but that was Martin's child.

A rustle of leaves from behind him disturbed his melancholy state. He shook it off.

He had a job to do.

He stood. Turned. Faced the direction of the quiver of leaves.

Shadows brushed the trees so faintly that a blink would have robbed him of the sight.

"I know you are there," he said. "And I know who you are."

He withdrew his cross from his pocket. Gently kissed it. Held it firmly. Gripping it. Clutching it.

Madelina was gone.

Martin was not here for her.

He was here to clean up Derek's mess.

When she had jumped, she had banished the demon from her body. But that did not mean it was not banished from this earth.

In the far blackness of the bushes two piercing red eyes appeared, then blinked back to nothing.

"You want me to be angry," Martin observed. "You want this to take the better of me. I know that. I feel it."

He paused. Held his head at an angle. Removed any emotion from his body.

"But I am the son of heaven, and you will not beat me. Nor will you intimidate me."

He stepped forward with a confident stride. His arm decisively rose as he presented the cross in the direction of the disturbances.

"Reveal yourself, you filthy dominion of hell."

The rustles punched leaves into the air and fluttered the branches of the trees. This happened again. And again. And again. Until eventually, bursts of leaves feverishly pumped into the air across Martin's eyesight as if being fired from a machine, painting the dark night before him with red and green flickers.

"You think that's going to scare me?" Martin mocked. "Throwing a bunch of leaves?"

Enough.

Time to rid this world of this child-eating monstrosity of the underworld.

"The spirit of the Lord is upon me," Martin began, holding his cross out before him. "I address you, Lamia, demoness of hell, as the one anointed to preach the gospel and preach deliverance to the captives. I preach the acceptable year of the Lord."

A screech shook the trees, the sound like a combination of a crow and a woman in peril. Birds fled the trees in which they nested, sensing the impending danger.

Martin was not scared. He was perturbed. But not because of this demon.

This was Derek's job.

And he was having to do it.

"For whosoever shall call upon the name of the Lord shall be saved," Martin persisted. "And I call upon the name of the Lord. And I am saved."

A ball of flames burst from the cross, firing into five corners of a pentagon that floated as his defence.

"Forgive me my sins, cleanse me, and give me the power to banish this demon."

Martin felt it. The strength. The power. It surged through him, an electrical charge pumping through his veins.

"Reveal yourself."

The screech repeated itself, this time deafening, but not deterring Martin. Its face appeared as an apparition, the face of a woman, beautiful yet twisted, an uncomfortably appealing haze. Beneath its naked chest was a snakeskin waist, above the tail of a serpent.

It shook its head with a cackle.

Martin knew this wasn't over. That this demon was part of the devil's plan. That its revenge would come back.

"Be gone," Martin spoke softly, trying not to think of the deceased pregnant woman lying behind his feet. "Be gone."

She faded away into a smoky haze.

One might be forgiven for thinking that Martin had won.

But, as he slowly twisted back toward the body that lay behind him, he knew it was not over. It was never over. The demon may have left, but its mission had been completed. It had torn him and Derek apart. This final appearance was just its mocking visage tormenting him.

As if to say, "Until the next time."

Martin didn't blame it.

And, as he lay by Madelina's sweet head, all he could think about was the man he did blame.

NOW

12

A FLICKERING AMBER GLOW OF THREE CANDLES ILLUMINATED the bedroom. One placed on Derek's bedside table, one on the desk opposite, and one on the windowsill. He liked being in a room lit only by candles. He told himself that it was because the light was natural, and it made him feel calm and serene. In truth, it was a habit he'd become used to as a way of detecting a supernatural attack; with the fights he had fought, he had become a vulnerable target, and if the candles brawled against a breeze in a room with a closed window and secure door, it would give him the first indication of an imminent presence.

As he sat on the edge of his bed, he ran his hands through his hair, which was damp from sweat. The process of walking upstairs had taken far more energy than he had to expend – he needed a few moments to mentally prepare for the energy it would take to lie down and pull the duvet over himself.

"Right," announced Julian as he barged in, placing a glass of water on the bedside table.

He opened the drawer and took out a pill box, arranging three pills from separate sections in his hands. He held them toward Derek.

"Here they are," Julian said in a thoroughly business-like fashion. "Do you want the glass of water?"

Derek took a moment to look at Julian's partially lit face. He was often short-tempered and snappy, such was his way; but there seemed to be something else. Something cold in the way he was conducting himself.

"Yes, please," Derek eventually answered, taking the pills from Julian's hand. He placed the first in his mouth, took the glass of water from Julian, and gulped it down.

"Good night then," Julian curtly grunted.

"Julian, wait."

Julian paused by the door.

"What?"

"Sit down."

Julian shook his head in a disdainful manner, huffing with annoyance.

"Derek, it's been a long day. I really don't have time."

"Don't have time for an ill man who taught you how to do the job you are so busy doing? Please, just sit."

As Derek took his second pill, Julian hesitated. Derek sure did have a way with words, and he knew it. What's more, he knew Julian, and he knew what to say to persuade him.

Julian gave another huff as he threw himself on the chair beside the door, slouching as if he were a teenager waiting outside the headmaster's office.

"What?" he barked.

Derek took the final pill and finished the water, placing the glass gently upon the bedside table.

"What's bothering you?" Derek asked, slowly and calmly.

"What's bothering me? We have dead kids, and probably more if we don't get moving, and we're pissing about, making me sit and listen to another lecture that I am bloody well sure is coming."

Derek nodded. Thought. Took his time.

"No," he decided. "No. That's not it. Tell me what's really bothering you."

"What?" Julian demanded, sitting forward, fixing his seething eyes on Derek.

"The way you spoke to April, to Oscar. I know you've had your differences with Oscar, but he came up big for us when we needed him. And April, I know how deeply you care for her. So why react like that?"

"This is pointless, Derek, I'm not going to–"

"Not going to what? Admit that you were unkind?"

"Damn it, Derek, they are children. Kids having kids. What do you want me to say? Them having a baby is bloody ridiculous. There. Said it."

"Right, fair enough. Now you've said it to me, you can keep it to yourself."

Julian glared at Derek. Not just stared, or gave him evil eyes – intensely glared. Peering his annoyance deep into Derek's retina.

"I can keep it to myself?" Julian repeated in a low-pitched growl.

"Yes. You can," Derek confirmed. "Because I'd bet that those two – being kids, as you refer to them – are bloody terrified right now. And they could do with some support. And that support needs to come from the one they look up to most." He pointed at Julian's heart. "You."

A lingering absence of speech hovered in the air, settling like a bomb exploding on the ground and rising into dust. Julian let it simmer, let his irritation grow. Derek could see Julian's thoughts working, could see Julian going from one annoyed retort to another. Trying to decide which vile insult or comeback to fire back with.

"You want to know what's really bothering me?" Julian spat.

"I truly do."

"You. You, who are so ill you shouldn't be anywhere but a hospital – but because you're so stubborn, you place the burden on *me* to look after you. Don't get me wrong, I have no problem doing it – you just have no idea what effort it takes. Because I have to run this business, solve a murder, defeat a child-killing demon, then force-feed you your sodding pills. And then I have to sit here and be subjected to a lecture about my manners and treatment of others, before you then go onto your incessant rambling about how good will always prevail, how good will go on, how good will do this, do that, yada yada yada. It's bullshit. All of it, it's bullshit."

Julian stood, unmoved. Hovering between Derek and the door. A flicker of apology for his outburst passed over Julian's eyes with the movement of the candle, then it was gone.

"Goodnight," he spoke, then left, shutting the door behind him.

Derek bowed his head.

Was he placing too much of a burden on Julian? Maybe this was a cry for help. Maybe the stress was getting to him. Maybe the pregnancy meant that the two people who were meant to be helping him were now going to be otherwise engaged, and this meant that the weight on Julian's shoulders was only getting bigger.

Either way, Julian couldn't know.

He couldn't know about the nine months Derek spent trying to rid that demon from Madelina. About how futile it was.

About how the demon's intentions were entirely to inflict this pain upon Derek. To find an innocent female victim, put something in that victim, something the victim would protect against even Derek, and let it consume that dreaded woman.

Madelina was lucky. She killed herself before she could release the demon's spawn upon the world.

What if it was happening all over again?

No.

Julian had many burdens, but this burden of knowledge was not for him. Not whilst he was in this state.

It belonged to someone who believed that this thing could still be defeated but good. By hope. By the same tools they had used and prayed for in every exorcism Derek had partaken in.

Derek decided, then and there, that Lamia's true nature would stay with him.

That was, until the day he had to fight it.

If he lived that long.

(6 MONTHS)

13

JULIAN SEARCHED THE SHELVES FOR WHAT MUST HAVE BEEN AT least the fifteenth time. Maybe even the twentieth. But it felt like the hundredth.

His thumb ran past the same rough edges of old, brown-paged sheets. The scuffed leather binding of ancient literature pushed out spurts of dust as he flicked past numerous titles adorning the sturdy shelf.

The Occult a History: 1400 to 1600.

The Demonologist's Handbook.

Exorcism: Alive and Well in the Twentieth Century.

None of these damn books had a single mention of Lamia. Not a drawing, reference, or even a mention in passing. It was like the demon either didn't exist, or all knowledge of it had been wiped off the earth.

Julian didn't even know why he was bothering.

Derek was once a great man. He was as good a mentor as Julian could hope for, and had taught him everything he knew. He was a legendary exorcist, having fought in the biggest war that mankind would never know it faced. He had saved thousands of souls, punished more demons than he was able to take stock of, and had saved more lives than most could achieve in a lifetime.

But that wasn't Derek anymore.

Derek was ill. Desperately, painfully ill. He wouldn't admit it, but his health was deteriorating by the day. What was once an astute, well-spoken, always smartly dressed, educated man was now a man who could barely walk across a room without needing to sit down.

The burden Derek placed on Julian day to day was more intense than the man could realise. Derek insisted he didn't need a hospital, saying he had no problem dying on his own terms – but what about those who cared for him? Those who were then left to do an inadequate job of what a qualified doctor should be doing?

It wasn't fair. And Julian was struggling to retain patience.

He dropped his weight into the nearest chair and slouched. He huffed. Then he huffed again.

He was tired. Exasperated. Irritated. Exhausted. Drained. Weary. Mentally full.

It was like someone just kept shovelling more and more into his head, filling it with stress, filling it with more burdens to worry about, then squeezed the top of his skull on tight and stapled it shut until nothing would be able to escape its bursting contents.

Dead children.

Derek.

A demon that didn't seem to exist.

But why would Derek claim it was Lamia if that demon didn't exist?

Why would Derek claim he'd had experience with this demon?

Why would he say anything?

Because he was delusional. It was the only explanation.

The illness had pushed to his mind. Convinced him of

things. Twisted the truth until it wrapped around itself so many times that it became convoluted, and there was no awareness as to what the truth was anymore.

It wasn't that Derek was lying.

But that he was not the man he was.

Julian dropped his head to his palm, shaking it to himself.

How could he be so curt?

The man Derek had been. The things he had done.

Julian wouldn't know any of this, be anything of the person he was, if it weren't for the effort and energy Derek had put into not only training him, convincing him, and moulding him – but finding him in the first place.

He hadn't even known what a Sensitive was.

No.

Mustn't doubt Derek.

Not him. Not that man. Not the one guy Julian respected.

He leapt to his feet, projecting himself back to the hefty cupboard. It took up the entire wall of Derek's study and was at least three books deep. It was a large collection, but that would make sense – Derek had, after all, been collecting these works his entire life.

He dragged his fingers across the next few spines.

Demons: An Intermediate's Guide.

How to Find the Truth – Demon or Delusion?

Modern Demons in a Modern World.

Titles he was familiar with.

All titles he had used at some point. All titled he'd subjected himself to for numerous hours slaving away at their words, reading them until they became jumbled nonsense falling through his mind. Read them until the words didn't even look like words anymore, but mystical shapes forming unfamiliar patterns that only highlighted how much there was to be known, yet how little of it he knew.

He could remember almost every word.

There had never been any mention of Lamia amongst any of them. He was sure of it.

He could ask Derek. Ask for more information. Ask to be directed to the right book.

But what was the point?

Time to be honest with myself.

It was bollocks, wasn't it?

All of it.

Just the ramblings of a fading mind. When a brain with such a mass of intelligence begins to lose its grip on reality, that intelligence only makes it worse. An unwise man would have little to delude themselves with. A genius would have so much information to fire through their mind, they would be bound to lose the ability to comprehend it, make sense of it, or to create the right links.

No.

Time to look elsewhere.

Julian would take care of Derek as best he could. He would be as faithful to his mentor as his mentor had been to him.

As for the nonsensical ramblings, he would do no more than nod along.

It was time for Julian to take over.

He was the one who must lead the Sensitives without help or guidance.

The burden was now to fall upon him.

14

A NERVOUS ENERGY BATTERED ITS WINGS AROUND OSCAR'S stomach. He straightened his shirt. His cuffs. His collar. Smoothed his hair backwards. Fidgeted with his hands. Anything to keep himself occupied.

To say his relationship with his parents had been rocky would be like saying his relationship with Julian was full of brotherly love. Before he'd met April and discovered his abilities as a Sensitive, he'd left school at sixteen and worked in the local supermarket. This was fine for him, but to his parents, who had bestowed ambitions of university upon him since he was old enough to comprehend what further education was, this was a grave disappointment. They had reminded him every day when he returned from work that this was not where he should be; he had just never had ambition to do anything else. That all changed once he pursued paranormal investigation and found a career he was passionate about – after which, he'd thought they would be proud.

If anything, they had stung him with more disappointment than they had before.

They were interested in what they termed 'educated

careers': teacher, accountancy, engineering, advertising, pharmaceuticals. Not what they had described as, "Hocus pocus nonsense," upon the announcement that he had a new, exciting career.

This had prompted him to move out a few months ago, which had led to him more recently settling in a new home with April. His contact with them since his moving had been minimal. Greeting cards, a text message on a birthday, stopping over when it was a larger family gathering – but nothing where they spent a substantial amount of time in each other's company.

It seemed that the announcement of an imminent grandchild had changed this. They wanted to make amends. And that started with a family dinner where they would meet the soon-to-be mother of his child.

He could just imagine what their judgemental impression would be upon meeting this woman. They would see the purple-dyed hair, the tattoos of Tim Burton characters on her arm, the baggy jeans – and they would instantly despise her, before they had gotten to know the beautiful, kind-hearted, wonderful human being that lay beneath. This punky image was what had first attracted him to her, and he loved it. He dreaded that his parents wouldn't.

"What's the matter?" April asked as they stood before his parents' front door. "You're sweating."

"I know. I'm just, y'know... mentally preparing myself."

"For what? Knocking on the door?"

Oscar turned to April, his face overcome with fear.

"Jeeze," April exclaimed. "I didn't even see you this scared when you were facing a prison full of ghosts."

"I just want you to know, whatever they say or do, please, just, don't take it personally."

She placed her arms around him.

"I love you, Oscar. And I've got skin thicker than anything. I'm more study than a Snickers bar."

"A Snickers bar?"

"Yep. I compared myself to a chocolate bar. And what of it?"

Oscar couldn't help but chuckle. He leant his forehead against hers. A gesture that had come to be special to them. A source of comfort they gave each other whenever they needed to make sure they knew they weren't alone.

"Well, you are nutty," Oscar joked.

April sniggered sarcastically.

"Now knock on the door," she prompted. "Come on."

Oscar nodded – more to himself than to her, as if preparing for the actions he was about to undertake – and turned to face the door. He stretched his arm out and placed four firm knocks against the wooden barricade between him and his elders.

Shortly after, they opened it. They held out their arms and greeted their son with an eager hug, then shook his girlfriend's hands with enthusiasm and energy he hadn't expected.

They were whisked inside and sat in the living room, where his dad made them a cup of tea and regaled them with stories of how the decorating of the room had gone wrong. They laughed. Oscar began to relax.

As the evening continued, they keenly questioned April about what they did and where she came from. She answered, and their prejudice toward his occupation had either gone, or was well disguised. Oscar's nerves faded with the setting of the evening sun outside, and before he knew it they were having a happy tea, engaging in willing conversation.

"So do you earn much from this business?" his dad asked April. "I mean, from your clients."

"Well, it depends on the client, really," April answered,

smiling at Oscar's mother as she placed a plate of chicken and vegetables in front of her. "Thank you."

"How so?" his dad continued.

"Well, I mean, the wealth of the client is a definite factor. We won't ask for money that they can't afford. Generally, we ask for a contribution toward our living, rather than a flat fee. After we finish and have helped them, they are usually so grateful that they try and shove as much money on us as they can. Sometimes they are even too generous, and we have to tell them to just give us what they are able, not what they want."

"Fascinating," his dad said, cutting a piece of chicken off the bone. "Really, fascinating."

"Do you find it rewarding?" his mum asked, then placed a scoop of vegetables on her spoon and directed them into her mouth.

"Oh, God yeah. I mean, it's tough. Particularly when we have to tell people there is nothing supernaturally occurring and they, you know, just need a doctor." His parents chuckled. "But when we do actually manage to succeed with a real case, it's rewarding to see the difference you have made to their lives."

Pleased that the conversation was flowing smoothly without his aid, Oscar cut a small amount of chicken and placed it in his mouth, ensuring he ate with his mouth closed. Their son or not, his parents were very middle-class people, and he did not want to seem rude with his table manners. It felt as if his relationship with them was repairable, and they were trying really hard; maybe he had to as well.

"So, tell us more about the baby," said his mum. "How far along are you?"

"Three months."

"And have you thought of any names yet?"

"Not really." April looked vaguely at Oscar. "We're still kind of dealing with the shock of it, I guess."

"Well, I bet. It must have come as quite a surprise. I remember when we had Oscar, we–"

A sudden, uncomfortable silence ensued.

Oscar stopped chewing. What had happened? Things were going so well? Why had...

He looked at April.

She had sunk her face to the level of her plate and dug her teeth into the side of the chicken, then ripped it off with her teeth like a lion feeding on a deer. She swung her head downwards again, sinking her teeth into the dead bird's flesh and ripping it away from the bone with such ferocity and such a large quantity, that it ended up poking between her lips as she chewed.

Oscar was astonished. If he ate his morning cereal with a slight opening in his mouth she would treat him as if he had just kicked her in the face and pissed on the table. Now, here she was, ravaging her meat like a hungry animal.

He had never seen her act in such a way.

"April..." he prompted.

She ignored him. Either that, or she didn't hear. She was too engrossed with grappling her teeth into the meat, engaging in a wrestling match between her and the bone, seeing who could win the most chicken.

"April," Oscar said again, a little louder.

Nothing.

She merely rotated the chicken – with her mouth, no less; her hands were securely on her lap – and devoured the other side with equal intensity.

Oscar looked to his parents, who were staring at this previously polite young woman, unsure what to do with their eyes. Do they stare? Do they look away? Do they comment? Ignore it? Demand her to leave?

It took her two more eager bites to rip away the remaining flesh. With sauce smeared across her cheeks, she picked up her cutlery and continued to eat her vegetables with the grace of a saint – never loading them up too highly, and munching with her mouth closed.

"Sorry?" she said, as if snapping out of a trance. "What did you say?"

"April," Oscar said. Once she looked at him, he pointed to his cheeks as an indication to clean hers.

"Oh, sorry, did I get some on me?" she asked, picking up her napkin and wiping her mouth. "What was your question?"

"Erm, yes, well," his father attempted to continue. "Where was I? Ah, yes. When we had Oscar."

"Well, I, uh," his mother tried to take over. "Yes. It was quite a shock. We were wanting children, but not quite yet."

The conversation resumed, and no more uncharacteristically rude gestures or actions were made. Oscar watched April intently, trying to figure her out, trying to understand what on earth had caused her bizarre actions. It was like he was on a hidden camera show, and someone was going to burst out any moment and reveal that it was all a ruse. A con, and they really did have him going.

But no one burst out. No comment was made, and she barely acknowledged it.

As the evening carried on, it seemed to be forgotten, and polite conversation resumed. At the end of the night, his parents spoke of how nice it was to meet her and how they hoped to see her again soon.

But Oscar did not forget.

He ruminated on it the whole way home, but decided to say nothing. It was gone. Done. Passed. And mentioning it would have done nothing but take away from the wonderful success of the evening – and that, for Oscar, was a huge achievement.

And he couldn't have asked for more – from April, or his parents.

15

DEREK HAD NEVER HAD A SON.

Once, he had been engaged, a long time ago. It had ended when he chose to pursue a life of fighting the supernatural, and she saw it as a joke. He had never had a prolonged relationship since.

Was it something he regretted?

The relationship – maybe, maybe not. He'd had many valuable relationships, just none of them prolonged romantic encounters.

But a son, or a daughter. That was something he regretted. And possibly a void he fulfilled in those he mentored, but a void nonetheless.

As he looked at Charlie, colouring in with a spritely energy he would not be able to sustain, he wondered whether Charlie and his unborn child would have ever been alike. Given, he had never imagined having a child with a terminal illness, but if he had, he imagined his child would have dealt with it with the same tenacity and resolve that Charlie had.

"What's this?" Derek asked, stifling a groan as he leant

forward from his chair to see what the young lad was colouring in.

"It's The Hulk," Charlie answered. "He's the best superhero ever."

"The best, huh?"

"Yeah! He's green, and when he's angry he gets bigger and he smashes things."

"He smashes things?" Derek repeated with feigned amazement.

"Yeah!"

"But what about the people whose things he smashes? Does he at least pay the bill for it?"

"No. He doesn't pay bills. He's too cool for that."

Derek couldn't help but laugh. If only he'd have been too cool to pay bills. It would have made life so much simpler.

"So how are things, Charlie?"

"Okay," he responded, continuing to colour in his picture.

"And this creature you spoke of. Has he been back?"

Charlie's hand stopped colouring. His eyes stopped scanning the black outline before him and his limp body grew tense.

"Has he, Charlie?"

"I – I don't want to talk about that."

Charlie's hand started moving once more, but far slower, colouring with a distant wariness.

"Why not?"

"Because I don't want to. I want to talk about good things."

"But aren't you afraid he'll come back?"

"I said I don't want to talk about it. And it's a she."

Derek allowed a moment of contemplative silence to hang in the air, and Charlie's hand resumed speed, until he was colouring eagerly once more.

"Okay, I understand," Derek finally affirmed.

As he sat watching the boy, Derek noticed something glistening around his neck. Something that sparkled in the light.

"Charlie, what's this?" Derek asked, pointing at what he had just seen.

"This?" Charlie responded, lifting a pendant from under his hospital gown.

"Yes, what is it?"

"It's from my mum."

"Your mum?"

"Yes. She isn't with us anymore."

"I'm sorry to hear that."

"It's okay." He opened it, showing a picture of a beautiful brown-haired woman with bright-green eyes.

"Is that her?" Derek asked, taking the pendant in his hand and gazing upon it.

Charlie nodded.

"She's very pretty," Derek said.

"She was. I miss her a lot."

"I don't doubt you do."

Derek let the pendant go and sat back in his chair. Charlie tucked it back beneath his hospital gown and resumed his colouring.

Derek watched it hanging loosely, wondering what he would give the people he loved once he was gone.

16

OSCAR MANAGED TO TURN THE KEY, OPEN THE FRONT DOOR, AND nearly slip on a pile of unwanted bills without acknowledging it with any thought. He rubbed his eyes, wiping the tiredness off his face, but he could feel his eyelids drooping. Success or not, the evening with his parents had been stressful, and it had truly worn him down. Anxiety was tiresome, and he had been full of it in the hours leading up to dinner, and he was looking forward to bed.

"I'm going to get ready for bed," he told April as she closed the front door. "You coming?"

"Mmhm," she answered.

He threw his jacket over the sofa and stumbled through to the bedroom. He meandered into the bathroom, pouring water into the sink without switching the light on; any illumination would be likely to highlight those tired features on his face and expose them in the reflection of the mirror, and a bout of insecurity was not what he needed to go to sleep on. He rubbed a handful of soap over his face, washed it off, and rubbed the water from his skin with his Batman towel. For the next three minutes he brushed his teeth without acknowledging the back and forth movement of his toothbrush, doused with a small dollop of minty refreshment, courtesy of the nearby tube of Colgate. Once he was finished, he went to switch the light off, and ended up switching it on, forgetting that it had been off in the first place.

He switched it back off, rubbed his eyes, then dropped his jaw as he feasted his eyes on the sight of April standing before him, as naked as the day she was born.

"Apr–"

He couldn't even finish saying her name before she had flung herself toward him and thrusted her mouth so hard against his he winced in pain as he caught his bottom lip in his teeth.

Was this pregnancy hormones?

Hell, does it matter...

Oscar engaged, putting his hands on her back and stroking gently up her spine. Before he could move his hands any further she had grabbed his wrists and shoved them back behind his back. He went to put his arms back around her, but she forced them behind his back once more.

"Leave them," she instructed with deadly assertiveness, twisting her head from side to side as she pushed and pushed her lips against his.

Oscar opened his eyes momentarily, taken aback by her abrupt nature. This was nothing like he'd experienced before. Given, yes, his sexual experience was vastly inferior to hers; but in the many, many, many times they had entered foreplay in the last six months, there had never been hands restrained behind backs or kissing so hard it hurt.

She grabbed hold of his arms, squeezing against his limp biceps so hard he felt her thumbs rub against his bones. She threw him onto the bed.

As he bounced on the mattress, he looked up at her as if to say something – but what? What was he supposed to ask? It was strange, yes, but in that fleeting second he had before her harsh lips pounded back to his, his thoughts could not formulate the words to express his confusion, or how taken aback he was.

She didn't even undress him. He went to take his top off, but she just shoved his hands back against the mattress above his head and held them there with one single hand. She used the other to unleash his belt and push his trousers down just enough for her to be able to grab his stiff cock in her hand.

Within seconds she had mounted him, and he had entered her.

It hurt. Hurt in a way it never had before. It didn't feel warm or pleasurable like it normally did; it felt rough. Coarse. Unprepared.

He knew this was due to lack of foreplay. She wasn't wet enough, and this meant that his penis was rubbing against the dry surface of her insides. He felt his foreskin scrape up and down against the force of her movement. He went to object, but her hand covered his mouth before he could open it fully.

As he stared up at her he felt himself tremble. Her expression was different. There was something carnal about it. Her lip was aggressively curled, twisting into a sneer, and her nose ruffled up into a leering snarl. Her eyes were distant, yet piercingly close. A sinister glare, as if she was doing this because she hated him.

Her hand sunk from his mouth, down his chin, and to his throat. Her palm spread over his neck and squeezed, tightening and tightening until he couldn't breathe.

He tried to speak, but she tightened harder until he couldn't. He tried to choke, tried to clamber for air, but she refused to allow him the luxury of oxygen.

She moved faster. Riding harder and harder. Rubbing her rough insides against him to the point that he was now burning, like hot rubber wrapped around his genitals, static pushing against his skin.

He wanted to cry.

This didn't feel like sex.

Sex didn't always have to be intimate, sometimes it could be playful, or even rough – but this felt worse. Like an attack. An invasion of his rights. Forced upon him until his voice was stifled and he couldn't make enough sense of what was occurring to object.

She loosened her grip, pulled her hand back, and growled. A low-pitched, sinister growl.

"Apri–"

She sliced her hand across his cheek. A slap with her nails, as if instructing him to shut up. To dare not moan. To never say a word against what this dominant force chose to do.

She stopped.

Suddenly. Her movement stiffly, abruptly still. She remained in position, him inside of her, poised in limbo.

She dismounted.

Fell onto her side. Turned, lying away from him, curled up tightly into the foetal position.

In less than a minute her breathing was deep, and a gentle snore whispered out of her mouth.

Oscar couldn't make sense of what had just happened. He couldn't react. He couldn't speak.

It's not that he didn't appreciate the surprise element, nor that he expected every movement of their sex life to be gentle and passionate, just that he should be allowed to talk. To voice his objections, or guide her in what felt good. So often he had gone down on her and allowed her to guide him, in either a gentle, soothing voice, or with the gentle nudge of her hands against his head. An action he had welcomed, as it allowed him to ensure he was giving her as much pleasure as he could.

This was different.

This was... something else.

He hadn't even been able to talk to her enough to even withdraw his consent.

It was hostile. Forced. Aimed at the destruction of his self-worth. The abuse of an intimacy both he and she had rights to.

The events soared round his mind as he lay there, listening to the faint purr of her breathing.

17

AN INSTANT LURCH AWOKE APRIL FROM A DEEP, DREAMLESS sleep. The light bursting between the lines of the blinds informed her it was morning, but she didn't have time to dwell on it as she ran to the bathroom.

She opened her mouth and vomit poured out of her. It burnt her neck, and left volatile lumps floating in her saliva. She spat, trying to get rid of the remnants, only to find herself violently heaving again, hurtling partly digested pieces into the toilet boil, with a small splatter decorating the toilet seat.

Morning sickness was a common trait of pregnancy, she knew that. But was it always meant to be this heavy? Even after she had drunk too much, her stomach would throw the contents of her stomach up her throat and out of her mouth in a way that left only a faint queasiness.

Yet, at that moment, she felt the need to fall onto her backside to avoid fainting. Blots of colours overtook her vision, masking the tiles of the bathroom with a hazy disguise.

Another gag jolted her body, along with another few gags, followed by a desperate sickness that made her sweat. She had already brought up most of the food in her stomach, meaning the final load had brought little more than blood.

She yearned for food to cure an eager hunger, but dared not eat. She had just emptied the contents of her belly and her body was requesting her to refill it, but she knew anything she put back in would just come up again.

She gagged once more. Except this time, she didn't feel the hot sensation of liquid and lumps pushing up her throat. It was something harder. Something small digging into her, giving a harsh, prickling sensation in her throat.

Another gag made it only intensify more. Her body convulsed a few times, and her mouth instinctively opened to allow the half-moon crescent shape of numerous nails to spew from her cracked lips.

She looked down at them with terror. They were thick enough to be toenails. They were yellow, as if they were infected, or long since dead.

Her eyes were transfixed.

Toenails?

She tried to justify it. Tried to convince herself that she had mistaken the sight, that they were something else. But there was such a large quantity of them that she was certain she wasn't mistaken.

There must have been a rational explanation, she was sure of it, but her manic thoughts could not clamber at one whatsoever.

Nails?

Had she swallowed them at some point that she didn't know?

She peered down at her bare feet. Her nails were short, as if recently cut – but she hadn't done that. At least, she had no recollection of it.

Was it something that you'd remember? Cutting your nails?

Or is it something you do without thinking, then forget

about, discarding the memory like the empty wrapper from a packet of food?

Except, how would they end up in her digestive system?

She had little time to dwell on it before her body fought against her once more. She gagged. Her body convulsed even harsher, even her arms and legs forced to twitch with the upward writhing of her chest. She coughed and spluttered as she felt something else push through, carving against the inside of her neck as if it were a knife marking a stone wall.

It was big. Thick. Coarse.

It grated against the inside of her throat. Against the passage she would use to swallow food, a passage that only seemed to be growing narrower and narrower.

It was long. Something rough, long, and...

The top of it came to her mouth. She could feel a tuft against her tongue, like numerous strings wrapped into a coil, brushing against her gums.

She reached her hand behind her teeth and grabbed hold of it. It was frayed. Harsh. Grating against her hand.

Another retch forced it further upwards and she managed to pull the end of it out of her mouth.

Rope.

She convulsed in an action somewhere between a choke and a gag. She could still feel it stuck, tightly wedged, blocking her breath. Bumpy, coarse, hurting her, frightening her.

She pulled it out further, reeling it through her mouth.

A small, yet thick, rough rope. Burnt at the edges, bristly along its edge.

The abrasive surface pushed itself further upwards with another gag.

Then her need to be sick stopped.

Her whole body tensed. She was no longer gagging, but it was still stuck, still lodged in her throat.

So she pulled.

She grabbed the edges between her fingers and yanked it out. In a sudden movement at first then, upon feeling its discomfort harden, a smoother, gradual pull.

It extracted, inch by inch, until the full length was out, at least the length of two long rulers. It was followed by a mouthful of blood that she spat into the toilet, but hit the floor as dizziness took over her aim. But she didn't care. A few drops of blood on the floor was the least of her worries.

Rope.

From her stomach.

How?

How had it—

She gagged once more, and her whole body convulsed into a violent jolt that sent her hurtling forward and sent her head smacking onto the side of the toilet.

As her skull combined with the porcelain of the toilet rim, a crucifix punched itself against the toilet bowl.

At least, that's what she thought it was.

Because that's the last thing she saw before she blacked out.

When she came around, she was still alone in the bathroom. Oscar was still enjoying a leisurely lie-in in the bedroom behind the en suite, completely unaware of the terror she was experiencing.

She peered into the toilet bowl, checking that she hadn't imagined it, checking that she had actually vomited those things.

But all she found as she moved her prying eyes was a clean bowl, and a complete absence of objects.

She stared, wondering whether she had really experienced it or if it had all been a dream.

She was tempted to believe the latter.

But the rough feeling of the inside of her throat, as if the rough edge of a rope had been dragged through it, made the nagging voice at the back of her mind believe otherwise.

(5 MONTHS)

18

A LOT OF TALKING TOOK PLACE. A LOT OF HYPOTHESISING, debating, and skirting around possible solutions without any firm decision – as most conversations intended to be decisive generally go.

Derek didn't care for a bit of it.

The whole time Jason and Julian stood debating the merits of extra security at the hospital, about how much to tell whom about the demonic aspect and what role Julian would play in all this. Derek sat still, staring across the children's ward and the ill young child stuck in the middle of all this nonsensical debating.

Charlie.

A bright young boy, aged ten.

Desperately unlucky.

He didn't deserve it. Derek was aware it would be unlikely you would ever attribute someone of being deserving of such an illness, but such a thought was ever more pertinent with this child. The lad had a zest for life, an enthusiasm in the mundane, and an infectious curiosity that had gripped Derek.

With the busyness of Julian's chaotic attempts to make sense of what does not make sense, he seemed to be missing out on that. That there was a child at the centre of this – no, that there were *children* at the centre of this – all of them longing for their opportunity at life. An opportunity nature had given them, then snapped it away like dangling thread before a helpless kitten.

"Do you know how much I've had to do to secure this?" Jason was saying. "With the budget the station's got, and with the way they look at me when I mention these damn cases, I never thought in a million years I'd actually manage to arrange for a permanent police presence here."

"It's not that," Julian responded, shaking his head.

"One officer. Stationed here, on rotation."

"It's useless."

"How, exactly?"

Julian sighed. He cupped his hands over his face. Derek could see how tired he was, you only had to look at his drooping eyes to see what the stress of this case was doing. But that was Julian – not someone to let a case go without doing everything he could to help the people involved, even if his ideas were irrefutably stubborn.

At least that was one strong trait that persisted in Julian. An unrelenting commitment to the cause.

"Just – what are you going to tell them?" retorted Julian. "That they need to look out for a demon? No, it's not going to work. If anything, we want to catch this thing – if we don't, we won't stand a chance."

"So we use a bunch of sick kids as bait?"

"That's not what I'm saying!"

"Then what is it you're saying?"

"I'm saying that a human police presence will not help, and if anything, will hinder. We want to see this beast found, don't we? We want to exorcise it from this ward? Well, we need it to show up again to do that."

"Oh right. I see. I'll just go make a phone call and say the children's ward with a potential ghostly serial killer doesn't need the extra protection I worked my arse off to get."

"No, Jason, you're not listening."

Derek's head dropped into his hands.

Their voices faded to a distant whine, like a muffle through headphones. His energy left him in a sudden spurt of pain, like some kind of vacuum had come along and sucked every piece of his liveliness out of him.

Charlie seemed so far away now.

The room stretched, pushing away from Derek, pulling further from his reach.

He tried reaching his hand out. Tried pushing his arm out and grasping it, but his arm didn't move. It just didn't move.

Charlie.

Colouring in.

Dropped his pen.

"You've dropped–" Derek attempted to say, but found his words coming out as a low wheeze, an old man's cough that stung his throat.

Charlie couldn't reach them.

The pen was on the floor. Charlie was too high up. The boy was leaning over, but he couldn't reach it. And he was too weak to get off the bed.

Derek reached out once more.

His chest stopped rising.

His arm held rigid, then slid downwards, falling down the spinning tunnel before him. Charlie turned to a blur, as did the floor, the luminescence of the lights, the faded corridor, the ceiling, the... the... the...

Derek fell.

Reaching his hand out for the pen, he toppled over and pounded on the floor.

The abrupt commotion that ensued around him turned to circles spinning over his mind.

He wasn't breathing.

He was sure he wasn't breathing.

Someone was by him. He could hear them talking, could feel their soft hands on his chest, but they weren't there.

They were, and they weren't.

He was pushed onto his back.

A haze of blurs.

Pumping.

His chest, pumping.

Lunging upwards. Lunging downwards.

No breathing.

Still no breathing.

Still no.

Still.

THEN

19

Another day, another answer phone message.

Martin was struggling enough without having to hear that voice again.

The same well-spoken, articulate, ever-calm voice.

"Martin, I know you've been ignoring my calls, but please, I implore you to respond."

He seethed over Derek's words. *I implore you to respond.* Who talks like that? That was the thing about Derek's evident education – it had always shown Martin what a difference in backgrounds they had.

And why was he ringing on a landline? Martin had a mobile. No one ever used landlines before. Derek was so stubborn.

Martin shook his head. Ran his hands over his face.

None of this had ever mattered before. He was looking for things to hate, and he knew it.

What did it matter if Derek didn't phone Martin's mobile? What's more, Martin had always found Derek to be accepting of anyone, of any background, so long as their intentions were noble. In fact, he'd…

Stop it.

Martin willed himself to hate his former mentor. To despise the man that he was.

The phone rang again.

"For fuck's sake," he muttered.

In a moment of sudden decision, he swung the phone from the wall and to his ear.

"What?" he barked.

"Martin?" came Derek's distressed voice. "Oh, I am so glad you picked up. Did you know it was me?"

"Of course I knew, no one else rings a landline."

"Oh. Well, I guess I'm still behind the times in some way. How are you?"

Martin huffed. How was he? After all this time, Derek had the nerve to phone him up and ask how he was.

"Derek, I don't want to speak to you, man," Martin said. "I told you."

"Yes, I know that. And if that is what you wish, then I will respect your wish, although it is against my own. I just thought I'd have one last try. As, well, I may not be able to for a while."

"Why?"

"Well, you see, I have myself in a little bit of a pickle. A girl called Anna, she died, and I... well, I needn't bore you with the details. I'm going away, and let's just say you wouldn't be able to find me. So I thought it best to find you. One last time, if that's what it is."

Martin looked out of his window. A young boy held his father's hand as they walked toward the park. Once there, the boy smiled at his father, running to the swing set. The father watched on with a smile that only a proud father would wear.

A father. Martin had never known what it was like to have such a thing.

Then again, he could have known what it was like to be a father. If Derek hadn't messed up. If Derek hadn't...

"Well, you found me," Martin observed after a few lengthy moments of silence.

"And? Would you permit me to meet with you? Perhaps introduce you to a few people who may be able to help you with–"

"I don't want anything from you."

A cold silence followed.

"I understand, Martin. Just know I had the best of intentions."

Martin laughed mockingly.

"Fuck you, Derek. Fuck you to hell. The best of intentions? You let that woman, and the child, die. You let them fucking die, you arsehole."

"I did not let them–"

"*Yes you did!*" Martin willed himself to calm down. He was breathing fast, pacing the room with an aimless rapidity. "Yes, you did."

"I promise you, Martin, I never intended–"

"Is that it?" Martin felt tears accumulating in the corners of his eyes, but he willed them away. He was not about to give Derek that.

Talking to Derek meant having to face up to what happened to Madelina. To his child.

It was easier to be angry.

It had always been easier to be angry.

"Yes," Derek said resolutely. "I guess it is."

"Bye then. Don't call again."

Martin punched the handset against the receiver.

He waited a few moments, then ripped the receiver off the wall, tearing the wires apart.

Now there was no way Derek could contact him.

He punched the wall.

His fist hurt, but not enough.

He punched it again.

This was all Derek's fault.

Madelina. His child. All of it. Everything. It was Derek's fault that Martin felt like this. That he felt like he didn't want to live. Like death would be the best answer.

He had no one. Nothing.

He used to have Derek. He was going to have Madelina. And a child.

Now he was alone, again. Alone as he had always been. No mother or father to take him in. No friends to open their arms.

No mentor to comfort him.

Alone.

Again.

Angry. Bitter. Fuming.

It was Derek's fault.

All of it. Everything.

He bowed his head.

It was Derek's fault.

If he kept telling himself that, he almost believed it.

NOW

20

An overhead light pushed its beams upon the plain room.

A steady beeping sifted into Derek's mind.

As his eyes gradually opened, the beeping continued. Until it made sense. Until he saw where he was.

A hospital gown. A bed. Sterile, cold, pale walls.

No.

This was not where he wanted to be.

He tried to lift himself, but his body was too heavy. He could barely lift a hand, never mind prop his torso up.

But this wasn't where he was meant to be.

It wasn't...

"It's okay," came a familiar voice. "You're alive, if that's what you're wondering."

With a great deal of energy that probably looked like nothing to a bystander, Derek flopped his head to the side and cast his heavy eyes on the concerned face of Julian.

"I said I didn't want to come here," Derek barked.

Well, attempted to bark.

His disdain wasn't as clear as he intended, such was the slow, struggling nature of the words he spoke.

"Well that's probably why you've ended up here," Julian said. "Because you refused to in the first place. Then look at what happened."

Derek didn't try to lift his head again. It was too much effort. Instead, he twitched his eyes back and forth.

He was in the ward adjacent to the children's ward. The cancer ward. He could see the children's ward through the window of the door.

"Why am I here?" he asked.

"You stopped breathing," Julian answered. "They had to perform CPR."

"Why did I stop breathing?"

"Why?" Julian's hands gripped the arms of his seat, and Derek could see it was all he could do to contain his fury. "Because you have cancer, Derek. Why won't you understand that?"

"I do understand that—"

"Clearly not! You almost—"

Julian looked away. He couldn't say it.

"Almost what?" Derek prompted. He wanted to hear it.

"Almost died," Julian replied. "You almost died, Derek."

"But I am going to die, Julian. And probably very soon."

"So that's it? You give up like that?"

Derek's lips managed to curl into a weak smile.

"I'm older than most people who survive this," Derek admitted. "I've made my peace with it."

Julian glared back at Derek. For a while they just sat there, an intense silence piercing the tension, so much firing around their heads.

"Well maybe you have," Julian said, full of venom. "But that doesn't mean everyone else has."

Julian stood up with full intention to storm out, but hovered in the doorway. He placed his hands firmly on his hips, dropping his gaze to the floor.

He looked over his shoulder at the weak man staring back.

"The nurses said to get some rest. Or you won't be getting out of bed."

Julian left.

But a shadow remained.

Derek frowned.

A shadow hovered. Lingering in the doorway. The shadow's head rotated, twisting toward him.

Derek peered into the doorway. Tried to see it. Tried to make it out.

But his eyes.

They were so heavy.

A face appeared on the shadow. A contorted, falsely feminine, narrow-eyed visage of abhorrence.

Its mouth opened.

Was this what they had seen? The children? Could he see it now he was so close to death?

His mind did not give him the luxury of dwelling on his thoughts. Thoughts often are unreliable and bizarre when in the place between sleeping and awake. And those thoughts drifted away into the submerged subconscious of his thoughts.

Yet, as he drifted back to sleep, he was sure he could hear, ever so gently, a low cackling.

(4 MONTHS)

21

MOTHERCARE WASN'T A SHOP OSCAR HAD BEEN TO BEFORE – the most obvious reason being that he hadn't ever expected a baby before, but also because he had found it a little scary. He was unsure why – it was hardly a place to dread, it was just full of children's stuff. It could have been that it made it real; not the lovely child on the way, but the huge burden that child was going to place on his finances. The stuff in here hadn't particularly received huge praise for its affordable pricing.

But, as soon as he crossed the threshold, he was taken aback by a delicate aroma of talcum powder that sent him back to his childhood. Nothing was crowded together; the items that helped with babies in all varieties of circumstances were arranged with aisles large enough to fit two prams down. The lighting was bright, but not too bright, with a slight orange-and-blue tint. It made him feel light, and gave him flutters of excitement for what was to come.

April, reluctantly attached to him via the sweaty palm clamped around his, looked less than impressed. He didn't take this personally. She looked immensely tired, as if she had been dragged through hell backwards. Her skin had come out with dark, splotchy patches, in the form of large, dark circles placed sporadically across her face and her arms. Her eyes looked weary, with barely a white space across her retina void of bloodshot veins.

Most grotesque of all – though Oscar would never verbalise such a description aloud – were her gums. They had dried up and bled, until the spaces around her teeth were prickling with flakes of dried skin.

"Hey," Oscar offered, doing his best to comfort her with a hand running down her hair. "You okay?"

"Fine," she answered in a low, raspy voice.

"I've got the list. If you want to sit down then honestly, it wouldn't matter."

"I don't want to sit down," she grumbled blankly. Her eyes did not rise to his, instead directing what small part of her pupil Oscar could glimpse from beneath her drooping eyelids at the ground. She looked absent of consciousness, like she was a zombie working on automatic. Honestly, if she sat down and remained really still, you would be excused for wondering if she was dead.

"Well, hey, we need prams first, and they are over here," Oscar said, trying to lighten the mood. He directed her to a few larger shelves that displayed some of the prams.

He had never realised there would be so many varieties and colours of one simple object as a pram.

Leaning forward, he took the price tag of the nearest item and turned it so that it was visible. He recoiled, and decided it was best not to show it to April, as it may just push her over the edge.

"Well, hey, maybe we'll go second hand," Oscar suggested. "Or look at a really small one. Like these over here."

He led her, dragging her like she was a pack of weights, toward a few of the smaller prams that appeared to be more toward their price range.

"What do you think of these, April?" he asked.

No reply.

"April?"

Nothing.

"Hey, April, what do you think?"

He turned to April, but she was not looking in his direction. Her eyes had opened wide, far wider than he had seen them in weeks, and her empty pupils were fixed on something. Something across the store.

He peered in the direction she was staring, trying to find what it was. There was no particular item that stuck out, nothing that took his attention.

Then he saw what she was staring at. Because he was staring right back.

It was a toddler. Barely able to walk. Rooted to the spot.

His mum was trying with all her might to drag the child away, but the child was immovable. Gravity seemed to be weighing him down with an irregular certainty, an anomaly of the human condition. For his mother dragged, and dragged, and dragged, but had to stop for fear of accidentally pulling the boy's underdeveloped arm from its loose socket.

"April?"

Nothing.

Her eyes were transfixed. The gaze between them was fixed with such rigidity, such stubbornness, that it seemed impossible to break. It was like an invisible laser had fired between their eye sockets and would not shift.

"April, come on."

Oscar waved a hand in front of her eyes.

No movement. No reaction. Her body was as stiff and as heavy as a box of wood.

She was not blinking.

Come to think of it, Oscar was sure he hadn't seen her blink for at least a minute.

"April, you're freaking me out," he tried, hoping he could reason with her. But his voice was like rain falling on brick. It did no damage, made no difference, and just glided off into a puddle on the floor.

"April, please, would you just–"

Oscar's voice shrivelled up, caught in his throat. He stared at the floor, mortified as he processed the sight beneath him.

He looked away, then looked back again, as if he had to convince himself it was real.

A steady stream of blood glided down the inside of her leg, and seeped from beneath her dress. It ran down her bare ankles, over her socks, and landed in a steady pool beside her Converses.

"April, we need to go."

Nothing.

"April, you're bleeding."

Not a flutter of the eyelids. Not a difference to the stone eyes that did not break or falter.

"April, we don't know what this is; we need to get to a doctor."

Her lips pursed. The first movement she had made whilst her and the child had been in this bizarre transfixion.

"April, are you–"

April muttered something.

"What?"

She muttered something again.

"What is it?"

Then, with an uncomfortable seething quality, a low-pitch intensity, with drawn-out syllables and vehement snarls, she spoke a few slow, specific words at the child:

"I. Am going. To fucking *kill* you."

Her eyelids closed, her body loose, and she fell to the floor. Oscar just about managed to catch her before she hit the ground.

He shook her, trying to wake her.

The boy she had stared at was gone. Finally relinquished his fixed stare and allowed his mother to drag him away.

Oscar shook April, terrified, petrified as to what may have happened to her, and the baby.

"Help!" he shouted.

He shook her again.

"Help! Please, somebody help!"

A crowd gathered, and from that crowd someone offered help, but Oscar couldn't hear them. It all turned to a distant buzzing.

All he could focus on was the love of his life, bleeding on the floor of Mothercare.

22

OSCAR'S NAILS HAD BEEN BITTEN ON AND CHEWED MORE IN TEN minutes than they had in his entire life.

He sat on the edge of the chair, eagerly awaiting the verdict, desperate to hear what the doctor had to say.

April lay back on the bed. Unresponsive. In a diluted vegetative state.

Her eyes were open, but beneath them was nothing. The spritely, friendly smile and sparkling eyes that she once had – her loving, doting smiles – were gone, replaced by coldness. By absence of life. By something taking over her that he could not quite understand.

The doctor finally returned to the room and sat opposite them. She gave her a calm smile, and allowed it to spread from bouncy cheek to bouncy cheek. It gave a small amount of reassurance to Oscar, which was quickly replaced by a reminder of why he was there.

"The baby is fine," she told him. "It's there, its heart is beating; there is nothing wrong."

"They why – why was she bleeding?"

"I know it's alarming, and you absolutely did the right thing by making the emergency appointment – but you don't need to worry. Sometimes these things can happen. They aren't common, but they are still normal."

"Bleeding is normal? Doctor, it was dripping down her leg."

"Well, yes, bleeding can be a sign of something very wrong. But we have looked, and looked, and she is okay. We've checked for signs of vaginal infections, placental abruptions, vasa praevia – everything we can think of. Nothing."

Oscar looked back at the doctor, unconvinced.

"I know it's unsettling, but we have checked everything, and the baby is fine. April is fine. It may just be due to cervical changes."

Oscar turned to April. Watched her vacant eyes stare across the room. Not moving. Not twitching. Her arms didn't move to fidget, her legs didn't move to gain more comfort. The only movement she made was the lethargic rising of her chest as she slowly breathed.

"You say she's fine, but – just look at her."

The doctor turned to look at April. She took a moment to take her appearance in, to allow herself to study April's absent eyes and pale skin. She sighed, deciding on what words she was to use.

"Doctor? Do you really think this is normal?"

The doctor turned her gaze toward Oscar.

"It's understandable."

"What?"

"Pregnancy is a stressful experience, and a difficult one. April is obviously tired, and obviously finding it difficult."

"Doctor, she's not even aware we're talking about her."

In a swift, unprecedented motion, April's head turned to face Oscar. Her eyes met his, and he saw nothing of her brightness casting a light over him.

"I'm fine," April stated.

"Is that all you can say?" Oscar replied.

"Don't talk about me like I'm not in the room."

"I'm not, I'm not," Oscar insisted, leaning forward and placing a hand on her leg. He was taken aback by how cold her skin was; it was more like he was placing his hand on an ice pack than on the leg of the loving mother of his child.

"I just need you to get off my back."

"I'm not on your back, April, I'm doing all I can to help you."

"Look," the doctor interjected, "this is a difficult time. For both of you. Why not just go home, go to bed, and have a relaxing weekend?"

Oscar sighed.

The doctor didn't know.

She didn't live with this. She didn't stare at this catatonic state every day. It was like this child had consumed her. It was like tiredness had taken over her body, and all that was left was a depraved, distant woman who used to be in love with him.

"Whatever happens," the doctor directed at Oscar, "you need positive energy."

"Positive energy?"

"Yes. And I'm afraid to say, it needs to come from you, Oscar. April will be difficult. Sorry if that offends you, darling" – April didn't react – "but she will be. And you just need to prepare for that."

"Prepare for it? How? What am I meant to do?"

"Get her a hot water bottle. Play soothing music. Promise her you'll do whatever it takes. Oscar, I've seen many pregnant women, and I promise you – you will be fine."

Oscar looked to April. He didn't feel like it would be fine.

But like she said, she'd seen many pregnant women.

He hadn't.

Maybe this was normal.

"After all," the doctor added, "you don't want to be stressed for when she comes along."

Oscar's head swung toward the doctors. His expression changed, overcome with joy and amazement.

"She?" he asked. "Did you say she? I mean, you were able to see this time?"

The doctor grinned.

"Yes, Oscar. You are having a daughter."

(3 MONTHS)

23

If Derek felt optimistic about escaping the hospital, those hopes diminished as soon as he stepped out of bed.

He'd imagined leaping out the window via a rope, dropping down to the floor, and running until he legs would not carry him anymore.

Or even sneaking down the corridor, perhaps disguising himself in a doctor's uniform, and finding a car conveniently parked with the keys haphazardly left stuck in the ignition.

Maybe he could re-enact *The Great Escape*. *The Shawshank Redemption*. Have an iconic soundtrack accompany his rapid progress as he dug a hole and appeared at the exact location he wished to be.

But, after making the decision to get a paper cup of water from the fountain outside his room, he had endured the struggle it took to get from his bed to his feet, to hobble across the wall to the door, having to lean his hands against the bumpy paint job of the sickeningly pale room, then reach the doorway, out of breath – it only highlighted to him how weak he was, and how much he depended on the help of the people in this building.

He used to be able feel the life dripping out of him by the day. Now, he felt it going by the hour. The more he tried to regain strength, the more he sweated, the more he struggled. Every movement seemed to take the effort of a marathon. His breathing quickened pace, his blood pumped, his sweat dripped down his forehead – all from walking across the room.

As he paused in the doorway, staring at the water fountain a few metres away, the target, the mission, he leant against the door frame.

It seemed so easy.

Just a few steps away.

Just a few steps.

Just a few.

Just nothing.

There was no *just* anymore. It was all an effort. All a drag.

If felt like death was waiting for him just past that water fountain. Hanging around, chilling out, hovering somewhere it could not be seen by Derek, but always had its beady eyes watching. Waiting.

Tasting the inevitable.

"Derek!" came the concerned voice of Julian, rushing down the corridor toward him. "What are you doing?"

"Water," Derek said between breaths.

"Here, let me," Julian insisted, helping Derek to a nearby seat.

Once Julian made sure Derek was sat comfortably, and wasn't going to slip off the chair, he strolled to the water fountain with a sickening ease, poured a paper cone, and handed it to Derek. Derek took it in his shaking hand, trying to steady his arms enough so he didn't splash the water over his lap. He brought it to his lips and felt the water cascade down his dry throat.

He was aware of Julian staring.

"What?" Derek grunted.

"Nothing," said Julian.

"I know what I look like. I know how I am. You don't need to look so concerned."

"You know that's not what it is."

"Then what is it?"

"It's just what's happened today, you know. It's tough."

Derek grew confused.

"What do you mean, what's happened?"

Julian's expression turned to that of perplexity, looking quizzically at Derek.

"You don't know?" Julian asked.

"Don't know what?" Derek knew he sounded impatient, but he couldn't help it.

"Oh. Well, I suppose you wouldn't have known. I guess we've been so busy dealing with it we didn't tell you."

"Busy dealing with *what*, Julian?"

Julian hesitated.

"Another child died. Was killed. It looked like it was whatever this thing is again."

Derek was stumped. Confused. It took longer than it would have done if he was healthy to comprehend what was said.

"Which child?"

"Oh, I can't remember the kid's name."

Jason's head appeared from the children's ward a few doors down the corridor.

"Julian, you need to come look at this," Jason called.

"I'll be right back," Julian told Derek, and rushed to the nearby door, disappearing behind it.

A child.

Died.

Another one.

Same demon.

Then it hit him like an elbow in the throat.

What about Charlie? Was it him? It couldn't be. It couldn't.

There were so many children on that ward, it was statistically improbable.

Still, Derek knew he wouldn't calm down until he found out for sure.

He used the chair to push himself to his feet. His legs buckled like two twigs trying to hold up a box of bricks, but he steadied them; with all the will he had, he steadied them.

Resting his hands on the wall, he pushed himself, dragged himself, pulled himself across the corridor.

The door was so close, but it felt like it was in the next building.

His breathing quickened pace. He wasn't sure whether it was his anxiety or his depleting energy levels, but he forced himself to ignore it, forced himself to keep struggling forward.

His hands clenched the door frame. The painting of a child on the nearest inside wall did not give him the reassuring sense of childish optimism he was sure was intended. In fact, the pictures of clowns and the scribbles and drawings hung up, decorations supplied by sick children come and gone, did nothing but push his fear upwards through his chest until it came pouring out of his throat in a quivering mumble.

Twisting around the door, he paused, looking back and forth.

Getting his bearings.

Adjusting his vision.

But he already knew the truth.

The sad thing about finding the certainty that truth brings is that denial is no longer an option. One has no choice but to be honest about what faces them.

And what faced Derek was police tape around the space that Charlie had once occupied.

Curtains were drawn, but they did nothing to disguise the

blood splashed against the inside. It pushed through, glaringly visible, multiple streaks of obvious red.

As he fell to his knees he felt his kneecaps pound, the bone punching against the solid floor.

He did not care.

Nor did he care about the multitude of doctors and nurses rushing to his side, dragging him to his knees. He'd have tried to object, to scream or kick, if he had the ability. But he didn't.

Because Charlie was dead.

Charlie. Was dead.

And he hadn't been well enough to save him.

24

Oscar's eyes sprung open like a hook had found its way under his eyelids and yanked them open. His eyeballs felt like they had outgrown his eye sockets. As he shifted his vision from side to side they felt swollen, like they had been ripped out and placed back again.

Darkness.

Bed.

April.

She was next to him, curled up into a ball, facing the outside of the bed. Calm.

Her belly was bigger. With his child inside. His daughter.

It was an incredible thought.

A human life lived inside of her. A person, soon to be born, soon to be loved. He was already bursting with affection for this girl, ready to take care of her, provide for her, and give her the love he never truly felt from his parents.

Not that they were bad parents, quite the opposite – they took care of him, provided him with pocket money, gave him a safe home. They never physically hurt him in any way.

But their love, their affection, it had always felt conditional.

Like he would only get it if he fulfilled their expectations. If he got straight A's, went to university, went to extra-curricular sports clubs – none of which he ever actually did.

But now, as he turned and leant his arm over the woman he loved, the woman he had only dreamt of meeting and being with, he placed his hand on her belly. Softly brushing the safe home where his child was being kept.

An abrupt whisper came out of April's mouth, and he retracted his hand quickly.

"April?" Oscar said softly.

Nothing. She was asleep.

He placed his hand on her belly once more, and the whisper started again.

She was saying something. There were words, he just couldn't make them out.

He leant closer. Took his hand away.

Listened.

Nothing. Then he placed his hand back again, and she whispered once more.

As soon as he managed to make out a few syllables, he realised it wasn't English. It sounded different. Old.

Latin.

He'd heard enough Latin incantations within his work to recognise it. But he didn't understand it.

He listened carefully once more, but she said nothing.

He placed his hand on her belly.

Her lips pursed once more, and the whisper came out.

Was this only happening when he touched his baby?

He listened. Took in the words she was saying, trying to make out the sound.

"Filia mea. Filia mea. Filia mea."

As he leant closer, his hand pressed more firmly against her belly, the whispering grew more aggressive.

"Filia mea. Filia mea erit tuae mortis."

Oscar leapt out of bed, put on a hoodie, and quietly left the bedroom. He entered the living room and made his way to the bookshelf, looking for the book he was after.

A Latin-to-English dictionary.

He found it and placed it on the table.

He flicked through the F's, found the word *filia,* and scribbled its meaning on a nearby piece of paper.

Daughter.

He flicked through to the M's and found *mea.*

My.

"Daughter? My?" he muttered, then realised the words needed to be switched around. "My daughter."

How strange.

My daughter? What a weird thing to be whispering.

He sifted through the pages to *Erit.*

Will be.

To *tuae.*

Your.

He paused. He was pretty sure he knew what *mortis* meant. It was too close to mortician.

He reluctantly turned the pages, finding the right one, and stared at it with a mind full of perplexity.

It was... strange. To say the least.

Death.

Will be your death.

Finally, the words she was muttering, bizarrely whispering to herself, oddly mumbling with no awareness, in a language she couldn't possibly be fluent in, sunk into place.

Oscar's mouth moved to the syllables, but they didn't sound.

He shook his head.

There had to be a rational explanation.

Finally, his mind took control. His mouth formed the

words, and he repeated her words in English as a reflection of what she was saying.

"My daughter. My daughter. My daughter."

He ran his hand through his sweaty hair.

"My daughter will be your death."

His thoughts struggled for a rational, coherent understanding, to form words that could make sense of it, to create a feeling of comprehension.

They came out with nothing.

It was then that he realised what he could no longer deny.

He needed help.

(2 MONTHS)

25

DEREK'S EYES OPENED FAINTLY FROM HIS AFTERNOON NAP TO SEE Oscar sat quietly at his bedside.

"Hey," Oscar greeted him, placing a cup of tea on the table next to Derek. "I got this for you."

"Thanks," Derek acknowledged.

Derek tried sitting up, and in his struggle, Oscar stood up and lifted Derek's pillows, helping him into a sitting position.

"That okay?" Oscar checked.

"Great, thanks."

"Would you like your tea?"

"Yes, please."

Oscar passed Derek his cup of tea, placing it into both hands. Derek lifted it to his mouth and let it sink down his parched throat, relishing the warmth and reassurance that a cup of tea always brings.

"Thank you."

"You're welcome."

"So what are you doing here?" Derek mused. "Haven't you got a pregnant girlfriend to take care of?"

"Yes, but I thought I'd take half an hour off to come and see you. Check you are okay. You also need help, after all."

"Well, I appreciate your company, Oscar, but I assure you I don't need help."

Derek realised how silly the words were as soon as they left him. He hadn't even been able to sit up and have a cup of tea without the generosity of Oscar. But, like a polite young man, Oscar allowed the comment to settle without objecting, allowing Derek his pride.

"So how are things taking care of a pregnant woman?"

Oscar blew an overinflated sigh out of his mouth to signal his answer to the question.

"That tough, huh?"

"This pregnancy, it's… Well, it's had its complications."

"They all do."

"Yes, but I imagine this one is particularly difficult."

"And how are you managing it? Are you taking care of yourself?"

Oscar shifted uncomfortably in his seat. He looked like he wanted to give an affirmative answer, but struggled to do so.

"I just keep thinking, you know. What if this child ends up with as much complications as the pregnancy?"

"And what if it does?"

"It'll be tough."

"Would you stick by her?"

Oscar feigned confusion.

"Are you kidding?"

"You two do seem to really get on."

"Man, we do, we just – it's great, you know?"

Derek laughed.

"No, I don't," he said. "I'm afraid I had my heart broken long ago."

"I'm sorry."

"Tell me about it, then. The way you feel. I'm curious what

earth-shattering love is like."

Oscar smiled and bowed his head for a moment, collecting his thoughts. As his head rose again, he seemed to have gained a new sense of vigour and enthusiasm.

"Like there's no one in the world but us."

"But this child wasn't planned," Derek said honestly. "How are you going to cope?"

"With great energy and enthusiasm, my friend," Oscar asserted with a large grin. "When I'm with April, it's like – I'm not just a better person, but the truest person I am. Like, everything changes."

Derek felt a sharp sting of happiness, in recognition of the evident happiness Oscar undoubtedly felt.

"The world just sinks away," Oscar continued. "And it's just me and her. Us against the world. And now it's going to be three. And, I – I can't wait."

"What if the baby–"

"I don't care. I know what you're about to say, and whatever the baby brings, I will do whatever to protect that child, and to protect April."

As Derek's eyes met Oscar's, he could see that he meant it.

"She changed my life. And I can never repay that."

His phone beeped. He glanced at it.

"I'm needed in the other room. Are you going to be okay?"

"I'll be perfect."

"See you in a bit," Oscar said with a warm smile, and left.

Derek watched him leave, thinking about him. Thinking about the excellent young man he was turning into. Thinking about how April could not have found a more perfect partner to support him.

Regretting that he would likely not live long enough to see him grow into an amazing Sensitive.

In that moment, Derek decided that Oscar was truly remarkable.

"IF YOU'RE SURE YOU'RE UP FOR THIS, APRIL," JULIAN REPEATED for the who-knows-what time, "and only if."

"I'm not a piece of glass that's going to shatter and break," April insisted. "I can still work."

Oscar wasn't so sure.

April was an independent person with a sturdy head upon her shoulders, and he did not doubt that she knew her own limits. It wasn't up to him to insist that she does or doesn't work, but he was worried. Especially with the complications of the pregnancy; the bleeding, the mumbling in her sleep, the staring at random children.

Not to mention how big she was. It was less than eight weeks until the due date, and she was having to push herself off every chair, lean over as she walked. To him, she looked stunning. But to Julian, she must look sweaty, uncomfortable, and downright short-tempered.

"Well, if you're sure," Julian went on. "We could really do with someone, just to tell us what we're dealing with here."

"I'll do my best."

The nurses and doctors hadn't taken as much convincing as

Julian thought they would. Jason hadn't had to explain the situation for long until they were setting up an area for them to work, and standing aside as they took over the children's ward.

Thing is, that shouldn't be so surprising. The doctors would know the cause of death; they would be able to see that it wasn't natural.

And anyone who spent more than a minute in that room would be able to feel the sickening cold that chilled everyone's bones. There was something there, and it was evil, no doubt about it. You didn't have to be a Sensitive to see that.

April stepped forward. She closed her eyes and bowed her head.

Julian nodded at a nearby nurse, who turned off the lights in response.

Doctors, nurses, police, patients – everyone in the vicinity stopped what they were doing and watched. Whether out of helpless dread, optimistic hope, or just sheer, unadulterated curiosity, all eyes were on her. The only sound was the beeping of the life machines. The only thoughts were of the unknown, of what was going to happen next.

Everyone's thoughts, that was, but Oscar's.

He wasn't as keen to put April in striking distance of whatever entity was at work in her state. She was heavily pregnant, and heavily stressed. But he remembered what she had told him the previous night.

"I have to work, Oscar. I have to. It could be the only thing stopping me going completely crazy."

Oscar was hurt, though he knew it was unfair. He had hoped to be the only thing stopping her from going completely crazy. Though, if anything, he felt like a hinderance. Nothing he did, however caring or with the best of intentions, seemed to make the slightest bit of difference.

He felt useless.

Worse than useless.

"I can do this, trust me," she had said. "I would not do anything if I thought there was a single chance it would hurt our daughter. But, fact is, children are dying. And I can help."

She was right.

Of course, she was. She always was. So much so, it was infuriating. But that was part of why he loved her.

And boy, did he love her.

Not just because he was infatuated. At first, maybe, yes. But it had become so much more than that, so much more than her being the only cool girl looking in his direction. His caring for her ran deep; it was in his blood, in his mind, in every thought. It affected every action. Everything he did, he wondered how he would tell her about it later. He thought about what their future could be like.

She was everything.

Julian lit three candles that formed a triangle around April.

"Okay," he softly spoke. "When you're ready."

April descended to her knees. She closed her eyes, lifted her arms, and remained motionless.

She waited.

Breathing.

Oscar watched her. Getting a feeling, deep inside of him, that this was wrong. This was all wrong.

"The entity in this ward," April spoke. "The entity within. I speak to you."

Every eye was on her. Poised. Watching. Waiting.

"My body is a vessel. Use it."

Julian stepped forward.

"There may be found upon us," Julian spoke, standing directly before April, outside of the triangle, facing her as her head bowed and her eyes closed. "Anyone that maketh his son or daughter pass through fire. An observer of times, an enchanter, a witch, a charmer, a consultant with familiar spirits, or a necromancer. These things are an abomination to the Lord, and Lord thy God will drive them out of here."

The whole room waited.

Waited.

And waited.

"I address you now, as the Spirit of the Lord is upon me, because he hath anointed me to heal the broken-hearted, to preach deliverance to the captives, and to preach the acceptable year of the Lord – so come forth. Use this vessel. Speak to us."

Julian looked back and forth. At the children leant up in the bed, peering at him. The doctors with clip boards held across their chest. The nurses, holding their crosses, tightly gripping pendants around their neck like their wellbeing was dependent upon it.

"Jesus came to free those under demon bondage, for whoever shall call upon the name of the Lord shall be saved – and I call upon the name of the Lord. And I shall be saved. And from the saved, I command you, use this vessel."

The candles flickered.

No one moved.

"I receive God's nature, and in his name, we command you, use this vessel. Tell us what your wish is."

April's eyes opened.

Everyone watched her.

Not just watched her – peered into her. Beheld her with such intensity that if eyes could pierce your flesh, she would be a bloody, skinless wreck.

Oscar sensed the danger.

He stood.

Julian held out his hand in a request that Oscar was to stay where he was.

Oscar halted. Watched. Waited.

April stood. Her eyes open, her pupils fully dilated, her

body hanging loose like a boneless animal. Like a ventriloquist's doll with only a loose guide propping her up.

"Demon," Julian continued. "You will remain within the triangle. In God's name, you will not leave it."

"Joanna," April mumbled.

"What?" Julian prompted. "Demon, repeat what you say."

April looked at a girl sitting up in bed behind Julian. The young girl's eyes were wide and alert, her body tensed, her young mind rendering her completely immobile.

"You will not leave that triangle, in God's name, you stand, and you tell us, who you–"

April stepped forward, out of the triangle made by the candles, and slowly stepped toward the young girl. Her bare feet made a gentle slap on the floor, the only sound that challenged the life machines – one of which was increasing in its frequency of beats. The one of the young girl April was stepping toward.

"Joanna…"

"You will stop! You will not move! You will–"

April sent her fist forward in a sudden, jolted movement. It settled into Julian's nose, which gave an audible crack as he fell back onto the floor.

Oscar was running immediately. Sprinting across the room, making his way toward her.

"Joanna…"

April approached the side of the girl. Barely older than seven. Her heart monitor was racing, her eyes ripped wide open, her body paralysed with illness and terror.

April reached her hand out toward the girl.

Oscar reached April's side and wrapped his arms around her chest.

"God, our Lord, King of ages," Oscar forced into her ear. "All-powerful and all-mighty, we beseech You to make powerless."

April's head rotated unnaturally, the only part of her body moving, twisting until it faced Oscar, inches from his desperate visage. In her eyes he saw nothing but black, nothing but terror.

This wasn't her.

This couldn't be her.

"You are powerless," its low, croaky voice whispered through April's mouth.

"Drive out every diabolic power, presence, and machination. Every evil influence, malefice, or evil eye and evil actions aimed against You."

"You think this will stop me?"

Oscar ignored it. He had to.

These things always said what they could to provoke.

He couldn't let it get to him.

He couldn't let it get April.

"Where there is envy and malice," he continued, "give us an abundance of goodness, endurance, and victory."

"I already have her."

"May You keep at bay and vanquish every evil power, every poison or malice invoked against us, by corrupt and envious demons."

"This has done nothing but bring forth the inevitable."

"Then, under the protection of Your authority, may we sing, in gratitude–"

"Your daughter is mine."

"–The Lord is my salvation!" Oscar screamed, his face scrunched up into a snarl, not letting it get to him, not letting its lies take him over. "Whom should I fear? I will not fear evil because You are with me!"

The demon's low chuckle forced her breath against him, stinking like rotting meat, and her body went limp. He caught her as she fell.

"My God, my strength," Oscar whispered as he took her to

the floor and waved a doctor over. "Lord of all peace. Father of all ages."

Julian began to sit up.

As the doctors descended on April, checking her pulse, checking her temperature, doing everything they needed to do to ensure her survival, Oscar turned to Julian, sat there nursing his wounded nose.

"Now," Oscar spat, "it is my turn to tell you how much of an idiot you are."

"Leave it out, Oscar. She's a big girl."

Oscar dove on top of Julian, grabbing his collar before he could stand.

"She does *not* belong to *you*! She is not your *pawn* you can use! She—"

"It's her," came a delicate voice.

Oscar stood and turned to the young girl. Startled, but speaking.

"I take it your name is Joanna," Oscar said. "Mine is Oscar."

"That was her. The thing that's been coming at night."

"Yes, I know. It was in her, now we've got rid of it, I promise—"

"No," the young girl insisted. "You don't understand. That is her face."

"What?"

Joanna dropped her head and refused to answer any more questions.

April had been lifted to a wheelchair and was being taken through the hospital. With a scowl at Julian, Oscar followed, taking her hand as he did.

THEN

27

IT WAS THE SAME ROUTINE. THE SAME CHAOS, THE SAME anarchy – but a new struggle.

As ever, Martin's exorcism consisted of flying furniture, shards of glass parading across the wind, lavish outbursts of elements that had no rational explanation.

And the girl, a young one, tied to a bed.

Only this time, Martin was on his own. When Derek had been there, they had worked together. They had battled the odds and made sure neither of them fell for the demon's taunts.

This time it wasn't so easy.

There was no respite. No point at which he could stand back and let someone else take over. No reassurance when he wondered if this would work.

"Soul of Christ, sanctify me!" Martin said, his voice trembling beneath his confidence. "Body of Christ, save me! Blood of Christ, inebriate me!"

He splashed holy water upon the writhing body beneath him, listening to the moans spew out of its wretched mouth with multiple pitches, each as unpleasant to the ear as the others.

The girl's face displayed numerous scabs. Cracked lips, bloodshot eyes, greasy hair – all of these were familiar sights to Martin. As was the blood around the crotch, the stains of urination over the bedsheets, and the wriggling of the body as its belly lifted into the air, rising upwards as it fought against is restraints.

But it was tougher. Those scabs were harder to look at, the blood harder to clean off, and the dried urine a smell impossible to escape.

He refused to think it. He wasn't going to wish Derek was there. He wasn't going to waste another thought on him. He would not.

Though he knew he could not do this alone.

"Water for the side of Christ, wash me!" he persevered. "Passion of Christ, strengthen me! Banish all of the forces of evil from me, destroy them, vanish them, so this house can be healthy and full of good deeds!"

A booming, croaky laughter sprang from the depths of the poor girl's throat and pushed itself to the surface of her lips. It filled the room, floating along the chaos, the bed quivering along the floor.

"You fool…" the demon's voice spoke, in at least five pitches and five distinct accents.

Martin would not listen. He knew better than that.

He had been taught not to listen.

"Burn all these evils in hell, that they may never again touch me, touch this house, or touch this girl, or any creature in the world!"

The demon's laughter announced itself once more.

"You never should have done this…" it claimed.

"I command and bid all the power who molest me!"

"Molest you?" The demon choked on its laughter. "The devil molests your mother in hell…"

It shook him for a second. The words, they made him pause. But he continued.

"By the power of God all powerful, in the name of our Saviour, leave this girl forever and be consigned to everlasting hell."

A sadistic grin spread wider than a grin could naturally spread.

"You never should have done this…"

"Lord, you said you give us peace, and peace you give us. Give us that peace now."

"You never should have done this… without *him.*"

Martin faltered.

She was right.

She's right? Get a grip.

A demon was never right. That's what Derek always reminded him – it was never right about what it said, only right in its choice of insecurities it senses.

"We may be liberated from every evil–"

"He's going to *die*, you know."

"We may be liberated from every–"

"You should have used him, but he's going to *die.*"

"We may be liberated–"

"And you aren't going to be there because you're a selfish little boy."

"*Shut up!*"

Martin regretted his outburst as soon as the scream had scorched his throat, and the demon's cocky laughter only made it worse.

"The devil has decided on its vengeance."

"Shut up," Martin repeated – this time as more of a beg than a command.

"Lamia will return."

"Please, just shut up."

Martin's head dropped. He covered his face.

What am I doing?

"You know it wasn't his fault; now look what's happened to you."

Martin shook his head profusely. Why was he listening to this? He knew better.

But this had been inside of him for a while. This wasn't just a taunt.

It was the truth.

"We are going to implant spawn," the demon continued with a singsong voice. "We are going to implant a demon child, and Lamia is going to infect it, and Derek is going to suffer to the last."

Martin fled the room. He pounded down the stairs and out of the house.

He ignored the family of the girl behind him, waiting to see if he'd had success.

He hadn't had success.

He wasn't going to have success.

Not without Derek.

Derek, of whom the demon had just revealed its intentions.

Martin would try to let Derek know. He'd try to contact him. He'd ring him, even show up at his old apartment.

But, just as Derek had promised in their last phone call, Martin would struggle to find him.

He vowed he'd persist. That he'd find him.

Somehow.

NOW

2 8

Folded arms, deadly frown, and furious eyes. Oscar did not disguise his anger from Julian one bit. If anything, he was ready to stand up to him, once and for all.

It had been too far.

"Honestly," Julian insisted. "She agreed to it. She insisted she could do it."

"Then you should have said no."

"In hindsight, yes, but—"

"To hell with hindsight!" Oscar said, standing up and throwing his arms into the air.

He'd had a few days to calm down, but he was still livid. April was fast asleep in their bedroom, and Oscar had reluctantly agreed to let Julian round to say his piece.

He wasn't at all interested in Julian's piece.

There were far heavier thoughts weighing down Oscar's mind.

"Look, children are dying, it was a tough call to make. And I gave her the decision entirely. I'm surprised she didn't talk it through with you."

"I'm not," Oscar blankly stated.

"What do you mean?"

Oscar went to speak, then found himself lost for words. He sat down on the edge of a seat, ran his hands through his hair, focussing on the corner of the room and staring at it.

"Oscar, what's troubling you?" Julian asked.

"Like you care."

"I do care."

Oscar grimaced at Julian. "You've been a dick to me since the moment you met me. I thought that would change after the prison, but ever since we've announced the pregnancy, you've come back more dickish than normal."

"I suppose I was just thinking about the strain it could put on the business."

"No, Julian, you were thinking about *yourself*. As always."

Julian pulled out a chair and sat beside Oscar. He allowed a few moments of reflective quiet to pass, allowing himself to mull over the words that had been said. Oscar kept his gaze fixed on the corner of the room.

"Maybe you're right," Julian admitted. "Maybe."

Oscar scoffed.

"What do you want from me?" Julian joked. "It's what I do. But honestly, I can see there's something troubling you. Something *else* troubling you. And I'm here to help. Really."

Oscar wiped his hands over his face, wondering if he should really confide in Julian. But who else was there? Derek was ill. His parents didn't particularly understand these things. It felt like his only option.

Fine.

If only for Julian's expertise.

"It's April," Oscar said. "She's been acting strange all the way through this pregnancy. Like, really strange."

"It's hormones, surely? I mean, pregnant women sometimes do crazy stuff."

"No, it's… other stuff."

"Have you been to the doctor's?"

"Yes."

"What did they say?"

"That these things were normal."

"Well there you go!"

Oscar stood, paced a few steps, then stopped and turned to Julian.

"But it all seems too strange."

"You think there's something paranormal at work?"

"Yes!"

"That's fair. You've seen too much; that's always going to be in your mind. But when there's a rational explanation, you still go with that one. And if the doctors are saying it's fine, then you've got a rational explanation."

"But what about... Anna?"

Even after everything that happened, Oscar still struggled to approach the subject, knowing how difficult it was for Julian. But Julian gulped, took a mature stance, and continued.

"Yes, I know. But that was an anomaly. You know how many of these possible hauntings we've been to actually turn out to be hauntings?"

"Jeeze. Less than five percent?"

"Far less. Are you sure it's not just you being paranoid?"

Oscar sighed. Folded his arms.

Julian had a point.

But it couldn't be so simple. It just couldn't.

"Right, let me tell you what's happened, and we'll see if you think it sounds like something," Oscar decided.

"Okay, go for it."

Oscar drew a breath, preparing himself.

"When she met my parents, and we were eating – I mean, April has a go at me if I so much as open my mouth slightly for a second with it full. She devoured a chicken with her mouth without even thinking."

"Okay," Julian acknowledged.

"She bleeds. So much she has to wear sanitary towels every day. She bled in Mothercare, after staring out a kid, then passed out."

"And the doctors said?"

"That it's rare, but happens. But, still. She's nasty toward kids. And, what the demon said to me the other day."

"You know they'll say anything to taunt you."

"Yes, but she said – the demon said it already has her. That my daughter is hers."

"Because it was a demon, Oscar; that's what they do. Demons are dickheads. They try to say nasty stuff."

"But – she whispered Latin in her sleep. And I translated it, and it–"

"April has used Latin a lot in her work. If she spoke it in her sleep then, honestly, it wouldn't surprise me."

Oscar bowed his head, collected himself, and sat down.

"So you really think it's nothing?" he asked.

"Oh, I don't think it's nothing," Julian responded. "I think it's a pregnant woman, who's perhaps an extreme example. I don't think there's a single thing demonic or paranormal about it."

"Really?"

"Really. And I think you need to relax."

Oscar nodded.

"Thanks. You're right, I guess."

"I'm glad I could help."

After a few moments, Julian reassured him once more, and said his goodbyes. Oscar walked through to the bedroom and watched April, watching as her chest slowly rose in her sleep, as her belly remained still, as she stayed at peace.

Maybe Julian was right.

The guy was a knob, but he did have an irritating habit of accuracy.

Maybe Oscar was being paranoid.

He lay beside her. Stroked her hair off her face. Placed his arm around her chest.

He slowly drifted off to sleep. All the time, ignoring those words coming out of April's mouth in a subdued whisper.

"Filea mea. Filea mea. Filea mea."

Eventually, they turned to dead, distant noise, and he dreamt of nothing but his happy family and his healthy, wonderful daughter.

(1 MONTH)

29

APRIL WAS HUNGRY. RAVENOUS. FAMISHED.

She could quite easily eat two dinners; that was how hungry she was.

She was fully aware that she was eating for two, and that the bump, growing ever bigger, needed more and more energy.

Not that it felt bereft of energy; it wriggled and bashed like it was having a rave in a cage! She had seen possessed victims having seizures that would likely cause less of a raucous in her belly.

But, such was the cost of pregnancy. In a month, she would arrive.

In a month, *it* would arrive.

She wiped a backhand of sweat from her forehead, then irritably dabbed it against her coat. She was sweltering. What's more, she knew that her humungous belly was creeping out from below her top – something she had always found quite gross in pregnant women. But, in that moment, she truly, unequivocally, unobtrusively, did not care. It needed to be released from the sweaty restraints of her top that was becoming more and more fitted by the day.

She huffed.

God, I'm ages away.

It was going to take her at least fifteen minutes to walk home, and that would have been without the extra load. She regretted telling Oscar she'd be fine, that she just wanted a walk, just to expend some energy. She wanted that boy there to carry her home. Or, at the minimum, drive her.

Glancing at a newsagent as she hobbled past, she felt her pockets for change.

Nothing. Nada. Zilch.

Not even anything for a packet of Freddos.

But, surely, they would not deny a pregnant woman a packet of Freddos?

I mean, what kind of psychopath are they?

She paused by a lamp post, reaching her arm out to support herself as she leant against it. Spotting a nearby park bench she wobbled from side to side, meandering her way over and plodding her expanded arse cheeks against the rusty seat.

A huge huff pushed out of her mouth.

I would murder for food.

A fluffy sensation brushed against her bare shin – a shin that hadn't been so bare a few weeks ago. How was it that even her shins were getting bigger? She had always been petite, and she knew she still was deep down, but as she gazed upon her body she saw nothing but excess skin pushed to its limits.

Her eyes wandered downwards, and the fluffy sensation appeared in the form of a cat. Its eyes peered upwards, sombrely reaching out to her with innocent, wide eyes.

She reached a hand down and brushed it across the cat's soft yet bristly fur. The feline closed its eyes as if to hint at its enjoyment in response to the attention it was receiving.

April was sure that, if the cat had the ability, it would be smiling.

There's always something a little magically triumphant in the ability to win the affection of a stranger's cat. Like, because that cat likes you, it means the whole world should deem you superior.

She pressed down more with her strokes, feeling its body press under the pressure, knowing that the cat would appreciate a rougher approach. Which it did. It lay down, flopped on its side, and rolled onto its back in order to expose its belly.

April tickled the cat's belly, watching as she or he closed its eyes once more and let its paws flop to the side in appreciation. It was lapping up the attention, and April was loving it.

She sniggered to herself. If only taking care of a newborn child was going to be this simple. She'd had enough unwarranted stories from anyone she knew with a child about what hell the first few months are. So much so, she was starting to wonder why any of them bothered in the first place, if it was such a treacherous time.

The hunger pain returned with a vengeance. A sharp pang in her empty stomach, sticking against her skin with a sharpened edge.

She looked down at the cat as it rubbed its head against her hands, fussing her with further unprecedented enthusiasm.

She placed a hand around its neck.

She placed her other hand around its legs.

She lifted the kitten up to her mouth.

Its confused eyes turned sombrely toward her, as if awaiting some kind of explanation. It anticipated the next round of fussing, the next tickle on the neck, the next rub on the belly.

That affection, however, was not forthcoming.

April gripped her hands tightly, so tight there was no way the cat could escape. It wriggled against the pressure of its neck, but such was her strength it found itself almost immovable.

April opened her jaw, prepared her teeth, and exposed the cat's belly toward her. With mouthful of anticipatory saliva, she sunk her teeth into the belly of the kitten, clamping down with all her might.

The cat moaned a long, unpleasant, high-pitched meow that only seemed to pick up aggression the more she bit.

But the cat couldn't move. April had clamped her hands too tightly.

She took her face away, chewed the first few mouthfuls until they were ready to swallow, then sunk them down her throat and into her belly.

Wiping some blood off her lips and onto her sleeve, she dug her teeth in once more.

The fur was annoying. It was a bit prickly against the top of her mouth, and it made her quite irritable for a moment. Then she allowed the flesh underneath to batter back and forth across her tongue, allowing it to shrink under the chewing of her jaw, and relished the flavour.

She lifted her head back.

Licked her lips, ensuring that she got every droplet before it fell down her chin.

She couldn't waste a bite.

She closed her eyes, feeling the pieces slip down her chest, feeling them feed her, give her energy, give her spawn energy.

When she next turned to the cat, its body had fallen limp.

How disgusting.

There was no way she was going to eat a limp cat.

She dumped it on the ground, discarded it, and made the jaunty walk home, feeling far better fed.

3 0

DEREK'S INCESSANT INSISTENCE THAT GOOD WOULD PREVAIL HAD been a major source of irritation to Julian, yes – but what he'd give to have him back at his full ability at that very moment.

He'd been at this case of the children's ward too long, and he was running out of ideas.

It was rare that one gets to a point in their life where they must decisively conclude – *I am completely and utterly stuck.*

It is typical that one should use a cliché to sum up such a feeling, so you'd have to forgive Julian's mind for forging a number of them together – but he knew that everyone, in their lives, comes to a crossroad. Everyone rolls the dice, and everyone sees a number come up that they do not wish to see.

Some people may even think they are stuck, but they aren't – they just aren't aware that either there is a solution upon their next stumble, or that there isn't a solution to present itself at all. Once they decide there will be no way going forward, they move on. They come to terms with it, and they readjust.

Julian could do no such thing.

Children were dying, and more children were at risk of death.

This wasn't a situation where Julian could throw in the figurative towel. This was a solution where he had to pick up that towel, look at it from all angles, examine it, and continue to hypothesise and test until he was blue in the face.

But what else could he suggest? Where else could he turn?

He had given Jason all of his 'I supposes and all of his 'I reckons – and he was out.

As he twisted in the chair in Derek's study, mindlessly rotating, spinning until his mind turned to a static race, he wished an answer would present itself to him. That an answer would throw itself into his lap. That it would give him something that would at least allow him to go to sleep. His mind needed rest, but until it reached a conclusion, it would not stop.

It was too dangerous to put April back in that position. She almost lost it before – and, what's more, that reluctant decision to encourage her to act as a conduit had not paid off.

He slowed down the spinning of the chair.

Or had it?

She had taunted Oscar. She had said, "I already have her." Followed by, "Your daughter is mine."

Logically, the demon would know it had a daughter...

He'd told Oscar never to listen to a demon's taunts. It was one of the greatest lessons Derek had ever taught him.

But the more he thought about it, the more something didn't feel right.

Or was he just trying to use the demon's words to provide a solution? Was he so lost that he was making them out of nothing? Was he so lost that–

He saw something.

Whilst mindlessly spinning himself around on the chair, his

eyes passed a vague blur in the bookshelf. Something small, a glimmer, something that didn't fit.

Behind the first layer of books on the bookcase that took up the vast amount of the wall, the dark-brown tint of the shelves mixed with the shadows of the second and third layer of books. But, in a flicker of light that caught a narrow gap as he spun, there was something discoloured. Something light brown. Something...

He leapt from his chair, grabbing books and throwing them out of the way. Derek would be fuming if he saw Julian treating his books this way, but if there was something in this bookshelf he had yet seen, something...

A brown piece of parchment, folded up more times than would be natural, was wedged behind a set of books. Behind the third layer, hidden away where someone did not intend it to be found.

Julian pulled the parchment out. He held it before him and read the message scrawled barely legibly on the front.

EXCERPT REMOVED *from Derek Lansdale's journal.*

JULIAN HAD READ Derek's journals – he'd studied them front to back, especially when learning about The Edward King War. Those were things he needed to know.

But he'd never realised that there were missing pages.

He unravelled the piece of parchment, and read each word quickly yet carefully.

27TH DECEMBER 2008

. . .

I WRITE this journal entry with a heavy heart, and thoughts full of regret. I feared writing this entry, unable to decide whether it was necessary. But I swore these records would be kept. I swore I would make note of what I know so that the world could be burdened with the knowledge when it was ready, or when it was needed.

BUT IT IS with great solace, and a troublesome mind, that my pen makes these scribbles upon the page.

I'M NOT EVEN ENTIRELY sure where to start. Outside my window, people are taking down wreaths. Packing away Christmas lights. Boxing their presents and taking them to their storage.

I AM NOT TAKING down any wreaths, lights, or boxing any presents. Because I never put any up. Nor did I receive any in the first place. Because I was busy. Working a case.

THE CASE in question is that of Madelina Esteves. A Portuguese woman in her early twenties, working in the United Kingdom as a nurse. She changed her location to Edinburgh, Scotland, as she was seeking me out. Seeking me to help her.

MADELINA WAS PREGNANT. But with what?

NO MEDICAL REASON existed for her frequent troubles.

. . .

SHE SAID it started with a need for meat. She would find a piece of chicken, or a raw steak, and she would devour it. Rip it off the bone with her teeth. Tear it to shreds until its contents were smeared over her cheeks.

THEN CAME the aggressive sexual urges. She would regularly have sexual encounters, then wake up the next morning with no recollection, with the only knowledge of what she had done being the marks on her lover's neck.

HER MORNING SICKNESS continued as per any normal pregnancy. But she found that she was passing objects she did not remember swallowing. Most notable were a set of rosary beads, and a crucifix.

SHE WOULD BE aggressive toward children, taunting them, even threatening them.

SHE WOULD BLEED from the vagina at regular intervals. The doctors told her this happened sometimes, but the baby was healthy and fine. But it kept happening. She said it got to the point that she wore a sanitary towel each day, and would have to replace it every hour, such was the frequency of the blood.

AND THERE WAS a constant murmur of Latin whilst she was unconscious, one that would chill anyone who was in the presence of her weary, sleeping body.

. . .

THESE SYMPTOMS all may sound like extreme hormones, or delusions. This is what she was diagnosed with.

I WASN'T SURE. I just wasn't sure. All of these things were, without a doubt, extreme – but could there be a rational explanation?

I WASN'T SURE. Until two weeks ago.

WHEN SHE KILLED A CHILD.

I KNEW THEN that there was something at work. My research led me to Lamia – a child-eating demon of Greek mythology.

BUT BY THE time I got to her it was too late.

SHE HAD DESCENDED ON AN ORPHANAGE. The sight that my eyes bestowed themselves upon will never leave me. Never. It was carnage. Reckless, unequivocal carnage.

PIECES OF CHILDREN lay about the house. Some of the bodies were unrecognisable. At times, you weren't even sure what you were looking at – whether it was intestines, muscles, or whatever else. It was sick. There is no other way to describe the mental image permanently tattooed onto the forefront of my mind. Sick. It was completely sick.

. . .

I FOUND Madelina standing on the edge of a hill, facing a steep drop to her death.

I KNEW this baby could be saved. I knew that there was a way. She was days away from giving birth.

BUT SHE WAS ADAMANT.

YES, I have saved a great many people, but this is the case that will stay in my mind.

I HAD to believe good would win. Because it normally does. It always does. I know it.

BUT THIS TIME...

THIS ENTRY WILL NOT RESIDE in my normal journal. It can't.

IT IS with great regret that I can't allow this to be common knowledge, and that I will be removing this page. If this is you, Martin, reading this, then I sincerely apologise for my cowardly actions.

IF THIS IS NOT Martin reading this, then I am still sorry to place the curse of knowledge upon you. Especially as the reason you've found this is because I have no ability to stop you – meaning that I am likely to be in a position that I can not respond to your questions or disappointment.

THIS IS a demon we can't defeat the normal way. This is a demon that can't be exorcised – it is not taking over a body, it is living within it. It is a child waiting to be born. But that child can still be good.

WE HAVE TO BELIEVE THAT.

THERE IS ALWAYS A SOLUTION. Always a way. Always something we can do.

THAT CHILD COULD HAVE BEEN BORN good. If only we'd have believed it.

I SIGN off from this note with great regret for my failures, in hope that you will not make the same.

YOURS IN SPIRIT,

DEREK LANSDALE

THE HANDS that held the parchment shook.

Julian's arms trembled. His thoughts distorted. His eyes not knowing where to look.

Who was Martin?

Julian buried such a question to the back of his mind and recalled a recent interaction he'd had with Oscar. A conversation where he'd reassured Oscar of all the things that he'd seen – where he'd reassured Oscar they were nothing.

Pregnant. Like Madelina.

The bleeds, just like Madelina.

The obsession with children, just like Madelina.

The whispering Latin in her sleep, just like…

Oh, God.

April.

HAVING SPENT HIS ENTIRE DRIVING LIFE OBEYING EVERY SPEED limit and braking for every turn – something that Julian was fully aware incensed the driver's stuck behind him, but insisted was the right choice, as it was safe – meant that his conscience was rejecting every action of his speedy, erratic driving. His breathing became so heavy he verged on hyperventilating, his arms shook like he was being charged with an electric volt, and his heart pounded like it was going to burst out of his chest.

He didn't care.

He had taken April off the streets. He'd found her. Shown her what it was to be a Sensitive. He had cared for her, been the big brother she needed, and had produced a damn fine, headstrong woman out of it.

He couldn't let whatever that thing inside of her was take control of her.

The thought was one he couldn't even bear. It brought tears to his eyes to even contemplate her demise, or even that she would be caused any pain.

After a half-hour drive spent clutching the steering wheel

and hoping for the best, he brought the car to a rough halt and leapt out of the door. Not caring whether it was locked or not, he made his way up the path to April and Oscar's flat, peering through the windows as he did.

All the curtains appeared to be drawn.

He pounded his fist against the door, feeling it battle against its hinges, and waited.

Nothing.

He pounded his fist against it once more, shouting her name.

"April! April!"

Nothing.

He placed his hand on the door handle, ready to barge the door down, only to find the door surprisingly unlocked. A gentle push sent it creaking open into a dark, lifeless corridor.

He stepped inside. Closed the door behind him. Edged his way forward.

"April?" he shouted, hoping she would respond.

Hoping *April* would respond.

Not something ungodly stuck inside of her.

"April, are you there?"

He used the walls for a guide, his legs inching across the carpet, until he came to the opening of the living room.

"April?"

A sudden jump impacted his body as he saw her. He poised in the doorway, taken aback by the calmness of the room.

She sat in a chair. Not a rocking chair so much, but a smaller chair that allowed her to sink deeply into it, and allowed her to rock slowly forward, then back, with such a slight movement that if it weren't accompanied by a sinister creak, Julian wouldn't even be sure he saw it.

"April?" he asked, quietly, almost worried he was going to wake some kind of beast, or already be engaging with it.

April did not look demonic. She did not look possessed,

wretched, or any kind of destitute. But there was something worrying, an undertone of disconcerting eeriness, in the way that she stroked her belly. She allowed her large, pregnant bump to proudly pronounce itself in all its nudity from beneath her top. Her hands brushed up and down, up and down, up and down, with such a gentle nurture that it was like she was protecting a precious item she had stolen and did not want to be disturbed.

"April," Julian spoke, "I just wanted to check on you. See if you are okay."

"I'm fine, Julian," she answered nonchalantly. "How are you?"

"Yeah, I'm good. I'm good."

"How's the case on the children's ward coming along?"

The first true pang of fear sent a shiver sprinkling up his spine.

If she was the one who had done it, then God knows how he was supposed to answer.

He edged slowly forward. Trying to get closer. He knew his crucifix was in his back pocket. He kept one hand behind his back so he was able to withdraw it at any time.

"I don't know, April," Julian replied. "Really struggling, I guess."

"Oh, I don't believe that."

He edged forward.

"Why not?"

"Wouldn't be the first time you lied to me."

"When have I ever lied to you, April?"

"I don't know. Right now?"

"How am I lying to you now?"

"Because you seem to be hiding a cross behind your back."

He stopped edging. His feet stuck to the floor like his trainers were part of the carpet. He was poised between attack and defence. Between getting the cross and going full pelt, or being cautious, as he did not know how much she knew.

"So, where's Oscar?"

"Oscar? Oh, he's out. Gone to get me some food."

"Oh yeah, what you eating nowadays?"

The side of her mouth lifted into a grin.

"What you are getting at, Julian?"

She continued to rock. Continued to stroke her belly. Continued to act so, so strangely.

There was only one thing Julian knew.

If this was April's ship, she wasn't the one steering it.

"I'm not getting at anything."

"Then get rid of the cross. You're freaking me out."

That was it.

He had to move.

He had to do something.

He flung the cross out from behind him – but, before he could present it or begin any kind of incantation, he found himself lifted into the air. His throat tightened, his chest rose, and his fingers shook until the cross fell to the floor.

April didn't falter. Didn't so much as blink. She simply remained, gently rocking, stroking her belly.

"April…" Julian whimpered between chokes. "Please…"

Like a bolt of wind punching him in his chest, he was taken off his feet, sent soaring out of the room until he reached the back wall of the cupboard.

He sat, slumped beneath a mop, his head spinning.

He couldn't make sense of it.

His head was groggy. His vision a blur.

His head smacked once more against the wall behind him. Then again. Then again. He tried to resist it, but he couldn't; something he couldn't see was pushing against his head too hard. Eventually, his awareness depleted to the point that he wasn't even able to acknowledge his head slamming against the back wall any longer.

The last thing he saw before he passed out was the closet door slamming shut, and April still sitting in her chair.

Rocking.

Stroking.

3 2

Oscar greeted the strange silence of his house as an infrequent occurrence. Normally, the moans and bustles of a pregnant woman would occupy the small rooms of their cohabited flat, but as he returned home in the darkness of late evening, it felt unusual to return to the quiet nights he and April used to have.

I suppose that will all change now.

In weeks, maybe even days to come, a new member of their family would greet them.

Family.

It felt strange to think it.

He wasn't just with a girlfriend anymore. He was with his family. His perfect life he could never have envisaged. He was the man of the house – the protector.

Although he knew April was far tougher than he, he still allowed himself a small smile at the thought.

He turned the key and stepped on that day's mail. He picked it up and sifted through the envelopes. Once he'd noticed they were all bills, he placed them beside the shoe rack and made his way through the hall to the only place that was lit.

The kitchen.

As soon as he entered, a wonderful aroma of perfectly cooked food took him aback. Just the right meld of bread and meat, combining into a perfect harmony of smells that made his mouth salivate in anticipation.

April sat at the table, smiling warmly toward him. Her hands caressed her exposed belly with small strokes, and a dish was placed in front of the empty seat beside her.

"Wow," Oscar said. "Is this for me?"

"Of course."

"But – you haven't got anything?"

"I've had mine. I just wanted to treat you."

Oscar looked playfully back at her.

It was lovely, but… odd.

It wasn't that April wasn't generous; in fact, quite the opposite. And it wasn't that the look on her face pierced through his eyes with an unsettling quality. Nor was it that there was no food in front of her. It was just…

She never willingly cooked. She had barely spoken to him over the difficulties of her pregnancy. He had felt isolated and alone, and this was a huge surprise.

"I – I don't know what to say," Oscar honestly admitted.

"I just wanted to do something," April told him with a calm, soothing texture that he wasn't used to in her voice. "Something to say thank you, to say I know how hard these nine months have been."

"Well, I… I'm speechless."

He hastily removed his jacket and sat at his place at the table. The dish below him, accompanied by a side plate adorning fresh, warmed bread, held a meat soup of the perfect colour, the perfect steamy temperature, and the perfect presentation.

He dipped his spoon, letting it sink, then bringing out a spoonful of liquid with a slice of meat, which he placed in his mouth and chewed. It was so fine. A delicacy one could only achieve with expertise in cooking. It was even still warm, but not so much that it would burn your mouth.

"Oh, wow," Oscar said. "This is amazing."

April said nothing.

She just watched him.

Watched as he took another spoonful and enjoyed the delightful taste of this home-prepared food.

Then he stopped.

Paused.

Wait.

This wasn't right. This whole situation, this whole scenario – it wasn't right. April barely liked putting pre-made pie and chips into the oven. She had never made something from scratch. How was it she had made something that tasted so perfect?

And how was it the right temperature just as he happened to enter the room?

"What's going on, April?" he asked. "You hate cooking. You can barely do anything with a saucepan. How did you make this?"

She shrugged her shoulders like it was nothing, not taking her eyes away from her precious belly.

"I'm going to be a mother. Time to learn to be a bit more motherly."

"I don't get it, this, just – it's delightful, don't get me wrong. I…"

He struggled for the words. Tried to snatch them as they floated around his head. But they were not forthcoming.

He couldn't articulate what was wrong, it was just…

Something.

"Please, have the rest," she insisted.

Reluctantly, he dipped his spoon once more, and continued to eat the rest. She didn't take her eyes from him, watching him with a sly smile the whole time.

"No," April grunted.

Oscar's head abruptly lifted.

April's face had changed. The smile was gone. She looked distressed.

"I said no."

"April?"

She turned around, placing her back toward him.

What was she on about?

"Said no to what?"

"I know you said it wouldn't kill him, I know you said it, but I can't, I can't..."

"April?"

Oscar stood, cautiously stepping toward her, his hand reaching out.

"Just let him live... Let him live and I'll do what you want..."

"April, what's going on?"

"Please, just leave him... I love him..."

"April?"

"I'll give birth to it now, if you just leave him..."

"April?"

April's face turned toward him. For the first time in months, he saw her eyes, her lost expression. Tears cascaded down her cheeks.

Her belly had gone completely red. It was kicking.

More than kicking.

It was throbbing. In multiple places, lumps came and went, quickening in pace.

"April, what's—"

His words got lost.

His vision unfocussed.

"I'm sorry, Oscar."

He fell to his knees.

"I'm so, so sorry."

He collapsed to the floor.

For a few seconds, he stared at her feet.

The throbbing lumps concentrated their attention on the lower part of her belly, reaching for him, as if trying to get at him.

He tried to say her name.

He tried. Even tried reaching out for her.

But he didn't manage to utter a syllable before his mind relinquished his consciousness to the depths of a blackout.

His hand stretched out, then flopped.

April was ready to give birth.

33

Luxuries.

They are things that we take for granted.

The luxury of food. Home. Family. Our working limbs. Our functional brains.

Then we have luxuries we afford ourselves. A fancy dinner out, a trip to the cinema with snacks, or buying that book you've been wanting for ages.

To Derek, life was the luxury he could feel slipping away.

Each breath seemed to take effort. Each move increased his struggling heartbeat. Each thought was thinking that it may be his last.

And as he lay there, attached to machines, staring groggily at the ceiling above, he could feel what the children were talking about.

They felt it because they were close to death. They saw it because they were close. For when we walk the tightrope between life and death, we can see both sides spinning beneath us. He'd been to hell. It was many, many years ago, but he had. Twice. He'd seen what it had to offer. And that feeling, that flickering flame lashing at his skin, that sense of dread that every step took, even the distant screams vibrating his prickly skin – he could feel it once more. Coming closer.

The entity in the children's ward had spread to the corridor, spread to his room. Its presence lingered there, but its body did not.

He'd witnessed Lamia before. He knew what it was after. And the children's ward was the perfect place. Souls that can't fight. Faces that would see Lamia in its true form – not the face of the host Lamia chose, but its true from. It relished the sight of vulnerable targets as their face melded into horror at the true form of the beast relinquishing that child from life.

That demon had chosen an orphanage before.

Now its next target was the children's ward.

He wanted to jump up and warn them. To rush into the other room, scream that they should arm themselves, begin the rites of exorcism. But his thoughts put so much of a strain on his weary head that the actual actions themselves may just be the very actions that removed the final breath from his body.

His head dropped to its side. The muscle in his neck strained.

Where was Julian?

Death was waiting around the corner. He had so much unfinished. So many thoughts, words, and lessons.

If he died doing it, he would insist to Julian his final lesson. Would batter this lesson into Julian's head until he could do nothing but agree. Would force him to hear it.

Good will always prevail.

He drifted out of consciousness, barely able to notice the nurse as she came in to check on him. He was awoken to the news that he needed to eat. She gave him morphine and adrenaline to help him sit up.

He barely touched the cheap, cold pie the hospital had brought to him.

"We have a visitor for you," the nurse told him. "A friend."

Good.

Julian.

He needed to know that Julian would not remain the cynic he was. He needed to know–

It was not Julian.

It was not human.

Lamia's true form unveiled itself. Long hair above elf ears, a naked torso trickling lines of blood down its naked breasts and to its waist, where a long, slithering snake tail took the place of its legs.

But this demon was not the size of a person, nor was it standing before him. It was far smaller than that. It hovered off the ground. Asleep. Its limbs entwined into a circle.

The size of a new born baby. The height of a woman's womb. Curled into a foetal position.

This demon was not hovering in the air.

There was something around it.

A body.

Walking into the room.

The nurse smiled at the body. Where the head would be. Welcomed it into his room.

"Hello, Derek," came a soothing voice. "Don't worry, I'm not interested in you."

What?

Its legs came out of the shadow.

Its belly.

Its face.

April.

Its face was April.

He finally saw what had been in Madelina. What had forced her to eat those children. What had killed those children. And was now within April.

Hidden in the unborn baby of a pregnant woman's womb.

But that child could be saved. He was sure of it.

That child yet to be born was home to the demon. It could be exorcized. Surely.

The nurse insisted it was time for rest and Derek reluctantly obliged, falling asleep in the midst of his objections.

He woke later to the terrible shrieks and mass hysterics that indicated a young girl called Joanna had been killed.

A STREAM OF PROJECTILE VOMITING AWOKE OSCAR FROM HIS daze. Once the shock of his rude awakening had diminished, he wiped perspiration from his brow and attempted to adjust his mind to his surroundings.

He sat up in the darkness of a small, cramped space. Faint light seeped through the outline of a door.

He was in a cupboard.

He stood, turned on the light.

A sudden lurch from his body brought up another mouthful of the soup April had made for him, forcing him to spew poison over a pair of stray shoes he hadn't worn in a while.

"Oscar?" came a faint voice.

He spun around.

Julian lay on the ground, rubbing his head.

"Julian?"

"Oscar..." Julian's distant eyes became abruptly alert as the dawn of realisation announced itself on his face. "Oh my God, April! April! Oscar, April, she–"

"I know."

Oscar could see Julian's eyes flicker as his thoughts raced.

"Oscar…" Julian's weary face mulled over a set of difficult words. "I don't know if we can save her."

"We can."

"We don't know–"

"We're both still alive, aren't we?"

Julian nodded.

"She spoke to it, I heard her," Oscar continued. "She argued with it."

"But she–"

"Julian – we are both *alive*. If she didn't want us alive, then that poison would have killed me, not just knocked me out. She's still in there."

Julian's phone beeped.

He snatched it from his pocket and brought it to his eyes, recoiling in despair as he read a text message.

"What is it?" Oscar asked.

"Another child has died at the hospital," Julian answered.

They shared a look of understanding. They knew who the murderer was.

"Help me get this door open," Oscar demanded.

Julian used the wall to steady himself to his feet. They stood back and barged the door together, managing to burst it open on the fourth attempt.

They both fell to the floor, still dizzy from their unconscious states.

"We need to get to the hospital," Julian stated. "Derek's fought this thing before. We need to talk to him and go from there."

Julian turned to Oscar. Saw the look on his face. A lost boy, scared, and worried.

"Julian…" Oscar whispered.

A tear edged out the corner of his eyes and announced itself on his cheek, glistening in the moonlight.

"I know," Julian said. "I know. But we are going to find her."

"But, my daughter…"

"We'll find her too. I promise."

Dragging Oscar by the arm, Julian took him out of the house and to his car. They sped to the hospital in silence, both of them too tense to talk.

By the time they pulled up, Oscar had managed to achieve a feigned sense of composure. Enough to be able to run the whole way to the children's ward.

35

Derek had recoiled at the memory of the bloody state of the children's ward.

The sight of April in his room. The appearance of the evil hidden within her. The screams that followed minutes after.

He hadn't wanted to see what April had done.

No – he hadn't wanted to see what *Lamia* had done.

But he'd had to.

The walls of the children's ward had been decorated in blood like never before. A mutilated body ripped to pieces of unidentifiable meat, spread over the bed and floor. But it didn't stop there; the spectacle had found itself onto every wall. Splashes of red stuck to the laughing faces of clowns and happy childish images. The floor was wet with red, and doctors were seeing to nurses who had been injured in the crossfire.

This felt bigger.

Like it was building up to something.

Like this was nearly the end.

Derek was sat up when Oscar and Julian ran into his room, eating a disgusting cream-coloured dish of hospital food.

"Derek, have you seen April?" Julian asked.

"I have not."

"Derek, I know. I know who Lamia is. I know what it did to the pregnant woman before."

"What?" exclaimed Oscar. "What happened?"

"It's got April, hasn't it?"

"What's got April?" Oscar persisted. "Who is it?"

Julian hesitantly turned to Oscar and told him who Lamia was. What the demon had done to Madelina. What Madelina had done to the orphanage.

As the initial shock subsided, Oscar's mind bombarded him with numerous unhelpful thoughts. As Derek watched Oscar, he could almost see the image of April clear in his thoughts, tearing children's skin from their bones with her teeth, much like she had the chicken. Watching her as she tore the children's ward apart.

"Where can we find her?" Oscar shot at Derek.

Derek shrugged his shoulders.

"Bloody hell, Derek, this is April!" Oscar rushed to his side. "Where woud she go? *Where?*"

"Oscar–" Julian tried to interject.

"Where would she go? Tell me, Derek, bloody tell me!"

Julian put his arms across Oscar and coerced him away from Derek.

"He is really sick, Oscar," Julian spoke in a low voice. "You're not going to get anywhere like this."

"Fine!" Oscar barked, throwing Julian's hands off him. He took to Derek's bedside as slow as his shaking, speeding body would allow him. "Help us. What do you know?"

Derek's mouth opened slowly and his words came out with difficulty.

"The child… can be saved."

"What?"

"The child is possessed, not her. But it still can be saved." Derek looked to Julian. "Good can win against it. It can."

"How do we find her?" Julian asked.

"I... don't know."

Oscar's hands ran through his hair.

"Where should we start looking?" Julian demanded, insisting that Derek should have something to help.

"Look... for places that mean something to you..."

Oscar nodded, thought, his mind jumping through all the locations he had ever been to.

"The pharmacy!" he decided. "That's where we first met."

"That's as good a place as any," Julian decided, and ran out the door, Oscar promptly following.

Derek remained still, waiting for them to go.

He felt bad about lying.

But he had to.

Julian did not believe in good. Oscar was too clouded by love.

And only Derek knew the true depths of this demon.

Madelina had taken herself to a place of suicide to prevent further death. To a steep hill.

That was where Derek knew April would be.

And, as he turned his body and placed his feet on the cold floor, he knew it would take the final energy he had left to get to her.

He took the clothes hidden beneath the bed and put them on. Once he had tied his laces, he made his way to the door, and checked that the coast was clear.

36

CLEEVE HILL. THE HIGHEST POINT OF ANY HILL IN THE Cotswolds. In the heart of Gloucestershire, next to Cheltenham, April's beloved home town.

The higher points meant steeper drops – and April had found the perfect height, with the perfect fatal fall.

It would be great.

The view before her brought back a sense of nostalgia. Memories of being a little girl, holding her daddy's hand as he guided her up here. Back in the years before he died. Before she was homeless.

She remembered one Christmas Eve in particular. She had been restless, eagerly anticipating the morning that was to follow. Santa Claus was coming and, although she didn't believe in him, she couldn't quell her excitement. So much so, she could not sit still. So her dad had brought her up here for a walk, a walk that lasted all afternoon, so she could expend that energy. It was one of the happiest times she'd had. Probably the happiest memory she had before the age of fourteen. When it all went so terribly wrong.

That memory made this location all the more ideal.

A perfect circle. A happy place to end a mostly happy life.

Oscar would miss her. Would he cope?

Surely, he must.

He had coped fine before she arrived.

Actually, that was a lie. He'd been a loser, spending his days working a dead-end job, playing on his Xbox all night, and jacking off in his room.

She gently snorted a reminiscent smile to her face.

You never realise the impact your mere presence or involvement in another's life has until you are about to take that presence away.

But did she have a choice?

It was not the demon inside of her telling her to end this. It was the human.

Just as it was the human inside of her that ensured she did not kill Julian. That she did not put enough benzodiazepines into Oscar's soup to be fatal. The human that had stopped her from killing more than the mere number of children she has killed so far.

But the children she had killed... that she had torn apart, unable to do anything but watch....

Her fingers were warily slipping. Her control over this part of her was being relinquished, and she could feel her thoughts losing any resemblance of sense.

What would happen to her once it had grown stronger?

What would happen once it had been born?

No.

She loved Oscar. She loved him more than life.

But that was why she had to do this.

That was why she had to save him.

He'd stop her. If he was here, he'd insist there was another way. He'd do anything to pull her back, to rip her away from the lethal drop.

She didn't even know what this thing inside of her was.

Was it a human baby?

A demon?

Some bizarre, deadly concoction of the two?

She rubbed her hands over her belly. She could feel it kick. Reacting to her touch. Responding with aggression.

She bowed her head. Allowed a rogue tear to drift into the wind.

She would not let herself cry. She would not let herself feel regret, remorse, or hesitance over what she was about to do.

So why hadn't she done it yet?

She stepped forward, the sight beneath her making her knees buckle and her stomach lurch. Such a drop, inches from her toes, staring back at her. Giving her the sense of imminent dread.

Her arms lifted out to the side like she was mounted to an invisible cross. She closed her eyes and spread her fingers, to allow the breeze to brush between them, to comb the air with its refreshing moisture.

It was a perfect day.

Not too cold, not too warm. A slight draught that did nothing to push her backward or forward.

It was the kind of day she and Oscar would enjoy spending together, climbing a hill like Cleeve Hill, revisiting through the memories that both of them shared. Some good. Some bad. And some with no emotional attachment whatsoever.

She dropped her head, her chin pressing against her chest.

She opened her eyes with a narrow slit.

The drop before her no longer made her knees buckle.

No longer made her queasy.

No longer frightened her.

It was the sight of inevitability. The sight of no going back. The sight of absolutely no choice but this one.

Choice.

It was a word people rarely acquired the meaning of in their life.

She was making a choice, but it wasn't hers.

It had never been hers.

She readied herself.

It was time.

SEEING THAT DEREK WAS STRUGGLING AND HOBBLING ON HIS walking stick, the taxi driver stepped out of the car and helped him to the backseat. He held the car door open and placed a helpful hand on Derek's back, waiting patiently as Derek feebly levered himself down using the headrest of the seat in front of him.

As Derek sat he readjusted himself and grabbed the seatbelt. Nodding at the taxi driver that he was ready, the taxi driver took to his seat as Derek put his biceps into work, pulling the seat belt across his front and pushing it into its slot.

"You okay?" the taxi driver asked.

"Fine," Derek responded.

"Where to?"

Derek thought. He knew the type of location he was going to, but his mind was already weakly racing across what words he could possibly say that would be more successful than with Madelina, and he hadn't yet thought which hill to go to.

"Where is the nearest, steepest hill?" Derek asked.

The driver thought for a moment.

"Cleeve Hill, I guess?" he offered with a quizzical look, as if it was the best answer he could give.

"Good," Derek confirmed, happy with the choice. "Then I would like to go there."

"Right you are."

The taxi driver turned, put his seatbelt on, rotated the key in the ignition, and pulled onto the road.

"Please, may we be hasty?" Derek asked. "My needs are desperate, and I'd appreciate some valour in your speed."

"'Scuse me?"

"Erm – please, can we be quick?"

Derek had always had a way with words that often left other people wondering what he meant.

"Right you are." The driver pulled into the fast lane.

Derek leant his head back, using the headrest to soften the blow.

How was it he felt so bad? That everything was such a task? That every action took the energy that would have previously been expended in a 5K run?

He had come to terms with death a while ago. The illness had only confirmed that the inevitable drew closer, and he was prepared.

The only thing he was not prepared for was leaving anything unfinished.

Madelina. April. Julian.

These were all unfinished.

He had to get there. He had to.

He allowed his head to loll, dropping onto his shoulder, and his mind drifted into an absent sleep. His mind filled with emptiness, allowing him a precious passage of time where imminent death or demonic spawn were not so prevalent in his thoughts.

He was awoken to the driver pushing him on the shoulder.

"We're here."

Derek looked out the window. There was a narrow road that went up the hill.

"Please, can you take me as far up the hill as you can?"

The driver looked at the path, then back to Derek, his eyebrows raised.

"Please. It is of the utmost importance."

The taxi driver reluctantly shrugged and did as he was instructed. Derek watched as the hills went by, peering into the distance, trying to see if he could spot a lonely woman on the verge of suicide.

What if he was too late?

What if all he'd see was a mangled corpse at the bottom of a steep drop?

"This is as far as I can go," the driver announced after a few minutes.

"Thank you ever so much." Derek scrambled through his pocket for a few wayward coins, and placed them in the driver's rough hand. "Keep the change."

"Cheers, mate."

Derek pushed the door open and moved across the stony ground, wincing at the bumps in the base of his shoe.

"You sure you're going to be all right?" the driver inquired. "You really don't look in the best state to be wandering around hills."

"I'll be fine."

"Are you sure, mate, 'cause–"

"I said I'll be fine!" Derek snapped, tiredness getting the better of him.

"Right you are!" the driver snapped back. He drove the car away at an excessive speed for a one-way country lane.

Derek paused, waiting for the energy to refill his legs. He peered across the horizon, over all the bumpy hills, seeking out a figure that would give him a direction.

He was going to have to use the final breaths he had. The

final stiffness of his muscles, the final twisting of his aching bones. He was going to have to force a surge of energy into his fading body, and will himself to battle on.

For everything he had faced, finding that required energy without collapsing was going to be the biggest battle he had yet.

Finally, his strained vision picked out something on the next hill over. An excessively steep drop, with a woman tipping gently over it. She looked ready. Like she was seconds from ending her life.

Derek had no time to waste.

He moved his walking stick forward and began his most trying journey yet.

OSCAR CHARGED OUT OF JULIAN'S CAR TOWARD THE PHARMACY, but all he found was a locked door and the dark interior of a shop shut for the day. He shook the door, battling against it, his frustration reaching the surface.

"Damn it!" he cursed.

Julian appeared behind him.

"Fuck!" Oscar continued to vent. "Where else is there? Erm, there is the coffee shop we used to go to, we could look there? Maybe we could go–"

"Oscar," Julian interrupted. "If she doesn't want to be found, chances are she won't go there."

"But Derek said–"

"Derek is delusional. He's ill. He doesn't really know what he's saying."

Oscar paused, trying to think of another solution. He didn't stay still for long before he was racing back to the car.

"Well, we've still got to try!" he insisted.

"Oscar," Julian said once more, forcing Oscar to turn around and throw his arms into the air.

"What?"

"We have to think about something."

"What? Right now?"

"Yes." Julian stepped forward, doing all he could to keep an air of calmness. "What are we going to do when we find her? *If* we find her?"

"What do you mean?"

"As in, what's our plan?"

Oscar shrugged.

"Do we need one?"

"Just an idea. What are we going to do?"

"We are going to save her."

"Save her?"

"At least try."

"What if she can't be saved?"

"You heard what Derek said–"

Julian rolled his eyes and let out a big, angry sigh.

"Stop quoting Derek to me!" Julian grudgingly insisted. "He was a great man, but now…"

"Well I believe him. I have to. Because I know damn well that if anyone tries to do anything but save her, they will do it over my dead body."

Oscar turned and resumed marching toward the car.

"Maybe that's why you should leave me to find her alone," Julian suggested.

"Are you kidding me?"

"After all, I've known her a lot longer than you. I know her better. I could get through to her more."

"Fuck you, Julian. Fuck off with your pathetic little ego! I've had enough of your cynical, constantly whiny attitude, especially not *right* now – especially with what is at stake!"

Oscar couldn't help it. His lip quivered. Prompting tears to edge out of his eyes.

"If Derek was able to think, if he knew what he was doing, he'd have sent us on this wild good chase for a reason," Julian said. "He's quite clearly sent us to the wrong location. Why do you think he'd have done that?"

"I don't know, Julian!"

"I would imagine because he knows we can't save her. That he knows he's full of shit."

"I thought you said he didn't know what he was doing?"

Oscar shook his head with uncompromising confidence, a sneer in his upturned lip refusing to accept anything but his own truth.

"I think *you* are the one full of shit, Julian. You're not right all the time. And if you think you are going to stop me from looking, however hopeless it may be, then you can go to hell. Because I will smash that car's windows down and drive it away myself if you are going to refuse."

Julian nodded. He walked to the driver's seat and got in, Oscar sitting beside him.

"Where to?" Julian asked.

"The coffee shop we used to go to. The little one with the curtains in the windows."

"Okay."

Julian drove, and as he did, they maintained a tense silence.

Oscar's fingers clawed into the side of his seat. He couldn't think. He couldn't do anything until he knew she was safe. By whatever means necessary, he had to know April and his daughter were safe.

A few minutes later, Julian pulled into a vacant space opposite the coffee shop.

It was closed. Pitch-black. Empty.

Another wrong answer.

Oscar's head dropped.

"Do you believe me now?" Julian asked.

"Wetherspoons."

"What?"

"The Wetherspoons toilets where she found she was pregnant. Try there next."

"Oscar, she isn't going to be–"

"Try there!"

Julian sighed and pulled away.

Oscar knew it was hopeless.

He knew she wouldn't be there.

But he didn't know what else to do.

His legs were seizing. Pain soaring through his throbbing muscles until they felt like they were going to fall to shreds. His bones wobbled as if the earth was shaking, but it was not; it was the feebleness of the bones that had already begun to decay. His body shook with a hot fever, quivering harsher than the worst flu he'd ever suffered.

But what hurt him most was the sight before him.

A lonely woman. Lost. With no other choice.

As Derek finally stepped upon the grassy verge leading to April's tormented body, his knees gave way and he fell onto his front.

But he did not pass out. He did not allow himself. He had to keep her talking, keep doing something, whatever he could to ensure she did not throw herself off that steep drop.

Her head turned to the side. Her body remained stiffly facing the edge of the hill, her face turned half over her shoulder.

She was not surprised.

"April…" Derek tried, his hoarse voice breaking under the

strain. It was rough like sandpaper, gristly in his sore throat. "April... stop..."

"What are you doing here?" her quiet, sombre voice replied as her face turned back to her fate.

Derek went to speak.

Why was he there?

He had expended such energy on the steep slope to reach her, his diminishing thoughts hadn't grasped any reason or words that he could use to justify her changing her decision.

He pushed himself to his knees, where he remained. He hoped she thought this was him begging. In truth, the edges of his vision were turning to black blurs, and he was unable to find the ability to stand.

"You can't do this," he said in the most compelling voice he had possible.

"You shouldn't be here."

Her body shifted her weight slightly forward, edging ever nearer to death.

"You don't think that," Derek claimed. "Or you would have done it already."

Fool!

He scolded himself for his poor lexical choice. Tempting her to complete her task was not what he intended to do.

Her foot stepped forward so that only her heel remained on solid ground. It knocked a few stones, sending them collapsing into the abyss.

"I once knew a girl. A sweet Portuguese woman, about the same age as you, who suffered the same trials."

April's head shook with marginal movement.

"I did," Derek persisted. "She was a nurse. She lived in Edinburgh. And by God, she was an infectious soul. A sparkling personality, enriching everyone she knew. Just like you."

"I've not been feeling very infectious lately," she replied, her voice remaining in a dull monotone. It was as if she had ripped all emotion out of her speech.

"I've noticed," Derek admitted. He allowed himself a few minutes to think, a few minutes to conjure the solutions that never clearly presented themselves.

"I see Oscar didn't come. Or Julian."

"They wanted to, April. Oh, they wanted to. But I sent them the other way."

"Why?"

"Because they aren't like me, you see. They don't believe that good can conquer the world. They don't believe that good can save you."

She shook her head, wiping her eyes on her sleeve.

"And *you* do?"

"Oh God, yes. Absolutely. I have always believed it. I wouldn't be good at what I do if I didn't."

A sharp pang fired through Derek's chest. A tingling shot up and down his left arm. His elbows gave way and he collapsed onto his chest.

Still, he remained resolute.

Still, he watched her.

"I can hear your heart," she told him. "It's fading. Getting quieter. Slower."

"I'm dying, April. I've known it for a while. The last few weeks, I've just been sitting in my bed, waiting for it."

She vaguely nodded. "I know what that's like."

"There's a difference. You have a choice."

"No, I don't!" she screamed, the first sign of anger coming from her.

This was good.

Derek could use this.

"This thing is inside of me!"

"No, your daughter is inside of you."

"No, it's not!"

"The demon is attached to your daughter, April. Your demon is not your daughter, it is attached, I promise, it is. We can do something about this."

"How?"

"Just like we've done with every other demon that's attached itself to a poor soul. We have… We've…"

He coughed.

"We've…"

He coughed again.

"We've… w…"

A splatter of blood dripped from his mouth, staining the moonlit grass beneath him. The flakes of green had turned to flakes of dark brown; dead plantation providing a rough bed for his chest.

"Please, April… I'm dy–… I'm…"

April turned her head to her shoulder once more.

Something ran down her thigh. Something wet.

She looked down.

It trickled down her leg.

Her water had broken. She was in labour.

She looked at the drop. This was it.

"Please, April…"

"Don't try to save me."

"We can help… You can be saved…"

She closed her eyes.

Spread her arms like wings.

Tipped forward.

"Goodbye, Derek."

4 0

"OSCAR LOVES YOU," DEREK SPLUTTERED BETWEEN MOUTHFULS of blood.

April halted. She could feel the pain in his chest. It reached out to her. It penetrated her heart until she felt it all.

She felt everything. Saw everything. Knew the longing of Derek.

Such was her ability to feel the pain of the dead. Ever since Julian had first taught her what her powers as a conduit meant, she had always been able to channel the deceased, in a way that—

Wait...

She leant back. Her arms dropped to the side.

Her thoughts repeated on her.

She was able to channel Derek's thoughts.

But I can only channel the thoughts of the deceased.

"Derek?" she asked.

No reply.

She turned to look at him.

She could feel his desperation to save her. His true, persistent belief in the good in her. His hope that his words could provide the encouragement she needed to survive.

She was a vessel for the non-living. Which meant...

She bowed her head. Closed her eyes. Denied it. However counterproductive it was, her thoughts denied it.

Derek laid on his front. Eyes closed. Chest still. Breath non-existent.

But she could feel him. Just as she had done with that old man who killed the girl for the very first time four years ago, she felt the dead close by.

Only this time, the feelings were different. They weren't of rage and anger.

They were of hope.

Optimism.

Positivity.

Derek sunk through her, filling her mind, filling her blood, pushing into her thoughts.

This was her gift. She could feel the emotions of those she channelled, could feel their lives.

She was in Derek's mind, looking through his eyes. In his sick bed. Alone.

She had a cup of tea in her hands.

She felt so weak. So weary. So empty of energy and life and–

Oscar.

He smiled back at Derek. Smiled back at her.

By his bedside. In the midst of simple conversation.

"But this child wasn't planned," she heard Derek's voice say through her lips. "How are you going to cope?"

Oscar's eyes twinkled with excitement as they looked back at her.

"With great energy and enthusiasm, my friend," Oscar asserted. "When I'm with April, it's like – I'm not just a better person, but I am the truest person I am. Like, everything changes."

She felt Derek smile. Felt his happiness. His appreciation of Oscar's feelings.

A tear fell down her cheek.

She fell to her knees.

She watched the memory. Felt the genuine love exuding from Oscar. Felt Derek's soul as it reached out to Oscar and his kind words, as Oscar's face melted into ecstasy at the thought.

"The world just sinks away, and it's me and her. Us against the world. And now it's going to be us three. And, I – I can't wait."

"What if the baby–"

"I don't care. I know what you're about to say, and whatever the baby brings, I will do whatever to protect that child, and to protect April."

Oscar's eyes focussed on Derek's.

After everything that had happened. Her absence from their conscious lives. Her troubles, her anger, her hostility.

After everything that had happened, he still spoke so clearly and so resolutely.

"She has changed my life. And I can never repay that."

She collapsed to the floor.

Derek's hope and enthusiasm fell out of her like water through fingers. He left.

She was alone again in her body.

Next to Derek's.

More alone than she had ever been.

She collapsed into a weeping mess.

This child could be evil.

But Oscar would do anything.

Oscar.

That boy. That strange, brilliant boy.

She cried uncontrollable tears, weeping, pushing them out of her eyes until there was nothing left to cry.

She turned to Derek. His face empty. His hollow eyes now open.

Her legs were covered in fluid.

This baby, whatever it was, was on its way.

She took her mobile out of her pocket and dialled 999.

"Hello, I'm at the top of Cleeve Hill," she said. "I've just gone into labour."

41

WHAT ON EARTH IS GOING TO COME OUT OF HER?

Since receiving the call from the hospital on his and Julian's drive away from the coffee shop, those were the words occupying Oscar's mind, spinning around like a bad animation on a PowerPoint presentation.

She was already in delivery. Whatever it was coming out of her, it was eager to arrive.

He burst through the hospital doors, charged to reception and, with a voice full of frantic anticipatory trepidation, he said to the receptionist, "Where is the maternity ward? My girlfriend's gone into labour."

"Down the corridor, up the stairs to the third floor, and to your right."

He walked as fast as he could without running, having to quickly adjust his path to avoid a few nurses. He directed himself to the stairs, and heard nothing put the patter of his feet quickly tapping against the steps.

Julian wasn't with him – something he was secretly glad of. This wasn't a time for Julian's cynical interference.

Although, the reason for Julian's absence wasn't so celebratory.

Julian received a call at almost precisely the time he had, from a separate department in the hospital, to be informed that Derek had been taken to the intensive care ward, and they were currently battling for his life.

Oscar hoped Derek survived.

It was a shame that such an occasion as a child's birth had to coincide with such a solemn turn of events.

Then again, the past few months had all been a solemn turn of events. And there was never an opportune moment to face death.

His shoulder barged into the door of the third floor and he gave up the hasty walk for a spirited run, aiming straight for the reception desk.

"Hi, my girlfriend's in labour."

"What's her name?"

"April Cristine."

The nurse looked at a sheet in front of her. Oscar wished she would hurry up.

"What's your name?"

"Oscar."

"Okay, Oscar, come with me."

The nurse led Oscar down the corridor, so slowly he kept knocking into her. It was as if nothing was happening. He kept thinking – *does this woman not know my child is being born?*

After a small walk that felt uncomfortably long, the nurse reached a curtain and pulled it aside.

"We have the father here," the nurse said.

"Send him in."

The nurse turned to Oscar.

"Here you are."

Oscar brushed the curtain aside and stood inside.

April was on the bed in a sterile hospital gown, her eyelids drooping and her head lolling to the side. A doctor sat between her open legs, the sight of a head in his hands. A nurse was by April's side, but as soon as this nurse saw Oscar, she moved aside so that Oscar could take her place.

He took April's sweaty hand firmly in his and brushed her hair out of her face.

"It's okay," he told her. "I'm here now."

Her fingers loosely flexed, then remained limp.

"How's she doing?" Oscar asked the doctor.

"Okay, but she's been in and out of consciousness. We've lost a lot of blood, but we're on the home stretch now."

Oscar turned back to April. Looked at her face. Her absent, pale face, her scabbed laps, her perspiring brow. She looked a state, to everyone else but him – to Oscar, this was the woman he loved.

"Right, April, you need to push," the doctor demanded. "I need you to stay with us, and push."

April groaned, her head turning to the side, her eyes remaining closed.

"Come on, April, I know you can do this."

Oscar kissed her forehead.

Then the fear returned.

What on earth is going to come out of her?

He pictured a demonic child. Horns. Flailing limbs. Snake tail for legs. Fire from its throat.

But as the doctor kept reminding April to push, he gave no indication of shock or horror by a strange appearance of the baby.

Oscar stayed by her side, holding her hand, whispering in her ear. She wasn't all there. Her eyes fluttered every now and then, but he knew she could hear him. He knew he had to keep talking to her, to keep her alive.

The piercing sound of a baby's wail filled the vicinity.

Oscar stared at the doctor, waiting for a reaction. A retort such as, "Oh dear God," or, "What the hell is that?"

The doctor did no such thing.

Instead, he smiled. Cut the umbilical cord and gave the child to the nurse, who checked her breath, clearing a small strip of fluid from her nose. She wrapped the baby in a towel, then turned to Oscar.

"Would you like to hold her?" she asked.

Oscar shook. He was nervous. He had a fluttering excitement in his belly, like he had on his first date with April.

Why am I so nervous?

He stepped forward, yet to see the baby's true form. He reached his arms out, slowly taking the baby, supporting her head, and brought her to his chest.

The baby stopped crying.

She looked up at Oscar with a perplexed look, as if to say, "I've never seen you before."

She was beautiful.

Her arms and legs wriggled like a tiny human. Her fingers reached out and clamped around one of his. Her eyes were big and green, staring up at his.

There were no tentacles.

No snake tails.

No horns.

She was an innocent, gorgeous little girl.

And Oscar could not have been filled with more love and adoration for the tiny person he cradled.

Being transfixed by her, his senses became suddenly aware of a commotion. The doctor was at April's side, shouting nonsensical instructions at the nurse that Oscar couldn't understand.

April's eyes weren't fluttering. Her fingers weren't lifting. Her face was blank.

"Is she okay?" Oscar asked.

He was ignored.

"Doctor, please, is she going to be okay?"

"Yes, but we still need to see to her – give us some space."

As a few more nurses came to the doctor's side, the maternity nurse who had handed Oscar his baby girl guided him away.

"Come on, let's get her cleaned up," she said.

"Is April going to be okay?" Oscar persisted, clutching onto his daughter, but desperately worried about her mother.

"Yes, but she has had a lot of difficulties, and we still have some work to do. We agreed before the birth that we would give her some Vitamin K to prevent haemorrhagic disease. Do you remember?"

"Erm, yeah, I guess," he answered, his mind barely registering what she was saying. But he let her guide him into another room, just hoping that April would be okay.

42

JULIAN'S LEGS CARRIED HIM BACK AND FORTH, FROM ONE SIDE OF the empty waiting room to the other. He wished he could halt his incessant pacing, but his legs wouldn't allow it.

The waiting room was decorated with blue paint and pictures of families. He understood why they had chosen such a calming colour, but the families he could not understand. This was the waiting room for intensive care, the place where families are most likely to be destroyed. Why would you want to see a happy family whilst yours is being ripped away?

He ran through every interaction he'd ever had with Derek. Every argument, every nasty word, every act of defiance. Every belittlement, every disagreement, every protest.

Suddenly, he felt like he'd been excessively cruel to his mentor. Made Derek feel guilty about Julian having to take care of him, despite Julian not actually being that bothered.

He knew his guilt was surfacing because he faced the possibility of losing him. That there were plenty of good memories too. It was just that, in that moment, his mind would not let him see them.

The door opened slowly and a doctor entered.

Julian stopped pacing. Stuck rigidly to the floor. Staring wide-eyed. The stillest he had been since he'd entered that room

"Julian?" the doctor asked.

"Yes," Julian confirmed. "How is he? Is he okay?"

The doctor's head bowed momentarily as he gathered his thoughts.

Julian knew what that meant.

He knew *exactly* what that meant.

"We did everything we could," the doctor said. "The cancer had spread too far. It had reached the lining of his heart – which made it almost impossible for us to start it again."

"Is he–"

Julian couldn't say it.

He couldn't say the word.

But he didn't have to.

The doctor faintly nodded.

"He lived longer than we expected," the doctor assured. "That last climb up the hill he did – it was one too many."

Julian didn't know what to say. His eyes remained focussed on the doctor.

"I'm sorry for your loss," the doctor said, and turned to go.

"Can I see him?" Julian asked.

The doctor hesitated.

"Yes," he finally answered. "The coroner is on his way, but you may have a few minutes first. Follow me."

Julian followed the doctor toward the operating theatre. Outside of it, Julian saw several surgeons, doctors, and nurses, all with solemn faces. They looked to Julian, understanding who he was, and all gave him an instinctive sympathetic smile.

He wished they hadn't.

They'd be back to work that next morning.

Julian wouldn't.

Not after this.

The doctor opened the door and allowed Julian to walk in. The doctor remained at the entrance as Julian slowly made his way toward a bed with a motionless body laid upon it. Numerous lights were fixed overhead, and surgical equipment remained on trays, still yet to be cleaned.

Julian reached Derek's side.

Derek's eyes were closed. Which Julian was grateful for.

A sharp pang cursed his chest, accompanied by the thought that he'd let him down. That he'd not listened to him. That maybe if he'd have paid attention to Derek's final lesson, things would be different.

Unsure whether he was thinking this out of grief or honesty, he willed the thoughts from his mind.

He took hold of Derek's hand. It was already stiff. Already cold.

He thought of what to say.

What his final words could be.

To the mentor he'd always wished for. The father figure he'd never before been granted.

To the man who taught him everything.

To the man who had taken more of Julian's shit than anybody else.

To the man who had never stopped trying. No matter how much Julian pushed, how much he tried it on, kept his own stubborn opinion, everyone else left. Hated him for his pessimistic outbursts.

Derek never left.

Never.

He remained. Loyal as a man could wish for.

What do you say to someone like that? What final words do you give them?

Deciding that he could never articulate the true lamentations of his affection, he settled for two very simple words.

"Thank you."

43

A GRAVEYARD.

Weeks and weeks of tracking Derek, which had turned into months, and turned into years, and that was where he found him.

Martin wished it wasn't so.

He stood over the headstone of his former mentor. The closest thing to a friend he'd ever had.

Truth was, he hadn't even found Derek. Martin was still listed as Derek's emergency contact. *They* had found *him*.

And now, with no face to look at, no skin to touch, he wondered what he was supposed to feel.

Anger? Not at Derek, but at his own stupidity. His own ridiculous, stubborn nature that meant Derek's attempts to reconcile had fallen on deaf ears.

Remorse? That his final words to Derek had been too harsh?

Regret?

No.

It surprised him, but he felt numb. It was as he was

expecting it. Like this was how he imagined his next interaction with Derek would be.

He turned and walked away. He wasn't one for sentimentality. He'd seen what he'd needed to see, now it was time to go.

As he made his way down a gravel path, he could see another man walking toward Derek's gravestone. He paused, and watched him.

The man looked sad, yet strong. Late twenties. Hands over his face.

Was this one of Derek's friends?

Had Derek moved on and found other people to help?

Had Derek even remembered Martin?

Ridiculous, really. A selfish thought. What, did he expect Derek to mope around for ten years, wishing Martin had ended the feud Martin had caused? Perhaps he just felt bitter that he'd been living alone all this time, and Derek had surrounded himself with people.

Derek always was more of a people person than he was.

The man's hands dropped. His eyes were red, wet with tears. His head slowly turned, and he looked at Martin.

Their eyes met, and held each other's gaze. No expressions, no hostility, no smiles – just watching each other across the crowded graves. Ignoring the bustle of the wind.

Martin wondered who this was.

A man trained by Derek, maybe. A man with a deep caring for him.

Did Derek rescue this man from a life of delinquency and potential crime, just like he had when Martin was young?

He tried to talk to the man. To open his mouth, give a message of condolence, to state that he was sad, regretful, morose. But he wasn't. He was numb. And he couldn't come out and say this.

The only positive Martin could find was that the demon's taunts were incorrect. The demon that had defeated him had claimed that the devil was preparing vengeance on Derek. That someone was going to be pregnant with demon spawn. That this would heap pain over Derek's weakening temperament.

But with Derek dead, there would be no point making someone close to him pregnant now. Vengeance against Derek would be pointless if Derek wasn't there to suffer through it.

So at least Martin knew that the demon was wrong.

Which meant he had no reason to stay. He needn't warn this man of anything.

He gave a gentle but definite nod to this man, who gave one in return.

Martin thought about what his next step was. Maybe he could reinvent himself. Find a life away from the demonic. Get married. Get a job. Fall in love.

But, somehow, he knew that the demonic would always find him.

Bury himself underground, then. Become a recluse. Be that crazy man who lives alone in a house that children run past. Maybe he could even grow a beard.

Finally ceasing eye contact, he stepped forward, directing his feet out of the graveyard and away from the life he left behind.

He'd tried to track Derek down because he needed to warn him.

But Derek was dead now.

Which meant, just as he expected, the demon was full of lies.

There was no demon baby. No vengeful demons. No warnings he needed to give.

There was nothing for him there. There never was. He was

a nomad without a purpose. A drifter without a home. A man without a soul in the world to care.

He reached the car park, got into his car, and drove away, watching the graveyard grow smaller in his rear-view mirror, thinking of nothing but regrets.

ONE MONTH LATER

4 4

Hayley's eyes remained soundly closed. Her delicate skin wrapped up, and the pram shielding her face from the sun. This was the quietest she'd been all day, and Oscar was grateful for the moment's peace as she slept.

Though, as tired as he was, he ended up missing the moments when she was awake.

It was tough doing this alone.

"Do you ever think," Oscar suggested, "that we could ever have a normal life?"

Julian, sitting on the bench beside him, smiled in a playfully dismissive manner.

"Us? Normal?" Julian joked. "We can't do normal anymore. We've seen too much."

"Yeah. Don't disagree with you."

Julian peered at the sleeping child. The sweet girl moving in her sleep. So cute. So tiny.

"So she didn't end up with tentacles then?" Julian mused.

"No," Oscar answered, smiling at Julian's incredulous humour. "She turned out to be a beautiful, wonderful baby girl. Whatever evil forces surrounded Hayley, I've seen no evidence of them."

Julian nodded, still watching the child.

"I'm glad," he said honestly. "Really, I am. I know I was a bit of a dick about it, but, honestly – you and April, you're meant for each other."

"Wow. Have you hit your head or something?"

"Don't push it. I've said something nice to you; that's mine done for another year."

Oscar chuckled. Then his face fell and his smile dropped.

He missed April.

"Have you seen her lately?" Julian asked, knowing exactly what the change in Oscar's face had indicated.

"Yeah, I took Hayley to see her yesterday."

"Any word?"

Oscar stuck out his bottom lip and aimlessly shook his head.

"I'm sure it's just a matter of time," Julian reassured Oscar.

"Yeah. I hope."

"She's strong. She'll fight."

"I don't know. Even the doctors don't know why she's still not waking up. She's fine, they just… can't figure it out."

"Here's a secret, and it's something I've learnt from a few years in our business – but the doctors don't always know everything."

"Yeah… that's what I'm worried about. What if it's not something of this world? If the thing that was supposed to have the baby now has her?"

Julian struggled for an answer. And Oscar knew why.

Twice now, they had denied that paranormal attacks on them were happening – Anna haunting Julian last year, and April's bizarre pregnancy.

It seemed like something was stepping up its attacks. Was targeting them.

And Oscar didn't blame them.

The work that the Sensitives had done against hell, against demons, had been brilliant so far. In truth, they had barely scraped the surface, but they had announced their presence as people to be reckoned with.

They couldn't have a few successes without expecting a backlash.

"What's next?" Oscar asked.

"What do you mean?"

"I mean, you've been targeted. Derek's been targeted. April's been targeted. That just leaves me."

"They won't go after you."

"Why not?"

"You're too strong. Too good. And they won't take a battle they don't think they can win."

Oscar looked at Julian, spiritedly bemused.

"That's two nice things now," he pointed out.

"Yeah, I know. I'm starting to feel sick."

They chuckled.

Hayley murmured, so Oscar placed his palm on her forehead and she sank back into her sleep.

"I know it was inevitable. I'm just worried about who it is that's coming after us. *What* it is. I mean, what's going to—"

"Oscar, Oscar," Julian interrupted, "just enjoy your successes. April is still alive. Your baby is healthy. You are here."

"Since when were you one to see the good in things?"

Julian smiled. "It was a lesson I had to learn."

For a few minutes, they allowed a comfortable silence to settle between them. The sun beamed against their skin, forcing Julian to remove his jacket. They watched people go by, minding their own business, dealing with their own problems.

Thinking they were safe.

Just as Oscar thought he was. Just as Julian thought he was. They had fended off the attacks that had come at them enough times to feel a sense of resilience.

Safe. For now.

Just as they assumed Hayley was too.

Oscar's baby had been born. She was a perfect representation of hope. The product of positive thinking. A wonderful child who cried and smiled like any other.

To Oscar, she was perfect. He stared down at her with no worries in his mind as to what she could be – they had all been quelled, and his mind was at ease.

A head. Two arms. Two legs. A round belly. A mouth that could scream and laugh. Normal as normal could be.

But she wasn't normal.

There was a reason this child's mother lay inexplicably comatose.

There was a reason the child gave the illusion of being perfect.

There was a reason the child had been born.

And her loving father, cooing down at her, was blissfully unaware of any of it.

THE SENSITIVES BOOK FOUR:
DEMON'S DAUGHTER IS OUT NOW

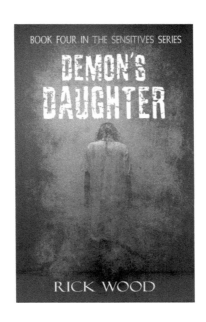